Praise for
Under Carico's Moons
Book 1: Distant Trails

"This thrilling sci-fi Western rides the open range of another world with complex characters caught in a web of conspiracy."
-Karen Eisenbrey
author of the *Rage Brigade* duology and the *Wizard Girl* trilogy

"*Distant Trails* is a roller coaster ride of pain and despair, love and redemption. Ballard's characters embody both frailty and resilience as they redefine their lives from tragedy to hope."
-Mikko Azul
author of the *Demons of Muralia* series

Under Carico's Moons

Book 2

Deep Canyons

by

Nan C Ballard

Copyright © 2022 by Nan C Ballard

All rights reserved.

Published in the United States by
Not a Pipe Publishing
www.NotAPipePublishing.com

Paperback Edition

ISBN-13: 978-1-956892-16-1

Cover art by Don Aguillo
Photo of Nan C Ballard by Jonathan Billing,
PNWPortraitEFX.com

This is a work of fiction. Names, characters, places, and
incidents either are products of the writer's imagination or
are used fictitiously. Any resemblance to actual persons,
living or dead, events, or locales is entirely coincidental.

To Mikko Azul
who gave me the right encouragement
at the right time
to get me to finish this
and actually submit it.

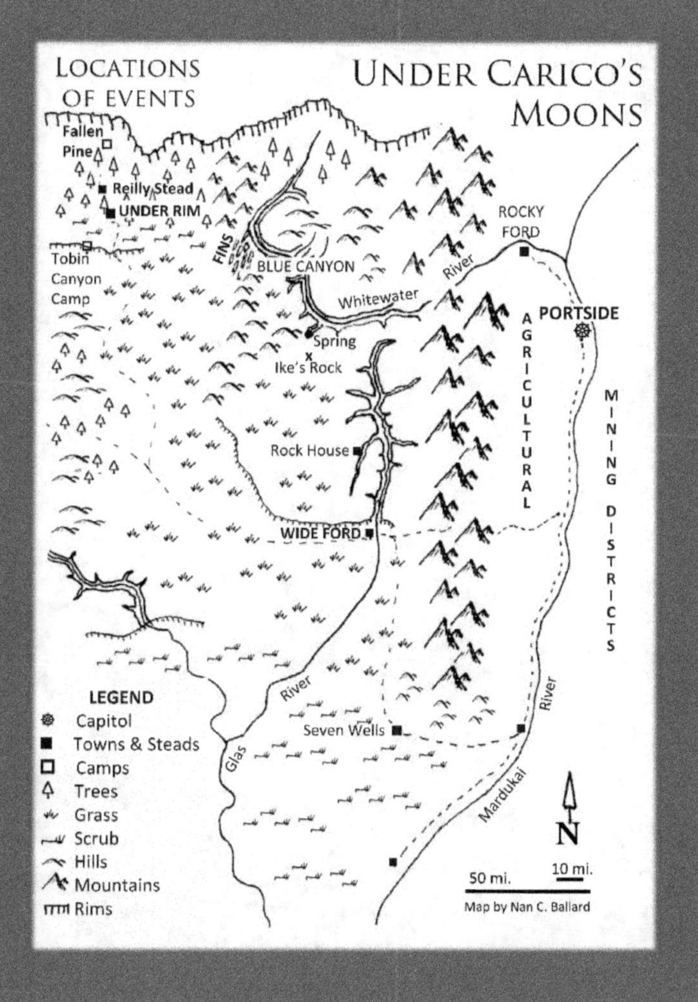
LOCATIONS OF EVENTS
UNDER CARICO'S MOONS
Fallen Pine
Reilly Stead
UNDER RIM
Tobin Canyon Camp
FINS
BLUE CANYON
ROCKY FORD
Whitewater
River
PORTSIDE
Spring
Ike's Rock
AGRICULTURAL
MINING DISTRICTS
Rock House
WIDE FORD
River
LEGEND
Capitol
Towns & Steads
Camps
Trees
Grass
Scrub
Hills
Mountains
Rims
Glas
Seven Wells
River
Mardukai
N
50 mi.
10 mi.
Map by Nan C. Ballard

Chapter 1

Lee

In the shade of the bulbous-trunked water-finder tree, Annalee "Lee" Vawn-Cory loaded the injector with a dose of immune booster for the injured tarbh calf. The mottled greenish-brown mother shook its head, displaying its helmet of horns with the wicked tips curling out behind its four yellow eyes. At five-two, Lee couldn't even see over its back. A man on horseback distracted the massive animal while another rider roped the calf by its hind legs and dragged it toward Lee, leaving the mama watching anxiously. The thought struck her that Carico was a long ways from the central planet city where she had grown up.

"Whatcha waitin' for, girl? Get in there." Ike Allred stepped past her with the spray bottle of temp-skin to seal the calf's wound. He showed every one of his seventy-three years of hard living as he shambled across the corral, tall, stooped, and determined. Lee followed him, injector in hand. The rider moved his horse closer to the threatening mother to give them a few seconds to doctor the calf and get clear.

Lee pushed the injector against the soft hide under the calf's neck, avoiding the tougher scales that covered most of the pale yellow and aqua body. With her knee on the animal's neck, she waited for Ike to finish spraying a coating over the gash in the calf's rump. He stepped away and pulled the loop off the calf's back feet. She took her knee off its neck and stepped clear as it bounced up and ran.

"Look out!" someone yelled. The mama tarbh charged the rider. His horse jumped aside, stumbled, and nearly fell. The tarbh headed straight for Lee and Ike.

As the old man scrambled for the fence at a snail's pace, Lee sprinted across in front of the tarbh's nose and drew it away from him. The animal swung its head at her. She dove away, rolled to her feet, and clambered up the fence rails. The tarbh made another pass, hooking at her with a horn, but she was out of reach. The animal laid claim to the center of the pen, raised its blue neck fan irritably, and locked its center two eyes onto Lee while its side eyes kept watch for anything else coming toward the baby now safely against its side. The riders closed in and herded the pair out the gate, clearing the pen.

Lee glanced through the amber-green cloud of dust to see Ike calmly putting the temp-skin spray in the med kit like he hadn't just missed being run down. She snatched the injector from the dirt where she'd dropped it.

"She about taught you who to pay attention to out there," Ike said gruffly.

"Yeah," Lee said. "Good thing I'm young and quick."

"Meaning I'm not?" He cocked a bushy eyebrow.

"Meaning one of us better be." She shoved the injector at him. He wiped it off and returned it to the kit. They had an uneasy partnership. He could out-grump a tarbh bull but aside from his sarcastic advice about how to live her life, he left her alone. And he had a wealth of knowledge to mine. They managed to get the work done. That was what counted.

A sharp whistle caught her attention. Kieron Dougherty, manager of the Seven Wells Stead, waved to them from across the barnyard. "Looks like the boss wants us," she said.

"So it does." Ike scuffed across the corral and opened the gate. She picked up the med kit and followed him, running her fingers through her short, dark hair to shed the dust.

Dougherty met them in the doorway of the main barn. "Come on in out of the sun," he said. The thick walls of verdigris-colored mud bricks could keep even the summer heat at bay, much less the gentle warmth of the spring morning. He led the way to the feed room, slight and wiry, two and a half decades younger than Ike and older than Lee by about the same. Crinkles from a ready smile and Carico's sun etched his mahogany skin.

Lee put the med kit away while she waited for him to explain what he wanted of them. Ike propped his lean frame on the counter. "I thought you were headed to Portside, boss," he said.

"I will be tomorrow." Dougherty grinned. "You two be packed and ready to go after breakfast. I want you to come with me."

"Us?" Lee said. Portside, Carico's one city, its capitol and space port, was half a day away by skimmer. She got nervous just thinking about all the people.

"What're you wanting us in Portside for?" Ike asked.

"The public meeting about the upcoming Settlement Plan evaluation. I want your ears and eyes."

"More off-world interference, if you ask me." Ike shook his head in disgust.

Dougherty shrugged. "Gotta live with it. The charter gives us one hundred planet years to prove up. We're coming up on year seventy-five."

"Only sixty-eight from first landing," Ike said. "I know. I was there."

"True, but the count starts with the date the Interstellar Coalition adjudicated settlement rights to the Sol-Terra Alliance. It took seven years for the Alliance to put the planet up for bid and for the Carico consortium to get together their expedition and make that first landing."

"I'm confused," Lee said. "Is it the Alliance we have to satisfy or the Coalition?" She knew something about how to evaluate a settlement plan but hadn't thought about the larger context since school.

"As long as we meet the base criteria required by the Coalition — self-sufficient, environmentally sustainable, with individual rights of our citizens guaranteed — the Alliance retains the settlement rights. But Carico has to meet the details of the settlement plan or the Alliance could put it back out for bid to new management."

"And we get kicked out and lose everything we've built." Ike gestured at the barn around them. "Lousy deal."

"I call it strong incentive to succeed. So you both come with me tomorrow."

Lee dreaded both town and the inevitable conflict and controversy that the evaluation would bring. "You don't need me," she said. "I've only been on Carico three years."

"You're coming," he said. "Your training with the Rangers gives you a better understanding of the environmental part of the evaluations than anyone else at Seven Wells. You can have your quarterly meeting with Ro Vinz while we're there."

"My ..." She trailed off. Pointless to argue that. She was still technically on medical suspension from the Central Services Rangers after her last disastrous assignment, and Rodahl Vinz, the Ranger Principal Advisor on Carico, refused to fully release her until he was satisfied that she had recovered from her 'trauma-induced reactive behavior.' Until then he insisted on meeting her face-to-face every quarter but hadn't pushed her to come back.

"Ike," Dougherty said. "Cook wants to know if you would get out that yeasty of yours and make a batch of biscuits for dinner."

"I'll go do that, boss. You have a little talk with the girl." Ike ambled away. Lee held her breath for a moment. Always 'the girl.' Would he ever give her more respect?

Dougherty watched him go before turning back to her. "Lee, you've been away from Seven Wells exactly three times in the year since Seth Reilly left, all to meet with Vinz, and you got him to meet you part way so you didn't have to go to the city. That's not going to convince him that you've recovered." He waited, arms crossed.

She gave in to the silence. "I like it here."

"Well, you're overdue to meet with Vinz again, and this time he wants you in Portside." Dougherty reached out and laid a hand on her shoulder. "More importantly, I do want your perspective on what's presented at this gathering. The evaluation is a big thing for Carico."

Something in his tone got her attention. "You're really not sure we'll pass?" she asked.

"We're behind on some milestones." Dougherty frowned. "This is our third review. The Alliance could opt to bring in someone who will move faster instead of letting us run our own affairs. We've been slow to occupy our allotted territory, and we still don't manufacture much of what we need."

"So that's why we do without." Lee had never gotten used to the lack of basic communications or simple global positioning technology, things that were routine on more developed worlds. Carico's one satellite only provided coverage in a limited area around Portside.

"Imports aren't only expensive, they don't look good for our self-sufficiency," Dougherty said.

She managed a grin. "And I thought it was just frontier pride at getting by."

"Well, maybe some of that too." He squeezed her shoulder lightly and let his hand drop away. "Anyway, the full review of our progress is about to begin, looking at economics, demographics, and a bunch of other -ics. They are bringing in a full satellite array to capture images of the whole planet over a full year to compare to the previous surveys. And you know a lot about that kind of survey."

Lee closed her eyes and sighed. "In theory." She'd rather let her past lie dormant. Carico's General Assembly of Districts contracted with the private provider Central Services for a variety of support, including law enforcement, medical, education, emergency services, and ecological studies, the latter provided by the Ranger Corps. There had been a time when she thought the Rangers would be her life.

"You want me to go, I'll go," she said. "For the Wells, but I'm not getting involved beyond that. I took my shot at public service a while ago. You know how that turned out." She veered her mind away from a racketeer named Jerdix, a man who enjoyed power and pain. She was still haunted by thoughts of his big, harsh hands; of the torturous pain-pleasure device he wielded with devastating effect; and of her relief at the sight of his broken body at the bottom of a cliff.

"You had a tough go and suffered for it," he said, "but you've become one of my best riders and you have some unique expertise. You can help me learn as much as I can from the survey data and help JT Land and Livestock expand their holdings, maybe into some of that unsettled territory."

"Okay, okay." She let her trust of Dougherty push back her reluctance. "You can drag me to town, for the Wells."

"Good. I'll see you after breakfast."

She and Dougherty left the barn. He headed up the lane toward the houses. Lee trudged across the dusty barnyard. Around it sprawled the office, store, cabins and bunkhouse, the cookhouse with its screened summer kitchen and a big garden plot, the barns and workshops, surrounded by a maze of corrals and pastures. The brilliant chartreuse of lush vegetation lined the ditches that spread the water from the namesake wells across the oasis. Under Dougherty's careful management, it was neat and well-maintained except for the inescapable dust that blew down from the arid, verdigris hills all around.

Lee liked riding for Dougherty. It was physically challenging but uncomplicated, and she was free of the constraints the Ranger organization had placed on her. Dougherty had taken her on when she had known nothing about being a rider and let her find her way. He had trusted her when she hadn't trusted herself.

As for Rodahl Vinz, what did she need to do to get him to release her? Was she suspect just because she liked her solitude? Or did he think, if he waited long enough, she would agree to go back to work for the Rangers?

The idea of Portside and the gathering about the evaluation turned her guts icy even though she had grown up in a far bigger metropolis than Portside. And she remembered a time when she looked forward to the energy and social interactions. Before Jerdix. She shook it off. He was gone, dead. And Portside had nothing to do with that anyway.

A day later, Lee followed Dougherty through the door into the lobby of the Steaders' Inn in Portside, and her feet quit moving. The Inn, like the rest of Portside, was packed with people there for the conference. Too many people. Anxiety fluttered in her chest, like her first day at the Ranger academy years ago. She tightened her fists at her sides and shook her hands out. It helped a little.

Ike stopped short of colliding with her. "Elements, girl, what's the hold up? Scared of a little room full of people?"

To herself, she admitted that she was. She sucked in air, trying to get her share. The voices rumbled; the mass of bodies merged, indistinguishable one from another. She shied from a hand on her shoulder, Ike's hand pushing her into the crush. She forced her feet forward.

She managed to slip between the clusters of people, trying to keep her boss's short-cropped, silver-laced hair in sight. She lost track of Ike behind her. Being only a year or two younger than the dusty hills, he knew about half the people in the room, and they greeted him warmly. Well, he was tall enough to see over heads. He could find her and Dougherty.

She caught up to Dougherty at the check-in kiosk and pulled her soft, green shirt straight. It was the only concession she had made for the trip to town. She didn't own a pair of dress boots like both Dougherty and Ike sported.

"Just in time," Dougherty said and stepped aside so she could press her thumb on the scanner to register for the room he had reserved for her. A bed, a bath, and privacy — something she had little enough of in the bunkhouse. Maybe this trip wouldn't be so bad after all.

"Meet me back here in half an hour," Dougherty said. "We'll go over to the Carico Serai for dinner. On JT Land and Livestock since this is business."

So much for her quiet evening. "How can I pass that up?" Lee said, wishing she had a good answer. Well, the food should be exceptional. He was feeling generous with the company's credit.

She saw Ike hitch his way past a group to get to them.

"How about you?" Dougherty asked. "Dinner?"

"Thanks, boss, but some of us relics are getting together. You're welcome to come if you think you can keep up with us."

"Stay out of trouble." Dougherty flashed a smile. He picked up his bag and headed toward the rooms.

"You've got plans?" Ike grinned at Lee. "Meeting your old flame?"

Another of his on-going jibes about her breakup with Seth Reilly. She wished he would let it go. Now it brought anxious quivers to her throat. She hadn't thought about Seth being in town for this. "Dinner with the boss," she said tightly.

Ike got an odd, almost sad look before he forced a grin. "If I see him, I'll let young Reilly know you're here."

Lee turned away without comment. No point encouraging him.

As she hurried to get out of the crowded lobby to the relative quiet of the hallway, she heard a woman's voice asking, "Are you Kieron Dougherty?"

Lee looked around to see Dougherty with a woman in Ranger brown, an impeccably neat, willowy figure with thick, blond hair confined in a long braid. Adel Verlane? With the whole Coalition to choose from, Adel was on Carico. Lee's mind hurtled to her years at the Ranger academy on the central world of Oasis where they had been classmates. Her hands clenched.

Dougherty was nodding. "Call me Kieron," he said with a smile.

"Kieron," Adel replied. "I've been wanting to talk with you. I am trying to meet as many of the larger stead-holders as possible." She turned a little and caught sight of Lee.

"Annalee Vawn-Cory! Is that really you?" The woman's glowing smile didn't reach her ice-gray eyes.

Annalee. Nobody called her that. Lee smoothed her face and forced a smile in return. "Adel."

Adel turned to Dougherty. "Kieron, excuse me. This is an old friend. I haven't seen her in what — four years?"

"Since we graduated," Lee said. She strolled over to stand next to Dougherty. "We heard Vinz found an assistant. I had no idea it was you."

"You know Kieron?"

"I ride for him."

"You're not coming back to the Rangers?" Adel's chin came up, and she looked down at Lee. "Well, lucky for me you are so settled in. I need local contacts. I'm in charge of the satellite survey."

"Congratulations," Lee said. "That's quite a coup for you."

"Thank you," Adel said with a smirk.

So that was what attracted Adel to Carico. The satellite survey would generate a huge amount of data — complete coverage of the planet every day for a full year — to measure progress on milestones in the settlement plan since the previous survey. And it was all in the hands of her old academy roommate and not-so-friendly rival.

"The Wells is glad to help," Dougherty said, drawing Adel's attention from Lee. "Blip me after the conference. We'll set up a time for you to come out."

"Good. I look forward to it."

"We'd better be going," Dougherty said. "Lee, I'll meet you back here in half an hour."

"Welcome to Carico," Lee said with a nod to Adel and headed for the lifts.

Impeccable Adel, with never a hair out of place, was racing up the Ranger ladder in quick time — four years out of the academy and in charge of a major project. As Lee strode away, she was acutely aware of the battered saddlebags hanging over her shoulder — the closest thing she had to a travel bag these days — and her scuffed boots. Just another rider among many; not much of a bragging right in Adel's world. Well, maybe that would keep her off the woman's scanners. She wished she had never agreed to come to this conference.

Counterpoint

Eta'ak

Truly our spirits were frayed near to unraveling that day. The Long Flight *— our ship, our home — had failed us.*

I remember well the day three of my companions and I watched from the planet's smaller moon as the Long Flight *limped away into the black of space. No longer capable of supporting us, its destruction in the corona of the system's sun would assure it did not reveal our presence to the others, the strangers who had already established themselves on the planet. For we were few, little over one hundred in all, and knew nothing of these others.*

When Long Flight's navigation system malfunctioned, Pilot had worked valiantly to bring us out of other-space to a planet that could support us. For that effort, Prime honored him with the responsibility of delivering the Long Flight to its final destruction. May we hold him in our memories always.

We had stripped the ship of what we could and exhausted the fuel for the pinnaces and escape craft transporting the materials and crew to the planet surface, saving only enough for that one last trip to send Pilot on his way and to complete placement of the communications equipment we would rely on for the foreseeable future.

And so we watched as we made the final checks on the communications vault. When the Long Flight was beyond our sight, we entered the pinnace for our journey down to the surface of the fourth planet in the system to join the rest of our shipmates.

Our new home would be a labyrinth of canyons with shallow caves and overhangs that met three criteria: to be hidden from the strangers; to be near enough to them for contact at some time in the future; and to have access to resources essential for our survival as ground-dwellers. Such a terrifying prospect to us who knew nothing but the corridors of a ship.

We dared not contact those others yet, not knowing if they would prove to be friend or foe. We were off our charts into the unknown. We could see that they were starfarers and not native to the world. Our scans revealed a sparse population on only a small fraction of one continent. They had only one spaceport with infrequent arrivals and departures, a single satellite deployed in geosynchronous orbit over their most densely settled territory, and little apparent concern for security. With the Long Flight gone, we felt safe from discovery. No one would be looking for what they did not know existed.

As the years passed, we succeeded, through our equipment on the smaller moon and the commitment of much time, in accessing the First-Comers' library files, news, entertainment broadcasts, and other information, allowing us to study our neighbors. We learned that we had arrived in what was for them the fifty-eighth year since their First Landing. For us, it was when we became Kelok — exiles — and began weaving the strands of our lives into a new fabric.

-From the Archives of Eta'ak, Information Analyst

Chapter 2

Lee

Lee took refuge in her lodging room, away from crowds and unexpected encounters. The snug room held a broad bed, a viewscreen linked to all the entertainment and information broadcasts available at the planet's hub, and a bathing facility, luxurious by bunkhouse standards. She decided to save a good soak until she had more time. She settled for rinsing off thoughts of the distant past along with the mostly-imaginary travel dust.

A glimpse in the mirror convinced her to trade the shirt for something dressier. It was the Serai they were going to. She put on a simple black tank top and pulled out a length of burnt-orange fabric almost as long as she was tall and two-thirds that wide. She had half a dozen of the wraps in different colors. They folded into next to nothing, served as everything from curtains to ground cloths to clothing, and looked pretty good doing it.

She draped the cloth around her shoulders like a shawl and felt like she was hiding behind it. She folded the fabric lengthwise and tried again. That was better, a nice scarf to dress up her rider's pants without getting too fancy. She ran a hand over the soft wrap. Somehow it gave her a feeling of confidence that she badly needed.

She checked the time display on the viewscreen. Better not keep the boss waiting.

She found Dougherty not far from the check-in, and he wasn't alone. The man with him was Rodahl Vinz. Vinz was short and stocky with the pale skin characteristic of humans from the planet Saaremaa. With its "tropics" arctic at best and the arctic regions too cold to be habitable, Saaremaa's people were over-represented in Central Services jobs that got them off world.

When Lee reached them, Dougherty and Vinz were deep in a discussion of fishing and not the usual catch-it-to-eat fishing. Vinz's hobby was the natural history of Carico's fish-like species, the smaller and weirder the better. His office wall was covered with 3D replicas of his finds.

"If it isn't Ranger Vawn-Cory," Vinz said with a laugh. "And here in Portside. That's promising."

"Now don't be trying to steal my rider right under my nose," Dougherty said. "Lee, is it all right with you if Ro joins us for dinner?"

"I, uh, sure," she said. What would he do if she said no, that an evening with Vinz was the least relaxing thing she could think of? But there were things worth standing up to your boss on. This wasn't one of them.

"We can call this our official review of your status," Vinz said. "Without the usual interrogation about your health and career plans."

"I'm fine, sir," she said. She was, at the Wells. Here there were too many people, too much activity.

As they walked across the wide central plaza of Portside's lodging district, Lee let the fresh coolness of the evening ease her tension. Around her, buildings rose several stories tall, resembling intricate origami creations folded to gather breezes and manage the sunlight to its best advantage. Gardens cascaded down the walls in places. She'd been raised in such a cityscape on a much larger scale, but it looked strange to her now after so long in Carico's mountains and deserts.

Her eye caught something half-concealed by landscaping — tarbh. She froze, then realized the animals weren't moving, that no living tarbh would be in such a setting.

"Those are new, aren't they?" Dougherty asked Vinz.

"They are. The artist did a fine job." Vinz led them past the statues, six of them representing a family group, one bull, three cows, two calves. Lee walked slowly around the life-size bull, reaching up to trace the feather-edged scales on its back. The animal was posed in defense posture, head low, one front foot poised to stomp, the wide blue fan of skin around its neck spread forward. Its horns wrapped down like a helmet behind its four eyes before hooking out and forward. It was immense, tall as a horse, with a high hump on its shoulders. The cows weren't much smaller. As she turned her back on the sculpture, she wondered about fools like her that faced the real thing on horseback and expected them to go where directed.

She hurried to catch up to the men. As she got close enough to the Carico Serai to smell the heady mix of spices, her mouth watered. The Serai catered to off-worlders looking for a taste of the best Carico had to offer, which made it the upper end establishment for locals as well. It was the kind of place where Adel would eat. Lee never had.

The restaurant was dimly lit with lots of native wood, stone, and copper. The host led them into the maze of tables and booths and ushered them to a small, private table surrounded by carved wooden screens.

"Your usual, Citizen," she said. "I made sure to hold it for you. I knew we'd be busy tonight."

"Thank you," Vinz said. "What's the special?"

"We have an excellent nutgrass pilaf with mixed meats and vegetables."

Vinz smiled broadly. "What do you say, Kieron, Lee? Shall we get the special for three?"

"Sounds good to me," Dougherty said. Lee just nodded, feeling like a tag-along.

"Fine." Vinz smiled at the host. "And have our server bring a bottle of the 66 JayTee Verdejo, well-chilled."

"Certainly, right away." She hustled off.

"The pilaf is a favorite of mine," Vinz said.

"How did you stumble on the verdejo?" Dougherty asked. "The 66 is the first bottling, if I'm not mistaken."

"It is. The import approval for those grapevines gave me a few sleepless nights, but your bosses were persistent. Turned out to be worth it for them."

Lee let that sink in. She had no idea JT Land and Livestock was in the wine business although she knew they had holdings other than the Wells.

Dougherty leaned back and smiled. "So, Ro, what do you need from me?"

"I already trust you to be a voice of reason in this evaluation," Vinz said. "Tonight it's a wayward Ranger I wanted to corner."

Lee looked up. "Me?" Cornered was right. A knot of anxiety rose in her throat.

"You know I have a new assistant to manage the environmental survey part of the project?"

"I heard." Lee swallowed nervously.

"She's going to need help from someone familiar with Carico. I want you to come back to work and do the ground verification of changes the satellite imagery shows. You'd be traveling a lot, not tied to the office. That should be a good transition back to full duty."

The arrival of the wine gave Lee time to stifle her initial response. In her experience, helping Adel meant doing all the grunt work, taking none of the credit, and serving as scapegoat when needed. On top of the stress of the inevitable disagreements the survey would generate among stakeholders. "I like the job I have," she said as the server poured.

"And I can't leave you in limbo forever," Vinz said. "You could be a big help with the survey part of this. Call it the last step in your recovery."

Dougherty swirled the pale gold wine in his glass. "Ro, you first came to Carico to run the environmental survey on the last review, didn't you?" Lee thanked him silently for the diversion.

"I did," Vinz replied. "This time I have Adel Verlane to do that. It'll be up to her to interpret the computer analysis of the satellite data and validate environmental impacts."

"I met your new assistant this afternoon," Dougherty said. "An old friend of Lee's, it turns out."

Vinz's sharp eyes pinned Lee. "So you know Adel."

"We were at the academy together," Lee said. "I wouldn't say we were friends."

"She was well-recommended by her last supervisor," Vinz said.

"I'm sure she was." Adel had always been good at polishing the brass one way or another.

"Ah," Vinz said, reading her skepticism. "Well, I almost envy her her part of this project. This time my job is politics — I promised Planetary Administrative Officer Emmerling that I would shepherd her through some of the other elements of the evaluation — balance of trade and self-sufficiency, demographics, civil rights — since she hasn't been through it before. And speaking of the PAO…" He stood up.

Lee looked around and saw a woman approaching. She was even shorter than Lee and about twice as broad with ebony skin and silver hair pulled up in elaborate braids. Her bright gold dress, accented with a malachite-colored shawl of whisper-light Jelwyn spider silk, stood out vividly in the muted tones of the room.

She stopped in the entrance to their booth. "Rodahl."

"PAO Emmerling," he replied. "We were just talking about the review process."

She laughed, her eyes sparkling. "Please, Ro, no need for formality here." Her eyes flicked from face to face. "I know Kieron, of course, and, if I'm not mistaken, you are Lee Vawn-Cory. I remember you from the Jerdix incident. Call me Charlyn."

"Hello," Lee replied, wishing she'd stayed at the Steaders' Inn. Jerdix wasn't what she wanted to be remembered for.

"I would love to impose myself upon your evening, but I am expected elsewhere. Ro, come by my office after the conference, and we'll compare observations."

"I'll call you." He watched her glide away before sitting down.

Kieron chuckled. "Was that a purely business invitation?" he asked.

Vinz cleared his throat. "She is an excellent PAO who listens to those around her." He placed his napkin carefully in his lap.

"Well, I don't envy her having to try and keep the General Assembly representatives filled in on the review," Kieron said.

"She's up to the task," Vinz replied. "Now, if I remember correctly, you were already at the Wells during the last review."

"Raised there," Dougherty said. "I didn't pay much attention to the process back then. I had just started as a crew boss and had enough to worry about."

Vinz stared into his wine. "The outcome this time is far less assured."

"We'll make it up in the five-year improvement period," Dougherty said. "A bad review should light a fire under people."

"It just might." Vinz finished his glass of wine and refilled it, topping off Lee's and Dougherty's too.

The server arrived with a steaming pan that he set in the middle of the table. It was heaped high with nutgrass pilaf generously mixed with chunks of meat and vegetables. Lee recognized blue-tinged tarbh along with pale grayish swine-deer and solid white pieces of frog-eel. She remembered how off-putting she had found the bluish colors resulting from the native, copper-based blood when she first came to Carico. Now it looked normal.

"Just smell that," Dougherty said, leaning forward. "The export of those herbs and spices ought to count for something in our trade balance."

"They do," Vinz said. "Along with the medi-botanicals. But refined copper dominates."

Lee found enough appetite to do the food justice in spite of the unsettling comments about the plan review. Settlements did fail, and neither the Sol-Terra Alliance nor the Interstellar Coalition had sympathy. Habitable planets were scarce in Coalition-controlled space. Another applicant would be waiting to take over management. Residents could be relocated or, sometimes, could negotiate to stay. The best guarantee of success was correcting deficiencies well before the review took place. Looming failure sounded like a good reason not to want to get involved. She didn't need the grief.

Faces flashed in her mind — Dougherty, Ike, Seth Reilly and his family, her aunt and uncle — all the people she knew and cared about on Carico. They'd paid in sweat and in the lives lost to the pandemic forty years earlier. She had to believe they would succeed.

She left the Serai with the two men late by up-at-dawn rider standards, although Portside was just getting its nighttime stride. They strolled across the plaza and watched men and women out for a night on the town — groups of riders, miners, and others crisscrossing the pavement, some rowdy, some laid back. The few off-world humans stood out with their extravagant clothing and garish colors. Caricoans tended toward slightly better versions of their everyday garb. The crowd was exclusively human. Carico was a long ways from the homes of non-human Coalition members.

"I don't like it," Dougherty said. "Feel that tension."

Lee looked around, noticing for the first time how different groups avoided each other. The evening's good time mood carried an edge.

Vinz nodded. "The review is sure to bring up all the old arguments — miners versus steaders, big steaders versus little steaders, botanical medicine folks feeling shut out. That's why we wanted to do this conference. Give everyone the same information at the same time and hope it stills the rumor pool a little."

"I'm glad I don't have your job," Dougherty said. "Like facing down one of these." He ran a hand over the tarbh bull statue.

And Vinz wanted her to get involved in all of that. Lee fell back a step from the two men.

"Ro, Kieron," a familiar voice called over the clamor. Lee's breath caught, but the man who separated from a group to greet them wasn't Seth Reilly. It was his father.

"Joe Reilly, good to see you." Dougherty laid a hand on the taller man's shoulder in greeting. "It's been a while. Here for the conference?"

"I am. And you brought Lee along. Alive and kicking, I see."

"I'm fine," she said. She wasn't sure where she stood with him since she and Seth had split. The problem was that almost everyone she knew on Carico had known Seth a lot longer than they'd known her, even her aunt and uncle in Under Rim where Joe was Marshal.

"A blip once in a while would be nice," Joe said. He pulled her into a hug. "You're family and don't you forget that."

"Thank you," she said. "That means a lot."

He kept an arm over her shoulders. "Ro, I heard you were looking for me."

"I am," Vinz said. "I've got a vacation coming before this whole review kicks into full gear."

"And you want some advice on where to go?" Joe asked.

"I have a couple ideas I want to run past you."

"Let's go someplace a little quieter. Wouldn't want too many people knowing where to find you." Joe gave Lee a squeeze. "You stay in touch, okay?"

"I will." She stepped away from him. "Tell my aunt I'll come visit when I get a chance."

"We'll hold you to that."

Joe and Vinz headed toward the Mardukai Lodging House. Lee and Dougherty continued to the Steaders' Inn. Once in the busy lobby, Dougherty said, "I'd better put in an appearance at the steaders' reception. And Lee, you think about what Vinz said about the survey. I'd be selfish to keep you chasing tarbh for the Wells when you could be helping. Carico needs local input."

"I'll think about it." She did, unhappily, as she watched Dougherty walk away. She wished they would just leave her alone.

A rowdy group of young riders crowded past, and she shivered a little. So many people. She shook the tension out of her hands and hurried across the lobby. As she passed the wide entrance to the lounge, she caught sight of someone she knew.

She froze like a swine-deer seeing a pack of wolf-lizards. But the tall, blonde woman at the corner of the bar was too occupied to look her way. Adel had changed out of her pants into a dress that looked like poured-on dark chocolate. And the capable hand that toyed with her heavy braid of hair belonged to Seth Reilly.

Lee fled to the seclusion of her room. Vinz pushing her to come back; Dougherty pushing her to do her part for Carico; now Seth flirting with Adel. How well she remembered the touch of that hand. She should have stayed at the Wells. Unable to sort out clashing emotions, she plunged herself into a shower so hot she could barely stand it and squeezed her eyes tight against tears.

Chapter 3

Lee

Lee perched on a chair in the summer kitchen, a screened patio off the Seven Wells cookhouse surrounded by the kitchen gardens. A peaceful spot. Spring was morphing into summer. In a few days, she and Ike would leave the increasing heat of the headquarters for higher country and a summer of watching over wide-ranging tarbh. And she might be able to leave behind unwanted thoughts of people from her past. Everything at the Wells was uncomplicated compared to the trip to Portside two weeks earlier. Except maybe what Ike had in mind for her morning.

"Time you learned to do this, girl," Ike said. He stood at the center island, bowls and ingredients spread around him.

Lee dragged herself out of her chair. Cooking instruction — make that baking. She should feel honored. His yeasty bread was known far and wide. But cooking was something she did to eat, not something she aspired to master.

"Wash your hands," he said. He lined up the containers of nutgrass flour, water, bean tree oil, and salt next to the crock with the yeasty starter. The yeasty and the crock that held it were his prized possessions. He fondly called the yeasty Beulah; Lee didn't know why. The magic yeasty crock maintained the perfect temperature and allowed air along with the critical native yeasts to get in while being spill proof.

He scooped out a sticky, goopy double handful of yeasty, measuring it by eye before dropping it into a big bowl. "Water next," he said. "About half as much as the yeasty to start, but you'll probably need more to get it right. And add a splash of oil."

A recipe would be nice, she thought as she checked the level of the yeasty on the side of the bowl and guessed at the water, poured a little oil on top, and stuck her hands in to mix it up. Ike watched over her shoulder, added a bit more water, and stepped back. "That's what you want it to feel like. See how much you've got? Now add that much more flour a little bit at a time. And don't forget the salt." He measured coarsely ground salt into the palm of his gnarled hand, showing her the amount before scattering it over the first flour she added.

She dug her hands in and began mixing up the big batch, enough to feed all of the dozen or so people at the headquarters at the moment. She discovered something satisfying in the feel as the dry and the wet came together into a soft, elastic ball. Maybe bread wasn't as difficult as she thought. Or maybe the tricky part came with what you did next, the rising and baking, but that should be all a matter of timing. She folded and kneaded, folded and kneaded, a soothing repetition. She began to understand why Ike enjoyed it.

"Isn't that your Ranger friend?" Ike tipped his head toward the woman getting out of a Ranger-marked skimmer behind the cookhouse.

"She's no friend of mine." Lee punched at the dough and noticed the flour coating her hands and wrists, not to mention the front of her tank top. *Scorch it.* She knew Dougherty had arranged for Adel Verlane to come to the Wells but didn't realize that was today.

Then Adel's companion got out of the driver's seat. Lee stared. She hadn't seen the man in three years, but she recognized Whip Willemsen. He'd been one of Jerdix's flunkies. Now he was driving the Ranger around. That made no sense.

Adel left him standing by the skimmer and strolled toward the closest building, the summer kitchen. Lee wiped her hands on a towel. "I'll take her to the office," she told Ike. "Why don't you take her driver over and let him wait on the cookhouse porch where you can keep an eye on him."

"You know him?" Ike asked as he covered the bowl of dough with a towel and set it aside to rest.

"We've met. Last thing I heard he was serving out a restitution work detail."

"From that mess you and young Reilly were in with a while back?"

"He was a minor player. A punk rider with more mouth than brains."

Adel spotted them and came to the screen door. Ike opened it for her. "Welcome to Seven Wells. I'm Ike Allred."

"Ike, my pleasure. I think Kieron mentioned you as someone I should talk to."

"Might be. I've had my boots in Carico dirt since First Landing."

"Then I'm sure I'll be interested in your perspective later in the process." She brushed past him. "I'm so glad to see you," she said to Lee. She waved a hand at their surroundings. "You gave up the Rangers for this?"

"And you've got a driver to chauffeur you around," Lee countered.

"Assigned to the office as part of a restitution. But he knows his way around this desolation."

Ike narrowed his eyes at that. "I expect it must look that way to a central like you," he said. "I'll go get your man out of the sun. You'll find him by the cookhouse when you're ready to go." He let the door bang behind him.

"A central? Me?" Adel smoothed her tunic.

By Carico standards Adel was. Lee had been too, three years ago, when she'd come from the heart of the

Interstellar Coalition to the frontier fringe. "All in your perspective," she said.

"I suppose." Adel smiled. "So, are the rumors true? You left your career for a man?"

Lee stiffened, staring at Adel's tawny braid lying on her brown shirt, remembering a gentle, strong hand toying with it. "Nothing to tell," she snapped. "It didn't work out." She felt the prickle of the horsehair bracelet she wore, a symbol of her relationship with Seth Reilly. She really should get rid of it. She turned to the sink, picked up a brush, and scrubbed the dough from her hands. "I'll take you to find the boss. He should be at the office."

Adel wandered around the kitchen, looking out through the screen walls. "This is a big place, almost a village all by itself."

Lee surveyed the familiar collection of mud-brick barns and sheds and the corrals surrounding the barnyard. "Everything we need," she answered.

"Isolated though." Adel shook her head.

"A little," Lee said. "Here comes the boss. He must have seen you come in." She watched Dougherty quick step across the dusty yard from the office.

"Adel, welcome to Seven Wells." Dougherty smiled. "My apologies, but we'll have to talk a little later."

"But you are the one I came to see," Adel said with practiced warmth.

"I've got some unexpected business at the big house, but it shouldn't take long. Meanwhile you and Lee can catch up. She can answer most of your questions." He gave Lee a look that said not to argue.

"Wonderful. I hoped we'd have a chance to talk. Although I do want the *steaders'* perspectives on the survey." Adel emphasized.

"And I, for one, am looking forward to seeing the survey results." Dougherty rubbed his weathered face thoughtfully. "It's easy to miss slow changes that happen right in front of you. The comparison to twenty-five years ago could show some interesting things, to the good, I hope. I'm glad I have Lee's trained eye to help me with that."

"Sure, boss." Lee said with tight lips. "Come on," she said to Adel. "Let me change my shirt. Then we can talk about raising livestock on Carico." She led the way across the barnyard to the bunkhouse.

"Did Kieron just brush me off?" Adel asked.

"Don't worry. He'll make time for you." Lee looked up the lane. One of the owners must have shown up unexpectedly. That's usually what big house business meant. "Here's the bunkhouse," she said, pushing the door open.

Adel looked around the long, narrow room with lines of curtained cubbyholes along the walls, each with a bunk above closet space. An assortment of tables and chairs filled the center of the room. "This place makes me appreciate my apartment."

"It's pretty quiet this time of year," Lee replied. "Only four of us right now. The rest are already out at the line camps for the summer. We had ten in here last winter."

"Hard to believe — you here like this." Adel perched on the edge of a table. "Lee Vawn-Cory, born and raised in Kasba-on-Oasis, headquarters of the Interstellar

Coalition, and Ranger to the bone. During training, you never passed up a chance to hop a ship to anywhere. I never dreamed you'd take frontier duty."

"My mother was raised on Carico," Lee answered as if it explained everything.

Adel stood up and drifted around the room. "When you vanished right after graduation, before most of us even had assignments ... well, chatter was you got assigned to some super-secret duty in the investigations branch."

"Something like that." Lee grabbed a clean shirt. She'd rather forget that first assignment trying to gather evidence on C.T. Jerdix. "Give me a minute to get cleaned up," she said and retreated to the washroom where she applied a wet cloth to her face and arms and got her head together. Flour-free shirt in place, she rejoined Adel. "We can talk out on the porch," she said.

Adel stopped in the doorway, looking at the cookhouse porch where Ike and Whip sat with two other riders. "Can we go somewhere quieter?" Adel asked. "More private?"

"Okay," Lee said. Pretty much anyplace away from the cookhouse would do but, if Adel wanted privacy, Lee knew just the place. "Let's go up where you can get a view of the place." She led the way between the corrals and out into a pasture beyond the barns, noticing with perverse satisfaction that not even Adel was immune to Carico dust. The Ranger's shiny boots carried a verdigris tinge.

Adel ignored the dirt. "You've settled in? Living out here in the wild?"

"You couldn't drag me back to Oasis." Lee shook her head. How many billion people now, human and otherwise, from eight member species of the Coalition and a couple others hoping to join or petitioning for something? No way. "Here I haven't seen ten strangers in the last six months."

"Except when you were in Portside for the conference," Adel said. "A lot of people showed up for that."

"People tend to be interested in things that bring change." Lee scrambled around a boulder pile and climbed the slope of a low rise. Reaching the hilltop, she stopped in the speckled shade of a scraggly copper tree and looked down over the headquarters of the Seven Wells Stead. "If you haven't figured this out already, we're pretty independent around here. We mostly deal with things ourselves. So anyone from Portside, much less off world, is suspect from the start."

"There did seem to be a lot of undercurrents," Adel said. "I was hoping you would help me with that."

Lee thought about all the little factions coming out to have their say. "That's the kind of thing to talk to my boss about," she said. "I don't get off the stead much."

"Oh?" Adel fanned her face with her hand.

"This is a big place." She swept a hand across the vista. Enough reason to come up here. Getting Adel sweaty was a bonus.

Adel came over to stand close to Lee. She looked down on the desert and the headquarters with the bluish-green soil and rocks, the yellow and chartreuse of the plants. "Do you ever get used to the colors?"

"It's the copper in the soil." Lee held her ground, uncomfortable with Adel's proximity. "It causes low levels of chlorophyll production by plants, and yellowish leaves."

"There is one patch down there that's truly green."

"The kitchen garden," Lee said. "The greener the leaves, the less copper, the better for human consumption."

Adel turned toward her. "Sounds like an analytical ranger lurking beneath the dungarees."

"Too well trained, I guess." Lee stepped away, out of the shade, and hoped Adel would finally get down to her real reason for coming.

"You are. That's why I want you to work on the survey." Adel closed in on her again. "I need people to go out on the ground and verify features the satellite imagery picks up, people who can navigate this desolation." She waved a hand at the surrounding country. "And it would be fun to work together."

"Us together." Lee had no idea where that came from. She watched Dougherty in the distance walking from the office up the lane toward the houses, a man she trusted. "I'm happy where I'm at."

"I hope you'll think about it anyway." Adel said, flashing an encouraging smile. "You've had time to get to know your way around."

"I thought you had a driver for that."

"He's very knowledgeable." Adel stiffened and moved away.

"Probably enthusiastic about extra-curricular activities too," Lee laughed.

"In fact, he is. What of it?"

That was unexpected. Adel usually flaunted her conquests. Lee changed direction. "So, besides trying to poach me from the Wells, what did you want to know?"

Adel sat on a boulder, her eyes on the desert. "You spent some time up north in Under Rim. That didn't go well, did it?"

"Not the way it was planned," Lee answered. Was Seth who Adel was actually interested in?

"I was sorry to hear about that. And you are still on suspension," Adel said.

"What else did you find in the files?" Lee asked. Her files should be confidential, including her medical suspension from the Rangers, and she trusted Vinz wouldn't have discussed a personnel matter.

"Sorry. I was concerned." Adel had the grace to look embarrassed about snooping. She changed the subject. "What can you tell me about Joe Reilly?"

"Joe?" That was unexpected. "He's marshal for the Under Rim District. Born and raised there. Married. Two kids and one on the way. In touch with what's happening in his district."

"You know the family?" Adel asked.

Lee couldn't forget Adel with Seth in Portside. "Well enough," she answered truthfully, then sidestepped. "My uncle is Joe's second-in-command at the Marshal's Office."

Adel's eyes widened with surprise. "I didn't know you had family there."

Something her confidential file hadn't revealed. "Aunt, uncle, and a cousin. I told you my mom was from

Carico." Lee paused, gathering her thoughts. "What's your interest in Joe Reilly?"

"Just looking for the power people in Under Rim and the other agricultural districts," Adel said. "People with influence behind the scenes."

Now that sounded like Adel. She liked being associated with important people. Her driver couldn't do that for her. "Outside of Under Rim, I can't help you much." Lee shrugged. "But power players aren't hard to figure out. Just sit in on the district arbiters' meetings. Districts elect their local arbiters; arbiters choose their General Assembly delegates. Sounds like you want the ones who show up at local meetings and influence the arbiters." What scheme did Adel have in mind? Experience had taught Lee to suspect the woman's motives.

"See, I knew you'd have it all scanned out." Adel twisted the end of her braid. "Remember those big dreams we had as cadets?"

"You'll never get famous from a First Contact here. We're a little short of non-human people, even from the known species." Lee quirked her mouth in a half-grin.

"First Contact? Fame and fortune?" Adel said. "I just want to do a good job with the survey. And I thought we could help each other out, me giving you some support getting back to work while you share what you've learned about this world."

Lee shook her head. "You thought wrong."

Adel gave Lee the strangest look. "Forgive me for trying to help." She walked away, down the hill toward the headquarters.

Lee followed her. She still couldn't figure out what Adel had hoped to get from her or why she had been so specific about privacy. Lee couldn't think of anything from their conversation to hide. Unless Adel had finally learned to be a little discreet about who she was jinking.

Lee waited to catch up to Adel until they got into the maze of pens and alleyways. Then she led the way silently. Dougherty was just returning from the big house when they reached the office. "Did you two have a good visit?" he asked.

"We got, uh, caught up on some things," Adel said. "But now I'd like to get your perspective on how a big stead like Seven Wells fits into the political landscape." She smiled and played with the end of her braid.

"Come on in." He held the door and raised an eyebrow at Lee. "If you've got a minute, please get us something cold to drink."

"Sure, boss." Relieved to let out of the discussion, she ambled across to the cookhouse, going in through the summer kitchen to avoid Whip. She had no desire to dredge up memories. Adel threatened that, poking around in her personnel file, her confidential file. And what had Whip, who had worked for Jerdix, said during their 'extracurricular activities?' Facing mad mama tarbh, or whatever else Seven Wells could throw at her, looked better than ever.

She returned with a pitcher of iced tea and let her boots clump on the wooden floor of the outer office to announce her entrance before she reached Dougherty's private office. Adel's voice cut off.

Dougherty met Lee at the door and took the pitcher from her. He waved her to a chair, filled glasses, and passed them to the two women. "So, Adel, what else can I tell you?"

Adel sipped from her glass and smiled. "You've been a big help. You're responsible for a large area. People like yourself have so much to lose if the review doesn't go right."

"I'm just the manager," Dougherty said. "A lot of folks have more invested in this than I do."

She glanced at Lee. "Well, once the satellites are up and the data is coming in, I'll have to come back, and you can show me the whole operation."

"Best call ahead," he said. "Make sure someone's around before making that long trip."

"Certainly. Now, I do need to get to Wide Ford." Adel rose.

"I'm sorry we didn't have more time today." Dougherty set his own glass down and stood. "Safe travels," he said. "We'll let you get on the trail."

"Yes." Lee got up and started for the door to encourage short goodbyes.

Dougherty called her back. "Once you've seen Adel off, we'll have that talk."

"Yes, boss." Lee gave him a puzzled look. What talk?

"You stay," Adel said. "I can find my way back to my skimmer."'

Lee stood aside. "Luck with the survey."

"Kieron, I'll be in touch," Adel said. She swept past, leaving Lee in a swirl of uneasiness.

Dougherty sat down. "You two have an interesting talk?" he asked.

"Oh, yeah," Lee replied, frowning. She waited for Adel to close the outer door before she went back to the chair she had vacated.

"She did seem concerned about you," he said. "In fact, unless I'm a spinxi, she was more interested in seeing you than talking to me."

"Then maybe you are a spinxi." Lee managed a laugh, picturing his face on the body of one of the lobster-armadillo-lizard creatures that kept barns free of vermin and provided tasty eggs for human tables.

"So she asked you to go work for her?" He raised his eyebrows. "Did Vinz suggest that to her?"

"Don't know, but she likes to keep a convenient scapegoat around," Lee said.

He gave her a long, assessing look that made her cringe inside. "Listen," he said. "I don't know the details of what happened to you and to Seth three years ago, but Ro Vinz thinks you are avoiding dealing with it."

"I'm fine," Lee said, too firmly. She didn't want to have this conversation, didn't want to think about the past.

"You are not fine. In Portside you were as nervous as a rock rat in a spinxi coop." He leaned forward and rested his elbows on the desk between them. "One of the reasons I took you on when you first came here was your commitment to seeing that Seth got the help he needed to move on. It took some tough love on your part, but you did it."

"And now you think I need a dose of that same medicine?" Her insides churned. He was going to take Vinz's side.

"Sending you back to the Rangers might be the best thing I could do for you. It's too easy for you to avoid the issue here."

"Boss, please." She hated herself for begging. Especially since she knew deep inside they were right. Seven Wells was her escape.

He studied her for a long moment. "All right."

She sighed with relief.

He stood up and turned to the map on the wall behind him. He laid a lean hand over an area somewhere north of the Wells, north of Wide Ford. He faced her. "It happens I have a job in mind for you here, something that will put your old training to good use for the Wells rather than the Rangers."

"What might that be?" Lee let herself relax a little.

"My meeting at the big house was with Tecknir and Johannesson."

Lee recognized the names, the two principal shareholders in JT Land and Livestock, the company that owned Seven Wells.

Dougherty continued. "They don't want to wait on the outcome of the review. They want to pursue expanding into unsettled territory. And maybe action now will look good toward meeting the development goals."

Lee remembered the discussion in Portside about settlement not having expanded into all the allocated territory. She was on firm ground now. "Do they have a place in mind?"

"We talked about the upper Glas River country, maybe for tarbh or maybe something else. I'm going up there tomorrow for a general fly-over and to get plans underway to send riders out to get a feel of the ground."

"Riders?" she asked.

"You and Ike."

Lee chewed her lip. "It'll be a long, tough ride. Do you think he's up to it?"

"You know he is." He sat on the corner of his desk. "He's got a good eye for what might interest the company, and he knows how to make a long trek. I don't have another rider right now that I would send with you for this. And it'll get you off Vinz's scanners for a while."

"When you put it that way ..."

"Good. I'll go up by skimmer and spend a few days getting the lay of the land. When I get back, we can map out exactly where you need to go."

"How long should we plan for?" she asked, already mulling over what they would need to take. She'd never made such a long expedition into unexplored territory.

"Let's see — on horseback, five days to Wide Ford and probably two more to the edge of the area I have in mind. Then a couple weeks — say sixteen days — on the ground, verifying water sources, vegetation patterns, anything of interest. Allowing for unexpected delays, plan for a minimum of thirty-five days. Back in plenty of time for Settlement Day."

"Won't that get us into the summer rains?" she asked. That would mean wet afternoons, risk of thunderstorms, and, on the plus side, short-lived pools of water in otherwise arid country.

"You'll have to take that into consideration in your planning."

"Why not do it by skimmer?"

He grinned. "I want you to taste the dust. Nothing like hooves on the ground to get to know the country."

She took a drink of tea, feeling the slick coldness of the glass in her hand. What was she getting herself into? Well, right now she was more interested in what he was getting her out of. A long ways from Vinz and from Adel's schemes. "All right, horseback it is," she said.

"There's one catch. I hope it's not a big one."

"What's that?" she asked.

"Your last supply stop, your last contact up there. It'll be Seth Reilly."

Counterpoint

Eta'aк

Ten cycles of seasons — ten years — have established us firmly in our caves and canyons, hidden from those others, but the time has arrived at last. We will not be able to remain undiscovered more than a few months longer.

Soon the First-Comers will put up satellites to capture images of the planet surface. They wish to document changes since the last time they did this, fifteen years before we arrived. Careful as we have been to conceal our presence from casual flyovers, I have no doubt our activities have marked the land with changes that will be revealed.

Some of us argue heatedly about old decisions, that we should have gone to the far side of the planet originally, forgetting that when we first landed, we hoped someday to make contact, even return to our old home. Such arguments waste time and energy on the past when we must move forward.

I have warned that this day would come and urged that we have a strategy for contacting the First-Comers before they come to us. But Prime disagrees, although she has offered no alternative ideas. On this she seems to be thinking like a male, content not to look too far ahead. It is the long future we must concern ourselves with. We do still have a narrow margin to take control of the events. Somehow, I must convince Prime and my fellow council members that we must act.

-From the Archives of Eta'ak, Information Analyst.

Chapter 4

Seth

Seth Reilly shifted the rock until it rested solidly on the ones under it. The wall was head-high now, good progress in the couple of weeks since he had gotten home from Portside. Finding this sheltered, south-facing pocket in the canyon wall had sold him on this spot when he'd been looking for a place for his own stead. He brushed his hand over the sandstone, pleased with the patterns of greenish-blue and brown in the blocks. The new room extended out from under the overhanging rock far enough to catch the sun all year.

He had a solar-heated water tank ready to install on the roof, a fine luxury for his primitive home.

The trip to Portside had inspired him to finish the shower house. The pure pleasure of unlimited hot water made that whole trip worthwhile. Leave it to his pa to think of showing up out of the blue and taking him to that conference. He hadn't seen anyone other than his neighbors for weeks, not since he had moved back after wintering in Under Rim.

Hot water wasn't the only thing he remembered from Portside. The image of Adel Verlane intruded on the rugged surroundings. He hadn't known she was the new Ranger when she'd first spoken to him in the bar. She was a tempting picture — tall, tawny, with curves in all the right places — and she'd definitely shown interest. But every time he looked at her, he'd expected brown-gold eyes instead of gray.

Seth rubbed his left wrist, missing the feel of the horsehair bracelet that had finally worn through from contact with the rocks he stacked for walls and fences. It had symbolized the commitment between him and Lee. He guessed it still did — now worn out, broken and set aside.

He'd seen Lee in Portside too, from a distance. But he wasn't going to push it if she didn't want him back. She was the one who sent him packing. It was up to her to change her mind. So he had avoided her.

Good thing he liked solitude.

From his perch on the ledge, he looked down on the floor of the canyon twenty feet below. Small canyons like this one cut into the sandstone plateau, rimmed by cliffs above talus slopes. Hard to find a place to climb out but plenty of good grassland on the flats on top. And where there was water, the bottoms were oases of vivid yellow-green vegetation.

Last summer he had made good use of the rocks from the talus slopes to build fences around a garden area and across the main canyon and several side-canyons to keep his horses from wandering too far. Good practice for the walls he'd built this spring in the cave. Slowly things were coming together, at least the things that only needed hard work to accomplish.

He gave the new wall one more stroke like it was the shoulder of a horse. The new shower room blocked the west end of the rockshelter from the late day sun and the worst of the winter winds. He had also walled in the deepest part of the shelter for storage. He planned to leave the rest open to take advantage of summer breezes and winter sun. He'd be able to stick it out here next winter rather than going back to Under Rim.

A distant hum turned his attention up the canyon. It sounded like a skimmer. He could have sworn it was tomorrow when he was supposed to help fix the neighbors' barn roof. Besides, Gabe Huff would have picked him up at daybreak.

He pulled on his shirt and climbed down the steep steps he had built to get to the floor of the canyon. Some emergency message for him, maybe? Gabe and Melinda had the closest communications antenna and let him have blips sent there. In return, he was glad to help them out, especially when Gabe drove up to get him, saving him the eighteen-mile horseback ride to their place.

He watched the craft come slowly up the canyon, hovering just above the twisted tops of the vine trees, like someone looking for something. It nearly passed him before the driver saw him and came around to park in the opening below the rockshelter. A Steadmaster 68, nearly new with room for six in the cab and open cargo space in back. Seth recognized the large JT on the side. Dougherty? Lee? His heart pounded.

It was Kieron Dougherty who climbed out and scuffed through the sand. "You got yourself out here a ways," he said, looking around.

"Well, you found me." Seth wiped his dirty, rock-scraped hands on his pants. "Welcome to Rock House." He nodded toward the ledge. From where they stood only the new wall and the steps showed there was anything there. "How'd you know where to look?"

"Your father. I saw you at the conference but never managed to catch up to you."

"You weren't alone," Seth said quietly. He'd seen Dougherty too but always with Lee.

"Thought that might be it." Dougherty hesitated and shook his head. "Your business. I came about something else. The owners want to expand and, from what your father told me about this country, I thought it was worth a look."

"That we can talk about. Come on up to the house."

Seth led the way up the steps, thinking hard. If Dougherty liked the ground and convinced the owners to establish a new stead nearby, he might just be able to make a go of this place. He needed more neighbors and knew the company well enough not to worry about them pushing him aside like some might. And he could use some day work so he could buy a few staples and maybe a new pair of boots. He could feel the rocks through the thin soles of the ones he wore.

They looked over Dougherty's computer maps and satellite imagery from the earlier surveys of Carico, and Seth pointed out a couple areas he thought had potential for a large stead. Northwest of him was the sandstone plateau. Tributaries of the Glas River cut into its eastern and southern edges, creating a labyrinth of canyons like the one he'd laid claim to. The broad flats on top grew thick stands of grass. Springs of clear, cold water hid down in the canyons, supporting wild tarbh and other animals. Tough country, but no more so than the lower desert where Seven Wells was located.

"Joe was right; that plateau does sound promising. And you're all right with the idea?" Dougherty asked.

"Plenty of room for my little horse-breeding operation and JT," he said. "Be nice to have more neighbors."

"I don't suppose you'd be interested in coming back to work for the company?" Dougherty asked. "We would need someone here who understands this canyon country."

"No thanks," Seth said slowly. The last year had been rough. Life would be a lot easier under the company's wing. But he wasn't ready to give up yet. Besides, Lee worked for JT. "Day work, maybe, but I've got my own place."

"Fair enough," Dougherty said. "You've made a good start."

Seth looked around. He had worked hard on the rock walls. The limited furniture he had built took advantage of the natural turns and bends of the copper tree wood. He liked the primitive artistry. "It's getting there."

"Any chance you'd let me stay here a couple of nights and maybe come along with me to look over the country?"

Seth grinned. "You're welcome to stay." Company sounded good. Better than being left with his imagination. "But I'll have to pass on riding along with you. I promised the neighbors to help with their barn roof tomorrow."

"Good enough."

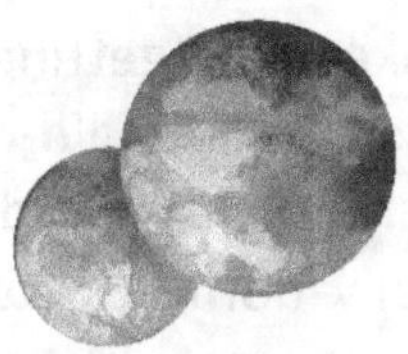

Dougherty stayed that night, left before Seth did in the morning, and was asleep when Seth got back from Huffs'. Seth took his time making breakfast the next morning, baking biscuits and making a thick, spicy gravy with swine-deer sausage, in no hurry for his visitor to leave.

"You liked what you saw?" he asked the older man.

"I did," Dougherty confirmed. "That spot you pointed out where the canyons come together would make a fine headquarters, and it's only a couple miles from here."

"I don't see much tarbh sign this side of the plateau," Seth said.

"They seem to like the hills on the far northwest side, clear up toward the Whitewater River. That's farther out than I'd like, but they aren't our first interest here anyway."

"Oh?"

"Time to diversify, find some new opportunities. Nutgrass for example." Dougherty sopped up gravy with a nutgrass biscuit before continuing. "Lots of it on the plateau. Probably some other plants of interest, especially hidden away in these canyon bottoms where there's good water."

"Farming?" Seth studied a pattern in the gravy on his plate. That would take some getting used to.

"With a light touch. Call it wild-crafting," Dougherty said. "Then there are the swine-deer. They could be hunted if not actually domesticated. It's not like the tarbh are truly domesticated either. And this side of the plateau would be a good place to raise horses — if a certain neighbor doesn't object." Dougherty eyed him steadily.

"Now that might be a problem," Seth answered, thinking of his own plans.

"The company might go for some kind of partnership with the right person, say a talented horse trainer familiar with the country." Dougherty carried his cleaned plate to the sink without waiting for a response. "Lots of possibilities," he said.

"Yup." Seth stood slowly. "I guess if I have to have more neighbors, I'll take JT over a lot of the alternatives."

"The company's always treated me fairly," Dougherty said. "Anyway, I'll send a couple riders up to take a closer look and map some of the details. The satellite imagery is a little iffy in these canyons. Then we'll see what the owners want to do."

"Makes sense."

"I could put you back on the payroll for a while if you want to go along."

Seth hesitated. He could use the credit. He was living off his savings from working at the Wells and what little he had earned at various jobs over the winter. His stead was a long ways from the day it would make him a living. "Sorry, but I can't afford to be gone," he told Dougherty. "With summer coming on, I need to keep my garden watered, and I have a lot of work to do before winter."

"Can I drop off supplies here for the riders?"

"Who …" Seth started to ask. He didn't really want to know if Lee would be one of them or the one delivering supplies.

"It'll be Lee and Ike Allred," Dougherty replied. "She needs something different for a while. And it'll be out of sight of the Rangers. They want her back."

"She isn't going?" Seth thought she would after he'd left the Wells.

"She probably should." Dougherty gave him a pointed look. "She's holed up at the Wells like a wounded wolf-lizard."

That bad? "Seeing me isn't going to help much," he said.

"She needs you," Dougherty said. "As bad as you needed her a while back."

Seth stumbled over his reply. "I tried. You know I did."

"I saw that. Look, you two never shared what happened with Jerdix, not the personal details, so I'm in no position to judge. Or to help."

"I can't share Lee's story."

"Not asking you to, though I can guess part of it. But you, well, I know it was bad. It took a lot for you to recover from where you were when you first came back to the Wells. I've got a lot of respect for that."

"Thanks ... thank you." Seth looked at the older man. "Have you ever heard of ..." He hesitated, then forced it out. "Of a pain-pleasure rod?"

Dougherty nodded slowly. "Nasty. Outlawed anywhere in the Coalition."

"Jerdix had one. He used it on me, on a random setting, repeatedly."

Dougherty was silent for a long breath. "Messes with your brain, doesn't it?"

"It actually causes physiologic changes but that's not the worst of it." Seth dug into his trust for Dougherty to voice something he'd never talked about outside of rehab. "Used like that, never knowing what a touch would bring? It left me ... I couldn't stand to ... even be ... be touched for a long time."

Dougherty frowned. "I saw that. And I saw you get the help, the treatment you needed."

"It's done." Seth straightened his shoulders. "I've learned to manage the residual effects. And no, he didn't do the same to Lee."

"I am glad to know that." Dougherty hesitated. "Just know I still wish you'd think about coming back. If you still care about her."

"If I ..." Seth gave a crooked grin. "Always. But I couldn't help her. She wouldn't let me."

"Maybe a year working with Ike has softened her up."

Seth looked him in the eye, trying to see where this was going. "That is an interesting team," he said.

"Something needs to knock her out of her cocoon," Dougherty said.

Seth's heart sank. "What about her old boss, Vinz? Shouldn't he be making sure she gets treatment?"

"He doesn't seem to want to force the issue. So the best I can do is give her a legitimate challenge to work on. She and Ike together have what I need for this expedition."

Seth shrugged, like it was no big thing. "No problem dropping supplies here," he said. "I can let you do that."

"Thanks. And think about what I said. I'm worried about her."

"Then this may be the last place you should send her," Seth answered. "It'll just bring up bad memories."

"Maybe she needs that before she can put them to rest." Dougherty laid a hand on his shoulder. "I'd better be going. I want to look over some of the canyons to the west on my way home."

Seth walked with him down to the skimmer, unexpectedly reluctant to be alone. It had been good to have somebody to talk to. Even if it stirred up the past.

"If I'm not around when someone brings the supplies, they can put them in the tack room." Seth pointed out the small stone building near where the skimmer was parked.

"Probably a week or ten days from now. I want to get this going. We're butting up against the summer rains as it is." Dougherty swung his bag into the bed of the skimmer. "Just know you have a place at the Wells anytime. I can't seem to find a good replacement for my horse trainer."

Seth managed a grin at that reference. "Thanks, I appreciate it. It's been good to see you."

"I'll let your father know I saw you. He worries." Dougherty climbed into the skimmer and pulled slowly away before lifting above the brush and heading up the canyon. Seth watched him until he was out of sight.

Maybe he should take the offer to go with the riders. He could build up a little more credit and buy a solar power array. Or trade for a couple more mares for his herd, the well-built, ground-covering horses that they bred at Seven Wells. He planned to cross those with his stout, mountain-bred stud to get smart, sound, versatile horses that would appeal to steaders.

If only it wasn't Lee. He could hear her laugh, see her trim figure at one with the horse under her, feel her ...

The canyon closed in on Seth. He looked across to the vine tree grove where his two saddle horses dozed in the morning shade. Driven by something he couldn't name, he grabbed a halter, caught the roan gelding, and saddled him. He headed upstream to a place the horse could climb out of the canyon onto the plateau. With the wide sweep of grass before him, he kept the horse in a trot until they both dripped sweat. Would he ever put Lee behind him? The memories still hurt like a smashed toe.

Chapter 5

Lee

Five days on the trail from Seven Wells, Lee didn't need the roll of maps in the case hanging from her saddle or the data pendant around her neck to know they had reached the Glas River. Ike stopped his brown gelding on the bluff where the trail dropped down to the valley bottom. "Better check the cinches," he said and eased to the ground, giving his creaky knees a chance to straighten before he went to his pack horse.

Lee swung off, checked her cinch, and rubbed Clown on the neck. The lean, little white-splashed gelding was one of two horses she'd selected for the trek. Her second horse, a stout, cream-colored gelding that had been in her string as long as she'd worked at the Wells, waited patiently while she made sure his packs were snug. She had argued for taking an extra horse or two, but Ike had overridden her as he had on pretty much every suggestion she'd made while planning the trip.

Ike climbed back onto his horse. "Let's do it," he said.

Lee watched the rhythmic motion of the sorrel rump ahead of her as Ike's pack horse disappeared from sight over the edge of the bluff. The broad valley of the Glas River stretched before her, a dozen braided channels, gravel bars, and brushy islands to cross to reach the tiny cluster of buildings that was Wide Ford.

In the time they had been on the trail, Ike had let her lead most of the time. Lee decided that was because his horse Tinker liked to follow another horse. But for the coming river crossing, he took the lead himself. She didn't mind. She'd forded here once before, three years ago, when she and Seth had come back to the Wells from Under Rim, and she still remembered the quicksand lying in wait for the unwary.

Ike waited for her at the bottom of the bluff. "Get those horses paying attention to you, and stay right behind me," he said.

She was nervous enough without another reminder. "Just stay with Clown, and you'll be fine," she told Creamy. She'd seen the pack horse get panicky about soft footing before. If Ike and his two bigger horses didn't stir things up; if Clown's narrow hooves didn't sink in. Counting what-ifs in her mind.

"Don't stop for anything," Ike said and headed across the gravel bar to the first water. Lee tugged Creamy's lead rope a couple times to get his attention and started Clown forward. The footing seemed good, but near the running water could be another story. Saturated sand couldn't support weight.

Ike sat a horse easily in spite of his age. However annoying she might find him, his horses trusted him. They walked steadily, entering the stream without hesitation or hurry. Her two followed calmly. They crossed three narrow channels without problems before coming to a wide, shallow flow. Rock cairns marked where the trail entered and left the water.

Ike started across, and she stayed close behind. Somewhere in the middle, Clown began to sink a little with each step. Lee held her breath and encouraged him to keep moving. They were nearly to the gravel island on the far side when Creamy wandered off Clown's tracks and hit a softer spot. As Lee turned in her saddle to see what was going on, the pack horse reared, lunged away, and buried himself to his belly in soupy sand. She gripped the lead rope and tightened it, hoping the pressure would help him pull himself out.

"Let him go," Ike shouted from the island. "Let go! Get clear."

Feeling her saddle horse struggling with his own footing, she released the rope and let Clown scramble across the last few feet to the bank, leaving her pack horse stranded. Creamy tried unsuccessfully to lunge free, then stopped fighting and stood still with worried wrinkles around his eyes and his ears flicking forward and back.

"Tie up your horse," Ike ordered as he secured his own pack horse to a tall bush. He didn't give her time to think. He shook down the long rope from his saddle. "Take the end of this out there."

She grabbed the end of the rope and ran into the ankle-deep stream with it. She was light enough she could stand where the horses sank. She slowed as she approached Creamy, grabbing his lead rope to steady him. He stayed still, watching her with trusting eyes.

"Get those packs off," Ike said. "I'll tow them to shore."

She worked her way around the trapped horse, rubbing his neck to sooth both him and herself. She freed the top pack, tied Ike's rope to it, and let it go. He backed his horse, pulling the pack onto the bank. Before she had the left-hand pack loose, he sent the rope sailing out to land across the horse's back. She snatched it up and tied it to the next pack. While Ike dragged it away across the water, she cautiously made her way to the horse's other side to free the last pack. They repeated the process, then Ike cast the rope back to her again.

"Now, tie the rope to the packsaddle," he instructed. "You dig out his legs. I'll lay him over on his side and pull him out."

She spoke softly to the horse, rubbing his shoulder as she positioned herself to free his legs. Starting on the side closest to Ike, she dug out his hind leg, struggling against the tenacious sand. Just when she didn't think she'd ever get it free, the horse extended the leg on the surface of the wet sand where miraculously it stayed.

She went to work on his foreleg, trying to stay clear of his hind leg in case he struggled. With the foreleg free and folded up, he rested on his belly in the muck. She stepped away from him, afraid she would end up bogged down herself as she moved around to the far side. Ike put slow pressure on the rope, pulling the trapped horse over on his side. She hurried to scoop sloppy sand away from the other foreleg and finally the last hind leg. Creamy lay still.

"Grab the lead rope and steady his head," Ike called. "Stay clear of him."

She kept a firm hold on the lead rope, waiting for the horse to panic or fight, but Creamy let himself be towed free of the quicksand and onto the gravel clear of the water. He lay quiet until she released the rope from the packsaddle with unsteady hands. Then he rolled onto his belly, got his feet under him, and scrambled up. He stood for a moment before shaking all over like a huge dog, sending water and sand everywhere. Lee encouraged him to quit with a tug on the lead rope. He walked forward, following her to where Clown stood.

"Is the horse okay?" Ike asked. "Anything in the packs that needs to be dried out?"

"I'll check." She shook with exertion and adrenaline. Wet clothes clashed with the midday sun, leaving her strangely hot and cold at the same time. She stopped to settle herself before approaching the horse. No time to panic earlier; now it was too late. She tied Creamy to a bush and ran shaky hands over him, looking for any injuries. Satisfied the horse was unhurt, she began to collect the packs from where they lay. They were all well-wrapped and had only been in the water long enough to be pulled to the bank. They looked fine. She began brushing sand off them.

"I'll scout the rest of the crossing." Ike untied his pack horse from the bush. "Make sure that horse is dry and free of sand before you load him."

"Right." She leaned on the packs as she listened to receding hoof beats, slowing her breathing and letting the adrenaline-rush fade away. Now she just had to wait until Creamy dried enough to get the sand off before reloading everything. It shouldn't take long in the heat.

She shrugged out of her shirt and shook it, scattering sand. Her wet tank top clung to her, just as sandy as everything else. She watched Ike, a hundred yards away crossing another channel toward Wide Ford. She had time, and she had the packs. She could change clothes while she waited.

The damp knots on the pack gave up reluctantly, but she got what she needed. She found a thicket of brush where she could change out of sight of any other travelers. By the time she had the sand shaken out, her damp clothes stuffed away, and the pack tied up again, Creamy was dry enough to brush. She scratched his favorite itchy spot on his chest. "Got us both cooled off for a little while at least," she told him. "Just stay behind Clown next time. If he's okay, you will be." She knew the horse wasn't going to want to get into the water again.

Ike wasn't back by the time she had the packs loaded on the horse. What was keeping him? It wasn't that far into town and back. She sat in the shade of a scrawny bush, staring at the next stretch of water she had to cross. If she kept that up for long, she would scare herself when she needed to be calm to reassure the horses.

Finally Ike reappeared, minus his pack horse. She tightened cinches, checked the pack lashings, and mounted Clown, ready to go by the time he got to her.

"Get 'em on across," he said in greeting. "I'll follow and give him a little encouragement if he needs it."

Lee steadied herself and led Creamy up and down on the island to relax him, then moved the two horses into a trot, and headed straight for the water. Creamy planted his feet and refused to go in. So much for that approach.

"Make him think about it," Ike advised.

She kept Clown in the river on a patch of hard gravel and let Creamy stand at the edge of the water for a minute. She played the lead rope carefully, slack when he faced the trail into the water and snug if he looked away. When he dropped his head to sniff at the footing, she let him, but he still wouldn't step forward.

"Try it again," Ike said.

She led the reluctant pack horse in circles on dry ground again, edging closer and closer to the water. With Creamy's head at her knee, she rode into the stream. He stopped again, but this time he stretched his head down and pawed, splashing them all. She asked Clown to take a couple more steps. Creamy locked up, tightening the rope between them. When the pressure didn't release, he jumped forward and bumped into Clown. She urged both horses into a quick walk through the water.

"You got this," Ike said. "I'll go get us rooms at the inn." He trotted off, splashing through the next channel without a look back.

"The inn?" It was only midday. Wide Ford was the last village they would pass through, but she had expected Ike to want to put in a full day anyway. She turned her attention back to the river crossing. Convincing Creamy to enter the water at each channel distracted her from getting nervous herself. She'd never quite believed the stories she'd heard about quicksand. Now she had one of her own to tell.

Ike was just turning his horses into a pen at the livery when she rode in. "Inn's over there," he said, pointing across the street. He slung his saddlebags over his shoulder, tucked his precious yeasty crock under his arm, and ambled off.

Lee took her time unsaddling and brushing her two horses off in the relative cool of the barn. She carefully cleaned both her saddle and the pack saddle and brushed off the saddle blankets. Once she finished all the dirty but necessary tasks, she had her mind on a shower and food that hadn't come out of a pouch. She left her horses munching grain and crossed the short main street to the inn.

Her room was barely bigger than the bed but that looked inviting after four nights of sleeping on the ground. She dumped out her saddlebags and shook out one of her wraps. She took it and the little bag that held her toiletries to the shower room down the hall. Getting the water as hot as she could stand, she let it wash a lot of Carico down the drain. Funny how a hot shower left her feeling refreshed on a hot day. Back in her room, she stretched out on the bed, consciously finding tense muscles and relaxing them. She didn't wake until the evening sun streamed in the window.

She picked out another wrap, this one purple and black with hot-orange swirls, all the colors that Carico was not, and tied it around her slender frame. She ran a hand through her hair to fluff it up. Why couldn't she look as good in work clothes as Adel Verlane always managed to? Well, tonight the simple dress felt cool in the evening heat and added a bounce to her step.

When she reached the dining room, Ike was nowhere to be seen. Lee drank a decent globeberry wine, the innkeeper's own vintage from his garden, and watched the sun set while she waited for her food. It didn't take long. Savoring the aroma of the well-seasoned meat, she neatly cut off a piece of juicy tarbh steak. She caught herself thinking of how she would describe the incident with the quicksand to Seth. It had been a year, and she hadn't quit saving up things to share with him. Well, she'd be face-to-face with him in a couple days. At least guess-what-happened-to-us gave her something to say.

Chapter 6

Lee

Lee got up in the gray before dawn and went to the stables. She grained all four horses and checked over her gear again to be sure everything was dry and sandless before returning to the inn to enjoy a good breakfast of spinxi eggs over hash-browned ball tubers with a chunk of bread fresh from the oven. From here on they would eat trail food that was mostly pre-packaged, often dehydrated to save on weight, and monotonous after the first few days. At least they had Ike's bread.

When she finished eating, Ike was visiting with the cook, crock in hand, sharing a starter from his legendary Beulah. He caught up to her at the barn.

They left the main trail at Wide Ford and headed north into new territory for both of them, climbing onto the plateau that the Glas River cut through before spilling out into the valley. A couple hours out of town, the trail dropped precipitously into a pleasant, yellow-green pocket walled by turquoise sandstone and skirted a prosperous-looking stead with a comfortable timber house, a large barn and stone-walled pens against the cliff. Beyond there, they entered the fringe where only a few scattered pioneers were trying to push back the edge of beyond.

The trail faded as they went farther. It rambled across the plateau, twisting in and out of draws and occasional cliff-sided canyons. Knee-high bunches of nutgrass, beginning to ripen under the summer sun, waved in the light breeze. The deeper drainages hid tiny springs and pockets of brush and trees, giving brief relief from the relentless sun. Lee liked the country but was thankful for the cairns someone had piled on the canyon rims, marking the ways in and out. Without those, a person might wander along the rims for miles looking for a crossing.

They saw the antenna tower long before they reached it. "Got to be the Huff place," Ike said. "The innkeeper said it was about a day's ride, the last comm site out this way."

Seth's neighbors. Lee immediately liked the looks of the stead with a small rock house built against the cliff and a long, low barn on a bench above a good stream. Evening shadows fell across the outdoor kitchen by the house where a tall woman about Lee's age watched them.

"Evening," the woman greeted.

Lee rode forward. "I'm Lee Vawn-Cory. This is Ike Allred. Out of Seven Wells."

"So you're Lee." The woman studied her until Lee wondered what Seth had told her. "Well, I'm Melinda Huff."

"We're checking out the headwaters country for JT Land and Livestock," Ike explained. "How far is it to young Reilly's place?"

"The better part of a day."

"Could we send a blip to Seven Wells?" Lee asked. "Just to let them know where we are."

"The comm is just inside the door."

"Thank you." Lee dismounted and handed her reins to Ike. "It'll just take a minute." She went to the cabin door and stepped inside. The temperature in the rock structure felt noticeably cooler than outside. She sent a short blip to Dougherty, one last check-in. A new voice outside drew her from the cool, pleasant room back to the porch.

"Gabe, this is Lee," Melinda said, putting an arm around her husband. He was short and stout with arms and shoulders that showed the time he had put into stonework.

"Hi," he said. "You're welcome to stay for supper if you'd like."

"Thanks, but I want to get farther on tonight." Ike answered before Lee could say anything.

"Remind Seth I'll pick him up day after tomorrow about midday," Huff said.

"We'd best get on our way." Ike held out Lee's reins. She went past the Huffs to take her horse.

"Thanks for the use of the comm," she said. Ike was already riding away. She mounted hurriedly.

"We'll be watching for you in two or three weeks," Huff said.

"Bye," Melinda added.

Lee rode after Ike, wishing she had had a few minutes to talk to the couple. From there on she and Ike would be on their own, not promising for good conversation.

They traveled another hour or more before Ike picked a spot to stop. They unloaded the packs and unsaddled. Lee hobbled the horses on a patch of meadow and strung highlines overhead between vine trees to tie the animals to for the night. Ike got a fire going and did the cooking. At times, they seemed like a good team. And he did cook up some marvels with Beulah's help.

Ike fed another branch to the licking blue-green flames of the fire. Lee knew the high levels of copper in the soil and consequently in the plants caused the flame color, but she still found it odd. No doubt those raised on Carico would look askance at a yellow-orange fire. It was all in what you knew.

"We'll see if we can trade that cream horse to young Reilly," Ike said casually.

Lee looked from Ike to the horse. "He's just a little sore from fighting the quicksand." She had been watching Creamy all day. It was subtle, but he was stepping just a little short. "He'll be all right in a day or two."

"Can't risk it, going back of beyond. We trade him." Ike grinned at Lee. "Give you a chance to negotiate with your old partner. Might be you'll have better luck getting him to deal than I would."

Lee shoved her hands into her pockets as the knot in her stomach hardened. "No." She walked out of the firelight to find her way to the horses. Ike and everybody else at the Wells had watched her relationship with Seth disintegrate. No point complicating things with another confrontation between them.

In the morning, the trail climbed out of the canyon and crossed another long stretch of grassland. Ike took it easy. They had time and a long way to go.

Lee watched her pack horse over her shoulder as well as she could. The gelding wasn't openly lame, but he tended to lag behind. Ike was right about replacing the horse while they could. Too bad he hadn't listened when she wanted to bring an extra. Now Seth was their last chance. At least they could leave the horse with someone Lee trusted to take care of him.

About mid-afternoon they came to a cairn of rocks where the trail dropped off the plateau again. They stopped, looking into the canyons below them. The one they had paralleled from Huffs' curved off to the east toward the Glas River. In front of them another canyon came in from the west. If the clear trail they followed down through a notch in the rim was any indication, Lee didn't think they would have any trouble finding Seth's place.

Seth … what would she say to him?

The trail switch-backed down the slope and led across the water to a gate in a sturdy rock fence that blocked the main canyon. Verdigris sandstone cliffs sheltered lush chartreuse vegetation. Vine trees clustered against the walls. Big-leaved bushes draped over the water, shading pools where frog-eels floated among the boulders. The summer heat barely penetrated into the sanctuary.

Ike lifted the loop off the post, swung the gate open, and rode through. Lee reached the opening and hesitated. She had no business crossing this threshold uninvited. She studied the gate and saw in her mind the strong, capable hands that intricately pieced together the copper tree limbs and vine tree poles; remembered those same beautifully gentle hands resting lightly on a horse's neck, caressing … She took a shaky breath, rode into Seth's stead, and shut the gate firmly behind her.

Chapter 7

Seth

Seth cocked the dun colt's nose toward him an inch, eased his weight onto the stirrup, raised himself up to lean over the colt's back, and rubbed his hand on the off-side shoulder. "This is it, colt. Your first ride," he said soothingly. "Nothing much we haven't done before; just putting the pieces together."

The colt stood calmly. Seth brought his right leg over and eased into the saddle, closed his legs softly against the colt's sides, and increased the pressure on the left rein. The colt took a couple tentative steps, found his balance, and walked forward. Seth grinned.

The colt locked up, head high, and let out a pealing neigh. Seth used his weight and legs to remind the colt to pay attention to him. Once the animal refocused and walked a few more steps, Seth asked him to stop and dismounted.

Two riders with pack horses came down the canyon, winding through the brush. Coming for the supplies one of the Seven Wells hands had dropped off the day before. The riders rounded a last corner and came straight at him. He caught a glimpse of the white-splashed face of the second rider's horse and knew it was Lee's Clown.

He looked away, vividly recalling her going cold in the midst of another loud argument about something that had nothing to do with their real problems. She had looked him dead in the eye and told him to get out of her life. She had stood there, arms crossed tightly, and watched him throw together his few belongings. He'd slept on the porch of the cabin that night, caught his personal horses before dawn, and been gone from the Wells by daybreak. Now, over a year later, she was riding into his home. But not by her own choice, he reminded himself.

A horse snorted. Remembering to breathe, he forced his eyes to the first rider. Ike Allred had been at Seven Wells since long before his time there. Ike's experience, Lee's training — obvious choices to scout the plateau.

The colt shoved a shoulder into him, eager to greet the strange horses. Seth pulled himself together and backed the colt off. "Mind your manners," he said, insisting on good behavior from his future herd sire. He waved at Ike and tied the colt to the corral fence. Ike stopped a little way off and waited. Lee hung back even further. Stomach churning, Seth walked out to meet them.

"The boss warned us you were out here a ways," Ike commented.

"Probably seemed closer to him in that nice skimmer," Seth said through teeth clenched to keep his turmoil from spilling out. Lee hadn't come forward yet. Couldn't she face him? "Your supplies are here in the tack room."

"Mind if we camp nearby tonight?" Ike asked. "I'd like your take on where we should be scouting."

Seth consciously relaxed his shoulders. "Help yourselves. There's a good spot with water just beyond the pens. Turn the horses loose in the little pasture there. Then come up to the house. There's a shower, and I'll fix something for dinner." He kept his eyes on the old man.

"Shower, huh," Ike said with a grin.

"Hot," Seth assured. "Get settled in and come on up."

As Ike started toward the path that led to the camp, Seth turned and strode to the corral without a word to Lee. He didn't even look until he heard her horses go by. Then he watched her stiff, unyielding back disappear into the brush that screened the campsite.

He unsaddled and brushed the colt, using the routine to steady himself. He tried not to pass his tension through the brush to the colt. Smoothing away the last of the sweat marks where the saddle had sat, he blocked out the memories that tried to flood in. Good thing Dougherty had warned him who was coming.

He untied the colt and led him past the garden plot to the fenced mouth of a side-canyon. He opened the gate and shooed away the two mares waiting on the other side. He let the colt loose with them and watched the three amble across the grassy bottom. There was a nice pool in the creek nearby where he had built a low rock dam to make it deep enough to soak in. Maybe if he spent an hour there, she would be gone.

He slammed the gate, pointlessly since it just swung through the opening and he had to pull it back to latch it. He thought back to earlier, to the feel of the colt under him, just starting to learn about balancing a rider's weight. He loved that stage of training when every little thing was an accomplishment for the horse. It was so simple, just him and the animal.

"You've got company," he reminded himself. Wishing wouldn't make them disappear. Thinking again how peaceful a soak in the creek would be, he hung the halter on the fence and started back to the ledge.

He climbed the steps, determined not to think about the past. He looked around at the newly functional shower house, sheltered kitchen area, enclosed storage, and the 'courtyard' with the few pieces of furniture he'd taken time to build. He only needed a couple of minutes to straighten his bedding, put his horsehair braiding and a few stray items into the pack boxes he used for storage, and check to see if there was enough hot water for a couple of showers. He picked up the horsehair bracelet, worn through now, that lay by the head of his bed. No point in leaving that where Lee might see it. He slid it under his pillow, trying to tuck his memories away with it.

Food — he had a swine-deer loin in the cold box to slice and grill. Better go see what he had in the garden ready for picking. Keep his mind on practicalities.

He fetched a bowl from the cupboard and headed for the stairs. The sight of Ike and Lee in the distance, turning horses out into the pasture, stopped him. He'd forgotten he could see over the brush to the campsite. They must be nearly done and would come any time now.

He gazed across the intervening space. His imagination had put her here so often over the months. But she'd had all winter to find him if she wanted. He'd been at home in Under Rim then, and someone would have told her if she'd asked.

"Don't be a fool," he said under his breath. Now she was just another visiting rider, no different than Ike. Fact was he had known Ike a lot longer.

He hurried to the garden, putting his jumble of emotions into physical action. Some of the early broadleafs were left, and the recent heat had brought on the blood roots and sweet galls. He gathered salad makings and some herbs to go with the meat. Crouched over the plants behind the rock wall of the garden, he saw Lee before she was aware of him, slender and pretty as a yearling filly. And about as flighty at the moment. He straightened and went to the garden gate, leaving it closed between them.

She stopped before she quite got there, looking down, tugging at her frayed shirt cuff. "Huffs asked us to remind you that Gabe will pick you up."

"Tomorrow. I remember." He could hardly believe how calm he sounded.

She looked around, everywhere but at him. "You found a nice spot. Your father said you had. I saw him in Portside a couple weeks ago." Her brown-gold eyes turned down, watching his hands. He could see the tension in her shoulders.

"Me too."

"I know," she said in a flat tone.

So she had seen him at some point during the conference. But she hadn't taken the chance to talk to him.

He stepped back from the gate. "Did you find the supplies?"

"Yes. Ike sent me to see how long we had before dinner."

"Whenever you're ready." He held up the bowl. "Just salad and grilled meat." He pushed himself forward, through the gate, and closed it behind him.

She retreated a couple more steps. "I'll tell him."

They hovered there, a few feet apart. If he just knew how to bridge the gap, what to do or say to get her to change her mind.

She shifted uneasily and ran a hand through her short hair. The sight of the bracelet she wore stunned him. In two steps he reached her and took hold of her wrist. "Why are you still wearing this?" he asked, pulling her arm up to bring the bracelet in front of her face. She was so close, between him and the garden wall. Her face was leaner than he remembered, with angles and shadows.

She twisted her arm free. "It hasn't worn out yet." She looked up at him with those brown-gold eyes. If he just leaned over, he could kiss her.

She stepped away. "Apparently yours has, though."

He held up his own bare wrist. "You're the one who wanted me gone. What did you expect?"

She turned her back and fingered the rock surface of the fence. "Nothing. I didn't plan to come here."

"I know. Your boss sent you." He recalled Dougherty asking if he wanted to come back to work for the company. "Are you supposed to convince me to come back to Seven Wells?"

"As if Dougherty's stupid enough to think you'd listen to me!" She slammed her palm against the rocks. "Well, I guess you did — once."

"I guess I did."

He glared at her; she kept her eyes on the rocks of the wall. Nothing had changed. Five minutes together and they were arguing.

Lee's head came up, and she stepped back. "What's that?" she asked. "A skimmer?"

Oh, Void. What now? She was right. He heard the distant hum. He couldn't see it, but it sounded like it was off to the east, not the way Gabe came. He saw Ike coming from the campsite, pointing toward the canyon rim.

"Somebody's lost," Seth muttered. Just what he needed — more visitors.

The craft came into view, swung around and dropped into the canyon to settle in the open ground between the garden and the steps to his ledge.

Lee glared at the skimmer. "A Ranger?"

"Yes." Seth puzzled over her reaction. "Looks like Adel Verlane. I met her at the conference." He handed the bowl of garden pickings to Lee. "I'll go see what she wants." He walked around the vehicle to the door then waited impatiently while Adel fussed with something in the cab.

She finally got out, smiling. "I'm glad I found you at home," she said. When she laid her hand on his shoulder, she made it more personal somehow than the standard greeting gesture.

He stepped back. "What can I help you with?" he asked.

"Just making rounds." She fingered the tip of her braid, reminding him of their encounter in Portside.

"That's a first," he said.

Lee came around the skimmer and shoved the bowl back at him. "What's this about?" she asked like it was her business.

The Ranger looked at her with surprise. "Lee! I just keep running into you."

Seth stiffened, caught between the two women. With the Ranger connection, he shouldn't be surprised that they knew each other, but Lee didn't sound very friendly.

Adel laid a hand on Seth's arm, smiling. "Lee and I were at the academy together, roommates in fact." She stepped past him to greet Lee with a casual hug that Lee returned stiffly. "What was it, only a couple of weeks ago that I saw you at Seven Wells? You didn't mention coming this way."

"Just passing through. Ike and I are looking over some country for the boss, going out toward the Whitewater."

"The Whitewater?" Adel said. "That flows through Rocky Ford, doesn't it?"

Lee ignored the question, turned her back to Adel, and greeted Ike as he joined them. "Ike, you remember Adel."

Ike frowned. "Sure."

"Hello again," Adel said. "Unplanned trip?"

"Nope," Ike said.

Seth stepped in to capture her attention. "What brings you all the way out here?"

Adel looked around at the three of them. "I am stopping at steads to warn people about a man the marshals are looking for."

"What man?" Seth asked.

"He was mixed up in some big case a few years ago," Adel said. "His name is Whip Willemsen."

Seth almost let the bowl fall. "I remember the name," he told Adel. He had almost forgotten Whip. Cocky little rider who thought he was going to be big in C.T. Jerdix's schemes.

"He walked away from his work detail in Portside recently." Adel's brow creased with concern. She put her hand on his arm again. "You're isolated here, and you have no way to report it if you did see him."

Lee grabbed the bowl teetering in his hand and smiled at Adel. "Escaped from under your nose. Must be lonely without your driver."

"He doesn't think much of you," Adel countered.

Seth eased out from between the two. What did Lee mean about Adel's driver? "Any reason to think Whip's out this way?" he asked.

"The marshals think he headed over to the mining districts but want people to watch for him anyway," Adel replied, stepping closer again.

"I can handle Whip if he does show up," he said.

"You sound like you know him," she said.

"We've met. He wouldn't get any help here."

Seth didn't miss Lee's eyes going to Adel's hand, hovering close to his arm. Lee said, "Good luck finding your stray." She brushed past Seth and climbed the steps without a look back.

Ike looked at Seth and shrugged. "I'll just go get that shower now. Up there?" He shuffled off after Lee with more speed than Seth expected of him.

Leaving him with Adel.

"They just got in," he said. Which was no explanation for anything. "To pick up supplies their boss dropped off for them," he added.

"She seems to know her way around," Adel commented, watching Lee disappear onto the ledge.

"She's never been here before," Seth said. Not that it was any of her business.

"I wish Lee and I had gotten along better. But she can be so capricious."

Capricious? Lee? "I think tenacious fits her better," he replied. Before Adel could respond he asked, "Will you be stopping at Huffs?"

"That would be my next stop." She twisted the end of her braid thoughtfully and smiled. "If I was in a hurry."

Seth remembered how Adel had flirted with him in Portside before turning her attention elsewhere in a blink when a group of mine owners had come into the lounge. "Just follow the canyon," he said. "I won't keep you any longer."

"I'd like to stop by again one day." She reached out but didn't quite touch him. "I'm interested in how small steaders like you operate. It will help me interpret the survey data."

"You know where to find me." He kept his voice flat.

"Tell Lee I said good luck with her exploration." She slid into the seat of her skimmer and closed the door. She waved as she drove away.

Seth walked to the stairs and sank down on the bottom step. His head spun. Morning — and having his place to himself again — couldn't come fast enough.

Chapter 8

Seth

Seth rubbed at the back of his neck as he watched Adel's dust settle. Before he could sort out what the Ranger really wanted, Lee tromped down the steps. "Have a nice dinner," she said as she stepped past him.

"Are you going back to work for the Rangers?" He threw out a wild guess.

She stopped and turned. "I am not," she said. "Does Adel stop by often?"

"Rangers come around quite a bit when you're building a new place," he said. "Making sure everything gets done according to plan." Lee didn't need to know Adel had never been there before.

"Sure they do." Lee turned away and headed for the camp.

Elements! That wasn't how he wanted things to go. "There's plenty of hot water," he called after her.

"Use it yourself," she said over her shoulder.

"Blast you, Lee, wait." He went after her. "Just come up; use the shower; eat dinner. We'll talk with Ike about your trek and nothing else."

She stopped, head up, shoulders square and hands clenched at her side.

"What?" he prodded. "You can't even be polite? You're the one who came here."

"I am," she said so quietly he could hardly hear her. Then more loudly, "I'll be there in a little while." She hurried away without looking at him.

He plodded to the steps and climbed to what was usually his retreat. Why had he pushed her to come back? He could have just let her walk away.

He set out the solar grill to heat so he could cook the swine-deer loin chops. Then he dumped the contents of the bowl from the garden onto the counter and fetched the meat from the cold box. The vegetables and meat suffered under his knife as he applied his frustration to getting food ready.

Ike came out of the shower house, toweling water from his thatch of silver hair. "You did a fine job with that shower set-up," he said. "Feels good on an old body."

"Grab a chair," Seth said. "Dinner's almost ready."

"I brought some bread." Ike retrieved half a loaf from his bag.

"Thanks."

"You're welcome to a start from Beulah, if you'd like."

Seth shook his head. "I've tried yeasties. I just don't bake enough to keep one going."

"Too bad. Something you should learn to do."

"Maybe when I get this place built up, I'll have time."

"It is a pretty spot," Ike acknowledged. "Nice breeze this afternoon. That's usual?"

"It is."

Ike settled into a chair made of copper tree wood with a rawhide seat. "You've done a lot of work."

Seth slowed down his attack on the salad. "I just finished the shower house. I piped the water from a spring for it and the kitchen. Got good shade from the overhang in the summer; protection from the rain as long as I remember where the drip line off the roof is; and the rock soaks up the winter sun. Couldn't ask for much more."

"One too many women." Ike grinned. "Best get that part sorted out if you want any peace."

"No women," Seth said. He chopped down on a sweet gall and nearly sent a piece of it flying. "I'll get my peace back in the morning."

"That Ranger — she's a good-looking woman, but did you notice how she never attracts dirt?" Ike laughed.

Seth let the tension go from his shoulders with a grin. "Now that you mention it."

"Something odd about someone who's never dusty." Ike shifted his chair farther into the shade.

Seth flattened his hands on the counter and slowly breathed in the evening air. His home, his life — back to normal in a few hours. "What's the plan for your trek?" he asked. "Where are you headed exactly?

"I want to go north across the plateau, more or less parallel to the upper Glas, then on as far as the Whitewater River and work back farther west."

Seth nodded. "Go to the canyon just outside my gate and up it about a mile where several canyons come together. Dougherty was interested in that as a possible headquarters. From there a trail climbs up onto the plateau." Seth said. "The Whitewater is fifty or sixty miles north. I've never been that far myself."

"We'll get the map out later and take a closer look at that mess of canyons," Ike said.

"After we've eaten. Lee should be back soon." If she came.

Ike stretched his legs out. "Shame to let one like her go to someone else," he said quietly.

Seth chopped through a blood root harder than needed. "Her choice. She sent me packing, remember?" As if he could stop her from doing whatever she pleased, Seth thought. He wasn't going to chase after her when she had made her feelings clear.

But had she? The bracelet around her wrist contradicted what she said, didn't it?

"Are those all the horses you have?" Ike asked, pointing to Seth's two saddle horses leaning over the rock fence some hundred yards or so across the canyon floor.

Seth shook his head. "Two mares are up the left fork of the canyon with the stud colt." He pointed his chin that way.

"Too bad," Ike said, sounding disappointed. "I need a replacement for the girl's pack horse, just till we come back. She got him mired at Wide Ford, and he's going short."

"She got him …" Seth bit back an automatic defense of Lee. He hesitated. "I guess I could let you take one of the mares. They're both saddle-trained."

"Nothing against mares," Ike said, "But one mare and three geldings? They'll be strutting around like idiots. You couldn't spare one of those two for a couple of weeks?" Ike pointed at the saddle horses. "You'd have mine in a pinch. You know that cream-colored gelding."

"Let me think about it." Seth didn't like the idea of loaning out either the roan or Jester. It would be like loaning out family.

Boots on rock warned him that Lee was coming. He checked the grill and laid the chops on it, stifling the urge to walk her around the place and show her all the little touches. He should have waited to cook the meat and let her shower first. Too late now.

She hadn't changed out of her rider's clothes: the loose, long-sleeved, light-weight shirt designed to reflect the sun and let any breeze cool the wearer and the tough pants that wore forever. She had washed her face and probably ducked her head into the water. Her damp hair stood up wildly. She looked around and headed for the kitchen cabinets to rummage for dishes. She was there as if she always had been, knowing where to find things without asking, setting out plates, filling a pitcher with water, just as they had always shared kitchen chores.

Ike cleared his throat. "Better turn those chops," he said with a grin.

Seth tore his eyes from Lee and nearly scorched his fingers on the meat.

She was there, going through the motions, but she kept her distance and rarely looked at him. He barely tasted the earthiness of the blood roots or the savory mix of herbs with the swine-deer chops. When the dinner was cleared away, she disappeared into the shower house without a word.

Seth tried to pay attention to what Ike said without much success. He did better once they spread out a printed map. The plateau was bounded by the Glas River on the east. It was upside-down country with relatively flat high ground dissected by canyons running down to the river. North of the plateau, the Whitewater flowed more or less west to east with just a few, short tributaries cutting through the rim. To the west, the tableland fell off into a jumble of walls, pedestals, and knife ridges with little vegetation and less water. Wildlife found good forage on the plateau's top when seasonal pools of water allowed them to spread across the expanse. Now, in the driest months just before the summer rains, animals stayed close to the good water found in the depths of the steep-walled gorges.

"Dougherty found trails down to water in a lot of the canyons," Ike said, pointing out marks on the map. "But those hills up toward the Whitewater look like the best country for tarbh. They want to be up high with shade and breeze on these hot days even if they have to climb down into some slot for water."

"If you stay west, you'll go around the heads of most of the Glas drainages," Seth pointed out.

"Might be hard to find water. I think we'll explore the Glas and its canyons on the way out. Then we can make a hard push back through the dry ground on the west. That way we'll know for sure we'll have water on this end."

"How long do you think you'll be?" Seth asked.

"Two weeks, three at the most. Depends on how long it takes to crawl in and out of all those trenches and how promising the hills are. And if Lee, here, doesn't slow the pace too much."

Lee, coming from the shower house, ignored the jibe. "I'm going to go check on the horses," she said. "Good night." She was gone before Seth could think of anything to say to her with Ike watching.

Ike rolled the tough, thin fabric of the map. "You should come along. We can hold up here a day if you need time to get ready."

Seth wavered, staring after Lee, but finally shook his head. "Already had that discussion with Dougherty. I can't do it. The garden won't take care of itself."

"Okay, your call." The older man stood up and laid a hand on Seth's shoulder. "Son, some things are worth saying, just in case you run out of chances."

"Not a chance left now," Seth said.

"You know how it is back of beyond. One little misstep is all it takes," Ike replied.

Riders took those risks every day. But it was a big, rugged, isolated country they were going into. "You'd better take care then." Seth shoved his hands into his pants pockets.

"Since you won't come along, I'll feel better for knowing someone here will bother to come looking if we don't show up on time."

Seth managed a grin. "If I don't see you in three weeks, I'll let Dougherty know, and we'll come. And keep your eyes open for Willemsen. He's got a nasty streak."

"Not likely he's way out back of beyond."

"You're probably right." Seth thought about what he knew of the man. "He'll be getting help from a friend somewhere."

"Still — you watch yourself too." Ike hobbled to the steps. "I sure am glad I don't have to climb in and out of this place all the time."

"Does that mean you're not coming up for breakfast?"

"It does. You come down to camp about daybreak." The old man made his way down the steps easily enough in spite of his claims otherwise.

Seth watched Ike leave the rock ledge before realizing they hadn't settled the loan of a horse. One decision he could put off until morning. He stood, facing down the canyon away from his visitors' camp, and watched the aerial antics of the little fliers feeding on insects above the water-rich strip of vegetation as the daylight faded. He began the practice forms of batayr, the martial art he'd learned as a moving meditation during his recovery from Jerdix's torture. The focus required for the prescribed movements invariably helped him let go of stress and find his own peace.

A pale ghost of a horse came from the corrals, floating in the twilight. He blinked and looked again, making out Lee riding the cream-colored gelding bareback along the well-worn trail. Curious, he stood still and watched as she approached the gate where his two saddle horses waited to greet the newcomer. She slid off and turned Creamy loose with them. The three wandered off like old friends with none of the fuss of strange horses meeting. A year apart meant little to them.

Lee closed the gate and made sure it was tight. She slung the halter and lead over her shoulder and stood for a moment, watching the horses it seemed. Then she turned and stared up at his ledge. She had changed into a tank top and light-weight pants, her usual camp wear. Crossing her arms, she plodded back the way she had come, stepping on the stones across the creek with none of the light grace he remembered so well.

"Evening," he called down without moving.

She froze and looked around, finally finding him. "You startled me," she said, catching the halter as it slid off her shoulder. "Ike said to put Creamy in with the roan and Jester."

She was too far away for him to see her expression. "I don't think we settled that," he said.

"I'll leave it to you two."

"Come up here?" he asked.

"No."

"Then I'll come down." He started across the ledge.

"No need. I'm going back to camp."

He hurried down the steps to catch up with her on the trail to the corrals. "How are things at Seven Wells?"

"Nothing new."

"Thanks for helping with dinner tonight."

She stopped walking. "What happened to Buster?"

"Buster?" His old brown gelding that he had used mostly as a pack horse the last few years. "I traded him to my sister for the sorrel mare."

"I was afraid something happened to him." She looked down and rearranged the halter and rope in her hand.

"Just turned into a kid's horse."

She looked up at him. "Why didn't you stay in Under Rim? I heard you spent the winter there."

"Why would I?" he asked. "I just didn't have this place ready last fall. But I will this year."

"You couldn't find a place a little closer to somebody else?"

He wasn't sure what he heard in her voice. "Not a rockshelter like this one. That saved me a whole lot of building."

"What happens if you get hurt or sick? What if Whip shows up here?"

"Are you worried about me?" he asked.

She threw up her hands and shook her head. "Not me. But some people are."

"Who would that be?" he shot back.

"Seriously, you are twenty miles from the nearest help. You don't even have a comm."

"It's only eighteen," he said, trying to lighten things.

"Hopeless, inconsiderate …"

"Hey," he broke in. "You're the one heading back of beyond with one crippled up old rider for company."

"Ike's doing fine."

Seth rubbed the back of his neck. He didn't want to fight. "I have a deal with Huffs to spend one day a week helping Gabe. If I don't show up, they'll let Pa know. Now, will you come up for a little while? Please?"

"So we can work out our differences; get back together again?"

"Yes, maybe, I don't know. I just want to spend a little time with you."

"Sure you do," she said. "Not tonight. I'm tired." She waggled her fingers at him and left him standing alone in the dark with the image of the bracelet on her wrist fresh in his mind. He was a fool to think anything had changed. But he hadn't expected her to still wear that bracelet after a year apart, not when she'd been the one who'd thrown him out.

He climbed the steps and watched her in the moonlight as she wound through the brush to the camp. She bent over the dying fire, probably pushing it together for the night. Then he lost sight of her. She always liked to sleep a little away from the heart of camp.

He dozed restlessly on his bunk, dreaming he was searching for Lee but always missing her wherever he went. Waking breathless from the dream, he got up and walked to the outer edge of the ledge. He took his stance there under the half-circle of Lander, the larger moon, and began the batayr movements again. The cool night air, damp with the promise of the water-blessed canyon, seemed to dance with him, an insubstantial partner fanning coals of anger at Lee for giving up on them and at himself for letting her. The anger fired his movements; fast and hard he let it burn through him. He repeated the series again and then again, letting the chatter and chuckle of the stream over rocks reach him. Little Damele, also at half, rose, adding its light to its larger companion and turning the stone to brushed silver. He completed the form one final time, feeling the roughness of the stone beneath his feet, rooting himself into its stability. As Lander dove behind the canyon rim, chased by Damele, he settled down to sit at the top of the steps with the light breeze and the chorus of nighttime creatures for company. And thoughts that no amount of meditation could still.

As the sky began to lighten, he gathered scattered chips of stone and pitched them off the edge, trying to hit a dead branch on a bush below, resisting the urge to pack up and go with Ike and Lee. What made him think he had any chance of getting her back in his life anyway? Just that bracelet.

Fragments of his dream nagged him, but taking care of the garden was more than an excuse; it was a big part of his food for the coming winter, the difference between staying there and having to go back to Under Rim or find a job somewhere. And traveling with someone who didn't want him anywhere near made no sense. Better to stay home and take care of business.

Lee and Ike knew what they were doing. He didn't need to tag along.

The ghost-pale gelding caught his eye, and he knew one thing he could do. Before dawn, when he saw fire spring to life in the camp, he caught his bay gelding, Jester, who had been with him for years and was utterly reliable under saddle or carrying a pack. He led the horse past the corrals to the camp where Lee was cooking breakfast and Ike was sorting through a pack.

"Here's your horse," Seth said.

Lee eyed him tensely. "Jester?" she said, looking from him to the horse.

"Jester," he answered.

"No," she said. "I won't take him."

"Ike wanted a gelding."

Ike left the packs and walked by him. "Now that's speaking louder than words," he said with a quiet grin.

Seth turned away from Lee and scratched the horse on the withers. "You be good, old horse. Watch out for her."

When he looked up, Lee was standing at Jester's head. "Don't do this," she said.

"You need him," he said. She was back-lit by the fire, her shoulders squared defiantly, but it was light enough to see her eyes looking up at him. He ran his hand through his hair. "The mares are both soft and lazy, not really up to this kind of trip."

"He's been with you for years."

"It's not like I'm selling him." He stepped away from her and held out the lead rope. "He'd better get back here safe and sound. Three weeks, and not a day longer."

"I ..." Her shoulders relaxed a little. "I'll take good care of him." She held her hand out for the rope. He passed it to her.

"Take care of yourself," he said and left her standing there before he decided he needed to go with them. As he strode away, a cold chill ran up his spine. He looked back and saw her reach up to rub at the back of her neck, like she felt it too.

Counterpoint

Eta'ak

Opportunity or disaster? Our hunters, in their monitoring of the First-Comers living closest to us, have discovered two people exploring in our direction, one young female and one elder male traveling with four of their horse-animals. They will be watched to see if they continue toward our villages. If they do, the hunters will divert them away without revealing our presence. Distractions, accidents — our males can be very creative in discouraging wanderers.

But is that the best choice now? I have a plan in mind to make us known to these First-Comers and use them to initiate contact with their leaders before the survey reveals us. Taking some control can only strengthen our position.

My chief spouse and his two brother-spouses will study these travelers and report to me. We will see if a contact can be conducted in a way that Prime and the others on the Council will approve. While the strangers are still at a safe distance from the villages.

-From the Archives of Eta'ak, Information Analyst

Chapter 9

Lee

Lee led Seth's horse over to the pack saddle she had taken off Creamy the night before, trying hard not to imagine what he meant by loaning her Jester. She kept her attention on brushing the horse, settling the pack saddle on his back, and adjusting it to fit him. She made each movement precise, smooth, and deliberate.

Ike passed her on his way to his own pack horse. "You'd be in a better mood if you'd spent the night in that nice little roost," he said as he dropped a bundle for her to load with her packs. She leaned her face into Jester's shoulder and held her tongue.

While the world was still black and gray, they started back along the trail they had come in on. Ike took the lead, leaving Lee to follow. She fought the temptation to look up at Seth's home to see if he was watching them go. He was doing so well, getting his dream of his own place, moving on with his life. Well, she had to bring the horse home. Maybe by then she'd know what she wanted to say to him.

Ike led them out the gate marking the boundary of Seth's stead and turned right into a wide canyon to wind through the brush on a faint track left by swine-deer or other wildlife. The canyon narrowed. The sun hadn't climbed above the rim yet, but grays were becoming lime and celedon and beryl. The air brushed coolly across her. She knew that it wouldn't stay that way for long.

In a few minutes, they came out into an open bowl about half a mile across, like a cupped palm with the incoming canyons as the fingers. They had ridden up the wrist and now stood at the base of the thumb looking across the browning grass and chartreuse brush.

"Here, this is it." Ike stopped his horse on a little rise. "Great place for headquarters for a new stead. Call it Five Canyons."

"Why not," she agreed. They were only a couple of miles from Seth's. He'd have neighbors, a place to use a comm, day work when he needed it.

"That way," Ike pointed. "Seth said to climb out between the two canyons on the right." He took the lead and found a steep path up the slope. "Back of beyond from here on," he said with evident satisfaction.

As far as Lee was concerned, they had been back of beyond since leaving the Huffs' stead with the last link to the comm system. But it was too late for second thoughts now. She tugged on the rope to encourage her pack horse. Ike's horses scaled the last precipitous opening in the rim, sending a small avalanche of rocks down. Lee held up to one side until the slope settled before letting Clown have his head so he could clamber up with Jester close behind.

They crested the rim just as the sun rose, washing the vast prairie before them in molten copper, just for a moment as smooth as still water. Then the light caught the edges of every small discontinuity in the tableland, tracing a shadow pattern of dips, draws, and ravines to the far horizon. The bright copper faded into the brown of dried grasses waiting for the summer rains to revive them, and Lee could feel the beginning of the day's heat.

"Now that's a sunrise," Ike said and waved a hand across the expanse. "This looks like good spring and fall range for tarbh as long as they can get to water. That will be down in those draws. We'll parallel the right-hand canyon. We should get around the head of it this afternoon and swing east toward the Glas. Then we'll have to find our way around or through all the canyons flowing down to the river." He turned in his saddle to study her and her animals. "How's that pack horse working out?"

"Fine," she said.

"Good thing the boy changed his mind. Nothing against mares, but they can sure upset a bunch of geldings."

"Sometimes," she said. He was right, but she didn't want to discuss the horse.

Ike rode on, and she moved Clown after him. The horses walked; the sun climbed; the coolness dissipated. She could hardly tell they were getting anywhere. Too much time with nothing to do but think, mostly about Seth and what she should have done differently. And what she wanted to do when she and Ike got done with their trek, when she returned Jester. Seth and Adel and Vinz would all be waiting. Now it was time to focus on the reason she was riding into the unknown. She pulled out the data pendent and started recording notes.

Every hour or so they stopped and let the horses graze while they unrolled the big map to check their location and add notes on the terrain, vegetation, and any wildlife they saw. Lee recognized a couple of species of grass from the Seven Wells summer range but also several new to her. They fell in two distinct categories: those with nothing more than a few wisps of leaves waiting for the summer rains to grow; and those like nutgrass that grew early and were seed-laden now. Shriveled broad-leafed plants also hung in that limbo between two growing seasons. Shrubs clung to rocky outcroppings with broad, waxy leaves drooping. The canyons, the oases of water, held more variety.

Between stops, she used the little recorder to keep track of observations. Things like nutgrass on the better soils and thousand-seed, a broad-leafed plant that could grow horse-high, around rocky outcroppings. The day got hotter.

"Swine-deer tracks," Ike said.

They weren't common around Seven Wells, but she'd seen a few. She leaned down to look at the scuffs on the dry ground. What told him they were swine-deer? She pieced it together. Too small for tarbh; too short-strided for wolf-lizards; not the right country for the mountain-dwelling cliff dancers.

Up ahead she saw the tops of the thousand-seed plants wave erratically. Ike trotted forward. A cluster of animals broke from the cover, too close together for her to count. The largest of them paused, hooked an antler-tipped snout at them, then trotted after the rest.

"They use those to dig up roots?" Lee asked.

"The antlers are mostly for display. Those snouts, now, those plow up a lot of ground going after roots and larva, even rock rats and their kin.

"They're heterothermic, like tarbh?"

"Yup. Let the environment regulate body temperature when they can and do it themselves when they have to. Efficient. Let's go. Should be water down below." He disappeared off the canyon rim down a barely visible track.

When she rode forward to watch him, she found that it wasn't quite as bad a drop as it seemed. The bottom was only fifteen or twenty feet down, but the trail was rocky and steep. They couldn't afford to hurt either rider or horse. She gritted her teeth and urged Clown forward.

"Looks like a good place to stop." Ike headed down toward a cluster of vine trees. In free-standing specimens, the lower trunks contorted as several thick vines wrapped around each other to form a single support, but here most reached to the cliff wall and the separate vines spread out across the face, climbing upward with only one or two drooping toward the ground.

"We made good time. We'll stop here, explore this area, and camp for the night," Ike said, surprising her. Midday was behind them, but it was a long time to dark. He eased down off his horse and began the daily routine of unpacking and setting up their simple camp. She did the same, hobbling the horses on a patch of grass by the trickle of water. The canyon felt like an oven under the summer sun until she stepped into the shade of the trees. She never ceased to appreciate how much difference that made.

"This water won't last much longer," she said.

"Won't be enough to show above the rocks," Ike replied. "But three weeks from now, I wouldn't want to be here. Might be more water than you'd like."

They would have no chance to escape a flash flood in this narrow trap. On the other hand, the thought of being out on the plateau in the middle of a thunderstorm sounded like a bad idea too.

"Will the summer rains make this country unusable?" she asked.

"They'll *make* this country," he replied. "Bring on good feed; fill natural tanks with water. You wait and see." He settled down, using his bedroll as a seat, and opened a packet of dried fruit. He looked at her like she was a puzzle to solve. "I just can't figure out why you aren't back at that nice little stead with Seth."

She clenched her teeth. He just wouldn't let it go. Why did he care what she did with her life?

"Good man, that one," Ike went on. "Skilled. And he has a plan for the future."

She bit back a sharp response about minding his own business. "He certainly does."

"It's good to have a plan. Good to have a partner too."

"His plan; his future."

"Boss thought this survey would be just the thing for you. Was he wrong?"

She straightened up, hot and out of patience. "Maybe it's the company I don't like. Maybe I'm tired of being second-guessed and lectured about what I should be doing."

He laughed heartily. "Finally she says what she thinks. *I* might start liking the company after all. But I still think you should be back at that stead."

"No, I shouldn't." She refused to say any more to him about it. She remembered her encounter with Seth the night before. They couldn't talk for five minutes without arguing. But she still wore the bracelet and still got all knotted up inside when she saw him. She was stubborn that way, not wanting to give up on something even if it had proven to be unworkable.

Before Ike could come up with any more comments, she stood up. "I'm going downstream." While she explored maybe she could find a place with enough water to soak and cool off.

"Keep your eyes open," he called after her.

"I'll be back for dinner," she said over her shoulder.

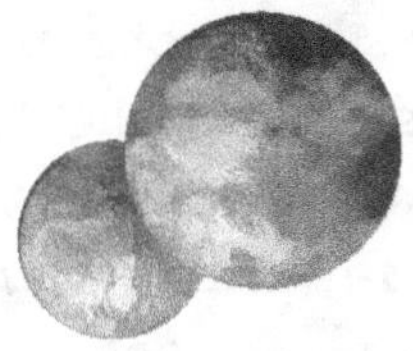

Early the next morning, they climbed back onto the plateau. The day was a repeat of the one before except a line of hills appeared far to the northwest. By midday they came to another canyon with a crossing Dougherty had marked on the map. They tied the horses in the shade of an ancient vine tree and explored the canyon to discover tiny pockets of chartreuse vegetation, a trickle of water that disappeared into the rocks and reappeared again, and not much else. Obviously animals came down for water but didn't stay in the oven-like cleft for long. Neither did they. They let the horses drink before they scrambled up a well-used trail to continue on their way.

The country changed subtly as they rode, everything except the heat and the dust that were unrelenting. The nutgrass thinned out, replaced with sparse, low-growing stands of feathergrass as the bedrock showed through the sandy soil more and more. Canyons became shallow draws. They were approaching the indistinct divide between the Glas River and the Whitewater River to the north of the plateau.

Ike stopped in a shallow basin at the head of a draw. "We'll camp here," he said. The deeper soil of the low spot supported good feed for the horses, and a few old water-finder trees suggested subsoil moisture. "We should cross the head of the main Glas River in the morning, not that it's much of a canyon anymore." He held the map up to study it in the dying light of the day. His brown horse, Tinker, watched the paper with wide eyes and flicking ears. The animal was a nervous sort at best. Pokey, his pack horse, ignored the fuss.

Ike swept a finger over the map. "Looks like no water near here since the early spring melt. That's why I made sure the horses had a good drink back there."

"How far to the next water?" Lee asked.

"Not too bad. Late tomorrow. We'll drop down into a canyon going north into the Whitewater. Boss marked a good spring there."

They wasted no time setting up camp before it got too dark. The horses seemed uneasy. Lee heard the distant growls and whistles of wolf-lizards. She paced the edges of the campsite, picking up firewood under the trees, while Ike got dinner ready. With no canyon walls to hold it in, the day's heat vanished when the sun went down.

Summer days were long. Hours in the saddle under the bright sun left her tired. Lee didn't wait for full dark to bring in the horses and tie them to the highline for the night.

Ike stretched his long, lean frame out on his bed. "Long ways from home," he said as she picked up her bedroll to find a place away from his snoring. "Sorry you came?"

"No." Where was he going with this?

"Me neither. Great country and lots of it." He yawned. "Quiet. A person can almost hear the music the stars dance to."

The what ...? Lee shook her head.

"You're good at this, you know."

"At what?" Had she heard him right?

"Most young riders would make a big thing out of it. You, well, you take on this trip back of beyond like it's just another day. No fuss, no chewing over what might happen. You pay attention to the details, but you don't miss the big picture. So, which way is home?" he asked.

She pointed back the way they had come.

"See, no hesitation. You didn't even have to look around. You scared of the emptiness? No, you were more scared walking into the Steaders' Inn back in Portside. Lucky day for Dougherty when you signed on."

"Lucky day for me," she replied. She didn't know how to respond to this kinder Ike.

"Guess it was. Maybe for Carico too. It needs smart people with an honest feel for the land." He cleared his throat. "'Nough said. Better turn in. Early start in the morning."

She hesitated, wanting to thank him for his confidence and sure he would just growl at her if she did.

"Go on then." He waved her away.

"Good night," she said.

"Yes, it is," he answered.

Lee settled her bedroll where she could see the horses tied to the highline strung between two of the water-finder trees. Ike getting poetic? With compliments no less. But he was right. She liked this country. Emptiness was a lot less frightening than people. And it gave her ample room to think. Maybe too much.

Tired as she was, she couldn't go to sleep. Finally, she pulled on her boots and walked up to where she could see across the plateau. The stars twinkled across the sky, dimmed by Lander, nearly full and high overhead. She walked slowly along the edge of the draw, knowing movement would help her relax. She could make out vague shapes of the horses, darker than grass. They dozed. She stood alone in the night and turned her thoughts to the stars and the hills far to the west.

In this strange country where the terrain cut down instead of jutting up, she felt the vastness of space more strongly than she had anywhere. Her view had always been limited by buildings or canyon walls or trees or the frame of a viewscreen onboard ship. Even Seven Wells was surrounded by hills. Here the ground stretched to the horizon.

And the silence. Away from the shuffling of horses' hooves, their breathing, Ike's snoring, in the deepest part of the night when not even the insects were active, she could hear her own heart beating if she held still. At that moment, the peace of the night overrode everything else. No haunting questions about her own past or future. Not even a question about what to have for breakfast. Just being.

A whistling howl broke the silence. She turned back and forth, hoping to hear another so she could tell where it came from. Another call, this one a long ways off to the east. Wolf-lizards. Then a full pack joined in. The bright night with the full disk of little Damele chasing the nearly-full Lander across the sky brought them out. She made her way back to camp and curled up in her blankets. She was nearly asleep when the wolf-lizards' chorus cut off like something interrupted them. She looked at the horses, dozing on the highline. They weren't concerned, so why should she be?

Chapter 10

Lee

Ike bent over the Dutch oven — actually a self-powered bread machine that controlled the temperature for both rising and baking. "Ingredients," he ordered, reaching out for her to hand him the yeasty, nutgrass flour, water, bean tree oil, and salt, one at a time. "Mix it up," he said and got up from the rock he sat on. While she buried her hands in the dough, he stowed Beulah's crock in a corner of a pack box, leaving room next to it for the machine. "Let the dough rest while we saddle," he instructed.

As if she didn't know that. They went through the bread routine every other day. Prep it in the morning, rest it until they were ready to go, knead it briefly, then let it rise while they traveled, stopping a couple of times to fold it in on itself. When it reached the perfect consistency, Ike would set the machine to bake, and they would have fresh bread for supper.

Another day of riding, stopping to make notes, and riding some more. A hot day. At least the hills grew slowly nearer. Lee took a swallow of water, feeling a little guilty that she didn't have enough for the horses.

Clown stopped abruptly, bringing Lee out of her water worry. Ahead of them Ike's horses stood still. The man was staring across a shallow depression.

"Look at that," he said. "Where did that come from?"

One rock the size of a big tarbh perched alone on the edge of the hollow, the only boulder in sight. "I have no idea," she said. She wasn't a good enough geologist to postulate how it got there.

"Like somebody just set it down." Ike shook his head. "It's a mystery."

She didn't answer. Something about the place made her uneasy. Ike must have felt it too. Instead of crossing the shallow depression, he skirted the outer rim on the far side from the boulder. They continued toward the north end of the line of hills where the map showed a canyon cutting down to the Whitewater River.

The ground changed as they approached the hills. The soil, so shallow and sandy around the canyon rims, appeared deeper and finer, more able to hold moisture when it was available. The nutgrass reappeared. Lee wiped sweat from her face with her sleeve and studied the hills for any sign of water. The horses hadn't had a drink in over a day. They weren't hurting yet but didn't have their usual energy.

"Tarbh," Ike said, pointing at the tiny splashes of blue against the verdigris hills. The animals waved the bright blue frills behind their necks to cool off. "I could sure use a fan myself right now." Ike waved his hat in front of his face.

"How far to that spring?" Lee asked. Tarbh could be half a day or more from water.

"The trail marked on the map takes off from that outcropping up ahead. Maybe an hour. I'll get us into the canyon with plenty of daylight left."

The hills cast shadows across the flats, and the temperature cooled slightly before they reached their goal. They found the trail easily enough. Even though it looked well-used by tarbh, it still plunged down more like a slide than a place to walk.

Ike started down first. Lee held back to let him get out of her way. Her normally well-behaved horses smelled water and danced anxiously. When Lee let them go, they charged down in a cascade of dirt and rocks. Heart pounding, she struggled to slow the animals.

"Let 'em go," Ike shouted at her. Against her own instincts, she gave Clown his head and rode out the slide to the bottom.

Her horses crowded in next to Ike's and plunged their muzzles into the stream to suck up water. The spring rose in the head of a narrow, rocky chasm. Only a faint trail meandered downstream. Apparently animals came to drink and returned to the plateau without staying.

Rocks clattered above. Lee looked up the trail to see a tarbh bull looming at the top. He pitched his fan forward to catch sounds and smells, reminding her of the statue in Portside. Tarbh weren't afraid of much, but this poor animal had never seen anything like horses with humans and packs. It folded its fan tight to its shoulders and spun back the way it had come. She wondered how long it would take the animal to return and get its drink.

She and Ike dragged the horses away from the water. The animals needed a little at a time after over a day without a drink. Ike led the way, looking for a campsite. As they followed the creek downstream, they let the horses have a few swallows of water at a time until the animals were finally satisfied.

They found nothing but rocks and the trickle of a creek in the bottom of a slot between curving walls of unbroken sandstone. She pulled out the recorder and snapped some pictures of the formation. No wonder the trail wasn't better. Nothing there to attract a tarbh. All she and Ike needed was a semi-flat place wide enough to camp, preferably before dark. It was going to be an uncomfortable night if they didn't find one.

Colors were fading to gray in the twilight when the left wall swung out in a 'U' with a tiny meadow in the middle and a bench with a few scraggly vine trees against the stone ramparts on the right.

Ike stopped on a flat, sandy spot below the bench. "Guess this'll do," he said as he eased off his horse. She unloaded the packs from Jester and Pokey while Ike found wood for a fire in the morning. She led the four horses up onto the bench, pulled off the saddles and set them on a half-fallen tree trunk, and hobbled the horses in the tiny patch of meadow. She found a good bed for herself against the cliff under one of the vine trees where years' accumulation of fallen leaves cushioned the rocky ground. Nearby she set up two short highlines between scraggly trees. With everything set for the night, she traded her boots for moccasins before joining Ike.

They ate a quick supper of fresh bread with cold tarbh from a vacuum pack. No need for a fire in the short while before bed. Both moons were up but blocked by the canyon wall. Their light brushed the cliff top with silver, leaving the camp and the horses in the dark.

"I'll find us a better camp in the morning," Ike said as he settled the bread machine with the leftover bread into a pack box. With gnarled hands, he tucked Beulah's crock into place next to it. He stacked the packs together on the sand near the wood for the morning's fire. "We'd best go back up on top, out of this trap, for a base camp."

Lee sighed with relief. The towering cliffs loomed over her. "Did you want to check out some of the hill country tomorrow?"

"Time to let the horses rest for a day. And us too," he replied. "Then spend a couple days around here before working our way back south." He sat on a pack box and drank the fruit drink they had mixed up. "I've never seen anything like this canyon. Those walls are like billowing fabric that froze in place."

She settled down cross-legged on the ground. Ike surprised her with these rare glimpses beneath his abrasive exterior. "Pretty unusual," she said.

"Maybe we'll see if we can follow this right down to the Whitewater."

"Horseback?" She was skeptical, in the absence of a well-used trail, that large animals could get through.

"Won't know if we don't look." He drained the drink container and set it aside. Something in the angle of his shoulders softened. She couldn't read his face in the half-dark. "You've heard of the Fever," he said.

"Of course." There was only one fever in the minds of Carico's residents — Immigrant Fever that had killed a huge portion of the population forty-some years earlier.

"My wife didn't survive it, back in the pandemic." Ike leaned his elbows on his knees and studied his hands. "Neither did the baby she carried. Your mom's parents didn't. Seth's grandparents didn't. Why I did is with the Elements." He took off his hat and fingered its copper and horsehair band. "When you find something you want, you have to fight for it. Don't let it get away." He didn't look up.

What could she say to that? She left him and caught the horses to tie them for the night. They hadn't had a chance to graze much, but they'd have plenty of time in the morning. She rubbed Clown's chest and a spot on Jester's neck before leaving them to find her bed in the dark. She hung her trail clothes on a tree branch and lay there, too hot even in just her tank top, wishing for the breeze that usually flowed down the canyons after dark.

Her mind spun. Ike's few words explained a lot about his life and all those who struggled to settle Carico. And he wanted something for her that he had lost himself — family. His prods about Seth got to her so badly because he was so right. The only man she could even imagine making a future with was the one she had driven away, so scared they would fail that she made sure they did. "Now you've done it, old man," she whispered. "You hit me with it often enough that it finally got through." She shifted restlessly, removed a couple of annoying rocks, and eventually drifted off to sleep.

Someone called her, just her name, over and over from far away. She tried to find them but, no matter which way she went, the voice was always behind her. And all around, hooves shifted restlessly in the rocks.

Clown blew loudly, clearing his nostrils, seeking some scent. Lee sat up; she had been dreaming. But the hooves clattering, Clown's snorting, and the voice calling her continued. She pulled on her camp pants and moccasins.

"Lee!" Ike's voice carried on the night air. "Here! Hurry!" She saw him in the moonlight, standing by the pack boxes below her, staring back the way they had come. She picked her way down through the rocks and brush to join him. Confused rumbles echoed off the cliffs and rolled around them. She couldn't make out anything to identify what made the noise or even where it was coming from.

"Flash flood?" She made a wild guess. They hadn't heard a storm.

"Hope not," he answered. He shambled closer to the entrance to their little cove. "Better get off this bottom, just in case." He hoisted one of the pack boxes and started up onto the bench where the horses were tied. It was the highest ground they could reach.

Lee grabbed a pack box and ran. They couldn't afford to lose their supplies. The noise grew louder; cracks of rock on rock rang through the general roar. She beat Ike to the foot of the cliff, left her box, and ran back. She scooped up Ike's bedding along with another box.

A wild grunting filled the canyon. "It's tarbh!" Ike shouted as he snatched up the pack that held Beulah. Faint rattles became the crashing of rocks under a hundred feet rushing down the canyon, reverberating off the surrounding walls. A wave of massive animals thundered straight for them, all horns and rock-solid heads bunched tight.

Get higher. Out of the path. Lee clutched the pack box and bedding. They ran. Feet slid in the sand. Ike stumbled. She dropped the box, grabbed his arm, and pulled him with her. He twisted free, pushed her ahead, his big, knobby hand on her shoulder. "Get clear!" he shouted.

She scrambled to the rocky slope; glanced back; saw Ike trip; go sprawling; curl in the shelter of the box she had dropped. With snorting, roaring breaths and thudding feet, a mass of bodies cut between them. Something struck her. She tried to catch herself, slammed into the rocks.

The sounds faded away, leaving a haze of dust in the air. She tried to get up. Pain stabbed her knee. She heard dancing hooves of frantic horses settle, go quiet in the aftermath. She lay back and sucked in a breath.

Ike! She pushed herself up, found she could stand. Just above her, she heard Clown stomping wildly with renewed panic. She saw him and Jester hit the ends of their ropes together, saw the highline snap. They fled past her and disappeared up the canyon. She ran after them but caught her feet in the brush and fell. Ike's voice called, "Girl, where are ya'? Lee —" Her legs wobbled, refused to hold under her; an acrid, musky stench enveloped her. The world spun her off into blackness.

Chapter 11

Seth

Seth stood in the dark at the front of the rockshelter he called home and let the light breeze wash over him. He shifted his bare feet on the sandpaper grit of the stone, seeking balance, grounding himself. He began the precise, familiar batayr movements, his mind on the details and the flow. Immersing in the meditation let him put the day behind him so he could sleep — sometimes.

Ringing neighs pierced the silence. Seth broke off his practice in disgust. "Now what has them stirred up?" He looked across the canyon and made out four horses, two of them outside the fence, one of them with splashes of white on its sides. Clown? He pulled on his boots and ran down the steps. Creamy and the roan greeted the two newcomers over the gate. Definitely Clown and his own Jester. Both wore halters with frayed ropes dragging from them.

"Well, I'll be a tailless rock rat. Deserters? You two?"

He wanted to believe the animals had simply wandered away from Lee and Ike. It wouldn't be the first time some rider got left afoot that way. But the lead ropes suggested they had been tied, not loose, and had broken free. At least they weren't saddled. So not a riding accident. And Ike's horses weren't with them so the two riders weren't completely afoot. Still, trouble.

Seth ran hands quickly over each horse. Remains of sweat left a slight roughness on necks and chests. He couldn't find any injuries.

He clamped down his urge to saddle up and head out. No point running around in the dark. He turned the two wanderers into the pasture with Creamy and the roan and tried to get his thoughts under control.

How long since Lee and Ike had left his place? He looked at the sky — his only calendar. Neither moon was up yet, but a tinge of light to the east told him Damele would be soon. It would be nearly full tonight, about what it was the day Lee and Ike had left, so eight or maybe nine days ago. From what Ike had told him by now they should be somewhere on the northwest side of the plateau. But he had no way of knowing where they had been when the horses got loose or how long the two horses had wandered. He would have to backtrack the strays and hope he met Lee and Ike coming after them.

His over-active imagination pictured the many things that could go wrong — falls, run-ins with wild animals, a fugitive like Whip Willemsen, even a simple illness. A little thing could be a disaster back of beyond, and losing half your horses was big.

He wouldn't take a pack horse, just Clown and Creamy since he was sound again. That meant he would only take what he could pack on his saddle horse, a blanket, a little food, some horse treats, the emergency kit that lived in his saddlebags. He hoped he'd find Lee and Ike on their way to retrieve the horses. But he couldn't leave yet. Little Damele was bright once it was up, but not bright enough to track by.

No amount of batayr practice or staring at the ceiling brought sleep. He went down and turned the irrigation water onto his garden to soak it well. It should be okay for a few days. By the time he had enough light to read tracks on the ground, he had the roan saddled and Clown and Creamy ready to go. He posted a note on the tack room door where he knew Gabe Huff would look when he didn't find Seth at home. Gabe would let Dougherty know that, if Seth wasn't back in a couple of days, someone should come looking. Seth trusted the Seven Wells manager to follow through. Dougherty took his riders' safety seriously.

Lee had better be hot on the trail of her missing animals, or he was going to get hungry. He only packed what he could carry on his saddle, enough for three or four days, and no extra feed for the horses. Enough to get by if he gave the horses time enough to graze, and he wouldn't risk tracking at night anyway.

He followed the fresh hoof prints in the dust past where Lee and Ike had camped and through the little pasture they had used. One trail more suited to swine-deer than horses twisted out of the canyon onto the rim. The gate at the bottom, designed to keep horses from going up, hadn't stopped Jester and Clown when they had slid down to it from above. He would have to fix that when he got home.

He kept trying to make sense of it. Two tied horses, well-trained and familiar with the routine of the trail, broke their ropes, left the horses they were with, and headed home, when normally both could be turned loose to graze without ever wandering from camp. Something must have spooked them pretty badly. What had Lee gotten herself into?

Tracking took time and care, especially on loose, dry ground that didn't hold an imprint well. He followed fairly obvious tracks for a mile or more where the horses had been traveling steadily toward home. Then the tracks faded away as the horses had apparently wandered randomly in search of feed. But the telltale marks of the dragging lead ropes gave them away. One sign led to another and kept him focused on the next few feet in front of him.

Too slow; too slow. He heard that ringing in his head all day. In spite of the slow progress, he found the first place where Lee and Ike had camped before dark forced him to stop. He could see evidence of the highline and the campfire laid out just as he expected Lee would set them up. It wasn't as if there was anybody else out there anyway. It had to be their camp. And now his.

The thought of another day inching forward made his stomach churn. Backtracking the horses was taking too long. He'd only gotten to Lee and Ike's first camp even though they hadn't been in a hurry.

While his horses grazed, he chewed half-heartedly on a cold biscuit and got out the map he had packed, looking for answers that weren't there, for a quick way of finding the riders. From what he had seen so far, it looked like the horses came back along the same route they had traveled going out. They weren't coming from the northwest where he expected Lee and Ike to be by now. How long ago had they gotten free?

He paced and studied the map and had a long, if one-sided, conversation with Clown about his travels, then made a guess at where Ike would have watered the horses next on the way north. He'd go straight there in the morning. If he didn't find horse tracks at that spring, he'd have to come back and follow the trail, but if he did find signs that the strays had been there, he'd be that much ahead. He gambled he was right.

He pushed the horses in the predawn cool, trotting or loping whenever the footing allowed. He stopped when he began to feel the heat of the day and switched the saddle to Clown to give the roan a break. Before midmorning he found the spring he had noted on the map. Plenty of tracks showed the riders had watered their horses before moving on and that the loose horses had come that way, but he found no sign of Ike or Lee coming after them. He watered the horses, filled his bottles, and followed the tracks long enough to get an idea which direction the horses had come from. Then he picked a landmark on the horizon and pushed on, walk, trot, walk, lope, trot, eating up the ground. He could hurry where Lee and Ike would have taken their time to study the country.

Tracks, both going out and the strays coming back, led him to Lee and Ike's second camp, a shallow basin at the head of a draw with no sign of water. Switching to Creamy, he walked the horses in the afternoon heat, studying the tracks and moving steadily, still north, still along their original route like they had never gotten to the home trip along the west side of the plateau before the horses got loose.

A few thunderheads built over the hills, reminding Seth that the summer rains would come soon. The sun painted the clouds purple and orange as it dropped toward the horizon. He needed to reach the next water, a big spring deep in the head of a canyon that flowed north to the Whitewater. They would have taken two days to reach it from where he had camped last night. He could, he would do it in one. No packs; no study of the land; just covering ground. He was eight days, one cycle of Damele, behind them.

He didn't need to follow tracks to find that spring. With the map he could go straight there. But what if they had never made it that far. Or turned west into the hills. Stay with the tracks. And hurry. Before he ran out of light.

He came to a broad hollow, a strange place with a lone boulder perched on its edge. Creamy stopped, ears pricked forward. The other two horses locked up tensely. Seth tried to see what they sensed. Then a shift in the breeze brought him the putrid smell of something dead.

His chest caved in. Don't let it be ... Reluctantly he urged the horses forward, circling the spot they were focused on, a solitary boulder. Or a carcass. A tarbh maybe. Hard to tell with the setting sun casting long shadows.

The horses relaxed a little as they passed the suspicious shape. He forced himself to dismount and tied them together, hobbling the roan to keep all three in place. He approached the lump on foot, covering his nose with his hand to cut the stench. It was a rock, but a body slumped against it, washed reddish by the sun. He hesitated, heart pounding. Please, please, not Lee; don't let it be Lee.

He moved closer and recognized Ike's copper-studded hat band. The man, or what had been a man, sat against the rock, facing the hollow and clutching a bridle in his hand, as if he had just stripped it from a horse's head. No need to check for a pulse. The dried, burned skin stretched harshly over the underlying bones in a caricature of a human face.

Seth turned away, struggling between shock and relief. It wasn't Lee. He swallowed hard. He had to figure out what happened. He had to find her.

Seth walked slowly around the body, concentrating on the tracks, trying not to think about Ike. He saw where a single horse had come from the hills. No sign that the horse had spooked or bucked. Ike, hurt or sick, had gotten off or fallen off and dragged himself to sit against the rock. The horse had stood close by long enough to eat down everything it could reach and to trample the ground next to the man. Ike must have kept hold of the reins as long as he could, then pulled the bridle off. The tracks showed where the horse had wandered back the way it had come. No sign of another horse or of Lee.

Seth's throat tightened, imagining Ike lying there alone, hurt, knowing help wasn't coming, freeing his horse before he died. "Last thing you did, old man?" he whispered. Days under the sun had wiped out any signs of what had killed him, sucking the moisture from flesh, leaving a shriveling husk.

Seth thought about leaving him as he lay and going on to find Lee. There was something clean about letting the sun and the air take the body but, in the end, he couldn't abandon Ike like that. He hurried to scrape out a shallow grave next to the boulder. He straightened the body carefully and wrapped it in a light emergency blanket from his pack. He eased the body into the hole as best he could and pushed the dirt back in. Securing a rope around the rock, he used his horse to roll it over onto the grave.

"Some marker you've got there," he said as he laid Ike's hatband on top of the rock where the copper pieces would catch the sunlight. It was a lonely place, open to the wind and rain and sun, just like a rider's life.

Between the fresh grave and the dying day, the place gave him an eerie feeling. Time to move on. Seth mounted Creamy in the twilight, struggling to decide what to do next. Ike had come alone from the hills, just him and one horse. That left his pack horse and Lee unaccounted for. Why would he have left Lee? Had they separated for some reason, searching for the stray horses maybe? Or was she dead too?

There would be water somewhere along Ike's tracks, whether it was the spring he saw on the map or something else, but now it was too dark to trust he could follow the hoof prints. His horses were thirsty. They hadn't had a drink since midmorning and had covered over thirty miles. Not good. He dismounted and switched his saddle to the white-splashed gelding. "Come on, Clown. You've been here before. Find yourself a drink." He started riding in the general direction Ike had come from and let the horse pick the way.

By the Void, when he found Lee he was going to kill her for putting him through this. "If I don't have to dig her up to do it," he told himself. He worked at controlling his breathing and the wave of anxiety that threatened him. He had known that feeling all too well in the past, but it didn't cripple him anymore. He could manage it now. He would.

And help would be coming. As long as Gabe called Seven Wells, Dougherty would have a rescue party on the way. He was a cautious man. That day or maybe the next, riders would gather at Seth's place and work out from there with skimmers. He should be easy enough to find on the wide expanse of plateau as long as he stayed out of the canyons.

The smaller moon, past full now, hurried across the sky, measuring time. The waning larger moon wouldn't rise until daybreak. He couldn't be sure how far he'd come, but Clown began to walk faster.

Up ahead he heard something. There, again. The neigh of a lonely horse. Ike's? It had to be. Clown and the others raised their heads but didn't reply. Seth caught movement, a blot on the moon-gray landscape, stopping, starting, neighing, slowly growing larger. It resolved into a dark horse, loping now, circling wide. He stopped, giving the animal time to recognize its friends. In moments, it came forward and sniffed noses with Clown. Ike's brown gelding, Tinker, still carrying Ike's saddle. Seth legged Clown into a walk, and Tinker fell in behind Creamy and the roan.

Clown brought them to the head of a steep trail and started down without hesitating. The others followed, scattering loose rock and dirt. Seth sat tight and let the animals find their way down into the darkness. Deep under the canyon rim, they reached a spring.

He let the horses drink, although not to their satisfaction. He didn't need a colicky horse. Looking around, he knew that Lee and Ike hadn't camped there. The canyon was too narrow and rocky. Above the spring was a sheer headwall, so they must have gone downstream.

He let the horses have a few more swallows and pulled them away, tying them securely to the single vine tree growing against the cliff. He unsaddled Clown before dealing with Ike's horse. He didn't know the animal or how easy it would be to catch in the dark.

All it took was a couple pieces of dried roundfruit. Tinker lipped the treats from his hand and stood while he freed the halter from the saddle and slipped it over the horse's head. He eased the saddle off and ran his hands over the horse's back. The animal had carried the saddle for days in the heat, had probably rolled, trying to get rid of it. The hair felt rough, and he found a few raw sores.

"Take it easy, Tinker. I'll take care of those as soon as I have enough light." He rubbed the horse and found an itchy spot on its neck to scratch.

He had to wait for daylight anyway. Much as he wanted to look for Lee, he didn't want to cripple a horse doing it or stumble all over tracks that might tell him something. He sat down with his back to the rock wall and forced himself to wait. He dreaded what he would find.

He should have gone with Lee and Ike on this trek. Dougherty and Ike had both given him the opportunity. Where, in the Black Void, had she gotten to?

Hot sun woke him. He scrambled up. His roan horse greeted him with a nicker. He watered the four animals and tied them again. Grazing would have to wait. First he needed to search for any sign of Lee.

A narrow path wound along the creek flowing from the spring. The sparse brush on both sides had been knocked down and broken, like a herd of tarbh had run through it. Heart pounding, he forced himself to study the ground.

He read a story of a stampede going down the canyon, Jester and Clown running up the canyon, then tarbh moving slowly up the canyon in file on the path, and lastly one horse going up the canyon. The tracks matched those he found around Ike's body. No sign of Ike's pack horse. Or of Lee.

Start where the horses had come from, where Jester and Clown had escaped, probably during the stampede. And see what he could learn. He hiked down the snaky, narrow slot, following the stampede until he reached a tiny, grassy opening. Lee and Ike's camp. And at least one person had been there after the stampede. Ashes of a campfire lay in the sand on top of the tarbh tracks. Two pack boxes lay with their contents scattered.

"Lee," he called. His voice echoed strangely off the rock walls. "Lee!"

No answer.

He walked around slowly. Near the campfire, the ground and a rock showed stains that looked like blood, as if someone, Ike maybe, had been injured and sat there for a while. Had Lee treated him? Or was the blood hers?

He found Clown and Jester's tracks where they had been tied against the cliff. The broken highline dangled from the trees it had been strung between. Two packsaddles hung over a leaning trunk along with Lee's riding saddle. Beyond he could see a second, intact highline with blood on the ground. From the missing pack horse? But where was the animal?

Lee would have slept near her horses. Under a vine tree, he found where a bed of dead leaves had been piled up. Her boots stood upright with socks hanging out of the tops. Above them her long-sleeved shirt and rider's pants hung on a broken branch, just as she would have left them. He dropped his head and closed his eyes, hope turning into a hard knot in his chest.

But her bedding and her saddlebags were missing. Someone had taken just those. Slowly he crisscrossed the camp area, gathering up gear that had been scattered. If the saddlebags weren't there ... well, if she could take only one thing, she would have taken her saddlebags.

He didn't find them or her bedding. He found no food and no first aid kit. Ike might have taken the kit but not all of the food they had carried. Wild animals would have left wrappings and scraps. He stacked everything he did find with the saddles — cook gear including Ike's precious yeasty and his bread oven, his bedding, a tent still in its bag.

Seth found nothing that gave him any clue where to begin to look for Lee. With a knot in his stomach, he searched for tracks all around the camp and down the canyon. A little way below the camp, the canyon widened again and the trampling from the stampede ended. He went beyond there until he came to a drop off that blocked his way. No sign that anyone had come that way.

He returned to the abandoned camp and sat next to the pile of equipment to think, drawing on meditation techniques to focus. He had to calm his thudding heart and the voice screaming in his head to do something, anything, right now. But the pieces wouldn't fit together into a picture that made any sense. She had vanished, not a track, not a hint of where she had gone. What did he do now? He had to make the right decision.

Chapter 12

Lee

Lee struggled through layers of sleep like a swimmer drowning in deep water, searching hazy, chaotic dreams for the surface, for wakefulness. Finally, her eyes cracked opened. Light glared, and her head pounded. Must have been some party.

She pushed herself up on one elbow and scrubbed her face with a hand, trying to clear the hangover haze. What party? Where was she? What in the Void had happened? She wished someone would turn out the lights.

Sunlight reflected off a rock wall into the shadows where she lay face down on her thin, self-inflating sleeping pad on blue-green rock. She had been ... she and Ike Allred had been exploring northwest of the Glas River. She lowered her face to her arm and tried to remember. No party, no hangover. A stampede. They had been trying to get out of the way of a stampede in a narrow slot canyon. Ike had fallen. Her horses had broken free and fled. Then ... nothing. She couldn't remember any more.

She rolled over, sore and stiff, and looked up at a ceiling of rock a few feet above her head. Had she gotten back to Seth's somehow? She sat up cautiously. Her ribs ached but didn't stab. Her head spun. She pulled her knees up to lean her head on them, but the right one didn't want to bend that far. When she tried to straighten it back out, she got tangled up, tugging her other leg out too. She reached down to get untangled and found something around her ankle. She opened her eyes wide.

A cuff a couple inches wide encircled her ankle. A foot or so of rope connected to a cuff on her other leg. She was hobbled, shackled. She covered her face with her hands, froze, forced herself to stay in the present. Jerdix was long dead. She was not back in a shack above Under Rim, waiting for that monster. There was heat and sun, not hail. And her hands were free.

That galvanized her. She fumbled with her bonds, trying to find a way to get loose. The cuffs and the rope were intricately braided from very fine strands of rawhide. She plucked and twisted them but couldn't find an end or a knot, like they had been braided in place. But that was an impossibility. She'd watched Seth with his horsehair braiding enough to know it took days of work to create that kind of fine interlacing.

The hobbles were a puzzle. The cuffs loosened and tightened as she worked at them but only to a point. She couldn't force them open enough to extract her feet. She was a captive. But of whom? Whip Willemsen? He was a fugitive somewhere. But the intricate rawhide work of the shackles wasn't his. From what little she remembered of him, he didn't have the patience. Was he working for someone, like he had for Jerdix? Some enclave of beyonders living outside the bounds of settled territory?

She looked around, hoping for some sign of Ike, some clue to where she was. The ledge was about fifteen feet from front to back and maybe twice that long, in a wedge carved horizontally out of the cliff by wind, water and time. The whole shallow rockshelter was in shade, probably facing north. At the back, the roof was barely high enough for her to stand, but it swept high at the front where the floor curved downward before disappearing.

She stretched and clenched her hands a couple of times, then shook them out, releasing a little of her tension. She saw nothing immediately threatening around her. She was barefoot. No sign of her moccasins. She had on the tank top and loose camp pants she had worn when the stampede hit, both dirty and torn in places but functional.

She ran her hands over her head but didn't find a tender spot that would indicate she had been knocked out. She had numerous scrapes and scratches, but the purple bruise on her right knee was the only real injury. She prodded it gently and tested to see how far she could bend the joint. Painful and stiff but not incapacitating. She still felt hung over, with a dry mouth, throbbing head, and gritty eyes. Dehydrated. Had she been drugged?

She got to her feet cautiously. The knee supported her weight although she suspected it wouldn't stand up to any strenuous action. Testing the shackles, she shuffled toward the edge of her prison. Someone had left her water bottle there next to a tray of the common roundfruit and spike roots. She bit into a roundfruit, savoring the juice in her dry mouth while she studied her surroundings.

Across the canyon, the opposite wall was about a hundred feet away. Not as deep and with a broader bottom than the slot where she and Ike had been camped. Trying to pick a point level with her on that wall, she thought she must be about twenty feet above the canyon floor. The sun reflected off the verdigris rock into her shelter. Huge old vine trees clung to that cliff, their chartreuse leaves bright in the sun, but none grew conveniently near her ledge. It was beyond her how anyone had hauled her up, or maybe let her down from above, to leave her there.

Low on the opposite wall, another rockshelter cut into the layered sandstone, shaded and half-concealed by the trees. She thought its sandy floor looked disturbed but couldn't pick out anything that proved someone occupied it. The canyon bottom, what little she could see of it, was devoid of people.

She went back and picked up the tray. It was actually a basket woven out of what looked like copper tree bark. She ran a finger along the rim. She'd never seen anything quite like it. Whoever these people were, they had both the time and skills to create beautiful crafts.

They were also secretive, it seemed. But, if they didn't want her to see them, why bring her here at all? An act of compassion when she was stranded, horseless, by the stampede?

She cupped her hands around her mouth and shouted, "Ike! Ike!" Her voice echoed in the silence. No one answered or came to see what she was doing.

She started to shout again but held back. The idea of someone coming to check on her made her heart pound. She clamped down fiercely on the memory of big, harsh hands taking hold of her. No matter that the man with those hands was almost three years dead. He had taught her what to expect from a captor.

She chewed the inside of her lip. She didn't seem to be in any immediate danger. She had food and water. She couldn't be sure if the water was drugged. The fresh fruit and vegetables seemed safer. Taking the bottle and tray, she shuffled back to her bedding, noting that the rope between her ankles was long enough to trip her if she was careless, but not long enough to let her do any rock climbing.

She put on a show of calm acceptance, assuming someone was watching. Mislead them into expecting compliance from her. Save fighting and escaping for the right time.

She picked up a spike root and bit into it. Another roundfruit next. As casually as she could, she ate her fill, keeping one of the roundfruits for later. She looked thoughtfully at the tray, then took it back where it came from. Maybe someone would take the hint and refill it.

She eased down onto the pad and picked up the water bottle. She sloshed the liquid around. It felt nearly full. She wasn't ready to risk another unplanned nap, so she used it to wet a corner of the blanket sparingly and wiped dirt out of her many scrapes. She found a lump and scab on her right cheekbone that she cleaned by feel. She must be quite a sight with the stampede's grime on top of a couple of days of sweat and dust. She hadn't had a chance to properly clean up since before the night they had dry-camped.

She counted back. The stampede camp, the dry camp, the camp in the canyon — three days out from Seth's, assuming the stampede had been last night. He wouldn't even begin to worry about them for almost three weeks. Unless Jester went home, but the horse could take days to wander back. Then Seth would have to get to his neighbors' comm unit to let Dougherty know they were overdue. Forget getting help anytime soon.

Her mind raced. "You're not stuck until you have to call for help," she muttered an old axiom. Two things she did know for certain. Panic would buy her nothing, and she had to get herself out of this. She began diligently picking at the braided rawhide of her shackles with her fingernails, seeking an end that would come loose so she could begin to tear the whole thing apart.

While she worked at the stubborn rawhide, she worried about Ike. She vaguely recalled his voice over the noise of the stampede. She had seen him fall and find the limited protection of a pack box. Even a stampeding tarbh avoided obstacles. At best, he was a prisoner too. Actually, best would be for him to be on his way to Seth's and help. Worst ... well, she didn't want to think about what that meant.

Shadows crept across the cliff. The heat penetrated her cave. Insects flew around, uninterested in her human blood. For the most part, they preferred locally evolved, copper-based blood. What was the word? Hemocyanin, rather than humans' hemoglobin. Somehow it pleased her that she could think of the technical term under the circumstances. A light breeze ruffled the vine tree leaves and soothed her, adding a normalcy to a summer afternoon.

Unable to make any progress with her bindings, she stretched out on her pad, rolling the blanket under her sore knee to elevate it. Waiting strained her patience. She wondered what the statistics showed. Did solitary confinement break a person more effectively than physical torture? She made her mind focus, retelling stories she had been told as a child, rehearsing what she would tell her family about her time at Seven Wells next time she saw them, picking out patterns in the rock overhead, anything to keep from imagining what might happen next.

Twilight replaced sunlight. Evening fliers swooped past on scaled wings in pursuit of insects. A grunting roar echoed through the canyon, answered by others.

She started in surprise, then relaxed. Just notalions. She hadn't heard one since she had left Under Rim. She had never actually seen one of the big-voiced, but apparently shy, little predators.

Something thumped against the rock. She saw the end of a log — no, a thick bundle of cane or reeds — appear above the edge near the empty basket. She scrambled to her feet, fighting the resurgence of memories of hands that had controlled her, held her down.

A hand appeared, an adobe-colored hand with two central, talon-tipped fingers and two opposing thumbs, one on each side. Not human; not like anything she'd ever seen before. She froze; waited.

The hand held a weapon that looked like a hybrid of a sling shot and a crossbow. Behind the weapon, two huge blazing-blue eyes watched her over a short snout tipped with a sharp, hooked beak. An upright, flaring headdress of dark red and cinnamon-colored feathers framed the face. The feathers folded down slowly — the creature's own crest rather than something it wore.

Without leaving the ladder, the creature held up a tall, cylindrical shape, set it down on the rock, picked up the flat basket, and backed out of sight. The end of the cane bundle vanished.

Lee shook her head in disbelief. Her thoughts whirled like a mob of tarbh milling in a corral. She couldn't sort one from another to give herself any direction. She had to be dreaming.

That creature should not be walking around unidentified on Carico sixty-eight years after first landing. The Coalition did not authorize settlement on worlds that already had indigenous cultures capable of any level of abstract thought, certainly not one capable of weapons manufacture and artistic expression. The careful pre-settlement evaluation of the planet should not have missed non-human people like the one she had just seen.

A first contact was a fine dream for students safe in the confines of the academy. But faced with the reality, so much could go wrong between alien cultures, not the least of which was her ending up dead. She would gladly let Adel have this coup, if only she could trade places with the Ranger.

She re-ran what she had just seen, looking for clues to help her. The creature looked avian with the feathers and the beak, but the snout was more reptilian. She hadn't seen below their shoulders, but they definitely had arms instead of wings. The weapon they carried showed no sign of metal parts, and there were the baskets and the rawhide shackles — all low tech but intricate and beautiful in execution.

What did the creature think of her? She was being treated as a captive. She was expected to recognize and respect a weapon when one was pointed at her. So she was more than a pet and less than a god. If the creature had any concept of either.

Her heart pounded. She had to escape but needed to undo the Gordian knot around her ankles first, and she needed to know if Ike was a prisoner too. So the only thing she could do for the time being was watch and learn enough to stay alive.

She picked up the new container, sniffed at the contents, and took a mouthful of the water. No unusual taste to it. Anyway, she was too thirsty to worry about it being drugged. She drank a couple more swallows. Carrying it with her, she walked along the lip of the cave looking for any evidence of occupation in the canyon. She couldn't see any sign of the creature, but brush concealed much of the canyon floor. She paced back and forth, slowly, like a sentry on duty; monotonous; holding panic at bay as twilight failed. All with a picture of sapphire eyes and a fierce hawk's beak fueling her imagination.

Chapter 13

Lee

Moonlight cast twisted tree shadows on the canyon wall. Lee paced slowly along the front of her little cave and thought about phases of the two moons, a prosaic consideration to help her avoid speculating on her future. At the dry camp, two nights ago, little Damele had been full. Lander had been waxing gibbous. So tonight, Lander would be full and Damele at half, not that she could see them. Both were too far south in the sky, hidden by the rock rim, but they lit up the canyon wall across from her. The night might be bright, but she was left in the dark.

She stopped at one end of her ledge and leaned against the rock wall. Her bruised knee ached, and her bare feet had been sanded by her pacing on the stone. She might as well try and get some sleep. Counting backward from a million might get her there. She eased down on her bed and stretched out, rolling the blanket to use as a pillow. She closed her eyes and focused on relaxing, muscle by muscle. Her heartbeat slowed. It seemed like she could feel it at the base of her skull, soft and gentle like a distant drum.

The beat intensified, a real drum, deep-toned so she felt it as much as heard it. She sat up and turned her head, trying to find the source, but the sound echoed through her rock chamber and the canyon beyond. She went to the edge to look out into the moon-washed night.

A flash of light down the canyon to her left caught her attention. Beyond a stand of straggling brush, she made out a greenish-blue flickering. Someone had lit a fire — no, torches, several of them, in a circle. Her captors were having some kind of get-together.

She could see four of them gathered between two torches on the far side of the circle. She couldn't make out details — they were a couple of hundred yards away, half-obscured by vegetation — but she could see their general forms. They were bipedal with narrow shoulders, two arms, and stout lizard tails that just reached the ground. Her childhood fascination with odd animals from her ancestral home world brought to mind comparisons like kangaroos with ostrich legs or the two-legged dinosaurs from Terra's ancient past.

The four tilted their heads back and burst into a cacophony of calls. Ten or fifteen more creatures came out into the circle of torches. About a third smaller and lighter colored than the first group, they looked more like the one who had brought her water.

They took places in the torch circle, leaving the first four together. A staccato drumbeat brought the gathering to order. Lee spotted the drum, a hand drum held by one of the larger individuals.

Two of the smaller figures strutted into the circle to face off several feet apart. They were slender and agile with long, snakelike tails. Lee couldn't begin to guess if the differences indicated gender, age, or separate species. But neither type bore any resemblance to any species she knew of.

The drum returned to a steady beat. The two in the circle began to dance, mirroring each other. The tempo increased; the moves got more complicated. Dance? More like a martial arts kata, like the batayr forms she had learned in the Rangers, that Seth practiced religiously. Chanting rose and fell, guttural sounds a human would have a hard time duplicating.

The two got closer and closer. At a shout from the watchers, the dance became a fight, a martial arts match that took Lee's breath. The antagonists whirled too fast to follow, using tails as much as hands and feet. She stared in awe and knew in her gut that few humans would stand a chance hand-to-hand against such fighters.

One went down and struggled to get up. The second spread its arms high and set a foot on the fallen one's neck. The drum and chant went silent, like a held breath. The crowd shouted something. Lee waited, expecting a death blow, but apparently concession was enough. The winner danced alone while the loser limped off to join the others in the circle.

Two more took their places. The whole thing was both unreal and familiar. She recognized the ritual nature, the demonstration of skill rather than intent to injure. But the speed and power of these fighters left her dizzy.

Cool night air brushed the opening of her cave and sent her for her blanket. She found a place where she could sit and still see through a gap in the brush. The drum and chanting resumed. She could feel it in her bones, rising, ceasing, rising for the next bout. The circle of torches dominated the night. The distance seemed to shrink as she watched, absorbed by the scene, so fierce and wild.

Finally the drum stilled for the last time. The larger creatures walked around inside the circle, and each selected two or three of the smaller ones to lead away. A last individual extinguished the torches and disappeared into the night.

The adrenaline drained away. Lee struggled to her feet, stiff from sitting so long, and hobbled to her bed. The sky was showing hints of gray. Morning wasn't far off. A new day and what then? She was tired enough not to care.

Before she could get settled, scuffling sounds brought her sharply into the moment. She hunched down, made herself small, a primal prey response. The cane ladder thumped against the rock and a face appeared, the same as before she thought, now darkened by a livid bruise. The creature pulled up a basket on a rope and took out a tray of food and another water container. She watched the creature's hand, the four long, strong digits in two opposing pairs like pincers, pale against the pattern of the baskets. The hand pushed the tray toward her; the beaked snout clicked; the face disappeared back down the ladder; and the bundled canes vanished.

She let out the breath she had been holding. She acknowledged the true magnitude of her position and was staggered by it. She had made first contact with an unknown species, unquestionably *people* as defined by the Interstellar Coalition.

More correctly, they had made contact with her, and they had complete control of the situation. They could feed her or not; let her drink or not; keep her alive or not. And she was completely isolated with no hope of rescue for days, if not weeks. She sought out the deepest shadow of the cave and huddled into the blanket, a child seeking refuge.

Daylight came and with it hunger, a clear reminder that she did have actions she could take on her own behalf, even if they were limited. She fetched the water container and the tray of food to her bedding and picked through the selection of fruits and vegetables. The only thing approaching meat was a pile of grubs that looked like they had been roasted. Well, protein was protein. Insect-like creatures in myriad variations topped any list of survival fare, not to mention high-end menus in some places.

She tasted one cautiously: crunchy with a gushy center, slightly sweet, seasoned with something she remembered her Aunt Teri using but that she couldn't name offhand. She popped several more grubs into her mouth and washed them down with juicy globeberries. Next to the grubs was boiled grain, nutgrass by the size and shape. Expecting dry and bland, she was surprised to find it sweetened with something that tasted like palm-pine sugar.

Settlers valued the useful sap of the palm-pine trees. Could these people be waterproofing the tightly woven water containers with it? Left over after the sugar was extracted, the sap made a tough, flexible coating used to protect horses' hooves among other things. She drank the last of the water she'd been given the night before, that she knew wasn't drugged, and inspected the interior of the container. The coating did look and feel like palm-pine sap.

So these creatures traveled far enough to gather from trees that didn't grow nearby. Or she had been taken a long distance from where she'd been captured. Palm-pines grew in the higher country. She and Ike hadn't seen any during their trek. One more little thing she knew about her captors. And knowledge was about the only power she had.

She hid some of the food under the blanket and didn't drink anything from the new water container. She would save it for later, when she was thirsty enough to risk drugs. She walked along the front of the ledge, seeing no activity in the part of the canyon within her view. The twenty or so beings from the night's festivities had to live somewhere nearby but not in this branch of the canyon.

No one came to check on her. Someone could be watching where she didn't see them, or they all could be sleeping in after the all-night party. It didn't matter much. The drop-off and the shackles would keep her where she was.

The day warmed up; heat reflected from the canyon walls into the shade of her prison; insects droned. She tried to sleep but couldn't stop chasing wild thoughts through her head at a full gallop. She began a batayr practice routine, but her bruised knee objected, and the shackles interfered with the movements. Her mind could see Seth flowing through the moves. What was he doing right now? Building another wall of rocks? Lounging in a deep pool in the stream that flowed through his new place? Most likely working with a horse. He wouldn't worry about her and Ike for weeks yet.

She stretched out on the bedding and studied the rock overhead, colors of verdigris and amber, the same colors in the braided tarbh rawhide around her ankles. Question after question — where was she, why, what would happen next — without an answer to be had.

"Ike, old man, where are you?" she muttered. Her one hope was that he was free and on his way to get help.

Chapter 14

Lee

The sound of something moving on the sand of the canyon floor brought Lee out of her pointless speculation. Midday and getting hot. She hadn't seen anyone since the food delivery before dawn. The clack of wood against wood got her to her feet and out to look off her perch.

One of the larger, dark-skinned creatures walked along the canyon floor toward the entrance to the shallow cave low down in the cliff across from her. Powerful legs took long steps. The body bent forward at the hips, and they raised their tail as a counterbalance. They stopped in front of the cave and straightened up, lowering their tail to the ground. A black fan as long as Lee's forearm tipped the tail. Feathers? Their head resembled an earless sheep, but the snout ended in a short, blunt beak like a turtle's. This creature looked a little less threatening than the hawk-beaked one, less predatory but no less alien.

Their head turned, and large, golden eyes met hers. Lee looked away awkwardly. Was eye contact challenging or threatening? Was looking away a sign of submission? She didn't speak these creatures' body language. She didn't even know what they were. Her guts went cold. Anything — everything could be misread. She looked back slowly, cautious not to focus directly on it.

The creature — the being, the non-human person — set down a large basket and a flat package. They unwrapped the reed mats covering the package to reveal a wooden frame about an arm's-length square. They folded out legs to stand the frame upright. The frame itself had several crossbars and was strung with cords from top to bottom.

A loom! A simple, portable loom.

The person settled onto their tail in a three-point squat. Lee watched, fascinated, while the odd twin-thumbed hands deftly shuttled threads back and forth, slowly creating a length of fabric. The person looked up at her again and the head bobbed slightly, as if to acknowledge her, before looking back at the loom.

They worked calmly and steadily, a strong contrast to the violent action between the smaller creatures the night before. Lee tried to study the weaver without openly staring. The smooth, leathery, mostly bare skin was raisin-purple. The fan of long, black feathers at the tip of the tail was closed at the moment although it had been flared out earlier. Shorter feathers lay like epaulets on top of the shoulders. The face was black around the eyes and down to the tarnished-silver beak, but Lee couldn't tell whether the mask was darker skin or feathers. The scaled feet had two toes with large, blunt claws. A multi-colored satchel hung across the body on a wide strap from one shoulder to just in front of the opposite hip.

Lee closed her eyes and pictured the being who had climbed to her ledge with food and water. All she'd seen close up had been their head and shoulders. The two beings were similar in general form but also very different. The small one had skin the color of adobe, the intimidating hawk beak, a crest of long feathers on their head, similar four-fingered hands but tipped with talons, and blue eyes with vertical pupil slits. And the tails the fighters used so effectively were longer and more agile than the weaver's and lacked the fan of feathers at the tip.

She puzzled over possible explanations: two co-existing species; adults and juveniles of one species; or even two sexes of the same species. Bad enough to have to figure out what to expect from one, let alone two species. She'd joked to Adel about never getting that student dream of a first contact on Carico. How wrong she'd been. A sick knot grew in her stomach, the kernel of panic trying to break free.

Lee stood up and shuffled along the ledge. Doing something, even just walking, let her fake being in control. So she searched once more for any place she might be able to climb down. She couldn't see off the sloping edge to even know how far the drop was, much less what she would land on. She might climb up the canyon walls. But they still looked much too smooth, just as they had the last however many times she had looked.

And the shackles reminded her she was truly trapped. She was stuck, by her own definition. She could not escape without help.

Was Ike in a similar perch somewhere along the canyon or was she completely alone? She closed her hand over her horsehair bracelet, pushing it into her skin, harsh and real, tying her to another person, a free person. She could imagine Seth working with his horses or in his garden. He was safe, and eventually, when they didn't return, he would come for them. Regardless of what had transpired between them, she had absolute faith in that.

Voices, harshly guttural and squawking, brought her back to her overlook. One of the smaller beings had joined the weaver. A loud voice, switching tail, and upright crest — she might be wrong but the hawk-beaked being looked upset about something. But they kept their eyes and sharp beak lowered — polite, maybe, or submissive. In contrast, the weaver spoke quietly, although the tip of their tail flicked back and forth, leaving sweeps in the sand.

The weaver stood up and reached out to the other, smoothing down the ruffled, blood-red feathers along the outside of its arms. Lee hadn't noticed those earlier. As the feathers settled, they seemed to change color, becoming the same dun as the being's skin. The being visibly relaxed except for a twitch at the tip of their tail. The weaver said something and pointed with their beak to a basket sitting nearby. The smaller being bobbed their head once, picked up the basket, and disappeared into the brush. The weaver settled back at their loom.

A moment later Lee heard the sounds of the cane-bundle ladder being lifted into place. The hawk-beaked being appeared at the edge of her prison-cave, this time coming all the way up and standing on the stone. Her heart raced. She held still, not wanting to incite any predatory action. Move suddenly, and predators chased. It was their nature.

The being snapped its beak and watched her. Testing her reaction? She didn't move. They took three small baskets from the large one they carried and set them on the stone, then pointed that viciously hooked beak to the water container sitting by Lee's bed.

She moved slowly toward the container. That seemed to be what they wanted. She picked it up, edged toward the being, set the container down, and backed away. The being picked up the container with their tail, dropped it into the larger basket, and exited down the ladder. That tail was more snake-like than she thought. She pictured it coiling around her, trapping her.

She pushed that thought aside. She had survived the first ever human communication with these non-human people. Not exactly a conversation, but they had exchanged information. They knew how to get what they wanted from her. She couldn't say the same.

She moved forward as the ladder disappeared and caught sight of the person crossing the canyon floor. They went to the foot of a vine tree growing near the weaver's cave and ran up it like a spinxi up a post. With their tail securely wrapped around the trunk, they perched on a horizontal vine about eye-level with her. Her guard? Observer? What? She shivered. She picked up the food containers and went back to her bed.

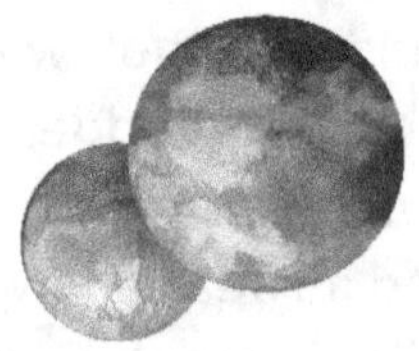

The next day began the same way, with the weaver at its loom, the guard perched across from Lee's cave. The guard brought food and water but, to her relief, never interacted with her beyond the exchange of containers. The beak and talons were enough to have her imagining less peaceful interchanges.

She thought they were the same two individuals. The guard's bruised face gave it away, but she couldn't be sure about the weaver. She assumed the guard remained nearby at night. Not that it mattered. She had no more clue how to escape than she had the first day.

She saw no sign of Ike or any indication her captors had another prisoner. Meddling, annoying old man, haunted by old memories — they'd be having some fine arguments about captivity and aliens if only he was with her. If he'd gotten away, he could be to Seth's by now.

Late in the afternoon, a sharp call from her guard disturbed her boredom. The being pointed toward the dance ground and leaped from their tree perch to the ground. Lee could see a line of the dun-colored beings crossing the open sand in pairs with nets slung between them. The nets held what looked like meat, maybe the quarters of a large animal like a tarbh, but she couldn't tell for sure. The final pair turned off and came toward her. Her guard met them and brought them to the base of its tree. They dropped their net, unrolled it, and stretched out the contents, the hide of a sorrel horse.

Pokey. Ike's pack horse. The only sorrel horse Lee knew of within miles. She sank slowly to the floor. If Pokey was dead, what about the rest of the horses? What about Ike? And what did it mean for her?

The bundled-cane ladder thumped into place, and her guard stepped off the ladder with their hands empty. No basket of food. The little crossbow-slingshot hung from a braided rawhide sash crossing from the left shoulder to right hip. A pouch hung the other way.

The being pointed its beak at her and then at the ladder. She froze. They repeated the gesture.

She was supposed to climb down? Then what? Her prison suddenly seemed to be a safe haven. Lee pointed at the shackles and shifted her feet to show her limited movement.

The being pointed a hand at the ladder and clicked their beak sharply. They pointed again, blue eyes boring into her. Lee shuffled toward the cane bundle. The being came closer, herding her with their body and tail. Upright, they were about her height. Bent at the hips with their tail extended, they were more like waist high to her and infinitely threatening. One swing of that tail would send her sailing off the ledge to the rocks below.

The bundle of canes rose about knee-high above the lip of the ledge. Lee had no idea how she was supposed to climb down with her feet shackled. She didn't want to think about why she was being taken down, now, with Pokey's fresh hide spread on the sand.

She peered over the edge and discovered the ladder had rungs of a sort. Crosspieces pierced through and extended out on each side of the bundle every foot or so. It was only ... *only* ... twenty feet to the rocky slope below. And the shackles hobbled her mind as much as her feet.

The being snaked their tail around her arm and pushed her toward the ladder. With her heart pounding, she locked her eyes on the top of the bundle so she wouldn't see the drop off and slid one knee to the far side as if she straddled a horse. She hugged the bundle with her thighs and stretched her feet down, seeking one of the crosspieces.

The being released their hold on her but let their tail lie lightly across her back, securing her. She had a momentary impression that it was soft-skinned, warm, and not the least lizard-like.

She closed her eyes and pictured the bundle of cane with the footholds sticking out. Her feet caught on rungs. She moved one foot and discovered the shackles gave her just enough slack to reach the next rung. She worked her way slowly down until she began to trust both the ladder and her own ability.

When her feet hit the ground, the tail lifted off her back, freeing her to move away from the ladder. Her guard dropped to the ground beside her, snapped their beak, and pointed toward the cave where the weaver waited. When she hesitated, the snaky tail switched forward to give her a push. She imagined what an actual blow from it could do.

Lee shivered in the hot afternoon air and did her best to walk steadily in spite of her sweaty palms, her tender, bare feet on the harsh ground, and the shackles. The spot between her shoulder blades crawled, and she kept glancing back at the hawk-beaked creature behind her.

The weaver held out a bone implement. Urged forward by her guard, Lee took the tool, avoiding contact with the weaver. They pointed their beak toward the hide staked flesh-side up on the ground. The guard prodded her toward the hide with their tail.

She turned the piece of bone in her hands. It looked like part of a scapula from a swine-deer maybe. It was oval and sharp on one edge. Scraper? A hide scraper? Well, work was better than some of the things she had imagined. She shuffled to the hide and sat down beside it. Her bruised knee wouldn't bend well enough yet to kneel over it.

The weaver came over, reached down and ripped open the tear in her light camp pants to show her knee. Lee froze, held her breath. The being touched the purple bruise with a finger before prodding more vigorously and taking hold of her leg to flex the abused joint. Apparently satisfied that she wasn't badly broken, they stepped away and mimed scraping. Lee let her breath out slowly.

Scraping flesh and connective tissue off a green hide wasn't easy, especially since Lee couldn't get into a position that gave her a good angle, but she did her best. No point fighting a battle with her captors that she would certainly lose. Pokey had already lost. She might be the de facto representative of Carico's human settlers, if not of the entire Interstellar Coalition, but she was also a prisoner and alone. She was walking a tightrope blindfolded.

Chapter 15

Lee

The next morning, the hide was gone. Her guard brought food and water to her perch but didn't take her down. The weaver worked at their loom; the guard came and went from Lee's view. Lee waited and wondered about what came next. She waited through that day, balancing between boredom and dread. Scraping the hide had at least given her a task to focus on.

The cave had been swept clean before she had been brought there. Not a pebble or a stick remained. No way to mark off days. If nothing changed, she would lose track. She couldn't see the ever-changing moons. They never came high enough in the sky for her limited view although she could see their cool light on the canyon walls at night. If she could remember what time they came up as they moved through their phases, she could track the days, but she couldn't.

Her purple knee turned yellow but still objected to too much movement.

No loose ends magically appeared on the braided rawhide shackles. She tore most of her fingernails trying to find one.

She grew tired of fruit, raw vegetables, and cold roasted grubs. Steak and Beulah-bread sounded like heaven.

It was seven and a half paces or fifteen steps from one side of her ledge to the other along the front, half that from front to back, but she couldn't stand up the last four steps. The ceiling came too low.

Her sleeping pad was too thin for comfort on bare rock. The weaver at least had sand to squat on.

She could count backward from one million to somewhere around eight hundred ninety thousand before falling asleep. Sometimes only to nine hundred ninety-five thousand. Sometimes just thinking about counting was enough. What was there to do but sleep?

On the fourth morning after the fight night, her watchers appeared early, barely after sunrise. That was a change. The dino-birds — that was how she was thinking of them — trotted through the brush, bodies forward and tails raised, one light and quick, the other deliberate. As they slowed to a walk, they stood more upright, although they kept their tails off the ground.

Weaver carried a couple of bundles to the loom cave. Guard crossed the canyon floor. Lee heard the now-familiar sounds of the cane ladder being lifted into place. She backed off to the far end of the ledge, knowing they wouldn't leave her food and water until she did.

But they didn't bring any. They directed her down the ladder instead. She straddled the bundle and got down without help this time. Once on the ground Guard pointed her toward Weaver.

Lee shuffled across the trickle of water in the midst of the canyon. Weaver reached into the satchel above their hip and held out Lee's moccasins, swept an arm to point up the little canyon, then pointed at Lee's feet before dropping the moccasins in front of her. Lee felt helpless as she bent over and pulled on the light leather footwear, trying to watch both of her captors as she did so. Where were they going?

Weaver bobbed their head once before handing Lee a large, empty basket with a single, long strap hanging from the top. They picked up a long walking stick with a broad, flat-bladed top and strode up the canyon, carrying a smaller basket by a loop handle. Guard stepped closer to Lee and swung their tail like a rider might swing a rope to encourage a tarbh to move. Lee followed Weaver, hyper-aware of the hook-beaked guard behind her.

There was no risk of her making a run for it. She struggled just to keep up. The shackles limited her steps and tangled on brush. Besides, her moccasins were little more than leather socks, not designed for hiking, while her two overseers' scaly feet seemed impervious to the stones and litter of twigs.

Weaver's purposeful lead and the baskets suggested this was a work party. They didn't go far, just around a point of rock and into a small cul-de-sac. Weaver stopped and studied the cliff above them. The rock was covered with yellowish ribbons the size of Lee's arm, twisting and rippling, making the cliff look like it was shifting and changing constantly. She wasn't usually squeamish, but it made her head spin. Then she remembered the ribbon worm colony at Tobin Canyon Camp, the first place Seth had taken her after they had met. This colony was much bigger, stretching along most of the rim around the cul-de-sac.

Weaver took the basket from her. They selected a place under the colony and slid the flat blade of the walking staff between the wall and the clinging end of one ribbon about as long as Lee's forearm. A quick twist pried the worm free and dropped it in the basket. Weaver waved Lee over and thrust the basket, with its squirming worm, at her. As Lee watched, the ribbon contracted, and its bright yellow faded to olive.

Weaver selected another ribbon and waved Lee into place beneath it. Lee ducked when the end of it slapped her in the face as it fell, but she succeeded in catching it in the basket. It lay twisting with the first one, shortening and fading into an olive slug the size of her foot. Lee couldn't make out any features except for the sucker that held it to the cliff. She expected them to be slimy, but their skin looked leathery and dry. They smelled surprisingly like fresh fish and thyme.

Another fell before she had time to study them closer. Weaver moved to another and then another. Guard disappeared somewhere, leaving them to their gathering. Lee let the tension out of her shoulders. She felt almost safe with Weaver compared to Guard.

Lee spent an hour catching and carrying, too busy to be bothered by the wriggling things anymore. Weaver harvested two or three, then moved along the rim to a new location for a few more until the basket was full. And heavy. Lee had to catch the last couple by hand because the basket became too cumbersome. She lost count but thought they had fifteen or twenty when Weaver walked away from the colony. Lugging the clumsy basket in her arms, Lee followed.

Weaver watched her struggling. The tiny feathers of their black mask flashed with ripples of blue and purple iridescence that Lee suspected showed laughter. Just a guess — she didn't even know if the creature did laugh.

Weaver took the basket from her, carried it around, and pushed it against her back. Another push clued Lee, and she reached back to support the weight with her hands. Weaver took the awkwardly long, wide strap attached to the basket, pulled it up, and settled it across Lee's head just above her forehead. Tentatively Lee pushed against the strap. When she leaned a little forward from the hips, the basket became a tolerable weight on her back and spine. Tumpline — the word surfaced in her mind. She'd seen pictures of tumpline packs somewhere, one of those useful, primitive technologies that had always interested her.

Weaver led the way back to the loom cave, stopping on their way to pick a variety of plant foods — spike roots, sweet galls, broadleafs, all familiar. There was no evidence of an organized garden, just a random scattering of edible plants in the sandy soil.

Guard waited for them by a small pool of water filled by the tiny trickle of stream. Weaver lifted the basket off Lee's back and set it into the water. Water seeped through the weave until the fibers swelled with the moisture and made the basket into a waterproof, evaporatively-cooled storage for the worms.

Weaver pointed at Lee and gestured downward with spread hands. Lee slowly sat on the sand. That seemed to be the right answer. The being held up an open hand, fingers up with the palm toward Lee. Stay? What else was she going to do under the gem-sharp eyes of Guard?

Weaver strode away toward the loom cave, left the vegetables there in the shade, and returned in a minute with an empty basket and a cluster of cane segments as long as Lee's arm. They quickly assembled an upright rack. They picked up one of the worms, slit it open, scooped the innards into the empty basket, and pierced the worm just below the sucker. They inserted a cane through the slit and hung the cane across the rack with the worm dangling. Weaver got another worm and repeated the process, then held it out to Lee.

Lee got to her feet and took the worm. Weaver pointed to the rack. Lee strung the worm on the same cane as the first one and left space between them, guessing the point might be to dry the meat. Weaver nodded and worked on another.

With Lee's own knife. The folding knife with a four-inch blade that lived in a pocket inside her saddlebags. Lee stared. So far she had seen no metal parts, not on the loom or on the guard's weapon. But obviously Weaver could appreciate the sharp edge on a knife. Weaver clicked their beak sharply and thrust a cleaned worm at Lee, bringing her attention back to the task at hand.

When the last of the ribbon worms hung from the drying rack, Weaver directed Lee to carry the empty tumpline basket and the smaller basket of guts to the loom cave. Guard then escorted her across to the cane-bundle ladder and followed her up to her prison ledge, helping her keep the shackles from snagging as she climbed. They left her there with food and water they must have delivered while she had worked. Fruits, vegetables, and grubs again. Not a ribbon worm to be seen.

Lee stretched out in the shade. The energy drained out of her. She hadn't realized how stressed she had been trying to interpret gestures and meet expectations. Alone now, her heart pounded, and her throat tightened anxiously. The two beings hadn't directly threatened her, but she admitted to herself that Guard with that hooked beak and powerful tail scared her.

They left her alone the rest of the day. Weaver worked at the loom. Guard perched in the vine tree. Lee gazed at the rock ceiling and told herself stories remembered from her childhood, leaving out the ones involving encounters with unknown aliens.

The next morning, Guard escorted her down from her ledge and to the loom cave again. Weaver took over and directed Lee to a heap of freshly cut bulrushes. The being settled into their three-point squat, selected one rush, pulled a flat piece of bone or wood from its satchel, and split the rush lengthwise.

Weaver handed another of the tools to Lee. Lee took it and turned it over, feeling the smooth surface and the thin tip. The whole thing was about the length of her hand. It felt like it was made from a piece of cane.

Weaver handed her a rush from the pile. Lee carefully started a split in the middle of the flat side. Weaver snatched it from her, slapped her with it, touched the edge of the leaf, and handed it back. Lee kept her hand away from her stinging cheek and swallowed rising fear. She tried again, this time splitting along the edge.

Weaver went back to work on their own rushes. Guard squatted nearby. The two beings didn't speak, and Lee noticed again that Guard kept their beak turned down or away from Weaver whenever they were together and took Weaver's orders without question. Then Lee recalled them arguing about something the first morning. So not completely compliant.

The heap of rushes slowly went into a neat pile. Weaver insisted they all lay with the tips in the same direction. Lee's hands ached from the unfamiliar activity. She stretched them and shook them out and went back to work slowly and deliberately. Was this what she had to look forward to — day after day of chores — slavery?

What about the rest of the beings? She had seen maybe twenty the night of the fights. Lee found herself thinking of Weaver as 'she' and Guard as 'he'. She wasn't quite sure why. She didn't even know if the beings had males and females as she knew them. She considered it an hypothesis she could test as she observed.

Once all the rushes were split, Weaver had Lee spread them out in the shade to dry. Then she was sent back to her ledge for the afternoon.

The next day Weaver brought already-dry rushes and showed Lee how to soak them to soften so they could be woven. Plaiting the flat lengths together into a simple mat proved more difficult than Weaver made it look. Lee decided a tail had advantages, an extra hand to hold things in place. She was a slow learner; Weaver repeatedly took the beginning of a mat away from her and tore it apart for her to start over. Not a patient teacher.

So her life went. Work gathering food items or weaving in the morning. Spend the afternoon on her ledge. Lee wanted tarbh steak, spinxi eggs with roasted tubers, a long shower, a cold glass of wine, to get up in the morning and know she could leave if she wanted and go anywhere. She wanted to know where Ike was. She had to live without the things she wanted. At least she had a way of keeping track of days now — fight night, first day watching Weaver, Pokey's day, another day just watching, then ribbon worm day, then rush-splitting day, then ugly mat day, then almost usable mat day, then ... even the projects began to run together.

Counterpoint

Eta'ak

For good or ill, I have instigated contact with one of the First-Comers. Prime placed many restrictions on my plan. The human is not to see our villages or know how many we are until Prime allows it. I question Prime's grasp of the nature of these people but will do my best to work within the edicts. I believe we would have done far better to approach an individual openly and solicit cooperation but, so far, the female we hold has proven more compliant than I anticipated. Perhaps that is only patience on her part.

Now we reap the reward of my years of observing the First-Comers through their broadcasts and from their archives. Acquiring access to their library files allowed us to translate their spoken and written language. We have analyzed their body language as well. We are not so different in expression of basic emotions, and I try to utilize some of their unique patterns — pointing with the hand instead of the beak, for example — in my interactions with her. She interprets our directions readily but has made no attempt to speak verbally with us, seeming content to observe us as closely as we do her.

The stranger learns mat-making slowly but prepared the ribbon worms acceptably, so can prove her usefulness in that way.

I listen to broadcasts nightly, expecting to hear of a search for her. Meanwhile our hunters return to the human's last camp to remove all signs of her presence. Give seekers a mystery to confound them.

-From the Archives of Eta'ak, Information Analyst

Chapter 16

Seth

Seth felt himself lifted from the hard ground, straight up like he was floating. He shook his muddled head and wished he hadn't. The world began to sway and jerk. He tried to roll over and something tightened around him. He was wrapped from head to toe. He couldn't see. Something across his face made it hard to breathe. He gasped for air, heart pounding, sliding toward panic.

He caught the hint of a scent, something safe; he searched for it, clung to it — the scent of herbs and something lightly spicy, of Lee when she lay sleeping next to him. Now, in the dark, trapped in an unstable cocoon, he had no idea where the scent came from, but it gave him what he needed to get control of himself. He quit fighting against what held him, forced himself to relax.

He focused on details, trying to piece things together. He had left the stampede camp, taken the horses up onto the plateau above the spring and camped. In the evening, he had led them down for water. Something had spooked them. That was all he remembered.

Fabric covered his head, over his eyes and mouth, and coarse ropes wrapped him like a hammock or net. His hands were tied together in front. His feet, bare feet, were brushed by cool air. Night then; it had to be night.

He swayed as footsteps rhythmically scuffed and padded on the ground, soft like moccasins, steady and quick. Runners' breathing matched time with the steps. Carried — he was being carried, slung between two runners. They obviously knew what they were doing, moving in step, carrying him smoothly. No horses. He couldn't hear hoof beats, tail swishes, none of the familiar sounds of horses in motion. Strange.

He shied from thoughts of who and why. His one hope was that Lee was at the end of this strange trip. He withdrew into himself, using hard-learned skills of meditation and mental control to calm himself and wait.

Hours later, if his stiffness was any clue, abrupt contact with the ground ended his journey. The net dug into him; he lay on rock. They — whoever they were — dragged him sideways until he began to slide downward. He sucked in a breath, held it until the net took control of his fall. He hung twisting in the air, felt a series of little jerks and slips, and landed gently on another stone surface.

Someone rolled him free of the net. His careful control cracked. He grabbed at the cloth, fighting to force it from his head so he could see, but it wouldn't come loose. He rolled to his knees, still struggling with the blinding fabric. Hands took hold of his, pulling on them. He jerked away, losing his balance and toppling onto his side.

"Stop," a voice said. "Hold still and let me help." But his urgency overrode the words, and he kept struggling.

"Scorch it! Do you want to fall off this cliff?" The voice grew firmer and finally shouted, "Whoa, whoa!"

He froze. That old command, the first he taught a horse, cut through the drive to fight his bonds. And the voice, he knew the voice.

"Lee?"

"Hold still," she said. He felt her hands fumbling, and the cloth came free. He still couldn't see much in the darkness. She held his wrists, working on the bindings until they fell away.

"Lee! Elements and All! You're alive." He pulled her close and wrapped his arms around her.

She tensed and pulled away. He knew better than to make her feel trapped, but he kept one hand lightly on her shoulder. She was alive.

A prisoner too. His heart caught. What had they done to her?

"Are you all right?" he asked urgently.

"I'm not hurt." Her brown-gold eyes glared at him. "So much for a daring rescue. What are you doing here?"

"Nice to see you too." Was she really angry? He decided that was better than defeated.

She stood up and stuck out a hand. "Be careful," she cautioned.

He let her pull him up, then nearly fell when he took a step. His feet were hobbled together. This couldn't be happening. He tipped his head up and threw his shoulders back to let air into his lungs. He held a breath, then let it out.

"Let's move away from the edge," Lee said.

"Edge?" He looked around. They were in a shallow rockshelter, much smaller than the one he called home. He couldn't make out details in the moonless dark. "What's going on?" He took her by the shoulders, keeping his touch light. "Who are they, and what do they want with us?"

"Come sit before you fall." She stepped out of his hold.

He followed, careful not to trip himself with the shackles. She led him to a sleeping pad on the ground near the back wall of the cave. He sat and tugged at the shackles. He identified the feel of braided rawhide and searched unsuccessfully for an end.

"Good luck with that," Lee said. "I've been trying for days."

"Give me light and a little time. I'll figure it out." He had confidence that what one braider could do, another could undo. "So tell me what's going on."

She knelt in front of him. "Have you seen Ike?" she countered.

"Ike?" He hesitated. "He's ... dead."

"Dead?" She didn't sound surprised. "What happened?"

"Trampled maybe?" he guessed. "I found him sitting against a big rock out on the plateau.

"That strange rock all by itself?" She swallowed. "What was he doing there?"

"No clue," Seth said. "It looked like the last thing he did was pull the bridle off his horse and turn it loose. He'd been there for a while." Something in her posture told him not to reach out to her just then. "I found your camp, what was left of it."

"Tarbh." She scrubbed her face with her hands. "I've never seen them behave like that. We tried to get the packs out of the way, but they came too fast. Something hit me and, next thing I knew, I woke up here." She stood and shuffled away. Seth realized she was shackled too. She faced him, silhouetted against the opening. "I thought, I hoped, he was here too, somewhere. I would have been run down if he hadn't pushed me away. He was only a couple of steps behind me."

Seth's mind flashed to an image of *her*, putrid and burned by the sun, lying next to Ike against that boulder. "A slot like that — bad place to camp."

"Yeah, well, it was late. We made do." She stood silently for a long moment, arms tight around her chest. "Now, what were you doing there?"

"You lost a couple horses." He gave the shackles a hard jerk. "Just trying to help. Stupid me."

"Stupid you," she echoed. Her voice went quiet and sad. "Selfish of me, but I'm glad you're here." She walked away, going to pick up the cloth she had pulled off his head. Shaking it out, she draped it around her shoulders.

It was one of her wraps. The smell of her, the smell that had kept him from total panic. "Jester and Clown," he said. "They showed up at my place. I couldn't leave you out here without a horse. I was worried." He rubbed the back of his neck. "And then I found Ike."

She sat down on the other end of the pad, crossed her legs and pulled absently at the frays on her pant cuffs. "It was late, almost dark, when we made it to the big spring at the head of the slot. Ike found the camp site. We were going to move back up on top in the morning." She sounded composed now, like some official report. "The tarbh came. I saw Clown and Jester break free. And I woke up here." She spread her arms and turned to take in the little rockshelter.

Seth struggled to find that same calm tone. "I found Ike's gelding but no sign of his pack horse. I left my horses at the big spring, walked down, and found your camp. Gear scattered." His voice caught. "Your saddles, your riding clothes and boots, all there except your bedding and saddlebags. I didn't know what to think then."

"You should have gone home."

He frowned and went on. "After I found your things, I made camp up on the plateau above the spring. In the evening, I took the horses down for water. Something spooked them. They knocked me down and bolted back up the trail. Next thing I knew I was wrapped in a net with something over my head, swinging along between a couple of guys on foot. It's mostly a blur. I don't know what happened to the horses."

"Probably halfway back to your place by now," she said. "So, no rescue party?"

"No." It seemed like the cave roof was pressing down on him. His throat tightened. "Well, maybe." He clung to that. "I left a message for my neighbor Gabe, so Dougherty might have people looking for us by now." He thought it had been three days since he left home or the start of the fourth.

"How far are we from the stampede camp?" she asked.

"Hard to tell," he said. He looked around, realizing that the darkness was lighter. "Looks like it took most of the night to get here, but I don't know how fast we went. I wouldn't think more than three or four miles an hour carrying me, but that's still fifteen or twenty miles."

She turned to face him, the wrap around her like a shield. "More … it could be a lot more. The ones who have us, they could have moved a lot faster than that."

Seth fumbled with his thoughts. "How?"

"Because…" Lee leaned forward. "They're not human, Seth. They are like no one I've ever seen before." She sounded somewhere between scared and in awe.

"Not human?" That was crazy. Non-humans rarely came to Carico at all. No way there were any living out here.

"Wait until daylight. See for yourself," she challenged. "This is not a cataloged species. Carico has its own people."

He bit back a comment about her sanity. "After three surveys and almost seventy years of settlement? Can't be, not this close to settled territory."

"I know what I've seen every day since I got here. You'll see."

He picked at the shackles, avoiding her eyes. She seemed coherent enough. Could her mind be substituting fictitious aliens as less threatening than real human captors? "How long have you been here?" he asked.

"I lost track," she said, settling back to sit cross-legged again.

"When were you caught?"

"Let's see. Lander was full. Damele was at waning half."

"Damele has come a full cycle, so eight days." He couldn't imagine what she had been going through.

"After the first few days, they started letting me down into the canyon for a while every day. To work — to gather food and weave mats. I'm not good enough for baskets yet."

"How many of them are there?"

"Just two with me. I've seen others, less than twenty in all, at a distance by torchlight. They have a community meeting area a couple hundred yards down this canyon."

"But there could be a lot more?"

"There must be," she answered.

He rubbed her shoulder reassuringly. "Once the sun comes up, I'll get out of these hobbles, and we can start planning how to get out of here."

Instead of relaxing, she pulled away. "I told you, I've been trying for days. They're geniuses with rawhide."

"I'll figure it out," he insisted.

"Well, thanks for your confidence in me." She scooted away from him.

"That's not what I meant," he said. If she was right … He waited for the line of her shoulders to relax a little. "Lee, what are we in the middle of here? You've had time to get a feel for things."

"Too much time." She waved him off when he reached out to her. "They haven't hurt me, but they could, easily. To be honest, I've just done what they tell me to do."

"They speak Sol Standard?" He shook his head. Delusions?

"No. They mostly point at where they want me to go and demonstrate what they want me to do."

"Oh." He pulled at the rawhide shackles, feeling the roughness. "Are you going to tell me what they want with us?"

"I would if I had a clue." She twisted a corner of the wrap. "Before I say too much, I want your first impressions. They are … well, you'll see." She hunched her shoulders and kept her eyes on the fabric.

She looked scared. He knew he was. If whoever held them had her this off base, they were in real trouble. "Okay, my first impression," he said as he stood up. "I need to think." He shuffled toward one front corner of the ledge, rolling his head to stretch his neck. The faintest gray hinted that dawn was not too far away. He wouldn't have to wait long. And he wanted to be thinking clearly. He wasn't sure which worried him more, to find that she had cracked and their captors were just humans or to find that she was sane and they were in the hands of unknown aliens.

He took refuge in the batayr routine, doing the best he could with the interference of the shackles. His fear ebbed, and he found the strong place within that kept him grounded. Halfway through, Lee joined him, picking up the routine and following along like they used to do every morning in the days when they were together.

As the light grew stronger, he could see the effects of her time as a captive — days' accumulation of dirt, stringy hair, torn knees in her pants, one shoulder of her tank top torn in two. But he saw no visible injuries, and she moved easily. If they could just get free.

He stumbled when the shackles interfered with the normal pattern of the routine. Then his concentration evaporated completely when something thudded against the stone. The end of a log appeared above the other end of the ledge. Lee gestured for him to stay still. She retrieved the water bottle and hurriedly set it near the log — no, it was a bundle of canes — and backed away.

A head came into view, a distinctly non-human head. Seth gulped. The creature looked around and focused on them with two eyes the color of blue flames above a beaked snout. They extended a hand and pointed some kind of a weapon at them before they climbed the rest of the way onto the ledge and slid a bag off their shoulder.

The creature was about Lee's height, slender and agile. They stood on two strong legs and swung a long tail. Without taking their eyes off the humans, they took three baskets from the bag and set them down near the empty water bottle. They picked up the bottle and stepped back, using their tail to locate the cane ladder. They slung the bag over their shoulder, dropped the empty bottle in, and backed down the ladder out of sight. A moment later the ladder disappeared.

Seth took a step back, aware that he had taken a fighter's stance, ready to defend himself. Lee hadn't been imagining things. Pictures of half-mythical creatures from old stories ran through his head. This was like a cross between a dinosaur, an ostrich, and a kangaroo. Smooth skin the color of his red dun colt; a predator's beak; a headdress standing up behind its head; powerful legs; and that snaky tail. Bag, baskets, but no clothing. The weapon they carried looked like a crossbow that shot pebbles instead of darts.

He edged forward as far as he dared, trying to catch sight of the being, to see where they went and what they did. No wonder Lee questioned the chances of escape. Seth knew confidence when he saw it, whether human, horse, tarbh, or unknown non-human, and he knew the creature was absolutely sure they were in charge.

Chapter 17

Lee

When the cane-bundle ladder thumped against the ledge, Lee hurried to put the empty water bottle in place and moved away. Then she studied Seth, anxious to see his initial reaction as Guard came into view. He hadn't believed her about the aliens. Well, now he would.

As she watched, Seth's expressive face revealed surprise, appraisal, distrust, and finally defiance. He fell into a balanced, fight-ready position. She froze, hoping he wouldn't start anything. He held still. Guard set down the baskets and never took their eyes off Seth as they backed down the ladder.

As the end of the ladder disappeared, Seth shuffled so close to the sloping edge that Lee held her breath. He peered off and watched for a minute before stepping back. He looked Lee in the eye and, emphasizing each word, he said, "That is a non-human, and I don't like him."

He paced along the edge in measured steps before finding a place where he could sit with his back to the wall and see as much of the canyon floor as possible. He went back to picking at the shackles with the complete focus he usually reserved for working with horses.

Lee shuffled to the baskets. One held the usual assortment of vegetables and fruit. In the other … she snatched up a cold, bite-size chunk of cooked meat, pale with a bluish tinge. She tasted it, then popped it in her mouth and chewed slowly. Tarbh, saltless but tender. She hadn't had meat since she had been captured, unless she counted grubs. Not even the ribbon worms she had helped gather had shown up in her food.

She took the baskets over and sat next to Seth. "Better eat."

He looked up, scanned the canyon, then inspected the contents before selecting a juicy globeberry. He could have all the fruit he wanted, but, to be fair, she held out the basket of meat. "Better have some before I finish it all," she said. "I guess you're privileged. They never brought me meat."

He took the food and studied the canyon as he picked at it. "We've got to get out of here," he said.

"You know, I have had that thought once or twice." She put down the basket she held and stretched out her hands, looking at her torn nails and grimy fingers. She had been through the how-to-escape exercise uncountable times over the days and never come up with a workable plan. Maybe with two of them they could figure something out. "Have any ideas?" she asked.

"Not yet," he said. She could read his mind by where his eyes turned, looking for places to climb up or down from their ledge, for hints to where their captors were, for anything useful lying around.

"Good luck," she said. The only new thing was that there were two of them trying to escape now. She picked a roundfruit from the basket and bit into it. Having Seth to worry about too tainted her relief at not being alone.

The sun rose; its light reflected off the far wall of the canyon to brighten their cave a little; the air warmed. They ate; drank the water; the day grew hot; the air smelled of dust.

"There's Weaver," Lee told Seth, pointing out the figure coming up the canyon. Again she watched his expressions.

Seth looked from Weaver to her. "You didn't say there were two different kinds," he said. "Same general design — beaks, tails, two legs — but they don't look much alike. This one's not itching for a fight. And look at the muzzle and beak. Not like a predator. The other one sure is. I don't think they're even the same species."

"Maybe not. I'm not sure," she said.

"You said you saw maybe twenty individuals?"

"Four of the big, dark-skinned ones like Weaver and the rest like Guard." She sat down, pulled her knees up, and leaned her elbows on them.

"Weaver and Guard?" he asked.

"I had to call them something," she said. She scrubbed her face with her hands, avoiding looking at Seth. "They watch me all the time. It was easier after they put me to work, not so much time to think. Weaving rushes is harder than you'd expect."

Seth reached out. She looked away from his hand. She couldn't handle sympathy just then. "Once I tried to hide a rock to bring back to cut through the shackles. Guard found it and didn't bring any food or water that night. The next night, when I didn't try anything, he brought extra. Like I'm some kind of specimen being studied and trained."

She straightened her legs and crossed her ankles, staring absently at the faded bruise on her knee showing through her torn pants. "So I study them in return, or Weaver at least. That's the only one I see often enough. Guard's around but out of sight a lot." She was thankful for that. Guard made her nervous, so she had even more trouble than usual figuring out how to weave.

"I'll give them something to study," Seth said, turning his attention back to the rawhide around his ankles. Lee watched him run his fingers carefully over the braiding, seeing by touch. "Let me look at yours," he said, pulling her feet into his lap, lifting them up and twisting the shackles on her ankles.

She leaned back on her elbows. "Be careful. That's me you're jerking around."

"So it is. Dirty feet and all." He made a face.

She bowed her head to hide her relief that he could find some humor in the situation. She hadn't been able to do that alone. "I haven't figured out how to ask for a bath yet," she said.

"If they haven't figured out that you need one, I have to question their sense of smell."

She pulled her feet away. She could hardly remember what it felt like to be clean. She stood and shuffled all ten steps to the end of the ledge. A slight breeze moved up the canyon. She let the air wash over her, hot and dry. That would have to do.

Seth retrieved her wrap from the bed and dribbled water from the container onto a corner of it. He came over and used it to wipe her face softly. Something in her started to melt, something she needed to keep firm. Snatching the wrap out of his hand, she turned her back and scoured her face herself. If he tried to hold her … but he simply laid a hand on her shoulder for a moment, then stepped away.

She looked at her hands, capable hands but without his skill to create beautiful objects or communicate with a horse. His hands could caress too. She could feel his presence, like all her hairs were tiny antennae tuned to him. The melting threatened to soften her again. She couldn't afford to be soft. "Listen, you need to know." She refocused herself. "The first night after I got here, they held a fight night."

"A what?" he asked with a puzzled look.

"Fights — match after match, almost all night long. Very ritualized, kind of like a batayr tournament, but so violent." She shuddered. "It was only Guard's kind that fought."

"And the others?"

"They watched. And cheered."

"Did anybody get hurt?" he asked.

"Not seriously that I could see."

"Well, that's a good sign," he said.

"I suppose." Lee sank down to lean against the wall wearily. Seth sat down close by, not touching her. On the floor of the little canyon, Weaver squatted in the shade. "Weaver's working on a basket today," Lee said. "Out of fine reeds it looks like. I think she's given up on me even making a decent rush mat."

"She?" Seth asked.

"It feels right." Lee shrugged. "She has a loom too. She's working on a scarf or something." She rambled on, talking about the kinds of plants she had harvested and her fumble-fingered attempts to weave, all the mundane details that had occupied her life for the past few days. She felt like she was hovering overhead, looking down at herself babbling on about meaningless nothings. She recognized it as a reaction to being alone so long, but she couldn't seem to stop herself.

Seth let her go on, asking a question now and then while he meticulously traced out individual strands of the braided rawhide, seeking an end he could work loose.

She started to describe her trip across the plateau with Ike and stopped at the thought that he was dead.

Such an irritating old man, but they had been a team, and her last memory was him pushing her out of the way of the stampede. "What did you do about … with Ike?" she asked.

Seth didn't answer. He had dozed off. She reached out with her foot to joggle his. He jerked upright and blinked.

"Go lay down," she said. "Nothing going on here."

He nodded and stumbled, half-asleep, to the bedding. Well, he hadn't had a restful night.

She watched him stretch out with the blanket bundled under his head for a pillow. Why had she ever told him to get out of her life? She studied the shape of his mouth, the fine weather lines around his eyes, the rise of his chest as he breathed, and she wiped away her unexpected tears. He was here, in trouble, because he tried to help her. And she was glad because now she could hope.

The thud of the ladder against the rock startled her. She jumped to her feet, feeling guilty but not sure why. Seth stirred, saw her, and got up, standing close to her.

"Guard, coming for the baskets," she told him. "Please, just go along with whatever he asks."

He rubbed his sleepy eyes. "Don't kick up the dust, you mean?"

"For now, until we have a plan."

"Your call," he said and straightened his shoulders.

As expected, Guard appeared, but instead of just taking the baskets he stepped off the ladder, pointed at her, and then at the bedding. She knelt down slowly.

When Seth squatted too, Guard pointed at him and waved toward the far end of the ledge.

"Better go," Lee said softly, hardly daring to breathe. What did Guard want?

Seth walked across the floor, careful not to trip himself with the shackles. Guard pointed at him, then took a posture Lee recognized as the opening pose of the batayr forms. Guard pointed to Seth again and completed the opening move.

"I think he wants a demonstration," Lee said. Seth took his position, watching Guard for confirmation. The being bobbed his head once. Seth moved through the first-level sequence as well as possible with the shackles, stopped, faced Guard, and bowed slightly.

Guard clicked his beak sharply and mimicked the opening pose again. Seth started over, keeping the moves slow and drawn out. Lee watched Guard study Seth attentively, the tip of his tail twitching. A few moves into the routine he gestured to Seth to stop, and he took the opening pose again.

Seth repeated the first few moves, still slowly but with sharp power rather than smooth grace. Guard followed along, not quite correct in form but echoing the power with more confidence than Lee expected for a beginner.

After a few moves, Guard put up a blocking hand. Seth stopped. Guard waved him back against the wall. Seth obeyed, head up with eyes locked on Guard's face. Guard's crest flared low and wide on the back of his neck, and his head pitched up in what Lee swore was a grin.

Guard backed to the middle of the ledge and began to dance in slow, deliberate motions. After half a dozen steps, he started over, eyes on Seth.

"I think that's the opening of their fight ritual," Lee told Seth, thinking back to the fight night.

Guard beckoned Seth forward, went into the first position, and pointed to Seth, indicating which foot to go forward, which arm to move.

With more arrogance than she had ever seen him display, Seth moved closer to Guard and copied the pose. He was taller by several inches, wider across the shoulders. Lee hugged her knees. Guard continued the instruction, moving smoothly into the next step, and Seth followed.

An image of two tarbh bulls posturing came to Lee. Any doubts she had about Guard's gender evaporated. These were two males strutting their stuff. Her heart raced. Seth echoed Guard, move for move, with concentration and power, until the shackles and lack of a tail defeated him. Guard stepped away, beak clicking lightly, and waved Seth toward the wall. Seth strutted over with casual disdain.

Guard danced the sequence again, this time at full speed with leaps and spinning turns. He finished an arm's length from Seth, bobbed his head, and sauntered to the ladder. He tossed the empty baskets off the edge and climbed down.

Seth watched until the end of the ladder vanished, then pointedly turned away. Lee shuffle-trotted over to him, her heart still pounding from the intense display.

"What was that all about?" Seth asked.

"I hope it wasn't an invitation to their next fight night," she said.

"That might get me out of these hobbles."

"Better hobbled than dead." She glanced toward the dance ground, remembering the ferocity of the fighting.

"I really do not like him," Seth said.

"You didn't look very intimidated." She had never seen that fiercely assertive side of him before. His power, his magic in her eyes, had always been in his quiet firmness with the horses. She could feel the heat from him flooding her. Her skin tingled, and her pulse beat in her throat. She hadn't felt that way in a long time. She moved closer, reached up to put her hand on his chest.

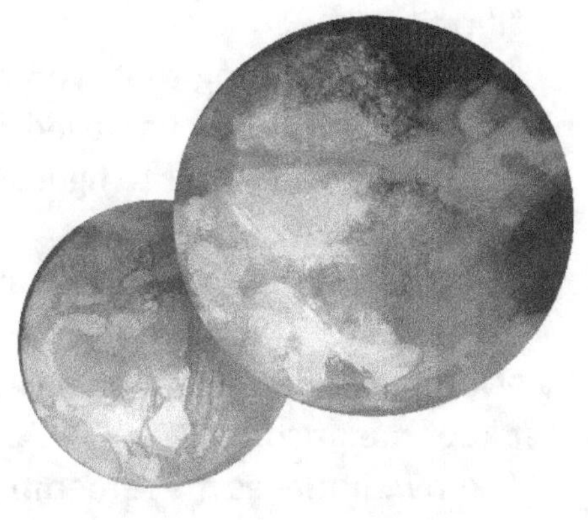

Chapter 18

Seth

Seth looked into Lee's sparking brown-gold eyes. Blocking the other, prying eyes across the canyon with his body, he cupped her face and slid his hand down to rest briefly just below her throat. He remembered the feel of her against him, how he used to caress her into responsiveness, slowly and patiently navigating the shields she put up after Jerdix raped her. She leaned into his hand, eyes half-closed, for half a breath before she dropped her forehead against his chest, and muttered indistinctly, "I'm going to go ... sit ... over there." She nodded toward the far end of the ledge.

"Don't," he said. "Don't get like that."

"Like what?"

"Shut down, locked away."

"I'm fine."

"I know — nothing that won't heal." He threw that phrase at her, one she had used so often. "You haven't healed. I gave you a year to figure things out. You've just gotten worse."

"I ... it's this, the situation. That's all."

"What have they done to you?" he asked gently.

"Nothing," she whispered. "They barely touched me. Just kept me prisoner."

"I know. It makes me remember too." He looked out at the canyon, at the here-and-now. "But it's different."

"I've done whatever they want. I've just let them control me."

"What could you do?" he asked.

She stepped back, turned away. "I just let them, like I let him," she said weakly.

"Him?" Seth prodded. Time seemed to bend back on itself.

She spun around. "Yes, *him, Jerdix.* I let him. I never tried to stop him. You know that. You know why."

"I don't know. You never told me."

She looked up at him. "Yes, I did."

"Never," he repeated. "I know he raped you. Your body told me that over and over again. But you never talked to me about it."

"I must have." She stared at him. "I rehearsed the words a thousand times. I said them again and again in after-action reports and counseling. I must have told you."

He shook his head, ran his thumb along her cheekbone, wiping away tears.

She kissed his palm. "I'm sorry. I guess I never actually said it out loud to you. You had your own hurts. And then it had been so long, and I didn't want to bring it all up again."

"Say it now. Say it and let it go. What did you let him do?"

She took a deep breath and let it out slowly. "Rape me," she whispered. "I stayed in my role — sweet little Anni — and let him and if I hadn't, if I had disabled him then, he could never have tortured you." Her voice strengthened. "And I got tired of listening to the experts tell me I couldn't have done anything else, that I was conditioned to stay in character. I failed myself, and I failed you. And now I've done what they want and didn't try to stop them and here you are again, neck deep in my shit."

He laughed, very softly.

She glared, startled by his reaction. "Now I know why I didn't tell you sooner."

"You know what our problem is?" he asked. "Our own expectations. We heard too many stories about the heroic exploits of our parents when we were kids. We think we should always have the right answer, do the very best thing in any situation."

"You think I was trying to be a hero?" she asked.

He took her by the shoulders. "I think we both survived, and Jerdix is gone, and I will not let him haunt my life. I also think you did exactly what you should have done here." He kissed her forehead and loosened his hold on her. "You survived. What else could you have done?"

"You've really put it behind you, what Jerdix did to you?"

"I live with it, and I don't lose sleep over it." He cupped her face in his hands. "You walked away from me once and jarred me into getting the help I needed. When I left you last year, I guess I was hoping to do the same for you." He stroked his thumb along her cheekbone again. "It's been a lonely year."

"Yes, it has." She leaned her face against his chest, very still, then took a step back. "And I hate that you are here just as much as I am thankful."

"Better get used to it," he said. "It doesn't look like I'm going anywhere soon."

"No, it doesn't." She looked past him across the canyon. "And Guard is watching over us to be sure."

"Yeah, Guard." He silently cursed the whole Void-spawned situation. But at least she had finally talked to him about Jerdix.

"I need to think," she said. "And you look like you could use some rest."

She was right about that. He let her walk away, then went to the bedding. He bundled the blanket under his head and looked at the ceiling, picking out the variations in color from tan to green to almost blue. Insects hummed in the heat of the afternoon. He willed his muscles to relax in a slow progression from feet to... He fell asleep to dream of a wild race across a plateau pursued by a tarbh bull with a long, snaky tail.

Something snapped him awake. "Did I just hear thunder?" he asked.

"Sounded like it." Lee sat in the middle front of the cave. She pointed across the canyon where the tops of clouds showed above the rim. "Looks like a little buildup to the north. Ike hoped for a couple more weeks before the rains came so we'd be off the plateau. Ike ..." Her shoulders drooped.

"I sure do wonder what he would think of this," Seth said. He stretched and got to his feet to look out into the canyon. Below him Guard trotted up to join Weaver in the middle of the canyon floor. Weaver said something, and Guard disappeared into the brush. The ladder thudded into place.

Guard stepped onto the ledge. He gave Seth a warning glare and held his hand in a blocking gesture. With his beak, he pointed to Lee and motioned her to the ladder.

Seth planted himself between Lee and the ladder. The end of Guard's tail tapped the ground impatiently. Lee started forward, eyes down, compliant, but Seth blocked her with his arm. She wasn't alone anymore. They needed to stick together.

Guard leaped forward, holding his claw-tipped fingers together as a weapon. Startled, Seth stepped back. Guard pushed Lee toward the ladder. As he turned to follow her, he swung his tail and took Seth's feet out from under him.

Seth fell hard, unprepared for the sudden strike. Before he could get up, Guard forced Lee to the ladder, clicked his beak once and slithered down after her. The ladder vanished.

Seth got to his feet and ran to the edge, tripping himself with the shackles. He saw Lee shuffle across the canyon to Weaver. Weaver led her to the shade of the shallow cave near the loom. Guard settled into a three-point squat a few steps away.

Seth caught Lee's eyes as she looked up at him before she sat down cross-legged near a pile of long, narrow leaves of some kind with her back to him and Guard. She focused on whatever Weaver demonstrated. He watched her fumble to hold the beginning together while she wove new strips into it. Weaver pointed, held, and redid Lee's work a couple of times. Once the construction held together, Weaver left Lee alone and went to the loom. Guard got up and trotted away down the canyon.

Seth shuffled to the end of the ledge where he could sit against the cave wall and see Lee. At least Guard wasn't hovering around. Next time that one came onto the ledge, he was going to … Seth told himself not to be stupid. Next time, just stay out of reach. He made himself sit still and watch with the patience he had learned training horses.

Thunder continued to rumble in the distance. The still, muggy air made it hard to stay awake. It had only been a day since he'd found the trampled camp. At least he had found Lee, and she was alive.

He was just awake enough to notice when Weaver approached Lee, squatted, and showed her how to finish off her creation, a basket the size of Lee's two hands cupped together. Weaver took it, pulled and prodded it, and set it aside, then pointed to a pile of rushes. Lee got up, stretched, and brought the leaves over. Weaver laid out another project, a mat Seth thought, and coached Lee until the form began to take shape, then went back to the loom.

Lee made quick progress on the flat weaving. Weaver came over to show her how to add in new rushes as the mat grew bigger but mostly left Lee to sort it out for herself. It looked like a simple process, especially compared to the horsehair work that Seth did. Feeding the ends in to finish the project took almost as long as creating the mat itself. When Lee smoothed it out, it looked about the right size for her to sit on.

Weaver held up the mat and inspected it. She tucked in a couple loose ends and laid the mat near the loom with the little basket. She gestured Lee to get up. The canyon floor was in shadow. Lee had worked the whole afternoon.

Seth held his breath as Guard appeared from somewhere to motion Lee toward the cave. When she got to the trickle of water in the midst of the mostly dry stream channel, Weaver called out something with a hoarse squawk. Guard stopped, pointed toward the water, and mimicked splashing it onto himself.

Lee looked from Guard to Weaver before dropping to her knees. She rinsed her hands, arms, and face and sluiced water over her head and through her hair before Guard tapped her with his tail and herded her away.

The ladder thudded into place. Seth met Lee as she climbed onto the ledge.

"I'm home," she said with a weak grin.

"Is this what you've been doing every day?" he asked.

"It may not look like it, but that's hard work," she said. "At least today's projects both held together." She began kneading her palms and stretching her fingers.

He took her hands in his to massage them. "How did you do it?" he asked.

"What?"

"Stay sane these last few days."

"Did I?" She smiled crookedly. "How do you, alone at your stead? By stacking rocks?"

"This isn't about being alone; it's the uncertainty."

"I think about something else," Lee said.

"Like what?" He stroked his thumb over her palm and stretched her fingers back.

"My report to Dougherty."

He circled her palm with his thumb. "That's all?"

"Seven Wells," she said. "And Under Rim."

"I think about those first days I knew you. When we laughed."

"Yeah." She pulled her hand away, dropped her head, and turned away. He let her go.

"What happens now?" he asked.

She watched Weaver walk off down the canyon. "Sometime before dark, Guard will bring food and water. And we'll be left alone for the night."

"Alone?"

"I never see anyone," she said. "But I assume someone watches."

"Makes sense." He studied the canyon wall across from them. Someone could see from the rim into their cave better than from the canyon floor. And who knew what kind of night vision Guard had.

Lee caught his hand. "Tell me about your plans, about your stead. Will you stay for the winter this year?"

"I plan to," he said. "But I could use a small solar array." He went on about the foals he expected next spring, expanding his garden, anything he could think of that had nothing to do with being held captive.

Chapter 19

Seth

In the pre-dawn cool, Seth went through his batayr forms, channeling his fear into fluid, powerful movement. When he couldn't control anything else, he could control himself.

Lee joined him as he finished the first section of the form. "Step me through what Guard was teaching you yesterday," she said. "I don't know how you followed him so well."

"Horses," he answered.

"Horses?"

"Reading and responding to body language. Like I do with horses." He pictured what Guard had taught or tried to teach him. "I can't really do what he does. No tail."

The thud of the ladder interrupted them. Guard stepped onto the ledge. He pointed his beak at Lee and then to the ladder.

"I guess it's time to practice weaving," she said.

"Be careful." He reminded himself she had been all right the afternoon before. And all the days when she'd been alone. But he didn't trust her hook-beaked captor.

She nodded. "Always." She hurried across the cave. Watching Guard for confirmation, she backed down the ladder.

Guard didn't follow her this time. He turned his attention to Seth, pointing to the far end of the ledge as he had the morning before. Seth did as directed, following Lee's advice about not stirring things up unnecessarily. As he crossed the cave, he glimpsed Lee following Weaver across the canyon.

Seth studied Guard closely. The being's style had a fierce, predatory origin, strong on offense, utilizing the tail as support as well as a weapon in moves Seth couldn't hope to copy or defend against. At least Guard hadn't used that hooked beak in any of the moves. A ritual prohibition maybe. Saved for serious fights, not formal displays? It was as fearsome a weapon as the claws he kept mostly retracted.

Seth wondered again why Guard was working with him. To intimidate? Make it clear they didn't have a chance? Yet Guard patiently taught him an approximation of the first half-dozen moves in the series, without the posturing that had characterized the exchange the day before. He was a demanding instructor. Seth had to repeat moves again and again.

The morning heated up rapidly. Seth shed his shirt early in the training session. When he used it to wipe the sweat from his face, Guard eyed him curiously. Guard didn't sweat, but his tan and red crest and arm feathers stood up, and he panted lightly.

Seth finally managed some nuance Guard was looking for. Guard stepped back with a bob of his head and walked away. He went down the ladder without a backward glance and left it in place. Seth hurried to it. Guard waited at the bottom, looking across the canyon. Well, Seth really hadn't expected him to go away and leave it.

Weaver escorted Lee to the stream, allowed her time to rinse her face and hands, and waved her to the ladder. Guard stood by until she climbed up, then followed, carrying a basket of food and another water container. This time, when he left, he took the ladder away.

"You look worn out," Lee said.

"I swear that one doesn't know the meaning of tired," Seth replied. He took a couple of swallows of water. "How was your morning?" Such an ordinary thing to ask, it seemed crazy.

"Baskets, little ones this size." She held her cupped palms together. "One finished and a couple Weaver shook to pieces in about two shakes. What about you? I don't see any bruises."

He frowned. "I don't know whether that was friendly sharing or I'm being groomed for a fight."

She froze. "Elements and All!" she whispered, shifting uneasily. "With the rains about to begin, it would be an auspicious time for an offering to the gods, whatever gods they may have."

"Offerings? That's pretty primitive."

"They are primitive." She faced him. "We have to consider that their belief system would be at a similar level."

"What are you talking about?"

"I'm not sure," she said. "But ceremonies to assure rain were common in human history. Including sacrifice."

He shook his head in disbelief. "You're imagining things."

She stared at him, her brown-gold eyes wide. Then she looked away. "You're probably right," she said. "The fights I saw the other night weren't to the death. And no one has actually threatened to hurt me."

As if Guard's presence wasn't threat enough, he thought. As much to reassure himself as her, he said, "He's been teaching me forms, not sparring with me. It's all display." Except for Guard knocking him to the ground without warning for not obeying, but he didn't remind Lee of that. "Now, I'm hungry. And we should eat when they give us the opportunity."

She nodded. "I'll see what Guard brought us." She collected the basket and water container, and they settled with their backs to the wall where they could see Weaver at her loom.

"If — when — we get away from here," he said, "which way do we go?" He wasn't even sure which way he had come from. Something disorienting about being trussed in a net in the dark with your face covered.

"I'm not sure," she said. "I must have been drugged. Last place I remember before I woke up here was the stampede camp."

"Well, any direction but north should bring us to settled country eventually." He sketched invisible lines on the rock. "So we have the Rim to the north; the Rocky Ford District and the Mardukai Valley to the east; Under Rim and the trail from there to Wide Ford to the west; and the Glas River District around Wide Ford to the south."

She turned a roundfruit over in her hand. "A long ways on foot in any direction."

He set aside the food and began to pick at the shackles. "What happens when the authorities in Portside find out about these people?"

Lee shook her head. "I don't know. There's no precedent I'm aware of. But I can't see humans being removed from Carico now, not without years of debate."

"What! Remove humans? What for?"

"It looks like Carico should never have been opened for settlement. Indigenous people — their world."

"But they aren't native. Can't be." He shook his head firmly.

She raised an eyebrow. "Because the pre-settlement surveys didn't find them? That doesn't mean they're not native."

"Missed in all the surveys and almost seventy years of settlement?" he said. "It's not like they're on another continent. It doesn't make sense."

"And a cliff-dwelling, pre-metal culture from off world does?" She pitched the roundfruit pit into the air and watched it sail off toward the canyon floor. "I've had days to figure it out. I'm still clueless. Not enough information."

"There must be a village. It's not just these two individuals."

"A village," she agreed. "But they've never let me out of this little dead-end canyon."

"So, what don't they want us to see?" That gave his imagination way too much to work with.

He had the afternoon to chase notions around in his head. Guard came and took Lee back to work with Weaver, then disappeared. Seth was left alone to watch Lee from a distance and try to keep his thoughts reined in. And watch thunderclouds building up.

Lee sat on a mat near Weaver's loom. Weaver set a large basket down by her, reached into it, and lifted out something long and narrow. Seth remembered Lee talking about gathering ribbon worms. Weaver squatted, placed the ribbon worm on what looked like a slab of wood lying on the mat, and picked up a knife. Seth couldn't be sure from his perch but thought it was a standard knife like many riders carried, Lee's own maybe.

Obviously familiar with the implement or one similar, Weaver slit the worm, gutted it, peeled the skin off, and dropped the skin into a basket. What was left was a strip of whitish flesh about as long as Lee's forearm and half as thick. Weaver diced the ribbon into small pieces, scooped them into a basket, and poured a little liquid over them from a bag. She got another ribbon from the basket and laid it on the cutting block. She held the knife out to Lee.

A weapon and given freely. Seth waited to see what Lee would do. Much as he wanted her to grab the knife and run for it, he knew it would be foolish. They needed supplies and something to give them a head start if they were going to have any chance of success. She hesitated, glanced up at him, and shook her head slightly.

Weaver extended the knife. Lee took it, knelt by the mat, and took hold of the ribbon worm. She copied Weaver's neat gutting and peeling of the body, diced it, and put it in with Weaver's pieces. Weaver mimed stirring, and Lee complied.

Weaver gestured at the basket of ribbons. Lee slipped the knife under another and transferred it to the cutting board. She cleaned and diced it under Weaver's watch. Weaver pointed to the container of liquid, and Lee added some to the pieces. When she was ready to start on another worm, Weaver bobbed her head and walked over to the loom, leaving Lee alone with a knife and no chance at all of escaping. Lee's shoulders slumped, and she went on with her task, one ribbon at a time.

Either Guard was psychic or he watched from someplace nearby. When Lee finished the last ribbon worm, he came to escort her back to the ladder even though it was only mid-afternoon. Without asking, she stopped at the creek to wash. He waited, tail twitching, until she finished.

Once she was back in their prison, Weaver and Guard trotted away, carrying the marinating ribbon worms and the bag of liquid. They only went a couple hundred yards down the canyon to the open area where Lee said the fight night had been held. There they met several others, all of Guard's kind.

"Another fight night?" Seth asked.

"I don't know." Lee wrapped her arms across her chest. "I hope not."

They watched Weaver, Guard, and the others, as much as they could see through the brush. Weaver came back to the loom cave and took away the baskets and mat that Lee had made. Others brought small mats to the gathering area and spread them on the ground, a row of five with a single mat in front.

"Like a tribunal," Lee said. "Five judges and an accused."

"Thanks for that," Seth said. The image made the back of his neck crawl.

"A petitioner in front of arbiters?"

"That's better." But he couldn't get the first idea out of his mind.

With the mats in place, Weaver led the group out of sight around a curve in the canyon. Clouds came and went. The air thickened with humidity, still and hot even in the shade of their cave. White clouds built towers into what sky they could see, and thunder rumbled.

Seth stretched out with the blanket under his head. Waiting again. "Are ribbon worms really edible?" he asked.

"I was cutting, not eating," Lee said.

"What did Weaver put on them? The liquid."

"Smelled like vinegar."

Vinegar, such a common thing — it made Weaver seem a little less alien to him.

"What would they make vinegar from?" Lee asked.

"Your Aunt Teri makes it out of a lot of things, mostly scraps when she's preserving fruit." The thought of her vinegar made his mouth pucker.

"Well, if they are planning a party tonight, it might just get rained out," Lee said. "Look how tall those thunderheads are."

The clouds shone white at the top but the bottoms were purple-black and heavy with rain. Thunder made a distant rumble all around.

"Good thing we are this high up," he said. "Even a little canyon like this can flood in a downpour."

Chapter 20

Lee

The afternoon dragged on. Lee sat under the protecting rock overhang. Lightning flashed. The first raindrops painted patterns of dots on the outer edge of the shelf. She breathed in the petrichor, the unique odor of rain on dry ground, the blood of gods upon the stones of the earth. For her it meant hope, the beginning of the summer rains that brought the desert to life, a good omen if she believed in such things. But the thunder strummed restless tunes on her nerves as the first sprinkle turned into a downpour. She got up and paced, unable to be still. She envied Seth who dozed on the bedding undisturbed.

The brief, heavy rain passed. Shadows climbed up the far side of the canyon as the sun dropped toward the horizon. Something caught Lee's eye at the gathering area. Weaver or one like her. Followed by four more, all stout, raisin-skinned, walking upright with tails carried just off the ground.

Lee nudged Seth's bare foot. He jerked upright. She said, "They're back. A bunch of them."

A group of Guard's type followed the first group. They clustered together so she couldn't tell how many for sure, except for one who stood apart. "They brought the kids," she added.

"Kids?" He stepped out where he could see better.

"I guess," she said. A pack of miniatures of both kinds ran across the opening and splashed in the shallow stream. "Looks like a family picnic."

"Predators bring their young to a kill to eat," he pointed out, chilling her optimism. "And where are the teenagers?"

She looked again. Full-sized individuals and small ones no more than about waist high on the adults, but none in between of either kind. "That is odd. Maybe they're coming later?"

"Guard and Weaver are headed this way."

"Bringing us dinner?"

"Or inviting us to join them," he said.

Just in case, she picked up her wrap and tied it into a makeshift jacket over her tank top. The rain shower left cooler air. Whipbrush danced in the gusty wind. Thunder grumbled. Not the evening she would choose for an open-air party.

The ladder thumped into place, and Guard appeared. He put a full net bag against the wall and pointed Lee to the ladder without giving her a chance to see what was in it. She gave Seth a worried look and complied, swallowing the anxiety that rose in her throat. She shinnied down the ladder. Weaver waited for her at the bottom. Lee looked back and saw Seth straddle the bundled canes. Weaver clicked her beak and hurried her away.

When they reached the gathering site, Weaver shepherded Lee to the single mat facing three other fantails waiting on the row of mats. One of the fantails picked up the final mat, carried it to one side, and placed it down in front of a fifth fantail who stepped onto it with a squared-up bearing that reminded Lee of a military officer. It — she? — gave Lee and Weaver a flat stare that chilled Lee more than the wind. One of the hawkbeaks stood at the fantail's shoulder, imposing even though he was only two-thirds her size. Standing where they were, they seemed more observers than participants.

The hawkbeak directed his sharp gaze past Lee. She looked around. Guard was straight behind her maybe twenty feet away, the only hawkbeak wearing a choker of braided rawhide. Weaver wore one too. A symbol of rank? But neither of the two observers wore them although they were obviously important.

Seth stood next to Guard. On both sides of them a line of hawk-beaked fighters closed the circle with the fantails. Lee felt like a swine-deer surrounded by wolf-lizards.

The fifth fantail and her companion watched from outside the circle. The little ones no longer ran and played. They clustered out of the wind against the relative shelter of the canyon wall. Lee counted four little fantails together and a larger group of little hawkbeaks. Amber and sapphire eyes gawked at her and Seth. Curious? Fearful? Expectant? Lee couldn't tell.

Weaver stepped into place at the end of the row of fantails. In front of her, four small baskets and the basket of marinated ribbon worms sat on a slightly lop-sided mat — the things Lee had made the last two days. Lee held herself still, half terrified and half curious.

Weaver began speaking, her voice carrying over irregular thunder. Lee listened, fascinated. She understood nothing of the harsh rasping, the gutturals and clicks, but recognized the rolling quality of fine oratory. Weaver went on for a minute or more, the fine feathers on her face flashing blue and purple, her hands enforcing her words.

When Weaver finished speaking, she beckoned Lee to her and held out the stack of small baskets. Lee shuffled to her and accepted them, wishing someone had given her a script.

Weaver took the top basket from the stack with a single bob of her head and pointed her beak at the next fantail in line. Okay, Lee thought. Take the next basket to that person.

Lee stood as tall as she could — a good six or eight inches shorter than any of the fantails — and took deliberate, if short, steps. Tripping over the shackles wouldn't help her image. She stopped before each of the three fantails in the line and presented the baskets. Each head-bobbed and held their basket in cupped hands before them. Oh good, no basket for the fantail standing apart, the one with eyes the same pale gold as the verdejo wine Lee had enjoyed at the Carico Serai weeks ago and just as cold. Lee was happy to keep her distance from that one.

Weaver gestured her back to the lone mat. When she stood before them again, the four fantails raised the baskets and displayed them to the watching hawkbeaks before setting them on the ground. Silence. Was that good or bad?

Weaver spoke again, this time directly to Lee, as she held out the basket of marinated ribbon worms. Clued in by the routine with the baskets, Lee took it. This time Weaver pointed her to the left, to the nearest hawkbeak.

Lee hesitated just out of arm's reach in front of him. He was her height and more muscular than Guard with a beak like polished bronze. He wore a satchel on a strap across his body. All of them did, hawkbeaks and fantails alike, and each satchel was different enough in shape and pattern to identify individuals.

The hawkbeak looked down, not meeting her eyes. He took a half step forward, and she steeled herself. With his crest held tight to the back of his neck, the hawkbeak scooped up a double-finger load of diced ribbon worms and ate. Then he bobbed his head once and looked to the person next to him. Lee took the hint and side-stepped from one to the next around the circle. Each took a single mouthful of food. All of them kept their beaks and eyes lowered.

When she reached Guard, he blocked her offer of the food to Seth. So Seth wasn't a guest? What was he? He looked calm but the set of his shoulders gave away his nervousness. She met his eyes and moved on.

She reached the first fantail and offered the food. The fantail took the whole basket and set it aside. Lee looked to Weaver for guidance. Weaver gestured her to come. Lee saw that a mat, her own lop-sided mat, had been moved into the row between Weaver and the fantail next to her. Lee took her place on it, guessing it meant some kind of change in status. She hated guessing about important things.

Weaver faced her and settled one of the satchels around her neck. Lee slid her arm through so it hung on her hip the way Weaver wore hers. Weaver took her by the shoulders and turned her to face the circle.

Guard stalked over without looking her in the eye and bent over at her feet. He inserted a talon into the rawhide braiding to release the mysterious fastenings on the shackles. Lee looked down at her bare ankles and fought the urge to run a victory lap. Seth gave her a subtle thumbs up.

"Thank you," she said to Guard. Guard, who had often looked her in the eye before, kept his beak lowered. He bobbed his head once, coiled the rawhide, and laid it in front of Weaver before returning to his place in the circle. Clicking surrounded Lee as both fantails and hawkbeaks stretched their beaks skyward and snapped them rapidly. Everyone but the two solitary observers. They stood statue-still.

Chapter 21

Lee

Two of the hawkbeaks lit torches set around the perimeter to add flickering, uncertain light to the cloud-darkened twilight. Lightning punctuated the gloom, and thunder echoed from the canyon walls, but rain held off.

Lee shifted her unshackled feet a little. She was free by that much, but she didn't imagine she could just walk away. Was she now somehow a member of one contingent of their strange captors? And what about Seth? Was he about to be initiated too? If that's what it was?

Two fantails picked up hand drums and set up a rhythmic counterpoint to the thunder. Guard stepped forward with a deep head-bob. The drums silenced.

He spoke to the hawkbeaks with gestures that came close to dance in their fluid rhythm. A declaration, a leader inspiring a team. Lee watched feather crests rise and flare, heard beaks ticking. Guard ended with a thud of his tail on the ground that the hawkbeaks repeated. Lee clenched her fists at her sides, anticipating another fight night. With Seth unarmed against beak, talons, and tail.

Guard strutted to Seth and reached down to take off the shackles. He laid them on the sand and stepped back. Seth looked him in the eye, spread his feet, and stretched.

Guard strode to the center of the circle and waved Seth to follow him. The hawkbeaks on each side closed in to fill the gap they left in the circle. Facing the hawkbeaks, Guard took the opening stance of his own martial arts form.

Lee forced her clenched hands open. Let it just be a demonstration.

Seth hesitated, and Guard waved him into position beside him. Guard led through the few moves they had worked on earlier. Seth stumbled through them like a one-armed man learning batayr. Those around the circle observed in silence. Light rain began to fall.

Guard said something to the hawkbeaks. Then he initiated the opening of the batayr form. Seth joined him, this time with confidence. Once they began, Guard stepped aside and let Seth continue alone.

Wow was all Lee could think. Unshackled, he could finally show the form as it was meant to be done, and he was flawless, flowing from stance to stance with power and grace. She stifled a cheer when he finished. Let that show them what you could do without a tail.

The silence hung until Guard raised his arms and crest and called out something. The hawkbeaks responded, some one way, some another. Lee's breath caught. She remembered an ancient tale of an arena where a fighter's life was determined by a thumbs up or thumbs down, and she wished she hadn't read so many old stories as a child.

Guard said something more, crouching forward and raising his tail in his balanced, fighting position. The hawkbeaks answered with a united krawing and rushed Seth. Lee gasped and took a step forward. Weaver's hand on her shoulder restrained her.

The wave of bodies surrounded Seth. The drumming started. The hawkbeaks encircled Seth in a tight ring, bouncing in place, higher and higher, straight up. Through the rain and bodies, Lee could barely glimpse Seth, turning in the center and then bouncing himself, easily outdone by the spring-action of the others' feet and legs.

Someone skrawked once. The ring broke, and the dancers ran to reform the larger circle, leaving Seth and Guard alone in the middle. The drums began again, and the hawkbeaks kept time with their snapping beaks.

"No," Lee whispered. Weaver gripped her shoulder. Lee wrapped her arms across her chest. She made herself stand when she wanted to run out and intervene.

Guard faced Seth and took the opening stance of the moves he had taught him. Seth mirrored him. Guard lashed his tail, moved sideways, drawing Seth to face him. He feigned a kick and beckoned Seth toward him, inviting. Seth settled into his own opening batayr stance and waited.

Guard kicked again, rib-high, making it a fight.

Seth blocked, spun away, bounced out of reach.

Get in close, Lee coached silently. Inside sweeping kicks and tail swings. Be careful, she screamed in her head.

Seth circled. Guard turned with him, waiting, teasing him in. Seth closed, drove a fist at Guard's side. Guard bounced away, swept his tail. Seth jumped over it, kicked as he came down. Guard blocked, connected. Seth staggered, regained his balance.

Lightning exploded with the deafening crack of a nearby strike. The afterimage from the flash left Lee half-blind. A whistle pierced the storm. Weaver ran into the circle and whistled again. Guard extended his arms downward, crossed at the wrists, and backed away.

Lightning flashed again; thunder crashed before the brightness died. The clouds opened up, and rain became a deluge.

Weaver squawked instructions. Lee stumbled through the pounding rain toward Seth. She saw the two observers trot away down the canyon. Adults gathered up the children and ran after them.

When she reached Seth, Guard laid a hand on his arm and pointed them up the canyon toward their prison cave. Two other hawkbeaks flanked him.

Seth didn't argue. He grabbed Lee's hand and ran. She did her best to keep up with him. In the dark with rain in her eyes, she wanted nothing more than to climb to the high, dry safety of their ledge.

Two of the hawkbeaks beat them there and had the ladder in place. Lee scrambled up it and barely got clear before Seth was up too. Easy without shackles. The ladder vanished. A flash of lightning showed the three hawkbeaks running down the canyon.

Seth pulled her back into the cave. A curtain of water poured off the rock overhang and flooded off the ledge, but inside was dry. "Are they gone?" he yelled over the pounding.

She nodded.

He picked up the blanket and ran it over his head before reaching out to towel water from her face. She took it from him and did it herself. "Are you okay?" she asked.

"No damage, aside from bruised feet."

"Me too," she said. She'd stepped on lots of rocks and sticks in that short run.

"What was that all about? Did you figure it out?"

She shrugged and shook her head. "Initiation?" She ran her hand over the tough weave of the satchel that hung over her shoulder.

"I guess we aren't fully accepted yet," he said as he waved a hand at their prison.

As she looked around, a shape caught her eye. The net bag Guard had left when he had taken them to the gathering. She bent over it in the dark and felt — "Boots! Seth, it's our boots. And saddlebags."

They fumbled to find the net's opening and empty the contents onto the floor. Boots with socks stuffed inside. The first one Seth tried turned out to be hers. She stripped off soaking moccasins, dried her feet with the blanket, and slipped on socks, blessed socks. She pulled boots on too and felt fully dressed.

Seth opened saddlebags and, mostly by feel, checked the contents. "I think everything is there," he said.

She identified hers by the buckle shape. "Even my knife." The one she had used to prepare ribbon worms, that Weaver had taken back.

"Hurry." Seth rolled the sleeping pad and shoved it into the net bag along with his saddlebags and Lee's water bottle.

"What?" She stood in the refuge of the cave, holding her saddlebags in her arms, feeling momentarily safe.

"We've got to go," Seth said.

"Go?" Flame and flood! He was right. And the thought hadn't entered her mind.

"Come on. Use the blanket to let me down. Before this storm lets up, and they come back."

"Go where?" She was slinging her saddlebags over her shoulder as she asked.

"Figure that out as we go. Over here." He dropped the net bag and stretched on his belly where the ledge ended against the cliff. "Brace yourself here."

Before she could argue, he had a corner of the blanket wrapped around his fist and was backing toward the edge. Lee grabbed the other end of the blanket, sat down, and braced her feet. It wasn't that far down, not really.

When his weight was gone, she dropped the blanket over the edge, followed by the net bag. When the ladder thumped into place, she clambered down. Seth pulled the ladder down after her and laid it against the foot of the cliff. He stuffed the blanket into the net, slung it over his shoulder, and grabbed her hand.

"Sure hope there's a way out of this canyon."

"Go that way," she said. "I saw a vine tree against the cliff when I was collecting ribbon worms."

The rain eased up a little as they struggled through the dark. The stream was several times its usual trickle. Brush and rocks obstructed their progress. But not far around a curve in the canyon, the dark, interwoven trunks of the vine tree climbed up the lighter stone of the cliff and offered handholds and places to wedge booted feet.

Lee settled the saddlebags on her shoulder over the satchel. Seth gave her a boost. She grabbed hold of the trunk and climbed, seeking out each hold by feel, wishing for enough light to pick a route ahead as the branches spread out across the rock. The vine-trunk quivered as Seth climbed too. The higher she got, the slenderer the vines became until she wasn't sure they would support her, much less Seth.

One bent in her grasp, leaving her teetering until she latched onto another. The vines she clung to shivered. She closed her eyes and held on, dragging air into her lungs as she froze in place.

She flinched when something grasped her ankle. Seth's hand — he gave her an encouraging nudge. With that mostly imaginary support, she found the courage to look for another hold. Lightning showed her a cleft within her reach. Pressing herself against the rock, she grasped the stoutest vine she could reach and stretched until she jammed her foot securely into the narrow crack. She thrust one hand as deep between the rocks as she could, wedged in her other foot, and scrambled up the last body-length to the rim where she sprawled in the mud, letting the rain pound down on her.

She savored her triumph for two breaths before she rolled over and sat up. Seth should be right behind her. The rain was just rain now, not the deluge it had been. And solid, if soggy, ground surrounded her.

Seth crawled over the rim at her feet. She grasped his arm and pulled him away from the edge.

He knelt next to her. "Are you okay?" he asked between gasps.

"Okay," she replied.

He grasped her shoulder. "We made it … out of the canyon at least."

She got to her feet and pulled him up. "Which way?"

"Straight away from that cliff we just climbed."

That would do until they could see the sky and surrounding terrain. Go far enough southwest, and they had to come out somewhere on the main trail between Wide Ford and Under Rim. If they could elude pursuit. Elude hooked beaks and powerful running legs. She grabbed onto the net bag and ran, pulling Seth with her.

Counterpoint

Eta'ak

The very elements seem against us tonight. And Prime and Second witnessed it to my chagrin.

The escape of the two First-Comers at this point is a sore disappointment. With the ceremony incomplete, I was not allowed to bring them with us to the village. I should have assigned guards. I clearly erred in my confidence that they would stay in shelter through such a storm.

I am proud of all my people. No one is seriously injured; most importantly the children are safe. The irreplaceable equipment survives intact. Only things we built with our own hands suffered. What we built once, we can rebuild — our water system being the most significant.

As soon as the storm lets up, hunters will go after our missing detainees. We must retake them before daylight if possible. Our hunters should not be on the open flats after sunrise. The risk of being seen is slight — those others who search for the two are far from here — but still to be avoided.

The First-Comers' broadcasts report that seekers are spreading out from the male's home. There appears to be disagreement between the riders and the Ranger female over who should direct the efforts. Such discord will slow them. We must monitor their progress.

Meanwhile hunters from our other villages have observed that the lone fugitive from the east moves closer to us, although without any pursuers. I can only hope he stays far enough distant not to raise the Council's concern.

I fear we have little time before we are discovered. We must take action to initiate contact first and, to do that, I need the human female.

-From the Archives of Eta'ak, Information Analyst

Chapter 22

Seth

Seth used a stick like a blind man to feel his way between the vague shapes of plants and rocks. He watched to be sure Lee kept close behind him. He didn't know which direction they were going except that it was away from the cliff and from their captors.

The storm moved off into the distance, taking what little light the lightning gave. Both moons were new, so the night was dark. They kept moving, one step after another. Where they didn't trip on the brush, they slid on the greasy clay mud that clung to their boots like ten-pound weights. The clouds parted enough to show the Great Tarbh constellation overhead, with the top of its fan pointing north. "We're headed southwest, like we thought," he said.

"Good," she answered.

With wet feet, soaked clothes, and boots heavy with mud, they trudged on. Seth was hardly aware that clouds had moved in again until the world lit up, and thunder crashed around them. Heavy rain pounded down.

He took hold of Lee's hand and turned ninety degrees to his right before stumbling forward, sending water splashing with every step. They struggled on through the downpour for several minutes before the rain eased up a little. Seth immediately turned left. "Keep raining," he muttered. He slowed down, feeling his way until the rain stopped.

"What was that all about?" Lee asked.

"I hope the rain wiped out our tracks."

"And we aren't on the same line anymore," she said.

"Make it a little harder for them." He could hope anyway.

"Can we stop for a couple minutes?" she asked.

"Okay."

She searched in her saddlebags and pulled out a pouch of emergency rations. "Hot dinner," she announced. "Left over from my Ranger days." She creased over the top edge, activating the heating element. She squeezed the contents around for a minute while it warmed, then sucked in a mouthful and passed it to him.

He swallowed the thick paste and felt the warmth going deep into him. Some off-world things were worth packing around. The restorative even tasted good.

They headed on, passing the pouch back and forth between them until it was empty. After what seemed a lifetime stumbling through the night, Seth pointed at the faint outline of higher ground. "There," he said. "Shelter." Good thing. They were both dragging. He tried to take her saddlebags to carry, but she refused to let them go. He knew her well enough not to argue.

They slogged on, leaving clay for sandier ground that at least cleaned pounds of mud off their boots. One foot in front of the other without stopping. Little by little they got closer to the hillock. A couple of centuries later, they staggered up its sloping flanks to the crown of boulders on top.

"What a rock pile," Seth said as they looked at the barrier.

"No way I can climb that," Lee said. "Not now anyway."

"No need." He took her hand. "This looks promising."

He led her to an overhanging rock with just enough room for the two of them underneath. He crawled in through the screen of brush and found the ground was dry. Their own little piece of heaven.

"Another good downpour to wipe out our tracks, and they'll never find us," he said. He spread the blanket on the ground. "Better leave the boots on for now. We might need them." Even tarbh hide wasn't water resistant enough to stand up to their hike through the slop, and wet boots did not go on quickly.

He watched her stretch out and relax into exhaustion. She said, "I can't remember the last time I did that much walking. Too used to riding everywhere." She shifted a little, getting comfortable. "You think we have a chance?"

"Dougherty and Pa will have searchers out," he said. "They'll be all over that plateau country. All we have to do is show ourselves."

"As long as it's to them and not Guard and his friends." She sat up with a groan and rummaged in her saddlebags to produce another of the ration pouches.

His body felt slack, drained, but his mind plodded on, still driven by fear that they would be found. The hawkbeaks could easily run them down, and his efforts to confuse their trail depended on the rain washing away tracks and scent.

He sucked down his share of the rations. Things would look better after some hot food and some rest. And they were free, for the moment. But the way his feet hurt, he didn't look forward to more walking. He wondered if the horses had hung around near the stampede spring or started for home. Maybe the searchers had found them. For all the good that would do. He hadn't found any clues to what had happened to Lee. He didn't expect the searchers would either. They had to get back to the plateau if they were going to be found.

He lay still, not wanting to disturb Lee. She slept restlessly with small shifts, cuddling against him in sleep. He listened to the tiny sounds around them, the drip of water, the scurrying of a rock rat. The thunder faded away. He closed his eyes and let Lee's presence warm him.

The next thing he knew the sky was pale with the promise of dawn. Back the way they had come, wolf-lizards greeted their favored hunting time with eerie whistle-growls, gathering the pack. He listened as their infrequent calls moved closer. Normally he wouldn't give them a second thought. They rarely approached humans. But it sounded like these were trailing him and Lee.

He put a warning hand over Lee's mouth. When she nodded to show she was awake, he let go. "Climb," he whispered in her ear. He pushed their saddlebags into the net bag, slung it over his shoulder, and crawled from behind the bushes that masked their refuge. She slid out, dragging the blanket, and accepted his hand, pulling herself to her feet.

He looked along the face of the outcrop and pointed at a sloping crack just wide enough to hold a booted foot. Lee stayed close to him as he picked his way over the rough ground to it. The crack led to a ledge about eight feet up.

He made a stirrup of his hands to give Lee a boost. She caught hold of the ledge, jammed a foot into the crack, and scrambled up. He passed the bag to her before following. She led the way along the ledge and ducked between two boulders on top of the outcrop. He squeezed through the space and found her crouched in a tiny opening, maybe three steps across, circled by rocks.

"Our own fort," she whispered.

She was right. He could see in all directions from within the jumble of boulders.

"Are they coming?" she asked.

"Not them; wolf-lizards," he answered. "On our trail."

"Wolf-lizards don't hunt people, do they?"

"Not where they're familiar with people." He frowned. "These may not know us from a tasty swine-deer."

"Oh, perfect." She ran a hand through her hair as she settled herself where she could see between rocks. "Dino-birds and now wolf-lizards."

"Dino-birds, huh. Good description." He scanned the fading stars and the country around them to get oriented. A few other outcroppings like their refuge dotted the immediate landscape. Far away to the south, maybe twenty miles, he could see the top of a line of hills.

He smoothed the sand between him and Lee and sketched the Glas River from south of Wide Ford northward past his stead to its head near the north edge of the plateau. He added the main trail that ran from Wide Ford west and north to Under Rim. He made his best guess at the L-shaped line of the Whitewater from Rocky Ford in the east, across the north edge of the plateau, then turning north to its headwaters under the Rim. Somewhere between where the Whitewater turned north and the head of the Glas lay the canyon with the spring and stampede camp. He marked that as best as he could, trying to remember from Ike's map how far south of the Whitewater the spring was. He added the hills running west from there.

"Does that look about right?" he asked Lee.

"Close enough," she said.

"We have to be someplace with cliffs in the canyons, here I think, north of the hills and west of the Whitewater." He drew a rough circle in the dirt. "If I remember the maps right, east beyond the Glas and north of the Whitewater you get out of the rimrock country. So, if we go south, we should cross those hills and be back on the plateau where Dougherty'll be searching."

"If we go anywhere," she answered, peeking over the rocks at their back trail. Seth looked, making out a line of wolf-lizards trotting across the flat toward them.

"Void!" he said. "The rain should have washed away our scent." He watched the animals uneasily. "Just hope they don't climb well. If we can sit it out until it gets hot, they might give up on us."

Seth saw the animals clearly now, long-legged and round-bodied, with a blue fin a hand's-breadth high running the length of their backs; flat scales like weathered bronze; bright blue ear flaps on broad heads with small ridges around the narrow muzzles; thin lips drawn up to show shearing plates in place of teeth; four eyes the color of ash.

The lead wolf-lizard sniffed the air. The pack gathered, rubbing shoulders before separating to surround the outcrop, whistling and growling as they stalked the base.

Lee swore under her breath, at least Seth thought she did. He didn't recognize the language, just the tone. He had other things he wanted to say, that he didn't want to risk leaving unsaid. "I missed you."

Her eyes widened. "You would want to talk about this now."

"Waited too long already," he said.

"I missed you too."

"Good." He stroked his thumb along her cheek. "Okay. Now, grab anything we can throw. Let's teach these wolf-lizards to leave humans alone." He began piling up small rocks. Not what he wanted to be doing.

The wolf-lizards circled the hillock like sentries, rubbing shoulders each time they passed another, whistling as if they were talking to each other. The big one stopped, looked to their back trail, and growled fiercely. It looked back again and rushed up the lower slope to jump at the boulders. The rest charged up from all sides, leaping and scrambling.

Seth leaned over the boulders and pitched fist-sized rocks at them, striking one on the snout, knocking another sideways with one to the ribs. The animals backed off, paced just below the boulder crown, and rubbed shoulders with their leader.

"Trouble," Lee called out, pointing. She braced against a rock with a bleak look on her face.

Seth glanced over the rocks and saw half a dozen hawkbeaks jogging across the muddy flat, heads down, tails lifted, powerful legs driving in long strides, intent on what the wolf-lizards had cornered — on him and Lee.

The wolf-lizards redoubled their efforts, but none made it up the rocks. At a drawn-out whistle from the pack leader, they regrouped on the flat. When Guard and the others got close, the wolf-lizards faced them. The hawkbeaks formed a tight line with slashing tails and snapping beaks. The wolf-lizards gave way slowly, then broke off and moved away to watch from a distance.

Seth crouched down. The sun was nearly up, and the last lingering clouds glowed pink and orange. It would be hot soon and muggy from the rain. He looked at Lee and grinned. "We tried."

"No way out, is there?" Lee leaned her head back against a rock.

"Grow wings?" He couldn't see any chance of them getting away.

"Here they come." Lee hefted a rock.

Seth thought about Guard's tail and talons and beak. This wasn't going to end well. "Keep your back to mine," he replied, weighing a rock in his own hand.

Then it was too late. Seth looked up. As the sun broke over the horizon, Guard poised on the rocks above them like some prehistoric, snake-tailed flier. The yellow light turned him to gold in startling contrast to the blue-green rocks around him. Steam rose in the sudden heat, wrapping him in mist. Then Guard tipped his sharp beak down, shook his crest feathers into place, and leaped down next to them.

The other hawkbeaks swarmed onto the boulders. Two held slingbows trained on them; one had a net ready to throw, but there was no room or need. Guard lifted his tail to pin Seth against a boulder. He paused, looking at the satchel Lee wore before he dropped his eyes as he did with Weaver. He waved her to climb onto the rocks. Seth twisted to get free. Guard pressed harder, under Seth's rib cage, until he could hardly breathe.

"Okay, I'm going," Lee said. One of the hawkbeaks dangled a net to her, and she climbed it like a rope. Guard eased the pressure on Seth. Seth pushed the tail away. Guard pushed back, pinning him again, then let him go. Looking Guard in the eye, Seth retrieved the net bag with their things before climbing up after Lee.

The hawkbeaks led the way down a narrow slot in the boulders. Lee's shoulders sagged. Seth stepped closer to her and heard her breath catch unevenly. "No weakness," he whispered. She nodded and straightened. Their captors herded them onto the flat at the base of the outcropping where they stopped.

Guard eyed Seth with his crest upright. The tip of his tail switched. Then he dropped his crest and motioned them to sit before he joined the other hawkbeaks in animated discussion. From the gestures, Seth thought it had to do with which way to go. The daylight and open ground seemed to make them uneasy.

Their captors didn't take long to reach agreement. One twisted the nets they carried into neat bundles. Another passed some kind of dried food around.

Guard flared his crest low and wide and clicked his beak. He reached for their net bag. Before Seth could stop her, Lee handed it over. "Let them carry it if they want."

She had a point.

"They're worried about something," she said.

"Searchers, I hope." Seth brushed Lee's shoulder with his hand. "At least we have a better idea of where we are." With the daylight he could see the hills far off to the south and was confident from their outline that the stampede spring was just beyond them.

"What good is that?"

Seth knew how she felt. That long, miserable trek through the mud for nothing. But he refused to show defeat in front of Guard. He said, "They didn't kill us outright. We still have a chance."

"To do what?" she said and got to her feet.

Three of the hawkbeaks trotted off straight into the sunrise. Guard pointed to Lee, with his beak and eyes lowered just a little, and swept his hand after them. Due east, not northeast where they had come from. Lee plodded off. Guard glared straight into Seth's eyes and pointed with his beak. Seth caught up with Lee and stayed close by her side. Guard and the last two hawkbeaks came behind them. The disappointed wolf-lizards drifted off to the west, looking for easier prey.

Chapter 23

Lee

Lee trudged along, leaving the rock outcrop and any hope of escape behind. Guard and two others were close behind her. She watched the other three hawkbeaks ahead of her jogging through a glowing haze as the sun filtered through steam rising from the wet ground. They looked around constantly, and their arm and crest feathers stood up.

She looked south toward the distant hills. Did the stampede spring really lie just beyond them? A long way off on foot but not so far for searchers in a skimmer, if they knew to come this way.

When she looked ahead again, the three leaders were disappearing over a drop. She came to a stop at the top of a dirt bank. Seth almost ran into her. They looked down on an unreal landscape of misshapen pillars and mushrooms of rock with the soil scoured away between them. The three hawkbeaks wove between the strange formations without slowing.

Lee looked at the five-foot bank in front of her. They had barely started, but she'd had enough of slogging through the mud. She folded her legs and sat down. Not one more step — she was ready to be about as mobile as one of the rock goblins before her. "They can carry me or leave me," she said.

"Are you crazy?" Seth whispered.

"Just too tired to care."

Guard whistled sharply, and the front runners came back to the foot of the bank. Guard stepped off the edge. Lee saw his tail snake around Seth and push him off the slick bank as he went. Seth lost his footing and slid down on his seat. He scrambled up and glared at the hawkbeak.

Guard pointed at Lee and beckoned. The other two hawkbeaks stood just behind her. Well, if she had to — she scooted forward off the edge and slid. Sledding in the mud on the seat of her pants struck her as hilarious. She struggled not to laugh. Some sane corner of her mind told her she was too exhausted to think clearly.

"Are you okay?" Seth asked as he pulled her to her feet.

"Oh, yeah, fine." She leaned against him.

Guard pointed his fierce beak at her and clack-clicked something. She gasped as two of his comrades pulled Seth away from her. They wrapped him in a net like a sausage, slung him between them, and started off.

Two more stretched out another net. Instead of rolling her into it, they held it open like a hammock. They were going to carry her, carry both of them. They scooped her up in the makeshift chair before she could move, leaving her facing sideways with the net cradling her back and head while her feet dangled off. She jerked her feet up and crossed her legs so they wouldn't drag. Her bearers jogged off between the wind-sculpted stones, faster now with their burdens than when she and Seth had been afoot.

The morning sun soon turned the valley into a steam bath. The hawkbeaks panted and flared their feathers but didn't slow down. Lee sweated and clung to the net. The cords dug into her; the net swayed; she swallowed and hoped she wasn't going to be motion sick. So much for being carried. But it meant their captors wanted them alive. If she could just figure out why.

The hawkbeaks trotted steadily, stopping only to trade off bearers, until they reached a river canyon. She thought about the map Seth had drawn in the dirt before they had been recaptured. It had to be the Whitewater.

The hawkbeaks climbed down a cleft and picked their way north along the base of the rimrock that capped the canyon wall. The sun beat down. Below her, Lee could see the water, muddy from the rain, rolling over the blue-green rocks. A long ways below. She held on to the net and closed her eyes.

When she thought she couldn't stand another minute in the swinging net, they stopped under an overhang of rock barely large enough to shade the six hawkbeaks and two stiff, sore humans.

The hawkbeaks lounged on their bellies, cornering Lee and Seth against the back wall. Guard passed around food — a mix of dried, pounded meat and fruits held together with a little fat. Then the hawkbeaks dozed. Lee pillowed her head in Seth's lap and slept.

Wind and distant rumbles of thunder woke her. The hawkbeaks roused too. They packed the nets away, and Lee sighed with relief. She dreaded being carried any farther, swaying in the net and staring down the long, rocky slope to the river. She saw Seth stretching and did the same before Guard herded them into line. Guard directed Seth after the leaders and followed him. Lee came next. At her own pace. She told herself she would not be hurried by the two hawkbeaks who brought up the rear.

She found she didn't need to worry. The hawkbeaks seemed at ease now that they weren't in the open, and speed didn't seem to be important. Good thing too. They picked their way along the upper edge of the talus slope over the rocky debris the rim had shed through the centuries.

Lee kept her eyes on the ground and picked her footing, always aware of the long, boulder-strewn slope below her. Not the place to fall. Somehow Guard's tail was always there when she needed a little support over a rough spot. At first she refused to touch him but, as she tired and he persisted, she took the help. Up ahead, Seth was on his own.

Lee turned that little puzzle in her head. Ever since they had been recaptured, Guard had treated her with more consideration than she could have expected. More than he showed Seth. He had consistently deferred to Weaver too. Subordinate by virtue of gender? Or some other cultural norm she didn't understand? Whatever it was, he hadn't shown her that deference before the ceremony.

The thunder stayed in the distance. Lee found herself wishing for a cooling shower. At least they were in the shadow of the rim now, not in the hot sun. Her feet hurt, rubbed raw in places by boots designed for riding. She had to think about each step, too tired for autopilot to keep her safe.

Evening engulfed the river canyon before the hawkbeaks came to a hanging canyon coming in from the side. It ran gently down from the left just below them before tumbling steeply to the river. The leaders scrambled down to it and wound upstream between clumps of whipbrush and screencane. Lee plodded on, her eyes on Guard just ahead of her and Seth in front of him. A few minutes later, the three hawkbeaks in the lead splashed across the wide, ankle-deep stream and clambered up a fresh scar on the side of the canyon where the recent storm had washed sand and gravel down.

Above them to the left of the scar, Lee saw a deep overhang of rock. Guard pointed his beak up the slide and made shooing motions with his hands. She looked up the steep scramble and then at Seth. With a shrug, he started up. She hesitated, measuring her exhaustion against the climb. Guard snaked his tail out, wrapped it around her arm, and towed her carefully but inexorably up.

Guard released her when they reached the base of the rimrock. She stumbled after him around a corner and stopped. She stood at one side of a great alcove sliced out of the cliff. She'd seen old, old pictures of places like this filled with multilevel houses of stone. No stone buildings here but to her right was a wall of woven-reed panels running parallel to the outside edge of the cave. The arching roof dwarfed the mat wall that was just high enough not to be able to see over.

"Wow," Seth said. "You could fit the Seven Wells barn in here twice."

Escorted by Guard and two of the hawkbeaks, they followed the mat wall past two curtained doors in it until it curved away from the front of the cave, and they entered a central plaza maybe fifty yards across. More mats closed off the far side and the back of the cave.

Villagers clustered together in the space, eight or nine adult hawkbeaks on the far side of the plaza and four adult fantails on the near side. Children peeked from behind adults. All eyes were on the two of them, the strangers.

A pack of knee-high creatures charged toward them. Lee flinched at the chorus of roars that echoed through the cave, almost deafening. She made out chitinous blue-green-yellow beetle backs over multiple legs as she was surrounded by the noisemakers.

She felt Seth's hand on the small of her back. "Notalions," he said in her ear.

"Notalions?" She'd heard the over-sized roars of the small predators often enough but never actually seen them before. She'd pictured something more like dogs than over-grown insectoids with armored heads and backs, soft yellow-green abdomens, runner's legs, and chameleon eyes on rotating bases.

Guard whistled sharply, and the pack silenced, running to weave around his legs and tail. He tapped the shiny shoulders with his tail tip then whistled again, a rapid trill. The pack trotted away toward the back of the cave.

Weaver stepped forward and stood tall. Guard strode to her, also upright but with his beak and eyes lowered a fraction below level. Weaver said something; he replied. She looked past him to Lee and Seth and gestured for them to come to her. Guard bobbed his head and stepped aside.

When Lee didn't move promptly, the two hawkbeaks behind her moved in, crowding her and Seth forward until Weaver held up a hand to stop them. Weaver reached out to straighten the satchel hanging from Lee's shoulder. She looked each of the humans in the eyes. No anger that Lee could see — the being's face stayed matte-black; her epaulet feathers lay flat.

Weaver said something, and Guard pointed a hand at Seth to wave him toward the hawkbeaks gathered across the plaza.

Seth put his arm around Lee. "We stay together," he whispered to her.

Guard's tail snaked around Lee's arm again and held her. The other two hawkbeaks closed in on Seth, grabbed him by the arms, and pulled him away. He dragged his feet and twisted, trying to break free. "Let me go."

Weaver held up her hand, and his captors stopped. Guard pointed one hand to Weaver and the other to Lee and brought his hands together. Then he pointed to Seth and to himself and used his beak to point across the plaza.

"Just go with them," Lee said. No point in getting in a fight they couldn't win.

"Are you sure?" he asked.

"Walk softly." She held herself as straight as she could manage.

He studied her face for a moment before nodding. "Okay," he said to Guard as if his captor could understand, and pointed across the plaza with his chin. Guard said something, and the two hawkbeaks released him. Seth walked ahead of them with Guard following behind.

Halfway across the plaza, a hip-high hawk-child ran forward, dodged around Seth, and squealed at Guard. Guard scooped up the youngster to ride on his back. Lee gaped openly, her exhausted mind slow to accept the child's welcome of someone who looked so fierce.

Weaver clicked her beak. When Lee looked at her, she pointed toward one of the curtained openings in the woven-reed wall. Lee forced herself to turn away from watching Seth and shuffled toward the doorway. If she could just rest for a while before Weaver had some task for her, just rest.

She pushed the fabric curtain aside and entered a space enclosed by reed mat walls on three sides and rock all across the back. Light filtered over the top of the mats. In the center of the space a tower of cane scaffolding supported shelves with baskets, bags, and various implements Lee couldn't identify without looking closer. On the floor under the shelves was a large, low-sided basket that seemed to be empty. Around the base of the tower were oddly shaped rattan chairs or chaise lounges, one on each of the four sides. They were very narrow at the lowest point and rose in a short, low arch on one end. The longer end swept up, widened, and curled over at the top. Lee couldn't picture how Weaver and her tail would sit on something like that.

Weaver led her past the central tower to the back corner where the mat walls met the rock. More racks lined the rock wall, with shelves above and mostly empty space waist-high underneath. Weaver pointed to a pile of rushes under the shelving. Lee pointed to herself and then the pile. Weaver bobbed her head.

Lee crawled under the shelves onto the makeshift bed. She had more head room than many ship-board berths, and she was too tired to quibble, even if she could.

When she sat down, Weaver pointed at her feet. Feet? Or boots?

Lee touched her boots. Weaver nodded and held out her hand. Lee struggled to pull them off her aching feet and handed them over. Weaver took the footwear and left her alone. She laid the satchel aside and stretched out on the rush bed. Their abortive escape had changed things at least. It brought them to a village, a very small village, complete with children. But no closer to home. And no closer to any clue to why these people wanted her and Seth.

Chapter 24

Lee

Eyes — the first thing Lee saw when she woke was four pairs of eyes peering at her from a few feet away. Four miniature Weavers, bodies poised to flee.

Lee had barely enough light to see around the room. The adult fantails reclined on their chaises — on their bellies, straddling the narrow seats with their tails draped over the low arches and their heads resting on the upper curves of the backs. Of course, how else would a tailed individual lie on a chaise?

She looked back at the young ones, and the littlest one squeaked. The largest tapped its tail on the little one's back. Silence. They stretched up straight and cocked their heads one way and then another curiously. They were featherless and slender compared to Weaver. Their faces were all eyes and blunt beaks. Their tails barely reached the floor.

Slowly Lee pushed herself up to sit with her back to the rock wall. That was too much for her audience. With squeals they scurried back to the basket under the tower, their nest apparently, safely surrounded by the adults. The adult nearest Lee raised her head and whispered something to the young ones. Their heads promptly vanished below the edge of their basket. The adult — was it Weaver? — stretched and dismounted from her chaise. She beckoned to Lee and walked softly to the curtained doorway.

Lee followed on bare feet. Her mouth was dry, and her stomach rumbled. She hoped that would be remedied before she was put to work.

Out in the cave, the sky was pre-dawn gray but light enough to let her see her surroundings. She looked straight out of the doorway across an apron of stone to the outer edge of the ledge. A row of tables filled the space.

To her right, the mat wall curved away toward the back of the cave. On the far side of the plaza, behind another mat wall, was where Guard and the others had taken Seth. Hawkbeak territory apparently.

It was a rockshelter, not a true cave. A wedge cut out of the cliff but not deep enough that daylight couldn't reach clear to the back of it. It was, she guessed, about a hundred yards from side to side. The plaza occupied the center third. The mat walls, just high enough to block sight, walled off rooms on each side and an area across the back. The center of the back half of the plaza was a work area with looms and weaving frames, bundles of reeds and cane, racks of nets, and rows of baskets. A broad aisle ran between the paraphernalia and the mat walls.

Weaver pointed Lee to one of the tables in front of them and gestured her down. Lee knelt. If she sat back on her heels, she felt like a child peering over the edge. It was probably just the right height for Weaver to sit at in her three-point squat. Lee stayed up on her knees, wishing for something between her and the rock.

The table was made of woven, split cane with bundled-cane legs. The table's surface was smoothed over with a thick layer of what Lee thought was palm-pine sap. How did they do that? The sap that riders used on horses' hooves stayed pliable, but this was iron-hard.

Weaver disappeared through a doorway in the mat wall. She came back out with a water container and plate of the usual fruits and vegetables, put them down in front of Lee, and went back inside.

Lee drank first, swirling the water around her dry mouth before swallowing. Too much hiking, not enough water the day before. She thought about a substantial rider's breakfast with spinxi eggs and tarbh ham. Oh, well. She took what was offered, starting with globeberries, tart and juicy.

She'd cleared half the plate when Weaver returned with two bowl-size baskets and a liquid-filled bag made of the cured stomach of something about swine-deer size. Weaver set them on the table, reached into one basket and pulled out a spiny pod big enough to fill her hand. She held up one of the flat cane pieces Lee remembered from the reed-splitting and used it to pop the pod open along a seam in the rind. Weaver dumped the contents into the second basket.

Lee looked to see what it was, expecting seeds, and grimaced. Grubs, the size of the end of her thumb, with yellow heads and white bodies fat from eating the heart of the pod. But it wasn't like she hadn't seen and eaten them or their like before — frequently in recent days.

Weaver handed her the flat cane tool and pointed at the basket. Lee picked up one of the pods gingerly and discovered the spines were soft enough not to stab her. She prodded one of the seams and twisted the splitter cautiously, afraid to break the cane. The pod popped open and spilled grubs on the table. Lee sighed and scooped them up with the empty pod to put them in the basket.

Weaver hung the bag of liquid from a cane rack at the end of the table and poured something over the grubs. Lee's nose crinkled. Vinegar like she'd used to marinate ribbon worms. The grubs curled up tight and sank to the bottom of the basket. Lee reached for another pod. Weaver bobbed her head. She watched for a minute before going back into what Lee decided must be the kitchen or pantry. She couldn't see any cooking area in the plaza.

As Lee split and emptied the pods, two more fantails appeared from the sleeping quarters, went into the kitchen, and came out with their own plates of fruits, vegetables, and small cakes that looked like pressed grain. They looked at Lee then walked away, going to the far front corner of the cave where vine trees grew up over the opening to create a sheltered arbor.

The fourth fantail herded the four juveniles out, saw Lee, and led the youngsters toward the arbor. Weaver came out of the kitchen with a tray. She waved Lee to her feet, handed her the tray, and pointed her after them. Lee walked across the long space with all the composure of a practiced server. Be nice to the customer no matter how you feel. She caught sight of hawkbeaks emerging from their doorway and watching her. Was Seth there, behind them?

She placed the tray directly in front of the fantail with the juveniles, took two steps back, turned, and marched back to Weaver. She glanced at the hawkbeaks out of the corner of her eye, hoping to see Seth, but no luck. The hair on the back of her neck stood up when a couple hawkbeaks followed her. Did they have their own kitchen or was that a shared area? She went back to her place at the table and continued opening grub pods without looking directly at them.

They went into the kitchen without paying any attention to her. They came back out a couple minutes later, carrying trays, and sauntered back across the plaza to join three others. They squatted in the space in front of their doorway to eat. No Guard and no Seth. Lee made herself relax her shoulders.

She emptied the last pod and stood up to stretch. Her knees ached from kneeling. Her feet hurt from miles of walking in boots designed for riding. She turned her back to the cave and looked out into the small canyon below. Bigger than the one where her prison-cave had been but just a small tributary to the Whitewater. If they had a boat, they could float away down the river all the way to Rocky Ford and then the Mardukai River and finally Portside.

Weaver brought her another basket of pods and a rolled rush mat. She dropped the mat to the floor next to Lee. Lee moved it into position to kneel on. Weaver bobbed her head, set the basket on the table, and left her alone. Grateful for the padding under her knees, Lee went back to removing grubs from pods.

On the other side of the cave, two hawkbeaks practiced fighting moves while four youngsters tried to imitate them. The largest of the juveniles only came hip-high on the adults. Half a dozen smaller hawk-children played a game that involved chasing and being chased by the notalions. But where were the "teenagers," the ones approaching adulthood?

Lee was nearly done with a second basket of the pods when a noisy group of hawkbeaks came onto the ledge past the arbor. In their midst, Seth stood out a head above them, shirtless and dirty but okay as far as she could tell.

Weaver clicked her beak sharply. Lee looked back at the pod in her hand. Dutifully she opened it and dumped its contents. When she looked up again, Seth was seated with Guard in front of hawkbeak territory. Two of the hawkbeaks strolled over, disappeared into the kitchen, and reappeared to carry loaded trays back to their companions. And Seth.

Weaver came out to check on her progress. When Lee popped open the last pod, Weaver whistled sharply. The two biggest fantail children trotted over with a water container and a basin-shaped basket, then scurried back to the arbor where it looked like story time or maybe lessons.

Weaver took the water and basin to the front edge of the cave, overlooking the small canyon. She waved Lee over and stepped away. Wash water? Lee poured water into the basin and scrubbed her hands together in it. With the worst of the vinegar smell gone, she dumped the water off the edge, hoping that was not forbidden, and poured fresh water into the basin to wash her face. When she finished, Weaver directed her back into the sleeping quarters without following her.

Any temptation to investigate got sidetracked by the sight of her saddlebags and blanket next to her pile of rushes in the corner. She couldn't believe it. They had given her back her own things, some of them at least. She wrapped herself in the blanket and pulled the saddlebags onto her lap. Like a gift, she held them and savored the anticipation before opening them, refusing to entertain thoughts about what it could mean.

Chapter 25

Seth

Seth sat among the hawkbeaks and ate from the plates they passed around from one to another. Since the first gray light, they had been repairing storm damage to a water system made of hollowed cane. They hadn't taken time for food until the job was done. They had kept him busy hauling lengths of cane while they artfully connected one to the next and glued them in place with good old palm-pine sap. Not exactly one of them — lack of common language made that hard — but they treated him better than he expected after the abortive escape attempt.

Across the plaza Lee was washing her face and hands. She looked tired and subdued, like she had in her role as 'Anni', Jerdix's meek clerk. He had hated the way 'Anni' had to grovel to that man. He didn't want Lee to fall into that old behavior. She needed to stand up for herself the way he knew she could.

All too soon, she went out of sight into the fantails' quarters. He pulled his attention back to the food. Guard took the last chunk of meat from the food tray and swallowed it whole. He and his fellows weren't equipped to chew. And time to chew put Seth at a disadvantage when sharing from a plate. He was going to have to learn to eat fast if he was going to get his share.

Guard rose to his feet, handed Seth the empty trays, and pointed to Weaver by the table across the plaza. Seth took the trays and delivered them, using the time to study the village under its sheltering rock overhang. He wondered if the fantails' side was as spartan as the hawkbeaks' area with simple cane racks and shelves for storage and a square of padded rush mats in the center they all slept on. Communal living.

Weaver took the tray and directed him back to Guard. Like a good errand boy, he did as she indicated. Weaver took the trays through a curtained doorway near the one Lee had gone through. He couldn't get a glimpse through either one to see what was inside.

The hawkbeaks he had worked with had dispersed except for Guard. The plaza was quiet. One fantail worked at a large loom, and a couple of hawkbeaks practiced their martial arts form. He watched them and thought about Lee's talk of fight nights. He studied their moves, the use of the tail, the reliance on kicks over punches. No grappling moves, but then they would be hard to throw with their weight in their legs and tail. His greater weight and reach against their speed, experience, and those tails — he didn't like his chances if he had to fight one of them.

He went back to Guard, a well-behaved prisoner. He admitted to himself that Lee's don't-kick-up-dust philosophy made sense at the moment. He could waste a lot of effort being stubborn and not gain anything except maybe bruises. He vividly remembered Guard's tail dumping him flat his first day in the prison-cave.

He was surprised at how gently they'd been handled during their recapture. In fact, Guard had been particularly helpful to Lee on the way back. Respectful almost, the way he was with Weaver. Always with eyes slightly down, maybe to lower the beak to be non-threatening. Clear deference. Seth had noticed the same with the other hawkbeaks around the fantails during the gathering before their escape.

Seth also recognized that the hawkbeaks had a definite hierarchy among themselves with constant interplay to reinforce it. But the signals were so subtle that Seth wouldn't have noticed if he hadn't been so used to reading tiny changes in a horse's body language.

When he reached Guard, the hawkbeak pointed him toward the two practicing the martial arts form. Guard said something to them that caused their crests to flare wide and low on their necks. The two stopped and beckoned Seth over.

They waited for him to reach them before beginning the form very slowly, just the first few moves that Guard had shown him. Seth suspected that the opening was designed as instruction in the most basic moves. Three of the older juveniles ran over, lined up next to him facing the adults, and followed along. The biggest of them came up to his hip.

Feeling like a clumsy giant, Seth copied them as best he could: overhand and underhand strikes with the fingers held together in a point, single front kicks, back kicks, then combinations of strikes and kicks to the front and back. No side kicks — couldn't they kick sideways?

Guard had taken him through all of those moves and stopped there. Seth quickly figured out why. The next move was a full spin with a tail sweep. Who needed to kick to the side when they had a tail to swing?

He substituted a spinning kick. That made an impression. He got slight head bows from the two adults before they went back to the beginning to start over. And moved on past the tail sweep to a double front kick while supported by the tail.

The best Seth could come up with for that was an attempt to kick, jump up and kick with the second foot as the first came down. That brought laughter from the juveniles with their short crests flaring. One of the adults snapped his beak, and the young ones stopped. Told to mind their manners maybe.

Determined, Seth repeated his spinning kick and the two front kicks. Better this time. He thought about trying a low-high roundhouse combination, keeping one foot planted, but decided to keep that to himself. He might need some surprises if he had to fight.

Guard whistled. Lesson over apparently. The two instructors gathered up the young ones and trotted off. But Guard took over and had Seth repeat the sequence through the spinning kick and the front kick combination, watching intently and bobbing his head slowly.

When Seth finished, Guard showed off the tail-sweep spin and double kick that Seth couldn't copy, ruffled his crest into place, and strutted back toward the door into the hawkbeak quarters, gesturing for Seth to follow. "Yeah, but let's see him ride a green colt," Seth muttered under his breath.

Guard held the curtain away from the doorway and waved Seth inside. He waited for Seth to go to the back corner and sit down on the sleeping pad that had been put there for him the night before — Lee's pad they had taken with them when they'd tried to escape. What had she slept on?

Guard left him alone and went back outside. Seth stretched out. He'd seen Lee, and she seemed to be okay. They might be prisoners, slaves even, but they were unharmed so far. Putting him to work he understood. Teaching him fighting moves made him think of the fight the storm had interrupted. He knew in his gut that he was going to have to finish that and sometime soon. Why? What was all this about? It baffled him.

There was enough space along the side of the room to practice the batayr forms. The practice with the hawkbeaks had made it clear to him that he needed to stretch muscles and tendons. Too much walking and being hauled around in a net left him stiff. He stood up. Lee used to accuse him of obsessing over his batayr practice as much as he did his work with young horses. Maybe, but the moving meditation kept him from chewing on what-ifs and maybes. He set his feet firmly on the stone and began.

He worked himself as he would work with some young horse, his whole world narrowed to what he was doing. He pushed aside his worry, the mental chatter. He moved in slow motion, pushing deep into the stretches until the stiffness and pain, the unevenness of his motions, eased.

The smell of roasting meat drifted in from outside, along with light thumps, scraping, and voices in conversation. The curtain slid back, and Guard stood in the doorway. He pointed at Seth and beckoned him out.

The plaza was busy with hawkbeaks and a couple of fantails moving the bundles of reeds, net racks, and other clutter from the center of the plaza and stacking them against the back wall. Looked like preparations for something more than a meal. Seth's shoulders started to knot. He pulled them down, working the muscles loose.

A sharp rattle on a hand drum brought the activity to a stop. The little ones ran past him into the hawkbeaks' quarters while the adult hawkbeaks spread out in an arc, making three-quarters of a circle about fifty feet across on their side of the plaza. Weaver, Lee, and three other fantails completed the circle on the far side.

Sixteen villagers counting Weaver and Guard. No sign of the two observers who had been present the night of the storm.

Guard led him into place between two of the hawkbeaks, across the circle from Weaver who stood next to Lee. She was equally spaced with the others in the circle, six or eight feet apart. He, on the other hand, had Guard right next to him on one side and another hawkbeak on the other. Making sure he didn't run for it?

The fantail next to Weaver rapped on a hand drum, a quick burst. Weaver raised her arms, and waves of blue and purple rippled across her face. She spoke to the assembly. The language was raspy, full of clicks and squawks, but almost musical in its rhythm. Seth couldn't begin to guess what it was all about except that it looked a lot like the night of the storm.

Weaver stopped; the drummer began a rapid beat. Seth braced himself as the hawkbeaks rushed him, surrounded him, and began their pogo stick dance. They shouted and waved at him to join them. Feeling silly, he bounced a few times. They whooped and sprang higher. So he gave it the best he could, surprising himself with how high he got with a few bounces. Pitiful by comparison, but he didn't have built-in springs like they did. It seemed to satisfy them though. The strange dance broke up, and they reformed the circle. Was he proving himself some way?

Across from him, Lee slumped and wrapped her arms tightly across her chest. Anticipating his coming defeat probably. He shook his head very slightly, lifted his chin, and brought his shoulders back and down. Slowly she imitated him, showing her tension in the way she clenched her fists. Seth exaggerated taking a deep breath. She copied him. He watched her pull her shoulders down and open her hands. "Steady," he muttered under his breath; he wasn't sure which of them he meant that for.

The drum began again, this time with a steady, rapid rhythm, the challenge drumming he had heard before the fight ritual that got rained out. His stomach twisted. He closed his eyes and felt the flow of air into and out of his lungs, deep and slow, blocking the panic. He straightened his spine and kept breathing. Lee smiled crookedly. If she believed he had it together, maybe he could fool the villagers.

Guard stepped into the circle and walked straight across to Lee. He hadn't done that the night of the storm. Seth's fists balled, but he stood still, all too aware of the villagers on both sides of him. The persistent drumming beat at him, a hard rain of sound that made it hard to concentrate.

Guard stepped around behind Lee, put his hands on her shoulders, and looked Seth in the eye. Weaver handed him a collar, an open weave three fingers wide, and Guard fastened it around Lee's throat with exaggerated movements. The drumming ran louder and faster, stopped for two breaths' time, then returned to a slow, steady tempo.

Lee reached up and tried to pull the collar off, but it stayed firmly in place. Guard made a show of checking the fit, like a man adjusting the halter on a horse. Seth took two steps forward. A look from Guard, and a slash of that snaky tail, stopped him. He glared but stayed where he was.

Guard strutted toward him, looked him up and down, and swaggered around him. The arrogant little rooster.

Don't let him rattle you! Seth heard that in his head as clearly as if Lee was standing at his side. Across the circle, Lee stood straight and still with one hand rubbing the collar and her eyes boring into him. He let his weight sink into his feet. He waited.

Guard faced Seth, upright crest feathers making him look taller. He began to bounce. Seth's heart thudded. No demonstrations today. What were the rules or were there any? Was Guard just trying to shake him or was Lee the prize?

Two could play that game. Seth ignored Guard's bouncing and swaggered — he hoped it looked like a swagger — into the circle. He tested the coarse sandstone underfoot, found it free of loose sand that could send him sliding. He strode over, stopped in front of Lee, and made a show of inspecting the collar. An open weave of rawhide with beads of a translucent, greenish stone he didn't recognize. The collar was wider in back than in front so it couldn't turn around her neck. It rested snug against her skin.

"Take care of yourself," he said. So much else he wanted to say. He didn't know if she wanted to hear it.

"Fight, don't spar." She locked her fingers together nervously.

He took her face in his hands, ran a thumb along her cheekbone, and resisted the temptation to kiss her. She didn't pull away. He said, "You might look a little more confident, even if you don't believe it. I could use the encouragement."

She managed a weak smile. "Stay in close. His power is in big kicks and tail sweeps."

"Right." He was out of time. Guard stalked impatiently back and forth. And he might never get another chance to tell her how he felt. "We should get new bracelets," he said. "If you want."

She slowly smiled. Working the worn horsehair bracelet from her wrist, she handed it to him. "Hold on to this for me until then."

He tucked the bracelet into his hip pocket. "Love you, Lee." Without giving her time to answer, he strode over to Guard where he waited at the center of the circle, crouched low, tail twitching. How did they start?

Guard stretched tall, then leaned forward, raising his tail. He switched it like a whip. The drumbeat built faster, louder. And stopped. Guard feinted with a kick. Seth stepped inside it and drove his left fist at Guard's body.

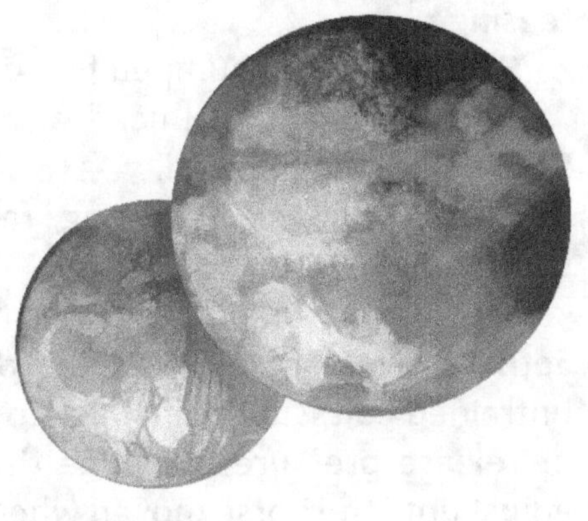

Chapter 26

Lee

Lee rubbed her bare wrist, her eyes glued to Seth and Guard in the middle of the circle of villagers. "I love you too," she whispered. She should have said so when she'd given him the bracelet. While she had the chance. So many chances the last few days, but they never talked about how they felt. As usual.

Don't hesitate. Fight. If he would. He whose success was in calmness. He couldn't win, not against Guard. Was there something else at stake, some status to be earned by fighting well even if he lost? She forced her knees to stay straight, her head to stay up, her lungs to draw in air.

Guard stood tall, his tail low. A heartbeat after the drums silenced, he opened with a kick, slow, almost teasing.

Seth closed in, thumped fist to ribs. Solid.

Guard grunted, bounced away, kicked. Thwack on Seth's side. Lee flinched.

They circled, slow, testing, feeling each other out. Like a held breath.

Lee leaned forward. It wasn't batayr she saw in Seth's movements. It was the dance he did with an untrained colt, subtle changes to either apply pressure or release pressure, to judge the colt's response and adjust until the horse moved when pushed without ever being touched.

Guard wasn't a horse. He didn't move away from Seth's pushing. He moved at Seth. Kicked; kicked.

Seth grunted; danced away.

Push in. Get inside. Lee threw her thoughts at Seth.

He was trying, but Guard blocked, kicked, pushed him back; strutted, head up, tail low and switching.

The hawkbeaks clacked, whistled, squawked.

Slow motion compared to the fight night. Why didn't Guard just finish it? He could.

Then Lee saw it. The attacks, the openings were all choreographed to lead Seth, showing what he had been taught, how well he'd been trained.

Guard straightened. Lee saw the opening, saw it suck Seth in.

Seth threw a low roundhouse, followed through with a high kick, a solid strike on Guard's shoulder. Not one of the moves Guard had shown him.

Guard spun, whipped his tail around.

Seth went down. Lee heard the breath go out of him.

Guard leaped in and set a clawed foot on Seth's throat.

Lee steeled herself, made herself watch. Not to the death — nothing she had seen made her believe it would be. But the fear haunted her.

Seth lay unmoving; Guard poised over him.

Beaks clicked all around the circle. The drums began, low, slow, steady. The hawkbeaks began to bounce, closing in around the two until she couldn't see Seth or Guard. Then Seth's head appeared above the others, rising and falling with them.

He was okay. She felt hollow — no hope, no fear, no relief. He had lost; they'd known he would. They were still captives; they still had no idea why or what came next.

The drums stopped, the dancers shouted, and the cluster dispersed. Seth stood straight across from her in the reformed circle, looked her way, and grinned. If he was injured, he gave no sign of it. She knew he wouldn't if he could help it, not in front of the villagers.

Weaver entered the circle, and Guard met her in the middle. She handed him another collar.

Guard dangled the collar from his hand and bobbed his head at Lee. She lifted her hand to the one around her neck. His crest feathers flared low and wide, and the skin around his eyes crinkled. He spun and strutted to Seth, reached up, and fastened the collar around the human throat. He shifted the collar until he was satisfied with its fit, then stepped into his place in the circle, leaving Seth alone.

Seth grabbed hold of the collar and tested it. Lee rubbed at her own and swallowed. Guard had claimed ownership of both of them now in front of the whole village.

Weaver beckoned Lee to the center of the circle; Guard brought Seth to join her. Conscious that every eye was on them, Lee touched him with only her gaze when she wanted to run her hands over every inch of him to assure herself he wasn't badly hurt.

The villagers closed in around them. Heads bobbed. Sapphire and amber eyes, beaks and feathers everywhere, all alike but different. Hands extended, touching them. So many hands.

Lee backed against Seth, her heart thudding. He wrapped his arms around her and sheltered her. She struggled to breathe. Guard and Weaver stepped in next to them and touched hands with those surrounding them. The mob broke apart. Lee leaned against Seth while her heart steadied.

As the villagers moved away, Guard herded Lee and Seth toward the back of the open area and motioned them to the ground. Lee went down on her knees.

Guard had to threaten with his tail before Seth knelt down with his shoulder touching hers. Then Guard stepped away and stood nearby.

Lee reached out to run her fingers lightly over a red patch on Seth's shoulder that would turn blue and purple soon. "How bad?"

"Nothing that won't heal," he answered, quirking a corner of his mouth.

The phrase she used when she didn't want to admit how much she hurt. "That bad, huh?"

"No, really." He squeezed her hand. "Nothing worse than bruises. I don't think he wanted to damage the goods."

Around them Weaver and the other villagers moved tables into a circle in the middle of the plaza. The children came running out from behind the mat walls; voices chattered; food was carried out.

"I can't figure this out." Lee spread her hands and looked around the plaza. "If we're Guard's slaves, why aren't we doing the work?"

"You're the trained Ranger. Aren't you supposed to know about interpreting other cultures?"

"I know it can get you killed if you aren't careful," she said. "Who knows how many customs we've already violated."

"Speaking of customs, the two groups seem to be mixing for a change."

He was right. All the activities they had seen so far had segregated the fantails from the hawkbeaks. Now they were breaking into groups of one fantail with three hawkbeaks and varying numbers of children at each table. The adults settled into the familiar three-point squat; children hopped up on stools. Conversations flowed around and between tables.

"Families?" Lee suggested. "One female with three males if we're right about gender."

"No idea." Seth put his arm around her waist. "I'm tired of puzzles. I'd like some answers."

"I would too." She shifted uncomfortably, feeling exposed under all those eyes. "What ...?" She put a hand to her neck where the stiff new collar firmly pressed. "These beads tingle. Odd sensation." She looked at his collar and ran a finger over the intricate lace of pale rawhide with a scattering of polished, translucent green stone beads intertwined. Extra width at the back kept it from turning around. A line of beads ran down each side of his spine. She felt her own and found the same pattern.

"Nice work," he admitted. "There's either some adjustment I can't see or these are custom designed to fit us."

"Much tighter and they'd be choking."

Lee felt invisible for all the attention the villagers paid to them. There had to be a purpose to their presence. The beings had put a lot of time and effort into taking and holding them.

"What did you say about spike roots?" she asked Seth.

"Spike roots? What are you talking about?"

"Hearing things, I guess." She looked around.

Guard joined Weaver at the table nearest them, along with two of the hunters who had brought them back. Lee heard a strange mix of words. "Working ... rrrwwwwkkk ... She kkkrrakk..."

Lee looked at Seth. He raised an eyebrow. "What?" he asked.

"You didn't hear that? I swear I understood about half of what Weaver just said to Guard."

"You're not making sense."

"Crazy. I know."

Lee heard a guttural sound from Weaver but somehow understood it meant "Good." Weaver crauked, and Lee understood "Soon."

Lee raised her hand to her collar. "Seth, I think this is some kind of translator."

"A translator?" Seth narrowed his eyes. "Then why isn't mine working?" he asked.

"I don't know. Maybe because I've had mine on longer. Weaver just said 'good' and 'soon'. Weird, like I hear her voice, but the words come out in Sol Standard."

"Maybe she just picked up a few words from us."

"No, I'm hearing her language, but I understand what she means." Lee sat down on her heels, thinking. How could these people possibly possess that kind of technology? But she knew what she heard. "Just wait and see if it happens to you," she said and concentrated on listening to the conversations around her. More and more became understandable, bits and pieces, like overhearing neighboring conversations in a public space. She didn't say any more until she felt Seth start.

"Crazy," he muttered. "Unbelievable."

Lee turned to Weaver. Weaver spoke to Guard, and Lee heard, "The devices are operating." Iridescence flickered across Weaver's face feathers.

Lee snapped her mouth shut. She glanced wide-eyed at Seth.

"Flaming frog-eels," he whispered. "How long have they been able to understand us?"

"All along?" She tried to remember when she had first noticed the chokers that Weaver and Guard wore.

The weird sensation continued, hearing a gabble of strange sounds but understanding more and more. Knowing she had some chance to communicate gave her confidence.

Weaver stood up and the conversations ceased. "Sisters and brothers," she said, looking around at the villagers. "Today our clan is gathered to celebrate, to share food and —" Her gaze, and everyone else's went to the corner of the plaza nearest the arbor.

"Flood and flames," Lee gulped. The two observers from the night of the storm stood there. Lee shivered at the sight. What was it about that fantail that she found so intimidating? She got to her feet and pulled Seth up with her. She was not facing this on her knees.

Weaver bowed her head to the newcomers. "Prime, welcome. We did not expect you."

"No?" Prime asked. "And why not?"

Prime? Was that what Weaver said? Name or title? Someone of authority in any case.

Weaver whispered something to Guard. He and the others at her table stood up and stepped away. Weaver walked toward Prime, her eyes lowered. "Food is prepared; the table waits. Will you eat with us?"

"I will not." Prime's face was dead-black without a flicker of color. "You will explain."

Lee couldn't understand the rest of the rapid-fire demand.

Weaver bobbed her head. "Yes, Prime. We have not yet finished the rituals."

"No matter. Bring the strangers." Prime marched to the arbor, shadowed by the hawkbeak who had come with her.

"Yes, Prime." Weaver turned to Lee and beckoned her. "Please come."

"Maybe we'll finally find out what's going on," Seth said.

"Careful," Lee said. "Don't push that one."

"I'll keep my eyes down," he said.

She nodded, glad he had picked up on that male behavior.

They followed Weaver toward the vine tree arbor where the children had gathered earlier. Guard came behind them. Lee's heart thudded, and she stayed close to Seth.

Prime waited for them. She reminded Lee of a commanding officer calling a subordinate on the carpet. Weaver approached with her head low. Guard waited behind Lee and Seth.

"You will get her answer to the question," Prime said.

"I have not yet explained to them," Weaver said distinctly. Lee wondered if she was speaking carefully to help them understand.

"Her answer," Prime repeated with a snap of her beak.

Weaver bowed her head, backed two steps away, and faced Lee. She held her hands up in front of her, palms toward her chest, and dipped her head. "Apologies for how we have treated you," she said. "We brought you here to ask for your help."

Chapter 27

Lee

Lee stared, stunned. Had she understood correctly? They were asking for help? From her? Anger flooded her. Then hope cleared her head. If they needed her, it meant she had power, and now, with the translator, she could communicate. She masked her rising confidence.

Seth didn't hold back his reaction. He met Weaver's eyes. "Help? After what you've done to us?"

"Silence the male," Prime said. The hawkbeak with her stepped forward.

Lee caught Seth's arm. "Let me do this."

He looked from Prime to her hawkbeak lieutenant. "For now," he said and placed himself at Lee's shoulder.

"Will she help or no?" Prime said to Weaver as if Lee wasn't there.

Lee stepped past Weaver to face Prime. "Explain what you want. Then I can answer." She put all the authority she could muster into her tone.

Weaver's hand touched Lee's shoulder. "Prime does not wear one of the devices," she said.

So Prime couldn't understand the words. But she understood submission. Weaver showed it. The hawkbeaks showed it. Lee wouldn't, not now. She kept her eyes on Prime's and told Weaver, "Translate for her."

Weaver bowed her head. "My new clan sister cannot answer until she understands what is being asked. I offer you the hospitality of my table while I instruct her."

Prime held Lee's eyes. "I will wait one degree's time." She stalked past Lee out of the arbor, followed by her companion, but not to the table in the plaza that Weaver had vacated when Prime arrived. Lee guessed that was a refusal of Weaver's hospitality.

"What does that mean — one degree's time?" Lee asked.

"The time it takes for one degree of planetary rotation, about four of your minutes. So listen, please."

Lee kept her surprise hidden. Degrees of rotation as a measure of time? Days made sense; hours could be measured with some kind of sundial; but individual degrees of movement was a new idea to her.

Seth brought her attention back to the real question. "What help are you asking for?" he asked Weaver.

Weaver held up her hand. "I will explain many things when there is time. For now you must remain silent," she said. "Only the females may speak." Guard, standing close by, bobbed his head.

Lee caught Seth's eyes. "Okay," she said. He nodded. She faced Weaver. "What help?"

"We need you to introduce us to your people, to shepherd us through that contact."

Lee let that sink in for a moment. A First Contact — an explorer's dream but a reality full of potential pitfalls. "Why would we speak for you? What do we know about you except that you have held us captive?"

Weaver bowed her head at that. "We do not ask you to sponsor us, just to introduce us. Your people plan a new satellite survey soon. That will reveal our presence. We would speak for ourselves before that happens."

Lee's jaw dropped. They shouldn't even comprehend the idea, or she had completely misjudged the culture.

Weaver's face rippled with flashes of purple and blue. "We do not have enough time to answer that fully but understand that we are not strangers to space. We are shipwrecked here."

Lee managed to breathe again. That explained a lot. She didn't miss Seth's little told-you-so grin. He had been sure from the start that they weren't from Carico.

Weaver went on before Lee could respond. "Also know that even though Prime joined the rest of the Council in agreeing to make contact, I think she did not believe we would succeed. Now she would prefer that you refuse."

So Weaver's people weren't all in agreement. Maybe she should just say no and give this Prime what she wanted. She didn't owe Weaver anything. But what would happen then, to her and Seth, not to mention when these people were found by the human settlers?

"I need to talk to Seth," she said.

"No time." Weaver looked toward Prime. "Trust me when I say it serves your interests best to say you will help."

"Even though that is not what your Prime wants?"

"Your help is of value whether she wants it or not."

And no help meant no value? Lee said, "Until I know more about your people and the situation, I shouldn't agree to anything."

"Is an introduction so much to ask?" Again Weaver glanced at Prime, then looked back at Lee. "You must hurry."

Lee considered what the best negotiator she knew, her father, would say. Probably to retain as much control of the situation as possible. "I will help you develop a strategy for contacting my people," she said. "I do not know if that will include me introducing you."

"So you say 'yes' but not to the question asked?"

Seth tapped Lee's foot with his, drawing her attention to Prime and her attendant approaching. Time was up. "How would you answer if you were in my position?" Lee asked Weaver.

Weaver bobbed her head. "With caution, as you do."

"I rely on you to translate."

Prime stopped only a step away from Lee, dominating with her size and her bearing, a commanding officer and an unhappy one. Prime clicked her beak. "The answer," she demanded.

Lee stood as tall as she could, keeping her eyes steady, drawing on her new sense of power. "I will help you plan how to contact my people."

Weaver translated verbatim.

Prime's beak snapped. "That is not what we ask," she said to Weaver.

Weaver started to answer, but Lee responded first. "I have not refused to help you." She waited for Weaver to translate before continuing. "In the time of one arc degree, I cannot know how to best assist you."

Prime's face went lurid purple. She looked past Lee as if she wasn't there and told Weaver, "She evades. She is of no value."

Lee's gut cramped with fear.

Weaver bowed her head low. "She is my clan sister and has demonstrated her usefulness as required."

Prime's cold eyes locked on Weaver. "They care nothing for the rituals."

Clan sister? So the ceremonies had been some kind of adoption. Lee followed Weaver's lead and lowered her head. "I will help my clan sister," she said.

Weaver straightened and translated, adding, "As the council agreed, I have initiated contact with representatives of the humans. With the information they will provide, we will improve the strategy. Is that not what you have taught us?"

Prime's tail slashed back and forth. "So be it. At this time tomorrow, the council will convene and hear your revised proposal. Then we will decide if we proceed or if we end this now." She stalked out of the arbor.

Her attendant hesitated, said something to Guard that Lee's device didn't catch, then trotted after Prime.

Lee watched as they crossed the plaza to an empty table, but not the one Weaver's family had vacated. One of the females hurried to fill a tray with food and place it in front of Prime while her escort stood back and waited. Apparently, they were staying.

Lee turned to Weaver. For all her confident front, she was confused and unsettled. She didn't like the feeling. "I think it's time you explained."

Weaver ruffled her epaulet feathers into place. "As I promised," she replied. "Come." She led the way to the table and stools where the young ones had spent the morning. She gestured to the stools. "Please, sit and wait. We were about to eat. I would let the others know to proceed without us." She left the arbor, but Guard remained.

Much as Lee wanted to talk to Seth, she wanted to do it in private, not in front of Guard. She raised a shoulder in a tiny shrug and tipped her head toward the stools. Seth dropped his head in a slight nod and escorted her over to sit, taking his place standing at her shoulder. "Do you know what you're doing?" he said with his back to Guard.

"Getting answers," she replied. "I hope."

He laid a hand lightly on her shoulder.

Weaver returned and squatted across the table from Lee, bringing her to Lee's sitting height. She spread her four-fingered hands on the table. "Thank you for your patience," she said. "The hearing facilitators do not handle names well so let us begin there. I am Eta'ak."

Lee heard it as a squawk punctuated by consonants with a break in the 'ah' sound.

"E-ta-ak," she attempted. "I am Lee. This is Seth."

"This is Trrk." Weaver touched Guard's arm.

Lee nodded and said, "We have been referring to you as Weaver because of your skill."

Weaver bobbed her head. "Ah, a nickname. You compliment me. Weaving is important. You may call me that. Eta'ak at home, but Weaver to the outside world."

"What name did you have for me?" Guard asked, tipping his head and narrowing his eyes.

Apparently the 'males-can't-speak' rule didn't apply away from Prime. "We called you Guard," Lee said.

"That is my task in this, to guard Eta'ak — Weaver."

Weaver spread her hands wide. "Welcome to Blue Canyon, home of the Kelok, and to this, the Village of Canes, where I am leader."

"There are other villages?" Lee thought there had to be with Prime's coming and going and the reference to a council.

"Five in all," Weaver confirmed.

Five villages; they'd seen sixteen adults in this one. That suggested around a hundred people. Not a big population.

"You called me your clan sister," Lee said. "So we are not prisoners?"

"I do not consider you to be."

Lee thought Prime might have a different opinion. "The rituals were an adoption ceremony?"

"We saw no other way." Weaver bobbed her head. "It is our custom to adopt new clan members through ritualized capture, carefully planned and scripted on both sides. Candidates are captured and brought into the village where they demonstrate how they will benefit the group by displaying some special skill. Since we had no way of explaining that to you, we had to improvise."

"That's why you had me plaiting mats and preparing food?" Lee asked.

"Yes. The custom goes back to a time in our distant past when the capture was forced, and survival depended on being useful to your captors." Weaver clicked her beak lightly.

"Fighting is considered useful?" Seth asked with raised brows.

"Our men fight," Weaver said. "It fulfills an instinctual need to establish their status and to compete. But now it must be done within the bounds of ritual. With a newcomer, outcome is less important than behavior."

"So my behavior was okay." Seth quirked his lips in a lop-sided grin and shook his head.

Weaver's face feathers flickered from black to violet and back. "You behaved honorably. And your escape attempt demonstrated admirable stamina and valuable knowledge of survival skills."

"Does my clan brother agree?" Seth asked, looking at Guard. "Did I fight well enough?"

"Not a fight. A demonstration," Guard said. "You were adequate."

Weaver's faced flickered with color. "As I said, our males are competitive."

"Ours too, sometimes," Lee said. She pointed Seth to the stool next to her. She had so many questions that she struggled with where to start. "How did you select us for your adoption?"

"Opportunity," Weaver replied. "We were watching, and you came within our reach."

"You took a big chance. You might have gotten someone who wouldn't even consider your request." What if it had been Ike, not her, who had survived the stampede. Lee tried to picture his reaction.

"We knew we would have to adjust our plans to fit the person. We might have simply let another go to carry word of our existence to authorities, though that would hardly give us the control of the meeting we would prefer. But fortune was with us. We had heard of you. We knew that you have traveled beyond the bounds of this world. We believed you would listen to us." She looked at Guard, standing beside her. "This one and I conspired to bring you here and carry out the adoption process as well as we could so that we could communicate clearly." Weaver fingered her own choker, similar to the ones Lee and Seth now wore. "Prime would not allow us to give hearing facilitation devices to strangers."

Seth confronted not Weaver but Guard. "You kidnapped us to get an introduction?"

Guard's feathers bristled. "We kidnapped *her* to carry our message. We took you to keep you from interfering."

Seth stood up. "And Ike? He's the one who died, or had you forgotten him?"

Weaver held up a hand.

Guard stepped back. "We only wanted the tarbh to disturb the camp and distract the two. We did not expect the animals to run as they did."

Lee tightened her hand on Seth's arm. So they had caused the stampede. And Ike's death.

Weaver spread her hands, palms up. "We would not have gone to these lengths if we did not believe it was critical to our survival. We regret the death of the elder."

"He was..." Lee considered her words. "He was of my clan, and I grieve for him."

Seth laid his hand on her back. She leaned into it, taking the comfort he offered, and said, "Why not just show yourselves and explain your situation?"

"How?" Weaver replied. "Even without the language barrier, what reception would we have gotten if we had walked into one of your towns?"

Lee tried to picture Weaver and Guard walking into Portside without warning, intruders on a Sol-Terra Alliance world. The little band of refugees would be swept up in a mass of red tape that would stretch from the Sol-Terra Alliance all the way to the Interstellar Coalition.

"Are you asking for recognition by Carico's government, or the Alliance and Coalition?" Lee asked.

Weaver bobbed her head. "We seek to be considered settlers here on Carico. We do not wish involvement with your Alliance of human worlds or the Coalition that includes many species."

"You want to be left alone, isolated?" Lee asked. She didn't know how they could avoid word getting out to the Alliance and the Coalition. "You don't want to be able to travel beyond your villages, or off world? To have access to resources beyond what these canyons offer?" Lee began to realize how complex this could get.

"Perhaps in the future, but we would begin here. Once we establish our place on this world, we can look beyond," Weaver said. She rose to her feet. "We have much to discuss but it can wait until tomorrow when you have had time to think. This day has already been long and tiring, and we still must complete the rituals so that Prime will have to accept you as members of the clan."

"What is left to be done?" Lee asked. What more was there? And under Prime's cold eyes?

"Nothing too difficult." Weaver's face rippled purple and blue. "We have yet to share the meal that has been prepared, but do not be concerned. I will bring food here and tell you our story while we eat."

Counterpoint

Eta'ak

This is the story that I told them, the same that we tell to our children and to ourselves lest the memories die.

Somewhere on the other side of the rumpled fabric of space and time lies the world that gave us birth, a harsh mother that shaped us for survival and pushed us out like hatchlings from the nest. The vastness of space became our home. Our ancestors built huge city-ships that never touched a world. From them our shrewd women ventured out in smaller ships to trade and transport goods among others in our region of space, always supported and defended by our valiant men.

The Long Flight was such a ship. Under the skilled leadership of our Prime and her Second, it traversed the systems. But changes came, as change is wont to do. Our city-ships competed among themselves for dominance. And those on the trade vessels were no longer always welcomed on any but their home ship, even for maintenance.

To travel the stars, one must risk following the twisted threads through other-space between place-times, for at light-speed it would take lifetimes. But in other-space, an error in navigation that sends a ship along the wrong thread is disastrous. And that is what happened to the Long Flight. Too long without repairs brought critical components to failure. When we emerged from the tangle of other-space, we could not find a single identifiable point by which to guide our return even if the Long Flight could have undertaken the trip.

Our scanners showed technologically sophisticated beings already inhabiting a tiny area on one continent of this world. We used the moons to hide our presence and, one pinnace-load at a time, we stripped the ship of what we could, exhausting our fuel as we did. Once the Long Flight had nothing left to offer us, it was flown into the sun. The only evidence of our presence we left was a carefully disguised communications array on the smaller moon. And we hid ourselves here among these canyons, close enough to the First-Comers to make contact if we determined it was safe to do so. We have learned to live *on a planet surface but paid the price in blood and sorrow.*

-From the Archives of Eta'ak, Information Analyst, sometimes known as Weaver

Chapter 28

Lee

"And here we stay," Weaver said. "Beyond any hope of returning to our city-ship, our birth-clans, all things that we knew. So ended one weaving, and we laid the strands for a new one."

Lee shivered at the thought. Jumps that went wrong, bringing ships out hundreds or thousands of light years from where they were headed, were rare with faster-than-light travel but the very thought gave travelers nightmares. "How long ago?" she asked.

"Ten planet-years. These canyons have concealed us while we studied your people, intending to make contact when we knew more."

Lee looked out of the arbor over the secluded canyon. How had they been studying Carico's settlers? Weaver had said something about a communications array on Damele. "I can understand your caution but ten years? Why not sooner?"

"Distrust," Weaver answered. "Some among us believe we should remain hidden. Some even regret not choosing to land on the far side of the planet. But we are here, and our children should not grow up ignorant of the wider universe."

Lee thought of the playful young ones. "All your children have been born here?"

Weaver bobbed her head. "Correct. Normally all hatchings would be on city-ships. But here, we must assure the future."

That explained the lack of teenagers, Lee thought. "I agree that children should have opportunities," she said. "And the Interstellar Coalition might be able to help you get home."

Guard spoke for the first time, his crest quivering upright. "We have made this place ours, paid for with the blood and bones of those who failed to survive those first years. Yes, we want much of what we have lost — technology to ease our lives, the freedom to travel the star lanes — but not at the cost of *this* home we have built."

Weaver laid her tail over Guard's like Seth would lay a supporting hand on Lee's arm. Her face feathers flared purple. "I believe that few of us would go back now if we could. It has been a long time, and the political situation was unstable when we were lost. We want to keep what we have built here. Although born a ship dweller, rarely setting foot on any planet, I, for one, enjoy free air and rain and dirt beneath my tail."

"How have you managed to avoid discovery?" Lee asked.

Colors played across Weaver's face as she hesitated.

Seth answered for her. "No one was looking."

Weaver's head bobbed. "Precisely. But the planet-wide survey will change that. We will not remain unknown for much longer, and we are few and uninvited. Our council agreed that controlling the initial contact is the only strength we have." She rose and walked to the arbor entrance, looking out to the village. "I have worked hard to bring that about."

Lee nodded. "And you want us to be liaisons between your people and ours."

"As I said earlier, only to introduce us, to open the way for us to speak for ourselves."

"That's all?"

"It is all we hope for. But having one such as you who knows what lies beyond this world — you are better suited than many to advise us."

"How do you know who I am?" Lee asked.

"We watch news feeds from Portside. You were prominent in those three years ago."

News feeds. What next? Truth was the Jerdix affair was only prominent briefly. Now her influence was non-existent beyond a tiny handful of people, and she didn't want to raise unreasonable expectations. "I'm still a newcomer to Carico." She turned to Seth. "Where do you think we should start?"

Guard's tail slapped the floor. "You ask him?"

"Of course," Lee said, puzzled by the reaction. "He was raised here. He knows more about Carico's government than I do."

Weaver laid a hand on Guard's shoulder. "She asks him as I would ask you if there was a question of technology or hunting." She turned back to Lee. "With us, the women have the skill as diplomats and politicians. We are the strategists. Our men are tacticians. It is sometimes hard to remember the same is not true for others."

Lee exchanged a glance with Seth. That was settled — one species. Weaver was female; Guard was male. But the gender segregation ran counter to Coalition standards and could complicate any official recognition on Carico.

Lee jumped to the heart of it and asked, "You prohibit men from leadership?"

"Certainly not," Weaver said, sounding upset. "They lead in many things."

"But not in government?" Lee continued.

Seth spoke up. "Carico's charter requires equality. That means all adults must be eligible for elected positions like district arbiter."

Weaver dropped her head and studied her hands for a moment. "When I say that Guard is a tactician, not a strategist, I do so with great respect. We fill the roles we are best at. Our survival depends on teamwork between our genders. You have only to look to understand how different our women and men are from one another."

"Forgive me," Lee said. "We have a lot to learn about each other."

"That is true." Weaver pointed her beak at the other fantails, all except Prime, walking past the arbor and out of the cave. "But let us wait to discuss strategy until morning. You have much to think about," she said. "The afternoon is hot. Please join us at the baths."

"And him?" Lee asked with her hand on Seth's arm. "Does he come too?"

"With the men."

"I would like to talk privately with him first." Lee tested a boundary. "Now, briefly."

Weaver hesitated then said, "Certainly. We will wait for you." She left the arbor. Guard followed, his crest wavering at half-staff, not agitated but not happy either.

Seth watched until the two stopped a little ways outside the arbor. "You are actually thinking about helping them."

"Do we have a choice?" she asked.

"Just tell them we're leaving," he said, keeping his voice low. "See what they say to that."

"I don't know about these two, but Prime is not going to let us walk away." Lee remembered the chill she'd felt when Prime had said she had no value. "Look, one thing is certain," she said. "They will show up on the satellite survey. Even if all the villages are tucked away like this one, they have done something that will show up as a change from the last imagery."

"And your friend Adel will find it."

Lee almost choked. "The perfect career builder, except she'd probably get somebody killed in the process." She shook her head. "You might not have noticed but unless she's dealing with someone she can seduce, she's not much of a diplomat."

Seth hesitated before answering, and Lee wondered momentarily about how well he knew Adel. He looked her in the eye and avoided the subject. "Then you and I will have to ride this out. At least we have moved up from captives to adoptees."

"Bottom of the local hierarchy no doubt." She ran her finger over the beginnings of bruises from his fight with Guard. "Be careful, okay?"

"You too."

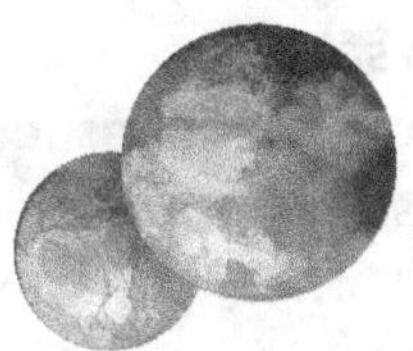

Lee followed Weaver past the arbor and out of the main cave on a narrow path against the cliff. She carried her saddlebags over her shoulder, everything she needed to get clean for the first time in days.

Weaver led her into a slot canyon, a deep, narrow gallery of aqua-colored sandstone frozen in ripples and sinuous curves. The afternoon sunlight barely penetrated the slender opening to the sky but painted the walls in light reflected back by the pools of water on the floor until the whole slot glowed. When a cloud slid over, the sharp contrasts vanished so that it was hard to tell wall from floor. A fantastical place.

They rounded a curve, and the floor of the slot widened out, like the bottom of a bottle. In the center of the floor, the trickle of stream fed a circular pool some twenty feet across and waist deep. To one side, Lee saw a system of overhead pipes made of hollowed cane stems, held up by scaffolding of the same material.

"The water should be hot now," Weaver said. "The storm damage has been repaired." She showed Lee how to turn on the water from the pipes, pointed out towels hanging from the scaffold, and handed her what looked like a peeled stalk of some kind. "Soap plant," she said. "The outer layer cleanses when wet. Save the inner fibers. We make cordage from them."

"Thank you," Lee said.

"Join us when you have washed." Weaver left her and walked a few steps to the pool where the other three females and the fantail youngsters already soaked.

Lee pulled one of her fabric wraps from her saddlebags, turned on the water long enough to soak it, then scrubbed it thoroughly with the soap plant. The fibers produced a surprising amount of lather and smelled wonderfully spicy. She rinsed the wrap and hung it from the scaffolding near the towels. Something to put on when she was finally clean.

Lee turned her back to the aliens in the pool, uncomfortable under the eyes of the Keloks. That was what Weaver had said they were called. She stripped off her filthy tank top and pants. The top was beyond hope, but she washed out the tattered pants and hung them with the wrap.

Armed with the soap plant, she turned the water on and stood under where it ran from many small holes in the pipe overhead. Hot water, almost too hot, ran over her as she scrubbed. It carried a sludge of soap and grime into a depression in the stone floor that took it somewhere away from the clear stream.

She shampooed her hair twice and then a third time, massaging through from root to end until it squeaked. She wished she had a stiff brush to get at the dirt ingrained into the soles of her feet and around her fingernails. She had to settle for repeated applications of the spicy-scented soap plant. Finally she quit scrubbing and just stood under the water for a minute before forcing herself to step away. However the Keloks heated their water, they seemed to have plenty of it.

She stifled her reluctance to face the strangers naked. Not that they would care or even know the difference, but she felt exposed and totally vulnerable. Nothing to do but put on her most confident face and join Weaver, three other females, and four girl-children in the pool. The adults lounged against the sides while the little ones swam and splashed in the middle. Everyone stopped and stared at her as she slid into the cool water.

Weaver's face feathers rippled blue and black. "Sisters, welcome Lee," she said. They were taller than Lee was by inches, closer to Seth's height, and took up far more room in the pool with their bulk and tails. Each differed a little in the tone of their bronze-plum skin and amber eyes and had features distinctive enough for Lee to tell them apart.

Weaver introduced each of them. Two bobbed heads and murmured welcomes uncertainly. One stayed silent, drew away to the far side of the pool, and looked at Lee with hooded eyes. Not a fan of hers, or maybe of Weaver's whole plan.

The children drew against the adults, peeking out at the strange creature who had invaded their play. "Why doesn't she have a tail?" one of them whispered, wide-eyed.

Weaver put her arm around the child and answered. "Remember what I told you about our new clan sister? That she is a different species than we are but still a person?" Weaver leaned closer to the child. "And she can understand what you say even though you cannot understand her." As always with the translator device, Lee heard the strange language but understood what was said.

The little one hid her face behind Weaver. Weaver stroked her gently. "Now go ahead and play. Which of you can stay under longest?" she challenged. "Show us." The children edged away from the adults and ducked under. By the time they sputtered back to the surface, they had half-forgotten Lee and continued to try and best each other's time. Maybe the males weren't the only competitive ones, Lee thought.

Weaver asked the others about routine things, how projects were progressing, what food sources were almost ready to pick, but the others were reticent to say very much. Lee schooled herself to sit silent and still, unsure how she could excuse herself from the awkward situation. She didn't believe her new status meant she was free to move around as she pleased, but she needed rest before she fell asleep where she sat.

She waited for a break in Weaver's attempts at conversation. "Please," she said. "May I return to the village? I am very tired."

Weaver bobbed her head. "Of course," she said without translating Lee's request for the others. She stood up and hopped out of the pool, water streaming from her smooth skin. Under the relieved eyes of the others, Lee climbed out and walked to where her clothes hung drying by the towels.

The towels were squares of fabric about the length of her forearm on each side. She discovered they didn't need to be big to dry her off. They proved very absorbent.

She pulled the wrap around herself, turning it into a dress, picked up the rest of her things, and made herself amble casually past the pool to where Weaver waited. She had learned one thing about these beings — rituals didn't necessarily mean acceptance. Not so different from humans in that.

She followed Weaver out of the slot canyon, along the cliff, and back to the village, wondering if Prime would be there, waiting, watching. The sun was dropping to the west, washing just the front edge of the giant alcove in gold. The village was quiet, empty. Apparently the men were still gone wherever they went to bathe.

Instead of the women's quarters where Lee expected to go, Weaver led her to the back of the plaza where several doorways opened in the mat walls. One in the middle of the line had a fabric curtain hanging across it. Weaver shooed away the pack of notalions from where they sprawled in front of the doorway.

"Your things are stored here," Weaver said. "I am returning them to you." She tapped the curtain. "You and the male may occupy this room together. That is something a mating couple would do for a short time."

"You think Seth and I …" Lee stopped. She had no idea what that meant in the context of such a segregated community.

"I think it will keep you out of Prime's view and will give you time to talk in preparation for our discussion tomorrow. My observations of your broadcasts make it clear that roles among your people are much different than among mine. Here his contributions will be better accepted coming from you."

"I will keep that in mind."

"The men will return soon. When they do, I will see that food is brought to you. Trrk — Guard — or I will come for you in the morning."

Lee got the message — don't run around unescorted. With Prime and her attendant somewhere in the vicinity, Lee decided she wouldn't argue that point; not yet. And she guessed that the notalions, quiet for the moment, would let the whole canyon know if she left her room.

Weaver held the curtain aside. "I regret the path we had to take to be able to communicate with you. Rest easy. You will not be disturbed. We have much to discuss tomorrow."

Lee half-bowed her head and stepped through the doorway. Weaver let the curtain fall behind her.

Lee looked around the tiny room in surprise. Their bedding was spread over a pile of reed mats against the back wall. A small table sat just inside the door. Along a side wall, saddles and packs were stacked. It looked like all their equipment, hers, Seth's, and Ike's. Ike's ...

Lee stepped forward to check through it and felt something beneath her bare feet. She looked down at a copper-red hide that covered the floor, a full horsehide with the hair on. "Oh," she murmured. "Pokey." Ike's pack horse — the hide she had worked on early in her capture, now tanned and soft.

She dropped to her knees and stroked the sleek hair. Ike, Pokey. How were she and Seth supposed to get out of this alive?

Chapter 29

Seth

Seth discovered that male bathing meant a swim in the river. The Keloks swam like fish, even the littlest of them. Swimming wasn't a skill Seth had much practice at, but he did manage to get clean and cool off without drowning himself. Returning to the village, he trailed behind the others except for Guard who brought up the rear. The scrambles, first from the river up to the hanging canyon in front of the village and then up the steep slope to the cave took about all the energy he had left.

When they reached the plaza, Guard pointed him away from the men's quarters and said, "Come."

Seth stopped. He'd had enough surprises for one day.

"Come," Guard said. "It is good."

Seth sighed and followed him to a curtained door at the back of the plaza. Guard held the curtain aside. Seth stepped through into a little, mat-walled room. The curtain fell behind him.

Lee was sitting on a hide on the floor, wearing one of her wrap dresses, her hair wispy in the dry air. She looked refreshed, but sad. She held a little leather-bound notebook.

"Are you okay?" he asked, dropping to his knees next to her on the hide.

"Pokey," she said. "Ike's pack horse."

Seth ran a hand over the horsehair. He remembered the steady little sorrel gelding. "I wondered about him when he wasn't with Tinker," Seth said. "What happened?"

She shrugged. "I don't know."

"I hope the rest of the horses are all right."

"Me too." She looked up. "I found Ike's journal in his saddlebags. Read the last entry."

Seth took the little book. The writing wavered across the page unlike the neat, tight script of earlier entries.

She vanished. Girl wouldn't have left me like that. Someone took her, and I'm too battered to go looking. So proud of her. Just want her to have what I had with Lori, my lovely Lori. So much alike. Should have told her she was my grand-niece.

The writing trailed off there. "Grand-niece?" Seth asked.

Lee shook her head slowly. "My mother had an Aunt Lori. 'Lovely Lori' — I had no idea."

"You can ask your Aunt Teri when you see her." Seth closed the book and handed it back to her.

"Yeah, *when* I do." She stroked the cover of the book and set it aside. "Hey, we have a bed." She waved a hand toward the back wall. "And our gear."

"Everything?" He looked at the pile.

"Looks like it, but I haven't gone through it yet."

"And they're letting us stay in here, not separating us?"

"Weaver says it's a place that 'mating couples' use." She managed a crooked grin. "Her excuse to get us away from Prime and let us talk."

He let her divert him from the 'mating' opening. "Okay." He stood up and offered her his hand. She took it and pulled herself to her feet. He let go and stretched with care, favoring his ribs.

"How badly are you hurt? Let me see." Her eyes ran over him, stopping at the red blotches that would start to turn purple shortly. He was shirtless as he seemed to be most of the time these days.

"Satisfied?" he asked.

She ran her hand over the largest bruise, low on his left side. "Is that the worst?"

"It is." He could think of other places she could touch him like that, if he wasn't almost too tired to stand. He brought his mind back to practicalities and opened the nearest pack box. "We'll have to repack," he said.

"Looks like they just put things in any way they would fit."

"The gear …" Lee looked around at the packs against the wall. "Beulah! I didn't even think about Beulah."

Oh, yeah, Ike's legendary yeasty. "Where is it?" he asked. "Which box?" He helped Lee dismantle the pile. Inevitably, the pack box she keyed in on was on the bottom. He stacked the rest back out of the way while she unloaded the contents.

"Here," she said. She brought out the yeasty crock.

"Well?" he asked.

"I don't know," she said. She opened the crock. "It smells okay but looks flat."

Seth laid a hand on her shoulder. "Lots of people have clones from Beulah."

"But this is the original. He and his wife started her when they got married."

"Lori. What happened? The pandemic?" he asked.

"Yeah," she said. "He lost his wife and baby both. I just found that out a couple days before …" She let that hang. "Get me the water bottle."

He handed it to her. "What are you going to do?"

"Feed her." She pulled a bag out of the pack box and took a handful of nutgrass flour from it to put in the crock, then added water. She found a small spatula and mixed the additions into the sticky batter. She covered the crock and left it on the table. "Come on, Beulah," she whispered. "For Ike."

"Do you want to sort through all this now?" he asked.

"Can it wait?" She stumbled to the bedding and let her legs fold.

"Sure." He came over and sat down next to her. "Hey, things are looking up. We have everything but the horses. And you got your shower."

"I did. How about you?"

"Swimming hole," he said with a quirk of his mouth. "I think I'm becoming one of the boys, but they say I can't really swim. No tail."

"I didn't know you could swim at all."

"I can keep my head above water, barely." He grinned. "Was there hot water?"

"Plenty. First hot shower I've had since your place. But I don't think all the women approve of me."

"Oh? Well, I approve." He remembered holding his breath when she stood up to Prime. Big change from her arguing for not kicking up dust. "Not a trace of 'Anni'."

She hesitated at that reminder of her past. "It helps to be able to communicate."

"Yeah. And they aren't from Carico. That much is clear."

She crossed her arms. "If we believe Weaver's story of a navigation failure."

"Hey, aside from a primitive, planet-bound tribe not being able to make up such a story, they have these." He touched a finger to the device she wore around her neck. "They also have feathers, two eyes, they even bleed red, in case you didn't notice that one good hit I got in on Guard. None of Carico's higher life forms have any of those."

She shook her head. "You're right. How did I miss that?"

"Maybe it didn't stand out as much to you as to me," he said. "You're used to seeing a variety of non-humans and animals from other planets."

"They must have quite a story to tell. Amazing that they survived, going from living on a ship to these canyons."

Seth cut off his response when the curtain shook, held by a clawed hand. When he pulled the curtain aside, Guard stood there with a cup-size basket in hand.

"For the bruises," Guard said, holding out the basket.

Seth took it and recognized the smell of herbs common in liniment and ointments used by the human settlers. "Thanks."

"We have much work to do, to discover how a tailless one might become a fighter, a proper clan brother."

"Now?" How much more could the day hold?

"Not now." Guard's crest flattened and spread fanwise, a gesture Seth was beginning to think was a smile. "Tomorrow maybe, while the women talk." He strutted away.

Seth turned back to Lee. "See, one of the boys."

"Give me that." She held out her hand. He gave her the ointment and stretched out, face down, on the bedding. Her fingers pressed into his skin, massaging the muscles underneath. She was slow where normally she would be brisk. It was all he could do to stay awake until she reached one of the bruises, and he flinched.

She lightened her touch. "Sorry."

He looked over his shoulder at her. "Why did you promise to help them?"

"Like I said, I don't see any other way out of this."

He nodded. "Something Guard said makes me think Prime sees us going straight to the Assembly to introduce them."

"She would want to go to the top. Leaders speak to leaders, not plebs like us." She worked the ointment into his neck. "Do you have another idea?"

"Maybe, but are we sure we should help them?" He rolled onto his side. "People ought to be able to hold what they've built — in principle. But what kind of neighbors will they be?"

"What? I thought you were one of the boys?"

He sat up and crossed his legs. "I'm not ready to invite them home for dinner with my family. Hard to forget being held captive."

"I can't argue with that," she said.

Thinking about the settlers being studied unknowingly for years gave him an itch between his shoulder blades. "Weaver seems pretty familiar with us. But what do we really know about them?"

"Very little." She stood and put the ointment on the table. "But they are here, and they will be discovered. We can't just wish them away."

He knew she was right about that. "Well, all Weaver asked for was an introduction."

"All I promised was to help them figure out the best way to make contact."

"All, huh?" He stretched out again. "Maybe if we sleep on it, we'll have some brilliant plan."

But he didn't sleep, not well. Sometime in the middle of the night he woke with a start, still half-lost in a dream he couldn't remember. He lay still, staring up at the rock ceiling overhead, sorting out where he was.

Next to him, Lee turned over and curled on her side with her back to him. The village was quiet. Not silent — he could hear movements of the residents, far distant thunder, the murmur of the river in the main canyon, the whisper of a breeze in the vine trees outside the cave.

No air moved through their little room. Careful not to disturb Lee, he got up and pulled back the door curtain. He could make out a lone male Kelok squatting at the front of the plaza, barely visible in the moonless middle of the night. A few feet in front of the door, a notalion lifted its chameleon-eyed head and watched him. He stepped back, and it lay down again. He got a saddle pad, dropped it just inside the doorway, and sat where a tiny tickle of air brushed against him.

"Everything okay?" Lee asked.

"Sorry, did I wake you?"

She got up and came over to sit beside him. "Maybe. Now my mind's racing."

"This is all way beyond my experience. The faster we can hand it — them — off to someone else, the better."

"But who?" she asked. "I don't see any way of keeping the Alliance and the Coalition out of it."

He looked out at the quiet plaza. "I've been trying to sort that out, the whole big political thing." For most of his life, what went on beyond Carico had never seemed very important to him. "What's their role in something like this?"

"The Interstellar Coalition allocates resources, like habitable planets, among its members," Lee said. "So they approved a trial area on Carico for settlement, and granted it to us humans through the Sol-Terra Alliance."

Seth thought back to his history and civics classes in school. "Okay. And the Alliance put the settlement effort out for bid. A private consortium won and mounted an expedition. That was sixty-eight years ago this coming Settlement Day." Now he was on more familiar ground. "Those first settlers, including our grandparents, set things up so the districts elect arbiters to settle local issues, and the arbiters send representatives to the General Assembly."

"And the Assembly's first responsibility is to make sure Carico is on track to meet the terms and conditions of the settlement plan, right?" Lee asked.

"That and mediate when districts need help to settle something." Seth couldn't think of anything in the plan that covered unknown alien castaways. And the Assembly didn't meet until fall. "It's the Planetary Administrative Officer who runs the day-to-day business," he said.

"The PAO — Charlyn Emmerling. I met her when I was in Portside for the plan review conference."

"Where do the Rangers fit into this?" he asked.

"The unit here now is contracted to consult and advise on ecological issues relating to the settlement plan, not handle inter-species relations, but Vinz would do the best he could to help until Carico requests a contact negotiator."

"So Adel Verlane has no authority?"

"That's never stopped her before." Lee dropped her head on his shoulder. "I don't want to talk about her."

He didn't either. The feel of Lee against him pushed away all thought of alien first contacts and Ranger advisors. "This afternoon did you mean it? About new bracelets. Or did you just think I was going to die?"

He felt her tense. She lifted her head. "I meant it. But do you really want to talk about it now, or do you just think we might not get out of this?"

Bounced it right back at him. Okay. He answered without hesitation. "Maybe these collars can substitute."

"Somehow I don't think they meet the intent since they are just on loan."

"There should be some leather lacing in my gear."

She eased away from him. "Maybe we should wait a little."

"Until life is back to normal?" he asked. As if he even knew what normal was.

"Well, at least a little more settled."

If that was what she needed, he could wait. The bracelets were just symbols, anyway. Somehow he meant to come out of this together with Lee for good. "About the strategy," he said, "how long before the satellites are in place, and these villages are discovered?"

"A couple of months probably. Plenty of time for us to get things rolling. The first meeting will establish their existence. After that discussions can take as long as needed."

"We could be home in five or six days," he said, "if we had the horses." He wondered if they had already found their way back to his place or if they had stayed around Stampede Spring. "It's a long walk otherwise."

"That's if Prime will let us to go alone," Lee said. "I have a feeling she won't like the idea."

"Probably not." He didn't think Prime liked anything about the situation.

She got to her feet, got a drink from the water container on the table, and stood staring at the yeasty crock.

"What?" he asked. "What are you thinking?"

"I'm thinking maybe we should give Prime a gift," she said. "They don't seem to make any kind of bread, do they?"

"The closest I've seen is those trail bars, but I wouldn't call them bread."

"Then find the lantern for me. I'm going to make Prime a treat."

"Worth a try," he said. "You do know how, right?"

"My Uncle Ike taught me," she said.

Smiling, he got up and dug into the packs to find her a light. She was on a mission, and he could almost feel the fire in her.

Chapter 30

Lee

Dawn gave Lee enough light to peek into Ike's magic Dutch oven. The bread had risen pretty well since she had started it in the middle of the night. She stretched and folded it in on itself and hoped it would be ready to bake in time. Good thing the Dutch oven did the baking so she could finish it without having to learn how the Keloks cooked.

She was looking for an opening, a little wedge, to get Prime to consider her of value. To give them some chance. But it was a risky idea, this gift of strange and alien food.

"Are we doing the right thing?" she asked.

Seth looked up from his seat just inside their door. "You seemed pretty sure of that last night."

"I'm sure I want to get home. I'm sure the survey will find these villages. But like you said, what do we really know about these people?"

He stood up. "There's a violence in them, the males at least. They will defend their homes. But they also respect rituals. Don't second-guess yourself now."

Lee laid her head on his shoulder and hugged him. He closed his arms around her, not too tight. "Thanks," she said.

"They're scared," he said. "I would be too. The less out-of-control they feel, the smoother things will go."

She looked up at him and stepped back. "Right. That's right. Weaver has been looking at this backward."

"What do you mean?" he asked.

"We're not taking it far enough. Instead of asking for a meeting, they need to invite the PAO to one. It'll level the field; give Prime a little more control and make her feel more secure."

"You've got something there."

The curtain shook. Lee exchanged a glance with Seth. He pulled the fabric aside to reveal Guard.

"You will come," the Kelok said.

"Okay." Seth stepped past him.

"Both." Guard led the way past the entrance to the men's quarters to another doorway that Lee hadn't noticed before. This one was covered by an actual door made of the ubiquitous mats in a frame instead of a simple curtain. She looked at Seth. He raised a questioning eyebrow and escorted her through. Then they both stopped.

The room was long and narrow with a mat wall on the right where the men's quarters lay and the rock wall of the cave on the left. A counter surfaced with sap-coated canes ran along the rock face. Lee stared in disbelief. On it sat more technology than she had seen anywhere on Carico outside of Portside — clear-sided cubes like 3-D broadcast displays, banks of what might be readouts except they showed colors but no symbols, flat pads the size of a dinner plate.

Weaver sat at the counter, straddling a narrow stool with her tail draped off the back side. "We have been reviewing media broadcasts. There is one that is of interest in our discussion today." She tapped one of the cubes with a claw and a static picture formed, a closeup of a face in front of a wall.

"Adel," Lee identified. "And that's Vinz's office."

"You know the woman?" Weaver asked.

"Yes." All too well. "Adel Verlane. An old acquaintance."

"This was recorded last night."

The sound came up, and the image went into motion.

"I am Acting Principal Verlane of the Rangers with an update on the pending satellite survey …"

"Acting?" Seth whispered in Lee's ear. Lee shook her head and kept her attention on the cube.

"… have received word that the satellite array will arrive sooner than expected, possibly by Settlement Day. It will take about three weeks to deploy and test

before we begin data collection. That is well ahead of our anticipated start date."

Weaver froze the display. "That leaves us little time before data collection begins."

"It seems so," Lee said. Eleven days to Settlement Day plus three weeks. But the satellites would be gathering data as soon as they began to be deployed, even if it wasn't a part of the official record. Better figure on just eleven days to get to Portside, deliver a message, and get a meeting set up. "It's the Planetary Administrative Officer we need to contact."

"Not your General Assembly?" Weaver asked. "Are they not your governing body?"

"Yes, but they won't meet until autumn. And the PAO has authority to prepare agreements for their approval."

Weaver considered that for a moment. "I can accept that protocol. But we must convince Prime, and soon."

Lee paused. "We still have to decide what the message should be and who should carry it."

Weaver stood up. "It is early and none of us have eaten. Let us get food and continue our discussion somewhere more comfortable. Guard, check for any additional information before joining us."

As they exited the room, Lee gave Seth's hand an encouraging squeeze. In a day or two they could be on their way home.

Weaver directed them to the nearby arbor. "I will bring food for us," she said and left them.

Adel as acting; an accelerated timeline on the survey; not to mention Prime. Complicated. "We need to stay focused," she said to herself as much as Seth.

"What's with the 'acting' thing?" he asked.

She remembered Vinz and Joe Reilly talking the night she'd gone to dinner in Portside with Vinz and Dougherty. "Vinz was going on vacation," she said.

"For how long?" Seth asked.

"He'll be back by Settlement Day. He does it every year." She paced and thought. "I had meant to have Vinz get us to the PAO, and, acting or not, Adel doesn't have the personal connection to grease that."

"Maybe Pa or Dougherty?" Seth said. "They'll be searching for us."

"So once we get out on the plateau, they should find us before we can even get back to your place." Lee stopped. "I wonder if Adel's involved in searching for us."

"It's been what, about eight days I guess since Gabe should have gotten my message."

"But they won't find anything," she said. "Guard and his friends removed every last thing."

"There was little enough sign to follow when I was there. They must be going crazy trying to figure out what happened to us."

"Time to get back," she said. "All we have to do is sell Prime on something she doesn't want to do."

Weaver arrived with a tray of food, and they settled around a table. Lee got right down to business. "You've had a lot of time to think about this. Tell me again exactly what you want to accomplish."

"The immediate goal is to claim this territory."

"You say you have studied my people from news broadcasts."

"And your library files." Weaver clicked her beak lightly. "That is what allowed us to program the hearing facilitators with your language."

So the devices just translated between pre-programmed languages. "May I ask how the devices work?" Lee asked, hoping that wasn't some classified secret.

"Guard could explain better than I," Weaver answered, "but in essence they convert the vibrations of what is said to vibrations of the translation and pass those to the skin for the receiver's body and brain to interpret."

"Sort of turning the skin into an ear?"

"In effect. We were very relieved when they worked for you. We could not be sure."

"They are impressive," Lee said.

"Without them, I do not know that we would have dared make contact."

Lee nodded. "Well, since you have studied our files, you understand that Carico was approved for human settlement and has limited authority to admit non-humans?"

"I understand that there are many obstacles to what we desire. Prime does not wish to hear of obstacles."

Lee wasn't surprised. "You had a strategy in mind before you captured me. What was it?"

"It was overly simple," Weaver said, "but the council accepted it. Find a representative of your species and have them escort us to your government."

"And what do you want to come out of the contact, I mean beyond holding your territory? The Coalition is very particular about first contacts. Newly encountered species have the absolute right to decide how much interaction they want." But did that apply to castaways on a Coalition world? Lee had no idea.

"The council has not approved a formal first contact, as defined by your Coalition. Just contact with Carico's government. Prime would prefer no contact at all beyond that necessary to establish our rights."

"Then we must be sure my people understand that." Lee appreciated a desire to stay safely hidden away but that had consequences. "You could ask for a border around your area that neither species crosses. But is that what most of you want? What about the future, your children and their children?"

Weaver looked at the youngsters playing in the plaza. "Our children are raised by the whole clan. We know they are cared for regardless of what happens to the one who hatched a child or sired a child. Still, the eldest of these is of my hatching, and I want her to have opportunities and choices she cannot have here."

"So what we do today and in the coming weeks should lead to becoming citizens of the Coalition at some point?"

"One step at a time, as your people say." Weaver's eyes stayed on the little ones. "But I believe we owe that to our children." Her face flashed blue. Then she looked back at Lee. "Prime does not agree."

"What does she want?" Lee asked.

"The impossible — to reverse time, to go back to our old life."

"And some others feel the same way?"

Weaver bobbed her head. "This exile has been most difficult for those of higher rank. They lost the most — careers, status they worked hard to gain. They carry the burden of knowing how many of our comrades did not survive those first years. And they will always deserve our respect, even though old ranks no longer have meaning."

"They make up your council?"

"No. Prime's command staff stayed together in the Village of Lichens, and the council has only one representative from each village. Others recognize that we must look to the future. But we owe a great deal to Prime and the others who led us. If Prime rejects a proposal outright, we would support her."

"So whatever is proposed must have her support?" This would all be a pointless exercise if Prime was just going to veto anything they came up with.

"Ultimately she remains Prime, our commander."

Lee had one more question, one she feared the answer to. "So if she rejects what we propose, what becomes of us?"

Weaver put down the piece of fruit she held and spread her hands on the tabletop, studying them as if they were of utmost interest. Colors played erratically across her face. She raised her eyes to Lee. "Our first law since coming here has been to prevent knowledge of our presence from reaching your people. None who know we exist may leave unless their memories are removed."

Lee held still, smoothed her face, tried to keep the depth of her reaction from showing. "You can do that?" No more messing around in her head. She had been 'conditioned' for her undercover role as Anni and still sometimes struggled to shed that persona even though it was supposedly reversed years ago during her debriefing.

"With particular drugs and something like what you call hypnosis. One will no longer remember specified events, places, individuals." Weaver looked down at her hands. "It is only to be used in dire need. It creates blanks in the mind. Individuals may still react to situations based on forgotten experiences with no understanding of why."

Lee stood up and leaned over the table. "But you knowingly violated that law when you brought us here. How was this supposed to turn out?"

"The plan to contact your people ended the requirement for secrecy — will end it."

"Unless your council changes its mind. Then we suffer the consequences." Lee pulled back, distancing herself from the alien. Seth stood up, his face bleak. Lee got control of herself. "We had better find a way of getting Prime's support."

Chapter 31

Lee

When the sun reached its zenith, the council convened in the arbor. Prime, with Second at her shoulder, waited at the far end. Weaver led Lee into position half facing them, half facing a long table along one side. On it were three of the plate-size pads that Lee had noticed earlier in the communications center. Guard entered behind them with Seth who carried a small table with the tray of bread and seasoned oil.

The breeze ruffled the edge of Lee's wrap dress. It was one Seth had given her, one she saved for special occasions, a whisper-light silk in a rich bronze shot through with gold. Neither of them had ever imagined it becoming diplomatic wear. But it was informal by comparison to Prime who wore a long, narrow stole-of-office around her neck like a human academic or religious figure. The stiff fabric had many multi-colored rows of stitching along its length, the finest fabric Lee had seen in the village. Prime also wore a choker of intricately woven copper wire with the same green stones as the hearing facilitation devices. Lee hoped that meant no translation would be needed this time.

She rolled her shoulders back, settled her weight into her feet, and stepped forward, away from Weaver, with her eyes lowered and her hands extended, palms up, as Weaver had coached.

"Honorable Prime," she began. "I present to you a token of my respect." She waited for Seth to place the table between her and Prime and back away before she continued. "It is called bread. It is made with nutgrass flour, water, bean tree oil, salt, and native yeasts grown for this purpose." She tore a small piece from the loaf, dipped it into the oil, and ate it. Still keeping her eyes low, she tore off a larger piece, laid it next to the loaf, and carried the tray and table the five steps to Prime, hoping her hands weren't visibly shaking. She kept her eyes on the delicate, many-colored stitching on Prime's stole and backed away until she stood next to Weaver.

Prime pinched off a tiny bit of the bread, sniffed it and touch her tongue to it. She ate it without expression, then waved Second to move the tray and table aside. But she had eaten it. That was more than Weaver had led Lee to hope for.

"We will begin," Prime said. She nodded to Second. The male walked along behind the long table, touching each pad. One-quarter-scale images appeared, three more females wearing stoles and hearing facilitators. The council was meeting by video conference. Weaver hadn't mentioned that. Lee marveled at the figures, crisp in every living, breathing detail, so incongruous with the rustic surroundings. All eyes were on her and Seth.

"Councilors," Prime said. "As you know, Eta'ak succeeded in bringing one of the First-Comers to us and has gained information to further develop her strategy for contacting their officials. She will explain now." No preamble. Lee wondered if that was typical of Kelok meetings or just Prime's style.

Weaver took a half-step forward. "Sisters, our plan is nearly woven. You see here with me Annalee Vawn-Cory and her escort Seth Reilly. They have provided insight into how to best approach their people to meet our objective to initiate contact and establish our claim to the territory we have settled."

Silence. If it wasn't for the eyes studying her, Lee would have wondered if the images were real-time or just static pictures. She stepped up next to Weaver and bowed her head.

The projected images exchanged looks. Their tails wrapped around their feet with the fans tightly closed; their epaulet feathers stood at half-staff. Stiff, uncomfortable. To be expected, Lee told herself.

"Explain your proposal." Prime snapped her beak.

Weaver's face flushed mottled blue and purple. "Yes, Prime. It is the Planetary Administrative Officer, the PAO, we must make contact with. She is our conduit to the General Assembly. Our new clan sister recommends that we do not ask to be granted a meeting, but that we extend an invitation." She paused, looking around at her fellow councilors. "We host a meeting with the Planetary Administrative Officer about matters of mutual benefit."

"Here?" one of the other councilors gasped. "Among our villages?" Tails twitched; colors rippled over faces.

"At a place away from any settlements," Weaver said. "Neutral ground."

Another of the councilors ruffled feathers into place. "I like it. It places us in the dominant position."

"As much as can be possible," another said, "when they control the planet."

"All the more reason not to introduce ourselves as supplicants," the first replied.

"How large a delegation would deliver this invitation?" Prime asked.

Lee kept her face still. This was the tricky part, the part she doubted Prime would accept.

"Just two," Weaver said. "Annalee and her escort."

"No." Prime snapped her beak. "We will not release these strangers so they can send their kind to remove us."

"With respect," Weaver said, "they are of our clan. And they can deliver the invitation without attracting notice."

"Of the clan?" Prime looked down her beak at Lee. "Rituals completed without commitment are worth nothing. They remain strangers."

Lee looked Prime in the eye. "You doubt my honor?"

"I do not doubt your loyalty to your own kind," Prime replied.

"Good," Lee said. "Because I believe a well-negotiated outcome is in the best interests of everyone."

Prime stood silent, not responding, just waiting. For what?

Weaver turned her attention from Prime to the other councilors. "Our time is short. We learned this morning that the satellites will be placed sooner than anticipated." She turned back to Prime. "We must act now."

"We must not act in haste," Prime countered. "For ten of this planet's turns our law has been that no First-Comer may know the location of our villages. You should not have brought these two into the village."

"Our villages will be revealed and soon," Weaver said, still addressing the other councilors more than Prime. "These two have agreed to help, to carry our message. Do we refuse that opportunity?"

The councilors shifted uneasily, looking to Prime. Prime's face went black. "They do not leave with memories of where we can be found. That is our law."

Lee tensed. No one was going to mess with her memories.

Weaver bowed her head to Prime. "Is it not also our law that memory removal may only be used on our own in the case of banishment?"

"It does not apply. They remain outsiders, not of the clans."

Lee raised her eyes to Prime's. "Do you set aside your own rituals? I have done all that is required to become one of Weaver's clan. You allowed me to wear the hearing facilitation device. You accepted my gift of food." She paused to let the council think about that before continuing. "I offer to carry your invitation to my birth clan without revealing any more than you tell me to. Right now, you can weave the pattern of the meeting. Very soon, others will do it."

Prime's eyes narrowed and her epaulets rose like flared wings, rumpling her stole against her neck. Lee was afraid she had pushed too hard but stood her ground and kept her eyes on Prime's.

She heard movement behind her, caught a peripheral glimpse of Guard leaving the arbor. Prime's eyes shifted to him.

"What is this?" Prime demanded. "Why does the male leave this council?"

"Permission to leave so I may learn the answer?" Weaver asked.

"Granted."

"Wait here," Weaver told Lee before striding after Guard. He waited just outside the arbor with another male. Both displayed twitching tail tips and upright crests.

Lee felt Seth close by her shoulder. "Any idea what's up?" he whispered.

She shook her head. Prime and the other councilors showed varying levels of irritation and curiosity in their demeanors. So much for her attempt to sway Prime into letting them deliver the invitation. Now the leader's attention was completely distracted. Then again, maybe it would give Prime a chance to germinate the idea and turn it into her own.

Weaver and Guard returned. Weaver bowed her head to the rest of the council. "Apologies for the disruption. It is a matter for the hunters to address; nothing requiring council action. I will release my escort to deal with it."

Prime ruffled her feathers into place. "No, you will explain the need for such an interruption."

"Yes, Prime." Weaver bobbed her head. "You are all aware of the solitary First-Comer making his way westward toward us beyond the river. Our hunters have attempted to divert him where he could pass without ever knowing about us."

Lee looked at Seth. He mouthed "Whip" silently. Whip Willemsen — her thought exactly. He had run away from his restitution work detail in Portside. Was he taking a round-about route to Under Rim? Or just staying in unsettled country, safe from the authorities? And what did Weaver mean about attempting to divert him?

"He has crossed the warning threshold," Weaver said. "We must take more direct action if he is to be prevented from discovering us."

"Your males are free to go," Prime said. "Second will accompany them. The stranger must not find our villages."

Lee didn't like the sound of that, even if it was Whip. Carico's legal system needed to deal with him, not aliens. With no chance to discuss what she was about to do with Seth, she stepped forward. "We will go with the hunters. We can deal with the intruder face-to-face if necessary so the hunters would not need to show themselves."

"He is of your kind. You would assist him." Prime's face flushed lurid purple.

Lee shook her head. "He is no friend of ours and threatens our shared goal for the future."

Prime straightened her stole-of-office and glanced back at Second. "It is for the hunters to decide whether the human male should accompany them. But the female may not go."

Behind her, Lee heard Seth whisper something to Guard. Guard took a step forward, kept his head lowered, and said, "A female could be useful to us, a lure to draw him."

Chapter 32

Lee

A lure? Lee glanced back at Seth. He gave her a discreet thumbs up. Whatever it was, it was his idea.

Prime turned aside and conferred quietly with Second. When she faced the holo-images of the councilors again, she said, "If that is what the males choose, be it so. They take responsibility for returning these two here to the Village of Canes. Then we will decide about any message to the First-Comers. We adjourn until that time."

The councilors all bowed their heads to her. The holo-images of the three vanished without ceremony.

Weaver went to Prime and said, "I will bring food for you. Will you return to the Village of Lichens this afternoon?"

"Yes," Prime said. "Second will have one of your males escort me. He will go with the hunters."

"As you wish," Weaver said. Lee followed her out of the arbor with Guard and Seth escorting them.

Once out in the plaza, Weaver stopped. "When do you leave?" she asked Guard.

"At dark," Guard replied. "We have preparations to make."

"Keep these two safe," she said. "We need them."

"I will."

Weaver stroked Guard's tail with her own before crossing the plaza toward the kitchen. Guard watched her go, then ruffled his crest feathers. "You will need horses if you are to keep up with us tonight," he said.

"The horses? They're here?" Seth looked around like he expected to see them magically appear.

Lee smiled to herself at the eager glint in his eye. Horses were his soul; without them he had been starving.

"Nearby," Guard assured.

"I need some things from our gear," Seth said.

"And I need to change." Lee wanted to make it plain that she was going along to get the horses.

"Gather what you require," Guard said. "I will meet you outside the men's quarters and take you to your animals."

Lee stood on a high spot on the plateau above the village. She and Guard watched Seth amble across the open ground not quite toward the horses where they stood in the shade of a copper tree a couple hundred yards away.

"He should hurry," Guard said.

"Not with that roan horse," Lee said. "He might walk right up to Seth or play tag for a while."

Guard squatted next to her, his tail wrapped cat-like around his feet. "Tag? Oh, the chase game, like our children play?"

"Yes. Not allowing himself to be caught but not running too far away either."

"I did not think the animals would play games with you." Guard bowed his head deferentially. "You used a word to describe the horse that does not translate," he said. "It is a name?"

"Roan? It's a color," she said. "A horse with a mix of white and dark hairs over its body. But a name too, I guess. It is what Seth calls that horse. I'm not sure why he's never come up with a proper name."

"It is customary to name animals?"

"When we work closely with them."

A sharp whistle brought her attention back to Seth. He stood in the open a hundred feet from the horses. The roan slowly came out from under the tree, head up and ears pricked. Seth whistled again. The roan trotted a few steps closer. The other three watched him without leaving the shade.

Seth walked slowly toward them. He was too far away for Lee to hear him, but she knew he was talking, some soothing patter. Clown started forward, but the roan blocked him with ears pinned back. Seth stopped and backed off a couple of steps. The roan dropped his head a fraction. Seth moved closer.

The roan circled the man, passing just out of reach. Seth turned with him. The horse halted, stretched his nose out to sniff at Seth's hand, ducked aside, and trotted past him. Seth walked after him, stopped, stepped back, waited. The horse turned back toward him. And they danced, slowly, subtly, linked together, the bond stretching and tightening.

Lee watched with a smile. She forgot the coming hunt for a stranger. She forgot messages to the PAO. She forgot the alien creature beside her. She loved the glimpse she got into his heart when Seth danced with horses, the patience, the strength, the exquisite, intimate exchange.

She started when Guard spoke.

"Why does he not capture it?" Guard asked. "He is so close."

"It's the horse's mind he wants," she said. "When he is given that, he has the whole animal."

"The animal trusts him then?"

"They trust each other," she said.

The roan's head came down level with his withers. He stood when Seth walked in next to his shoulder, and he accepted the treat Seth held out to him. Seth slipped a lead rope over the horse's neck and rubbed the horse's shoulder before holding the halter open and waiting for the horse to drop his nose into it. He stood there, scratching the neck and chest while the dark head came around and leaned against his body.

Lee ran a hand through her hair. She'd gotten lost again for a minute. "I'll go help him get the others."

Guard bobbed his head. "Take them where I showed you. I will go ahead so as not to frighten them."

Lee left the Kelok and strode down the slope with a bounce in her step. They had the horses, their equipment; soon they'd be headed home. A restless breeze wrapped around her, taking away some of the afternoon heat. Seth waited for her, surrounded by the horses, all with noses extended for treats. All but Tinker, the uneasy one, the one who didn't know yet that Seth was half-horse himself.

"The roan was pretty easy," she said.

"He was." Seth scratched the horse's face. "I wasn't sure what he would do after being chased way up here in strange country by tailed monsters."

They haltered Clown and Creamy. "I'll get Tinker." Lee handed Clown's lead to Seth. Ike's brown gelding watched them, head high, ready to run.

"Don't worry about him," Seth said. "He'll follow the others."

Seth stood there, just a step away, with the three haltered horses around him. The roan's nose was inches from his hip. Lee knew if he moved, the horse would go with him, attached by an invisible force, a trust and something deeper that she couldn't name. Seth reached out his hand to her, and she was as drawn to him as the horse was. He was the part of her that had been missing for far too long.

His eyes met hers, smiling. She took his hand and let him pull her in against him. She laid her hand behind his neck, inviting his head down, starved for him.

When she thought their kiss would never end, he ended it, kissed her on the forehead, and wrapped her in his arms. "I'm afraid if I let you go, you'll be gone again," he said.

"Then don't let me go."

But he did, slowly. She pulled him back to kiss him again, quickly this time.

"Guard said to take the horses to the pen they made," she said, regretting the lack of time and mostly her own past foolishness.

He cupped his hands for her to step in and boosted her onto Clown's back. In one smooth movement he swung onto the roan. "Let's get these horses safely corralled. Then we can find out what we've gotten into by offering to help with Whip."

"Assuming that's who it is," she said. She rode next to him, feeling the movement of the horse beneath her, the sweat starting between her and the bare back. Reality. "It's an opportunity to build some trust. Prime would just as soon wipe our minds and get us as far from here as possible."

"Or worse." He was looking at her so intensely that she stopped her horse.

"What?" she asked.

"Dougherty said you wanted no part of 'public service.' That was the phrase he used. About you not going back to the Rangers to work on the survey. So what changed?"

"Nothing," she said. "Well, the situation," she added. "This isn't about going back to the Rangers."

"And it isn't just about you and me anymore either."

"Okay, it isn't. I can't let all of Carico be thrown into chaos when I can do something about it." She shifted uneasily.

"Or let the Keloks make Whip Willemsen vanish into the wilds?"

"That …" She legged Clown into a walk. "That is more tempting." But she knew she couldn't be responsible for letting it happen, not even to one of the men who had delivered Seth into Jerdix's hands once upon a time.

Seth chuckled. "I'm with you." Somehow she knew he meant more than agreeing about Whip's future.

They followed Guard's directions to get the horses down into the village's canyon farther upstream than they had been yet, then down to the dance ground. They turned up the side canyon past their prison-cave where the Keloks had strung hunting nets across the canyon to make a pasture for the horses.

When the horses were secure, they met Guard at the dance ground, and he led them to the village. They climbed up a trail through a bean tree grove to pass the arbor and enter the plaza. No sign of Prime or of the loaf of bread. Had she actually taken it with her? Maybe Weaver had put it somewhere.

Second was squatting by the door into the men's quarters with several of the village males. Guard stopped, eyes lowered politely to Lee. "Please go gather what gear you and my tailless brother will need while we discuss how to proceed."

Lee got the message. Clear out and leave the men to plan tactics. Live by the home rules. At least they were letting her go along. She squeezed Seth's hand and left him with the males.

She stepped around notalions, who barely noted her presence before going back to their siesta in front of her doorway. Inside the room the air was still and muggy. She pulled gear outside the door and laid it out along the mat wall — saddlebags with first aid and emergency repair kits, lightweight rain jackets, water bottles, tack for the horses. It was too fascinating. The notalions had to investigate along with the Kelok children, both males and females.

Weaver came over and shooed them away. She handed Lee a basket. "Trail food," she said. "One never knows how long hunters will be gone." She looked at the gear with a little shiver of her feathers. "It feels very strange to have a female going with them."

"You don't go away from the village?" Lee asked. Prime certainly traveled.

"We go together to gather, sometimes for several days, or escorted by a spouse to visit another village. But not on the hunt."

"You consider this a hunt?"

"Of course," Weaver answered. "Does not 'hunt' mean to seek for? Or is it defined by outcome?"

"Sometimes one; sometimes the other," Lee said.

"For us it is the action. The outcome is separate."

"What outcome is the goal of this hunt?" Lee asked.

"Diversion," Weaver said. "If possible." She hesitated. "I am concerned that the males' need to protect you will distract them."

"They don't need to protect me,"

Weaver clicked her beak. "They are Kelok. Our women are few. One female egg, then male eggs in the next three or four hatchings. Our males must take extra care of the females."

Biologically it made sense. Culturally it was hard for Lee to grasp. "Would it be appropriate for the males to assign one the task of protecting me and free the rest of them?"

"I will suggest it to Guard."

"And I will do what I can to stay out of their way."

Chapter 33

Seth

Seth and Lee left the Village of Canes under the light of two moons. The slope from the hanging canyon to the river fell away like a huge slide, small stones distorted into boulders by moonlight and shadow. Seth led the roan down and down, always listening for rocks kicked loose by Lee and Clown above him. Hooves clopped and thunked; dust rose. Below, two Kelok hunters crossed the river, dark shapes in a dizzy dance of swift, silver-rippled water sliding sideways. Above, unseen, unheard, Guard and Second followed.

They reached the riverbank, mounted, rode the horses into the Whitewater, knee-deep, its bottom hidden by the dazzle of light on water. Horses splashed through, bounded up the far bank, pushed into the brush.

They rode on, a relentless journey of trotting horses, slapping, snagging brush, rock and dust. The two moons crawled westward. Hours, miles, moving toward an unfamiliar meeting place to protect their captors from discovery a little while longer; to protect a stranger from their captors. Up the river; up a narrow side-canyon; up onto a ridge, horses digging in hooves, noses nearly to the ground, scrambling, leaping.

They stopped on top to let sweating, blowing horses recover from the climb. Grasses and low brush dotted the ridge top. Copper trees clung to the rocky edges with weird, contorted limbs black in the moonlight. Seth took his feet out of his stirrups and stretched his legs to ease joints and muscles aching from the hours horseback.

"How much farther?" Lee asked.

Seth looked at the moons. "An hour maybe. About the time Lander sets. That's when Guard expected to meet the hunter who has been watching the stranger."

Abruptly the roan tensed and crouched under him. When the horse leaped sideways, Seth went with him, gathering the horse with legs and reins before he could run. "Whoa, whoa," he ordered. A glance told him Lee had Clown under control. Both horses locked eyes on something coming onto the ridge behind them.

"Second and Guard," Seth said. He saw the two Keloks in the moonlight. They sank down into the brush as he watched. "Looks like we're holding things up."

It took him a bit of gentle persuasion to get the roan to turn away and move on. The horse kept his head cocked to one side, watching behind. Clown was even worse, walking almost sideways.

"Fun having horse-eating monsters for trail companions," Lee said as she worked to get the horse straightened out.

"I told Guard it would be better if they were in front where the horses could watch them, but Second doesn't trust us." The feeling was mutual.

Slowly the horses quit seeing stink bears in every bush. Seth trotted to stay ahead of their escorts. The larger moon won the race to the horizon, leaving just Damele to light their way. "There, the palm-pines. That's where we meet them," Seth said. These were the first palm-pines he had seen in this country. They must have climbed higher than he realized.

"What do we do with the horses?" Lee asked.

"How about there?" He pointed to a clump of copper trees on the edge of the ridge top near them. "That should keep them far enough from the meeting place. I wish we'd had time to get the horses used to Guard and his friends before we started this."

They turned aside and dismounted at the edge of the trees. "Leave them saddled till we find out what's happening," he said. He caught a glimpse of Guard and Second slow-sneaking through the brush, trying not to spook the horses. When the roan looked around, the Keloks froze. Not seeing anything, the horse relaxed.

Seth tied the roan to a solid tree trunk. "Let's hobble them too, just to be safe," he said. "Don't want to lose them if they get spooked."

Guard and three others — the two who had come ahead of them and the one who had been watching the stranger — waited for them in the palm-pines. Second stood to the side. All of them carried satchels and slingbows. Seth noted that only Guard and Second wore translators and touched his own. He barely noticed it anymore.

"The stranger is still there," Guard told Seth and Lee as they joined the group. "Camped at the head of the valley to the east. He has only one horse. He killed his other after it broke a leg in the rocks two days ago. It seems the animals have fragile legs."

"Is that what happened to Pokey?" Lee asked sharply.

"Pokey?" Guard asked.

"The one you butchered."

Guard's crest rose slowly. "Yes, that one was injured during the stampede."

Second intervened. "Make the female comfortable. Then you may plan."

"I'm fine," Lee said.

Seth laid a hand on her arm. "She wants to hear what will happen so she won't get in the way."

"She will not be in the way. She will be protected." Second ruffled his crest uneasily.

"Certainly," Guard said. "But we brought her so that she can assist."

Lee shrugged off Seth's hand. He stepped back, letting her stand on her own, not sure what she had in mind.

She faced Second, eyes on his until he dropped them slightly. "Thank you for your concern," she said. "I am still new to your ways. Please guide me. I will stand with you and observe, if I may."

"You may."

Seth gave her a slight nod. She'd gotten that just right. She squeezed his hand before walking a few steps away.

Guard squatted down in a patch of weak moonlight and smoothed the dirt. "This is the ridge we are on," he said, drawing a double line. "The rim beyond the next valley to the west runs like this." He added a single line parallel to the double line. "The valley beyond that drains more westward although its head is very near this one." He drew a line making a 'V' with the single line. "If he goes down that valley, he will cross the river upstream from all of the villages and can continue west."

Seth looked at the crude map and at the country around him. "So we need to make these two canyons uninviting."

"Or the far one more inviting. You said that he will not want to encounter riders," Guard said. "If you appear, he would leave."

"That was before I knew he needed a horse," Seth said. If the man wasn't walking with everything packed on the one horse, he must have packed very light and be headed for someplace he could get supplies. Seth couldn't think where that could be this far back of beyond.

"You think he would want to take one of yours?" Guard asked.

"I do."

"Then we lure him rather than pushing him." He outlined his plan, using horses rather than Lee as bait.

The next couple of hours were the hardest of the whole night — waiting until time to put the plan in motion. He and Lee went back and unsaddled the horses then rejoined the others to eat a little and rest. The Keloks, except for one on watch, stretched out and dozed. Lee did a better job of imitating them than Seth managed. The plan sounded simple enough. If the stranger behaved predictably; if Guard's hunters stayed out of sight; if the unexpected didn't happen.

At the first gray hint of light, he and Lee found a place near the horses where they could look across the next valley. "Up there," he said, pointing toward the dip in the far ridge that led to the canyon they wanted the stranger to go down. "You can see the tops of the palm-pines on the far side. Leave the saddles in those trees and stake the horses out on this side where he'll see them. Then you watch from out of sight."

"I'm surprised Second agreed to this," she said. "Doesn't it violate his views on separation of duties?"

"I guess as long as you are just delivering the bait to its proper spot, it's okay." He hated the thought of their horses as bait but better the animals than one of them. "Second said he will go ahead of you and find a spot where he can watch over you."

"Leaving the rest of you to intercept the stranger if he goes the wrong direction?"

Seth nodded. "That's why I have to stay with them; so I can confront him face-to-face if I have to."

"I'd better get going then." She cut through the trees to the horses before he could say any more.

They saddled both horses, and he brought the roan to her. "Once he heads toward the horses, you get them and lead them —"

"I know," she said. She laid a hand on his chest. "I draw him off over the ridge then get out of the way so Guard and his hunters can spook his horse down the canyon without me losing ours."

"I'd feel better if I was with you."

"I'll be fine."

He put his arms around her, giving her time to push past her hesitation, that holdover from her past, before hugging her close. "I, well ..." He kissed her then forced himself back. "Be careful," he said, running his thumb along her cheekbone.

She kissed his palm. "You too." She swung up on Clown and took the roan's lead from him.

Seth watched her ride along the rim and follow Second across the open valley, trailing well behind the Kelok. The horses were focused on the creature ahead of them. Once Second disappeared over the ridge, they moved more easily. Seth paced and watched. He wished he was with her or had left her with Guard and gone himself.

He waited until Clown's vivid white splashes disappeared over the ridge. As he turned to join the

Keloks, he saw something coming into the valley from his side, a horse with a rider heading after Lee. The stranger had broken camp early.

Chapter 34

Lee

Lee crossed over the ridge into the far valley, watching for Second, hoping he was hidden. The horses were still looking for monsters behind every bush. She wanted them calm before she staked them out to graze and be bait. Bait! She'd rather do that herself than risk losing their horses.

The canyon ahead of her ran off to the west, with a bowl at this upper end, narrowing between rims farther down. The palm-pines hung like an eyebrow on the ridge to her left. Lower in the bowl she saw what looked like a good spring surrounded by big clumps of the whipbrush that created a maze of grassy openings.

She stayed high on the slope and rode into the pines, working her way far enough in to be out of sight. Sunrise wasn't far away. She had enough light, even in the trees, to see what she was doing.

She pulled the saddles off. Leading the two horses, she started back toward the ridge top. The roan kept his head high, still nervous. She worked the lead, tight-loose-tight-loose, to keep his attention on her. Clown crowded on her other side. She stopped at the edge of the trees, struggling to keep control of the animals. "Easy, boys, no monsters, just Second." Lying close by like a predator-in-wait, no doubt. "Think about all that grass waiting for you."

Clown leaped past her. The roan went with him, ripping the lead ropes from her hands. Scorch it!

They ran down toward the spring, stopping well out into the open to stare back her way. The roan snorted and blew, like he had a rattle in his nose. She took a deep breath and let it out before starting after them, forcing herself to walk casually like she wasn't thoroughly scared. She would catch them eventually, but she didn't have time to out-patience them. "Silly boys," she soothed. "I'm calm; you should be too."

"Hsssss," she heard from back in the trees.

She turned and saw Second. "You were supposed to stay away," she said.

Second dipped his head apologetically. "The stranger is approaching sooner than expected. He saw you cross the ridge."

She muttered a few choice words, none in translatable Sol Standard. Did Kelok women curse in front of their men?

In quick assessment, she looked at the ridge where the rider would appear anytime, then down at the horses, still standing at full alert, eyes glued on the Kelok. She faced Second. "I need to catch those horses," she told him. "Now, before that rider can get to them."

"Was it not the plan for him to find them?"

"See them; follow them this way. But not get them." Was this a time when a male Kelok would do what he was told by a female? Worth a try. "Go," she said. "Tell Guard what happened. I need enough time to get the horses out of the way before he and his hunters follow."

"Leave you alone?" Second seemed honestly shocked.

Weaver had told her that Kelok women didn't go off on their own, at least not far from the village. "That is what must happen," she said. "The plan is working; the rider is heading this way instead of toward the villages. Once I have our horses out of the way, all that is left is to keep him spooked enough to keep moving down the canyon instead of coming back for them."

Second's crest stood up high and wide. He bobbed his head. "You show great courage. Go hunt your horses. We will be back to watch over you soon."

"Go," she said. "Hurry." And this time keep your distance. But she didn't say that out loud.

He vanished into the trees. At least he had done what she'd told him to. She started down the hill after her horses. She needed her hands on them before a strange horse appeared on the horizon or a bunch of Keloks began slinking around. Act casual, no hurry. Easy to say.

Both horses were grazing, snatching a mouthful of grass, then looking around. They watched her warily. The roan trotted away a dozen steps before turning back to lock his eyes on her. Clown mirrored him.

Lee changed direction, angling to go past them, kept her eyes off them. She recalled watching a pair of wolf-lizards pass a herd of tarbh, heads low, all attention ahead as if their sometimes-prey didn't exist. In return, the tarbh gave them no more than a glance. "I'm not interested in you; you're not interested in me," she said quietly.

Clown might have come to her if he'd been alone. But the roan edged away, trotting a few steps, stopping to watch. Well, one was better than none. Lee stayed on line to pass Clown, slowed down, and began to wander a little, like a grazing horse. Clown started grazing, leaving the roan in the background.

"Hey, Clown, silly beast." She kept talking, low and steady, as she moved closer and closer. Clown lifted his head and watched her, took a step her way. She waited; he stood still. She eased up to his shoulder, putting her boot down on the dragging rope. "That's my good boy." She rubbed his neck and got hold of the rope just below the halter. One down. Running out of time.

The nearest place she could tie him was by the spring. She strode rapidly down the hill to the taller vegetation around the water and pulled together a bundle of whipbrush stems to tie him to. "You wait here," she said, "while I go get your partner."

The roan had followed them to the spring. He stood with his forefeet in mud, drinking. He lifted his head to look at her. "Go ahead, finish," she murmured. "Now why hasn't Seth ever given you a proper name? Pretty boy like you deserves a proper name." She moved slowly, aiming for the rope that trailed on the ground behind him rather than for his head. Quietly she picked it up and slowly tightened it. "Come on, good horse, let's go see Clown." The roan stepped out of the water and came to her, obedient to the rope. "Oh, thank you," she said.

She got Clown and let him drink before leading both horses deeper into the clumps of tall brush. She and the horses needed to get out of the way, so Guard and the others could spook the stranger's horse down the canyon. With luck, he'd believe she and the horses were ahead of him and go without paying too much attention.

Clown and the roan threw their heads up tensely. Up the ridge, Lee heard the ringing neigh of a lonely horse. Flood and flames — they'd been seen. She had to move, now. Taking a firm hold of the two lead ropes, she headed down the canyon bottom, keeping the clumps of whipbrush between her and the stranger, looking for a place where she could work her way to the side, up into the palm-pines, without being seen.

After the one neigh, his horse was quiet, but the alert attention of her two warned her that he was getting closer. She heard galloping hoof beats. He was passing between her and the palm-pine forest, trying to get below her. She changed direction, back toward the spring, looking for an opening in the brush that would take her out of the bottom. She grabbed hold of Clown's mane to swing on him and run for it, get enough of a lead that the Keloks could cut her pursuer off.

Clown spun away from her, leaving her struggling to keep hold of both leads. She got him turned back and saw a man step out of the brush, about her age, compact, smaller than Seth, dressed in dark clothes. Whip Willemsen. He hadn't seen her in three years and knew her then as meek little Anni, his boss's office help. He might not recognize her in rider's clothes in a place he had no reason to expect her to be.

"I'll take the horses," he said.

"I've got them," she said gruffly. She turned her toes in a little to add a different swing to her movements and stepped between him and the animals.

"I wasn't offering to help," he said.

"Good, because I don't need any." She kept her voice low and rough. "I was just hunting these strays. We're camped on down below a ways."

"We?" He came toward her. "Who? You and the Reilly cub?"

"Reilly?" she said, trying to sound puzzled.

"Didn't think I recognized you? After you two ruined everything? If you're here, he's not far away."

"My name is Lee," she said as casually as she could, hoping he couldn't hear her thudding heart. "Rider for Seven Wells."

"I don't care what you call yourself these days."

"Look, whoever you are, we're out here scouting some new grazing. Come on back to camp, and you can talk to the boss about a horse if you need one." If he would just believe she was part of a crew not far away … She stepped closer to Clown.

"Why ask for what I already have," he said. "I figure a couple horses is a small price to pay, considering what you owe me."

"I owe you?" She shook her head in disbelief. "I don't know who you think I am. Just back off."

"You may dress like a rider, but you're Anni all right. I had a good job with Jerdix. I had a future. And you took all that away."

She gave up the pretense. "You ran errands for a crook."

"What about you? Jerdix's office sow. You did a lot more than run errands. Real close, you two — before you turned on him."

"Not so close." Never, not the way it had looked. "If I remember correctly, you're the one that told the marshals about his plan to blow things up. So who's the betrayer?"

"I had to look out for myself. You'd already ruined everything."

"Poor you."

"Give me the horses," he said, reaching for Clown's halter. "Or don't you pay your debts?"

She was not going to let him lay a hand on her. She turned loose of the roan, slapped him on the neck to move him out of the way, and got her feet squarely under her. Whip was a bunkhouse scrapper. The only way she could take him was if she caught him by surprise and made her strike count. He wouldn't expect it; not from Anni. She held out Clown's lead rope. "Here, take one horse and clear out while you're ahead."

He lunged for her. She drove her hand forward to catch him under the ribs, but Clown leaped away, pulling her around.

She let go of the lead as Whip grabbed her from behind, one arm around her throat and the other around her ribs.

Her mind blanked. She was back in Jerdix's clutches, waiting for the assault she knew was coming, feeling those huge, harsh hands on her.

"Hold still," the voice said in her ear. Whip's voice, not Jerdix's.

She shoved back against him and went limp, a dead weight sliding down to the ground, one thought in mind — do damage. She slammed her head back as she dropped, hoping to hit his crotch. Missed.

She rolled, drove her boot heel into his kneecap, and scrambled to her feet. He bent over, clutching his knee. "Bitch lizard!" He straightened and hobbled toward her.

She faked a kick at his groin and followed with one over his block to slam her boot into the lower edge of his rib cage. He folded over with a groan, and she brought her knee up into his nose, feeling a satisfying crunch. She backed out of his reach and waited to see if he would stay down.

Blood streamed from his nose. His knee collapsed when he tried to get up. "You crippled me," he yelled. "I'm going to —"

"Just sit down," she said. He tried his knee again and collapsed on the ground, forearm to his face, catching blood.

Scorch it — this was not the plan. With one eye on Whip, she caught Clown before the horse wandered off. "What do I do with him now?" she asked. Clown just snorted, blowing snot.

She could leave Whip where he was, take the horses, and regroup with Seth and Guard to figure things out. Whip was down for now, but she didn't think he'd stay that way. Given a chance he might go back to his horse and clear out, which is what they wanted in the first place. Or he might come after her and their horses.

"My nose." He tipped his head back. "I think you broke it."

"Good for me," she said. Shaking her head, she tied Clown to a clump of brush. "Sit up and lean forward," she instructed. She risked getting within his reach, pushing him forward. "Now pinch your nose closed and hold it. It'll quit bleeding in a few minutes."

"It hurts."

"Just do it." She stepped away and looked him over. His knee was swelling against his pant leg. She knew from experience that his ribs probably hadn't made themselves fully felt yet, but they would. "Where's your horse?" she asked.

"Down there," he said with a nasal whine. He was pinching his nose gingerly.

"If you aren't here when I get back, I will leave you to walk out of here on your own," she told him. She caught the roan, grazing calmly a short way off, and came back to untie Clown. With her own horses safely in hand, she headed down to find Whip's horse. Easy enough once the lone animal saw other horses. Leading all three, she hurried into the palm-pines. She tied the horses well below where she had left the saddles, away from Keloks coming over the ridge into the valley.

All that and the sun still hadn't climbed above the ridge. No sign of Keloks or Seth yet. She looked down at the canyon bottom. Whip still sat in the opening in the brush holding his nose with one hand and prodding his knee with the other. She hesitated to leave anyone half crippled in the back of beyond, but she really wanted to put him on his horse and send him down the canyon, not have to deal with him anymore. He must not see the Keloks, must not learn about the villages, and wasn't going to get one of their horses. He was a scorching inconvenience.

He'd actually had hold of her. She remembered his breath on the back of her neck, his arms forcing her against him. Her hands started shaking. She sank down, pulled her knees tight against her, and waited for her heart to slow to normal. She'd done it. She'd defended herself, and she'd won. A lock deep inside her opened, and she felt ready to face anything.

She got to her feet. Time to deal with the consequences. Whip was waiting, broken nose, jammed knee, damaged ribs, and rotten attitude. And she saw Second sneaking through the brush near the spring. She whistled to get his attention and held her hands up, palms out, in a stay-there gesture that she had seen

Guard use. Second understood — he sank down on his belly and lay still.

She hurried to dig a leather thong out of Seth's saddlebags. That was all she needed to make Whip pretty helpless in his condition. She glanced toward Second. A blindfold! A hood would be better. Something to make sure Whip didn't see Keloks. She pulled one of her wraps from her saddlebags. Like the Keloks had used on Seth when they had captured him. She strode down the hill.

Whip managed to get to his feet somehow, but he wasn't putting much weight on his injured leg. His nose had quit bleeding. "Where've you been?" he said. "There's something up by the spring. I heard it moving around."

"Nothing for you to worry about. Put your hands behind your back."

"Aw, you don't have to do that."

"You had your chance to go on your way. That's all we wanted." She pulled his hands back and tied them together securely. "Now we are stuck with you, so I guess you're headed back into custody."

He spun around, nearly falling, his eyes wide. "You can't. Please, don't take me back. Just give me my horse, and I'll be gone. Never saw you; you never saw me."

He was scared. Would he really go? "Not up to me," she said. She shook out the wrap, folded it, and draped it over his head.

"Ow! What's that for?"

"Maybe you're not the only one who doesn't want to be seen." She tied two of the corners together around his neck to make a hood. It was going to get blood stains on it. At least it was an old wrap. "Now stand right there. I'll be back."

"But …"

She left him balancing on one leg, turning his head as if that would help him see, and wound her way through the brush to the spring. Second rose out of his hiding spot when she approached.

He bowed his head and clasped his hands. "Are you safe?" he asked, keeping his voice soft. "I was near the ridge top. I saw him lay hands on you."

"I am fine," she said, meaning it. "He is tied up with a hood over his head, but I think it is best if you and the hunters don't get too close to him. Oh, and he has some injuries. Nothing too serious, but he won't be running off."

"What kind of injuries?"

"Bruised ribs, bruised or sprained knee, and damage to his nose."

"You fight well." He hesitated, his crest rising and falling. "Our females do not fight, not physically."

"I prefer not to," she said. "He gave me no choice."

"You should not have been unprotected."

"Many things should have gone differently this morning," she said. But she'd taught Whip Willemsen to think twice about taking hold of a woman. The question was what to do with him now.

"You must not allow him to become aware of us," Second said. His concern for her, the female, seemed to be fading.

"So far, he isn't," she said.

His crest rose. "The hunters will assure that does not change."

She wished she understood the Keloks better, but she was pretty sure letting Whip go wasn't what Second had in mind. Memory wiping? Or would they resort to killing to protect themselves? "He is my prisoner," she said firmly.

He studied her with narrowed eyes. "Then stay and guard your prisoner. I will join the others to decide how to salvage this." With a sweep of his tail, he turned and trotted away up the ridge toward the upper end of the palm-pine stand.

Lee followed him out into the open, far enough that she could be seen, assuming Seth was up there in the trees watching. She stood there for a minute before going back to Whip, taking a path that kept her in view as much as possible so Seth would know she was all right. She found a place to wait where she could see Whip, a place where she didn't have to talk to him. Bad enough she might have to protect a waste of space like him from the Keloks.

Chapter 35

Seth

Seth sat against the base of a palm-pine, staring down toward the spring. He saw Lee lead three horses — three — into the trees and then return to the canyon bottom where she disappeared into the brush. A minute later he caught a glimpse of her moving toward the spring but couldn't see where she went.

"Patience," Guard said. He stretched on his belly behind Seth, out of sight of the spring as long as he was still. The other three hunters rested at the upper edge of the trees not far away.

"She had his horse," Seth said. "So where is the rider?"

"We will learn that soon."

"I'm going down there." Seth pushed himself up.

"Second is there. He would have warned if anything was needed."

"It doesn't matter if *I'm* seen."

"Perhaps, but we do not know enough to act. Wait for Second to bring us information. Sit."

Seth sat and fidgeted with the bracelet, Lee's bracelet that she had given him before his initiation fight, that he carried in his shirt pocket. He should never have let her go alone to bait the stranger.

Guard held out his hand. "May I see that? It is braided from what?"

Reluctantly Seth passed it to him. "It's horsehair, a bracelet."

Guard turned it slowly. "You made this?"

"Yes."

"It is delicate work. It has meaning?" He handed it back.

"For Lee and me it does. There were two, one for each of us." Seth put it in his pocket. "But things changed."

"So you must make new ones."

Seth shrugged. "Maybe. If I was sure we are back together, not just … Not just because of this situation," he finished.

"You must have new ones." Guard clicked his beak lightly. "Although the thought of a family without brother-spouses is very strange to me."

So he and Lee had been right about the groupings at the feast, the single females and multiple males. "We usually settle for one partner at a time," Seth said.

"Yes, I think your siblings and other family provide much of the sharing and support we males get from co-spouses."

Wondering what it would be like to have to share that way, Seth looked down the hill. "There. Second's coming alone. And there's Lee by the spring. Why isn't she coming this way?"

"You see she is safe." Guard got up and shook dirt and leaves from his fine down. "Wait for Second to explain."

Seth didn't want to wait, but Guard stepped in front of him, reminding him of his low place in the Kelok hierarchy.

Second came straight to them, trotting easily. Not worried about being seen. "The plan has failed," he said when he reached them. "The stranger is now captive of the woman."

"Of the woman!" Guard's crest stiffened straight up.

"She is the one who defeated him in combat and claimed him." Second clicked his beak and shook his head. "A female. Extraordinary."

"Why didn't she come up here?" Seth asked. "Is she okay?"

"The woman is unhurt, but the man suffered some injuries that require minor care," Second said. "She guards her prisoner."

"Has the stranger seen any of us?" Guard asked.

"Only the woman."

"You have a recommendation?" Guard deferred to his senior.

"You lead this hunt," Second said. "I came only to observe."

"I should go down there. She may need my help." Seth wanted to hear the whole story from Lee.

"She is in control," Second assured.

"Before you go, let us be clear on our objectives," Guard said.

Seth ran his hand through his hair. "He doesn't know about you. We can keep it that way."

Guard looked down the canyon. "Is it possible that he could still be sent on his way?"

"Unknown," Second said. "I do not know if his injuries will allow him to travel unaided."

"So we may be forced to wait until he can travel and assure he leaves the area as originally hoped, or drug him and take him with us," Guard said.

"There is another way, more final, though not one we have resorted to previously." Second paused. "It is your decision."

Guard's crest rose and fell uncertainly. He didn't say anything.

More final? A knot tightened in Seth's throat. He faced Guard. "We can take him with us without him seeing you or the villages. Lee and I could take him to the authorities when we take Prime's invitation." Seth planted the idea without much hope they would go for it. Prime hadn't committed to that plan yet.

Guard glanced at Second. "We will rest here for the day and make a decision before leaving," he said. "You may go to the woman. After my hunters and I go to the spring for water, we will keep watch from a distance."

Right. So we don't take Whip and run off, Seth thought. "I need to let the horses graze."

"Of course. We will stay away from them," Guard said. "You will come back at midday to tell us more about the prisoner's condition and how cooperative he will be. Go now and move the prisoner away from the spring. We will wait for you to signal us."

Seth set off down the hill as fast as he could walk, wishing and doubting whoever it was would be glad to leave the area as quickly as he could.

Lee came out of the bushes to meet him with a bounce in her step and a limp.

"Second said you were okay," Seth said. "What happened?"

She put her arm around his waist and led him down the canyon. "I bruised my knee. It's just a little stiff."

He stopped. "Tell me. Is it Whip?"

"It is," she said. "He waylaid me and thought he could take the horses."

"And?"

"He seems to think I owe him something for putting him out of a job with Jerdix."

"And?" Seth was losing patience. "Second said you defeated him in combat."

"Whip grabbed me. Now he has some bruised ribs, a swollen knee, and probably a broken nose. The nose is why my knee hurts."

He stopped and turned her to face him. She was grinning, almost smirking.

"His mistake," Seth said.

"I did it," she said, her grin straightening into satisfaction. "I stood up to him. He'll think twice about laying hold of a woman again."

He caressed her cheek with his thumb. "You made quite an impression on Second."

"Good." The energy seemed to drain out of her. "I am so tired."

He put his arms around her gently. "Me too. Guard says we'll stay here until dark." She was soft against him. No resistance; none. "They are coming for water. Then they'll leave the bottom so the horses can graze."

"Good," she said. "When we get the horses, we need the aid kit for Whip."

"That's what you want to do next? Fix Whip?"

"Absolutely not." She leaned into him for a moment before stepping back with a laugh. "But better take care of business before we get too distracted."

Seth followed her to an opening out of sight from the ridge. Whip sat on the ground with his back to a clump of brush and with one of Lee's wraps around his head, covering his face. His hands were behind his back. He shifted uncomfortably. Seth could see one knee was swollen against his pant leg.

"Aren't you a picture," Seth said.

"Hey, help. She's crazy." The man pulled at the thong binding his hands, groaned, and cradled his side with his elbow. "She crippled me."

"You'll heal," Seth said.

"Reilly? Is that you?"

"That's right."

"Get this hood off me." Whip tried to shake it loose and groaned.

"Maybe later. Sit quiet while we decide what to do with you."

"Just let me go. I'll clear out, forget I ever saw you."

"I thought you were crippled."

Whip tried to get his good leg under him and fell back. "I'll crawl out of here before I'll go back to that work detail."

"What do you mean by that?" Seth asked.

Whip settled back and sat still. "I don't have to explain to you." And he shut up.

They left him where he sat. Seth waved to Guard waiting up the ridge to come to the spring, then followed Lee into the trees where the horses were tied, the roan, Clown, and a gaunt, raw-boned bay that looked like it had seen too many miles and not enough feed for quite a while. Before they entered the woods, Seth saw Guard and his hunters trotting swiftly down to the spring.

"How far to our saddles?" he asked.

"Almost to the upper end of the pines," Lee said.

"Leave them there for now," Seth said. "But go grab our saddlebags and our picket ropes while I take care of this." He began unsaddling Whip's horse.

By the time she returned, Guard and his hunters had left the spring. Seth and Lee led the horses into the meadows along the little creek that ran down from the spring and picketed the three on long ropes so they couldn't wander.

He put an arm around Lee and drew her back into the brush. "Second is thinking about eliminating the problem, killing Whip I think," he said.

"I got the same impression. What about Guard?"

"I don't think he likes the idea, and Second says it's his decision, but I'm not sure about that."

She leaned against him. "I hate to say it, but we need to come up with a way of protecting Whip. If they kill one of us now, what are the chances of ever establishing peaceful coexistence?"

"And it might encourage some of them to decide that is the easiest answer for us too?" He hoped that Guard wouldn't agree with that. He didn't know about Second. Or any of the ones who thought they could stay hidden.

"Prime has already thought about that," Lee said. "I'd bet on it."

He ran his thumb along her cheekbone. "We're going home," he said. "You and me. My place, the Wells, wherever you want. We are going home."

"Then we had better get Whip out of this so we can concentrate on the bigger picture."

Seth stood over their captive while Lee pulled off the wrap and washed the blood off the man's face. Next she slit open the outside seam of his pant leg from mid-thigh to mid-calf, revealing a knee already showing signs of purple. Whip sighed with relief when the pressure was released.

"Tape?" Seth asked.

"You have some?" she replied.

He dug into the emergency kit in his saddlebags and found a roll of light, strong tape and a sheet of fabric the size of his open hand, an emergency cold pack. He soaked the fabric in the little creek running down from the spring, impressed by how cold it felt once it was wet.

Lee applied a final strip of tape to Whip's knee and opened the front of his shirt, prodding his side to find the sore spot. "Breathe," she told him. He did, carefully. "I don't feel any crunching," she said. "What about you?"

"It hurts."

She put the cold pack on and used tape to hold it in place and stood up.

"Hey," Whip said.

"What?" she asked.

"Water. Can I have some water?"

Seth got a water bottle from the saddlebags and watched while she gave Whip a drink. Playing nursemaid to Whip Willemsen. This whole fiasco just kept getting crazier.

She looked up at Seth, holding the makeshift hood. "What do you think?"

"Back on," Seth said. He didn't want to take any chances.

"Tarbh's clackers," Whip said. "I'm not going anywhere."

"Listen carefully," Lee said. "We aren't with any crew of riders. They're beyonders, and they don't like strangers. So it's best for all of us if you don't see any of them."

"What beyonders?"

"The ones watching from up on the ridges." She secured the wrap around his head, careful not to put pressure on his injured nose. "Just take it easy for a while," she said, pulling his shirt closed over the cold pack. "We'll be around."

Seth picked up the saddlebags. They found a spot in the shade of a brush clump where they could see both Whip and the picketed horses, and where the Keloks could see them so Second wouldn't feel the need to make sure they hadn't run off.

"I think we can convince Whip to go away," she said. "Across the river and maybe north above the rim. He does not want to go back to Portside."

"Sounded like it was the work detail, not custody that he was afraid of. Any idea what that was?" Seth asked.

Lee nodded. "He was assigned to the Ranger office. He drove Adel out to Seven Wells for a meeting with Dougherty. And she was enjoying some after-hours benefits. So I would guess that he crossed her somehow. Maybe overheard some scheme she didn't want known."

Adel and Whip? "Must have been something serious."

"To Adel anyway," Lee said. "She does like to handle things personally."

Well, they had more immediate problems than Adel Verlane, wherever she was at the moment. "I don't know about you, but I need some sleep before I try to figure anything out." Seth could hardly remember everything that had happened in the last day — the council meeting, recovering the horses, the all-night ride.

"You and me both." She pillowed her head on his shoulder, draped her arm across his chest, and relaxed against him. "I trust the hunters are keeping watch," she said, turning her brown-gold eyes on his.

"'Fraid so," he answered.

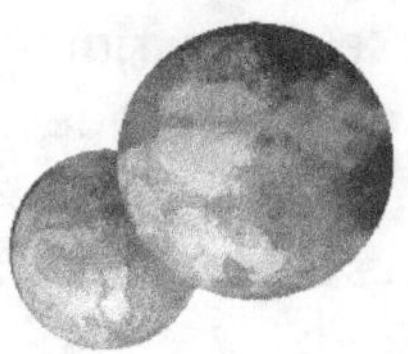

At sunset, Seth boosted Whip Willemsen onto his horse and stepped aside to leave Lee to deal with her prisoner. Her prisoner — she had made that point very clear to Guard earlier.

"Repeat the instructions," Lee said.

Whip nodded. "Cross the river, go upstream past where the rim meets the river canyon, climb the trail to the top, follow the first drainage going away from the rim."

"The trail and the drainage will be marked with cairns."

"I know." He shifted uncomfortably in his saddle. "And I'll find supplies at the spring in the head of the drainage."

"Your own stuff, retrieved from where you left it," she said. "Stay at the spring as long as you need to heal up."

"If I can stay on a horse that far."

"Hey." She took hold of his horse's bridle. "You can stay here and either get delivered back to Portside or turned over to very territorial beyonders."

"Okay, okay. From there I go west and stay above the rim until the snow drives me down. I got it."

"Earlier you seemed to think we owed you something. Well, you'd better call it even after this." She let go of his bridle. "Now get out of here before they change their minds."

He reined his horse away, riding slowly, one leg free of the stirrup to keep his knee straight, one elbow against his sore ribs.

"You think he can stay on as far as that spring Guard described?" Seth asked.

"He's going to have a long, uncomfortable ride." She came over and took Clown's reins. "I can hardly believe you convinced them to agree to this."

"Your female strategy; my male implementation," he said. "Anyway, the hunters will follow him and make sure he follows directions."

"Now we can focus on Prime and the whole diplomacy thing."

"We'd better get going," he said. "Guard and Second are waiting for us."

She stretched up to kiss him with a hint of passion, a promise for a day when they could focus on each other. "By tomorrow at this time, we'll be packing up to head home."

"With a little luck." He gave her a leg up onto Clown and swung onto the roan. They had a long night ride back to the Village of Canes where they would have to account for the decision and convince Prime to carry through with the invitation.

Chapter 36

Lee

At midday the next day, Lee stood in the arbor at Weaver's village with Seth at her shoulder and Weaver and Guard beside them. They hadn't had much sleep after riding all night to get back. Prime looked about as welcoming as the gunmetal blue clouds that blocked the heat and wrapped the canyon in stormy half-light. Sheets of rain moved toward them. A flash of lightning back-lit Prime and momentarily paled the holo-images of the other councilors. Second stood to one side as escort to Prime.

Thunder echoed through the cavern, strumming Lee's taut nerves. Weaver stepped forward and waited for the thunder to die before speaking. "The hunters report success. The intruder traveled out of our territory and is being monitored."

"Not without contact," Prime said. "Why was he allowed to go?"

Weaver lowered her eyes. "His only contact was with our human clan-mates, as was planned. He offered no threat to our villages."

Lightning haloed Prime. "You cannot be sure of that. What did he learn from them that the hunters were not present to hear?"

Lee stepped forward, separating herself from Weaver. "We aided in diverting a passing intruder according to clan laws. When we deliver your invitation —"

"*If* you go." Prime straightened her stole-of-office. "Councilors, we have remained undiscovered for ten years; we have taken great care not to leave marks of our presence visible from above. One, only one, of this council has argued for making contact now, but what do we know of these people that we call First-Comers that should give us hope for fair treatment? What do we know of this individual that should make us trust her to speak for us to her own people?" She paced the length of the arbor, looking Lee and Seth up and down.

She turned away from them and faced the holo-images. "None shall be allowed to spread the knowledge of our presence. We have lived by that. We should continue to live by that. So say I, who once commanded the *Long Flight*. What say you who have been chosen to speak for your clans? Do you stand with me to abide by our code and strip their memories before returning them to their own territory?"

Silence. From the storm. Within the arbor. Lee waited, barely breathing. Would even Weaver openly defy Prime? She touched her shoulder to Seth's, glad for his presence while wishing he had never come looking for her and gotten into this. He leaned into her, solid and steady.

"With respect," Weaver said, her head deeply bowed. "These people were brought here with this council's approval. They have offered a strategy that places us in a position of greater control than we had hoped for. Do we set all that aside now?"

None of the other councilors seemed willing to speak up. Lee could read uncertainty in their shifting postures, ruffled epaulet feathers, and unsettled face colors.

"Where do you stand?" Prime looked from one to the next.

"With you," the first said without hesitation.

The second looked from Prime to Weaver and back. "I ... I stand with initiating contact as we agreed previously." Her feathers drooped under Prime's glare, but she stood her ground.

Lee's heart pounded.

The third councilor responded slowly but also stood with Prime.

Two with Prime. One against. Did they follow a simple majority rule?

Weaver's turn. She settled feathers into place, her face matte-black. "I have made my position clear. They will discover us. I cannot stand with you."

"Three out of five against contact. It is decided," Prime said. "This is your village. Take charge of the prisoners and carry out the order."

Lee leaned back against Seth. He put his arms around her, sheltering her against him.

Weaver's face flashed purple. "It is the decision of the council. We ..." She hesitated through another crash of thunder. The wind swirled through the arbor.

Guard stepped past her, turned to face her. "It is within the Council's right to countermand its previous decision," he said with his head bowed. Then he raised his eyes to meet Weaver's. "But the males reserve the right of refusal when we cannot implement a decision." He paused, glancing aside at Prime. "Implementation would violate our honor. We will not act so against a clan-brother."

Prime pointed her beak at Weaver. "Control your male."

Second stalked forward, drew up to his full height, and spread his crest high and wide. Lee felt Seth's arms tighten around her. Better in Guard's hands than Second's.

Second faced Prime without a hint of lowered eyes. "He has the right. We do not wipe memories of our own." Without waiting for Prime's reaction, he turned to Weaver. "And if the females do not support the other as clan-sister, we will take her in as a clan-brother. She has earned her place among us through combat."

The ruffling epaulet feathers, purple faces, and switching tails told Lee a lot about how drastic a suggestion that was.

"Combat? This female? This was not reported." Prime snapped her beak. "More evidence that contact with First-Comers threatens the fabric of our lives."

"As change often does." Second lowered his eyes and turned to her alone with bowed head. "You have led us through our trials with courage and determination. Lead us now as we navigate this new challenge." He looked up. "You have a good strategy, well thought out. Trust my faith in our newest clan members and invite the First-Comers to meet with us on our terms."

Prime held herself stiff and tall. "This is your recommendation as leader of the males?"

"And as your spouse whose task it is to protect you to the best of my ability."

Prime's pale gold eyes scanned the councilors. She caught Lee's gaze and moved on to look Seth up and down. Then she faced Second and raised her beak high. He touched his sharp beak to her exposed throat, then stepped back into place at her shoulder.

Prime straightened and smoothed the stole-of-office that she wore. "I change my vote. It is three against memory wipe. I now propose sending our new clan members to the planetary authorities with an invitation to meet with us to discuss matters of mutual interest. Councilors, do you concur?"

"Yes, Prime," Weaver answered with bowed head. The other three hesitated before bobbing their heads and echoing her.

"Then I leave it to Eta'ak of the Village of Canes and her males to arrange the logistics." A crack of thunder and a deluge of rain cascading across the cave mouth drowned out whatever else Prime said. She swept out of the arbor and away into the storm. Second stopped to put his hand on Lee's shoulder. "Speak well for us."

"I will," Lee said, her head spinning. Then he was gone after Prime.

Chapter 37

Lee

Prime and Second were gone. The holo-images of the councilors were gone. Lee stood with Seth's arms around her and looked at Weaver and Guard. "That's it? We really get to leave?"

Weaver bobbed her head. "We have permission. You may carry the invitation."

"And Second was the one who changed her mind." Lee eased out of Seth's arms, keeping hold of his hand.

"You must have impressed him greatly." Weaver ruffled her epaulet feathers into place. "I suggest you go and sort out your gear now. Later we will discuss the details of your message and the meeting."

The storm passed as quickly as it had come, leaving bright sun and muggy heat in its wake. Lee and Seth moved everything outside the door of their room where they could spread it out. Still stunned by Second's support, Lee began sorting through things, something routine, normal.

"We can get out of here first thing in the morning." Seth looked at the saddles lined up along the wall.

"Sooner. I think Weaver wants us gone before Prime changes her mind," Lee said.

"We'll pack Creamy and Tinker. I guess we'll have to leave Ike's saddle here. With Pokey dead, we don't have a horse to put it on."

"Yeah, the packs are more important." She closed the lid on the pack box she had been loading.

"Will you and Weaver have time to decide on the message to the PAO?"

Lee nodded. "I think so. It doesn't have to be long."

"Okay. Guard and I will start hauling things down to the overhang where Weaver had her loom set up. It's close to the horses. We can spend the night there and leave early in the morning."

She put her arms around him. Even in the heat, she wanted the feel of him against her. "We're on our way home."

"Hmmm, I like the sound of that."

Scaled feet scuffed on stone and Guard said, "You are ready?"

Lee stepped away from Seth.

Seth pulled her back and kissed her lightly. "We'll take the saddles first," he said to Guard.

Lee stowed things in the pack boxes. She knew where everything went. Ike had made a science out of it, making sure nothing would shift, rebalancing weights each time they packed. Now the boxes were lighter than they had been. A lot of what she and Ike had carried, especially food, had gotten trampled in the stampede.

Weaver came from the kitchen, carrying a basket. "I brought some trail food for your journey."

"Thank you." Lee took the basket. "I was a little worried about having enough to get us back to Seth's."

"That is how you will go?"

Lee nodded. "There's a good chance the searchers will pick us up once we get onto the plateau."

"I believe it will be better for all if your PAO meets with Prime soon."

"Me too." Lee looked forward to handing off responsibility to someone with some authority and diplomacy. She and Seth had gotten lucky so far.

Weaver settled into her squat. "I never got a chance to thank you for the bread."

"The bread? That I made for Prime?" Lee asked.

"She did eat it. And shared a little. We do have a fondness for ferments."

Ike's yeasty in its crock was sitting at Lee's feet, waiting to be packed. She picked it up. "Would you keep this for me? It is a colony of living organisms used for making the bread. You would need to use and replenish it regularly. My friend Ike named it Beulah."

"I would be honored to care for it, for Be-u-lah."

Lee smiled at the translator's handling of the name. She got out the Dutch oven. "Better take this too."

Weaver bowed her head. "Let us go find a place to keep these where they will be seen and used. Before you go, you will explain the process to me."

They put the crock and Dutch oven on a shelf in the kitchen where Weaver said she would be reminded to use it and to feed the yeasty every day. What would Ike think if he knew what she had done with his prized possessions?

"We need to talk about the message to the PAO," Lee said as they crossed the plaza. "Where and when will the meeting take place?"

Weaver led the way to the shade of the arbor where a light breeze cooled the afternoon. Lee had a hard time picturing it as the same grim, dark place it had been during the council meeting a couple hours earlier.

It didn't take her and Weaver long to reach agreement on the basic message:

> *Prime, leader of Kelok Gra'a Tral — the Exiles of Blue Canyon, invites Charlyn Emmerling, Planetary Administrative Officer of Carico, to meet together so that we may discuss our peaceful coexistence on this world.*

"You must deliver this to your leader only," Weaver said.

"I'll have to go to someone else first. Someone I trust, who can get me in to see her without explaining to her staff." Rodahl Vinz, she thought, but she'd have to get around Adel first. "I won't tell him any more than absolutely necessary to get him to take me to the PAO," she told Weaver. "I will have to tell the PAO who you are and how you came here before she will accept the invitation."

"She must know our story," Weaver said, "but not too much."

Lee nodded. "I will be discreet and leave it to Prime to reveal details like your location and how many of you there are."

"I am in your debt. My strategy nearly failed," Weaver said. "That you convinced Second to trust you says much about the honor and integrity you showed dealing with the intruder."

Lee shifted uncomfortably under the praise. "I am acting as much in our interest as in yours. Now, this message should be in writing."

"Ah, a difficulty."

They went in search of materials for Lee to write the message out in Sol Standard. She settled for a piece of thin rawhide and the marker she and Ike had been using on the map of their trek. Weaver promised to provide a copy in her language. Lee went back to the arbor to draw out each letter carefully. Writing wasn't something she did often, at least not more than notes scrawled on a map, and this was destined to be a piece of history. The beginning of relations between two species.

Apparently details like the place and time for the meeting were logistics and in the male domain. "Ike's Rock," Seth explained when he found her a while later. "That's the place. The Keloks can camp near Stampede Spring. Guard thinks that is a safe distance from the villages."

"Ike's Rock?"

"Where I buried him."

"I like that," Lee said. "When?"

"No more than eight days, one cycle of Damele, after we deliver the message. Weaver will monitor the broadcast message boards to find out exactly when."

"I don't mind being an envoy. I'll just be glad when the responsibility is on someone who actually has some authority."

"You've faced down an alien leader and convinced her second to support you. You've got this in hand," he said, "even if you got into this trying to avoid the responsibility of getting pulled into the whole plan review thing."

"Vinz." She had a horrible thought. "Seth, he's never released my medical suspension. What if they don't believe me, if they just think I'm imagining things?"

"Didn't Weaver say she'd give you a copy of the invitation in their language?"

"Yes."

"That should back up our story."

"It should. Here she comes now."

Weaver set a tray of food down on the far end of the table away from Lee's document. "I thought we would eat here where we can talk," she said. "Guard will join us soon."

Lee held up the rawhide she had been writing on. "What do you think? Does it look formal enough? We'll square the edges. Maybe Seth can add some lacing to pretty it up."

"I know little about what your written documents look like, but I am sure this is distinctive, as is fitting." Weaver reached into her satchel and held out Lee's data pendent. "You will want this back. I added images that you may find useful in convincing your leader to accept the invitation — children playing, women working at the looms, men repairing nets, enough to show that we do exist."

"I thought this had gotten lost. Thank you." Lee slid the recorder into her pocket. "It should help. This is a pretty incredible story."

They ate a quiet supper of fresh fruits and vegetables with fish the hunters had brought from the river, and they talked about little details for the meeting, things Weaver said were male responsibilities but needed her protocol oversight. How many people should accompany the PAO? Should there be food and drink available during or after? What to do for shade from the sun? Lee found herself feeling truly at ease with the Keloks for the first time.

When they had finished eating, Weaver gathered up the remains of the meal to return to the kitchen. When Lee got up to help, she was waved back to her seat. "Remain here. I will return," Weaver said.

Weaver brought back a tray with a chilled container of liquid and small cups. She carried a satchel, this one of stiff rawhide rather than fabric. "I must formally dispatch you on your errand according to an ancient tradition." She gestured to the container and cups. "This is a distillation from what you call buttonweed. You are familiar with it?"

Lee grinned at Seth. They knew the weed well. "We chew the seed pods as a mild euphoric," she said, "but I don't know of anyone distilling it."

"My studies have shown me that we have in common a custom of drinking to the success of a coming endeavor," Weaver said as Guard poured the pale liquid and distributed the cups. "Let us wish success in bringing our leaders together for the first of many meetings."

Lee thought of Guard's and Second's bold actions earlier and added, "And may they always have wise council at their shoulders."

She let the chilled liquor rest mellow on her tongue before swallowing. She didn't want to worry about the miles of wilderness between them and home, the challenges of even getting to see the PAO much less getting her to take them seriously, or all the things that might go wrong once she did. Leave those for another day. It was enough right now that they were going home.

Weaver set her cup down. "Now please stand. These are for you to carry with you." She opened the rawhide satchel and took out a folded cloth. "First a gift from our council to the Planetary Administrative Officer. In our writing, we use colors rather than symbols. This documents our story. Someday soon we hope that Leader Emmerling will learn to read it for herself." She laid it in Lee's hands.

Lee felt how finely woven it was and could see its many colors but couldn't distinguish a pattern. "This is what you were weaving before our initiation?"

"Yes," Weaver said. "In hope that we would need it."

"I will deliver it into her hands."

Weaver took another piece of fabric from the satchel and shook open a long, narrow, multi-colored stole-of-office like the one Prime and the other councilors had worn. "This is a symbol of your authority to speak for us. Wear this when you meet with Leader Emmerling, then pass it on to her. She should wear it when she meets with Prime to signify her intent to meet in peace."

"I will explain its meanings to her."

"And finally, this. The invitation itself to go with the one you prepared." Weaver laid out a piece of rawhide about the same size as the one Lee had copied the invitation on. Colored dots, streaks, and swirls covered its face.

Weaver put the stole and the two copies of the invitation into the rawhide case. "Carry these swiftly and safely to your destination." She handed it to Lee. Lee added the story cloth and secured the flap on the case.

Lee looked at the two aliens with her and at the neat, well-lived-in village around them. Captors, clan mates, enemies, friends, catalysts provoking her to step up to responsibility. She laid her hand on the rawhide satchel. "We'll do everything in our power to bring about this meeting before the satellite array is in place." Together she and Seth could do it.

"It is set in motion," Weaver said.

Lee nodded. "We should go now." Before Prime had second thoughts. "Watch for our broadcast." She hated goodbyes. She never knew what to say.

"I will. One last thing, my sister." Weaver bowed her head. "We must keep the hearing facilitators here."

"Oh, of course."

Guard stepped forward and bowed his head to Lee first. "Fare well on your journey. The clan is lessened by your absence."

Slowly she turned so he could unfasten the choker.

He moved over to Seth and said something she could no longer understand. Seth grinned and said, "I look forward to it." Then his choker was gone too.

Lee dared to lay a hand on Guard's shoulder before she bowed her head to Weaver. She slung the rawhide satchel over her shoulder, took Seth's hand, and left the arbor. The villagers were gathered in the plaza, watching. Lee bobbed her head at them.

"Come on," Seth said and put his arm around her waist. They headed out into the evening light, accompanied by the pack of notalions weaving around their feet.

They took the trail down into the canyon. The notalions abandoned them among the whipbrush, off on a hunt or whatever they did when they left the village.

"Do you want to load up and go a ways tonight?" Lee asked.

"How's early in the morning sound? That's what Guard and I talked about."

"So back to my prison ledge?"

"The ladder is gone. We'll have to make do with the overhang where Weaver worked."

They crossed the dance ground and turned up the side canyon into shadows. It all seemed unreal now, being held alone in the little rockshelter unable to communicate with her alien captors. From that to being an envoy for those same people in two cycles of Damele.

"What did Guard say to you?" she asked. "Before he took your facilitator."

"Just to hurry back. That there is still the matter of figuring out how a tailless one can fight as a brother should."

"We're tied to these people, aren't we?"

"Maybe so." He stopped and faced her. "But right now, there are just two of us here. What do you think of that?"

"I think it's been too long since we could say that." She took his hand and led the way to the sandy-floored overhang where Weaver had tried to teach her to make mats and baskets and where their packs and gear were stacked. Looked like Seth had thought ahead. Their bedding was already spread out. Something lay in the middle of the blanket. "What's that?"

Seth knelt down and held up a pair of bracelets. "Guard's been busy," he said.

"Guard?" She dropped down next to him.

"He was asking about your horsehair bracelet one day, about what it meant. He said we needed new ones."

"Oh, he did." Lee sat back on her heels.

"I'll just…" Seth glanced at her and down at the braided rawhide loops in his hand. "Just put them in the packs I guess."

"Can I see them?" She held out her hand. He passed them over. She turned them over, feeling the delicate strands and the slide of one end into the other. "I wonder if these latch like the shackles. Want to see?"

"See what?"

"Do you want this or not?" She took his hand and held one of the bracelets up.

"You know I do. I just wasn't sure about you."

"Didn't we have this conversation?"

"Back when we weren't sure we'd survive."

"Hold this." She dangled one of the bracelets. He lifted it from her fingers. She put her hand halfway into the loop and held up the other one. They slipped the bracelets on each other. "There," she said.

"We'll have to thank Guard when we get a chance." Seth adjusted the bracelet around her wrist. Sure enough, once snug it didn't pull open again.

She did the same for his. "Ike would be happy."

"Ike?"

"He told me we belonged together. Over and over." She gave Seth a push, toppling him onto the blanket.

He pulled her after him, laughing. "How fast do we have to deliver the invitation?"

"Soon. It should only take us a day or two to get to where a search party will find us."

"Wouldn't do to vanish back of beyond for a little longer, just the two of us?"

"Probably not, but ..." She set aside the diplomatic pouch with its looming responsibilities and turned her attention to making up for lost time here and now.

END

About the Author

Nan C. Ballard's *Under Carico's Moons* series of science fiction cowboy stories reflects her love of places where vehicles yield to cows, towns are hours apart, and hills climb clear to the sky. She's written and edited environmental  assessment reports, written an arts column for a small town paper, and collaborated on adaptations of plays for community theater. Her poetry has been published in the online *Willawaw Journal* and the anthology *Mount Shasta Reflections.* She supports her fellow writers as a chapter co-chair and online Coffee co-host for Willamette Writers. She does quick pen-and-colored-pencil doodles to practice mindfulness. Her current just-for-fun project with her husband is to visit interesting places in every county in Oregon.

You can find her at nancballardwriter.blogspot.com or @NanCBallard on Twitter and Instagram.

Also Available from Not a Pipe Publishing

THE STAFF OF FIRE AND BONE

BY

MIKKO AZUL

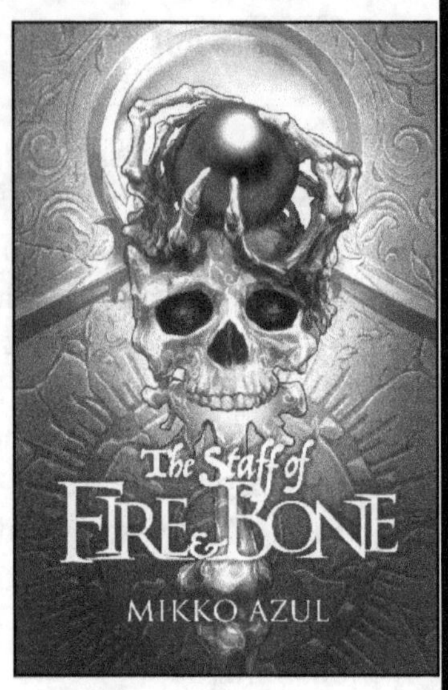

This sweeping, exciting high fantasy epic tells the story of Cédron Varakas, already isolated as the Regent's son, who has a Shäeli demon for a mother. Approaching manhood, his demonic powers manifest. Blamed for the earth shakes ripping through the land, Cédron races against time to find the real cause of the destruction. He must become a hero or join the great demon and embrace his true heritage.

"…a complex world fraught with danger and magic. I highly recommend Azul's work to anyone of any age who enjoys high fantasy and exciting adventure."
-Amy Jarecki, award-winning author of the *Lords of the Highlands* series

Wherever Fine Books Are Sold

Also Available from Not a Pipe Publishing

Once Upon a Fang in the West

by

John Dover

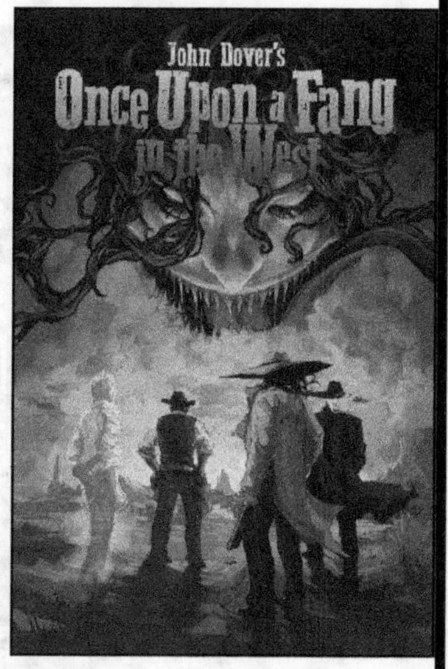

The Braided Pony saloon is no stranger to gun fire and blood stains on the floor. But when a mysterious gunslinger turns up dead in Ruby's room, it's up to the town's drunken sheriff to investigate. Lucky for him, Samuel, a fast-talking vampire, arrives looking to settle a score and attempting to resurrect his dead friend. Now they're on the hunt across the rocky plains of the Wild West to recover the life that was stolen.

"...a hilarious page-turner Western, as well as a very explicit, gory vampire tale that binds the genres. Just pour yourself a shot of whiskey and wear an apron before reading."

-Ivonne Saed, author of *Triple crónica de un nombre* (*Triple Chronicle of a Name*).

"Can a story with this much blood and gore be called 'pure'? Because this is pure fun!"

-Benjamin Gorman, author of *Don't Read This Book*

Wherever Fine Books Are Sold

ALSO AVAILABLE FROM NOT A PIPE PUBLISHING

**The Grigori Cycle:
Book One**

UNRELENTING

by

**Jessi Honard &
Marie Parks**

A mysterious disappearance. A glowing symbol painted on a crumbling wall. Sentient smoke that chases, chokes, and burns.

Bridget Keene practically raised her little sister. Then Dahlia vanishes. Her car is found submerged in the river, and nine months later, everyone has given up hope. Everyone except Bridget. She's determined to revive the case and bring Dahlia home. Except her search reveals something far more sinister than a typical missing-persons case—a carefully-guarded plot tied to powerful, ancient magic. To uncover the truth about her sister's disappearance, Bridget will confront a secret world that threatens to drag her under, too.

"The sibling bond is stronger than supernatural power in this high-energy thriller."
-Karen Eisenbrey, author of the *Daughter of Magic Trilogy*

"...brimming with twists that unravel into something far darker and more chilling."
-Michaela Thorn, author of *Tooth and Claw*

WHEREVER FINE BOOKS ARE SOLD

ALSO AVAILABLE FROM NOT A PIPE PUBLISHING

GhostCityGirl
by
Simon Paul Wilson

Serial killers, starvation cults, and spicy noodles – just another day in Nihon City.

It's been one hundred years since Tokyo was ravaged by a ghostquake and talking about the supernatural was forbidden. To escape her unhappy family life and mundane job, Kichi Honda

spends her days off visiting Mister Tanaka, an old man who tells her illegal tales of haunted Japan. But when Kichi gets stranded on Level One, she meets an impossible girl who claims to have come from Tokyo.

Kichi learns the truth about what really happened all those years ago ... and discovers history is about to repeat itself.

"*GhostCityGirl* is immersive and haunting, pulling you into Kichi Honda's world from page one and not releasing its grip on your psyche even after the wild ride is over. Every detail, from the mundane to the supernatural, is deliciously written, and the story kept me guessing at every turn. I highly recommend *GhostCityGirl* to fans of horror and the macabre, and am very much looking forward to reading more of Simon Paul Wilson's work."

-Jessie Kwak, author of *The Bulari Saga*

WHEREVER FINE BOOKS ARE SOLD

ALSO AVAILABLE FROM NOT A PIPE PUBLISHING

Sparks

by

Maren Anderson

When Rosie and Patrick, her mysterious new ... friend, get drunk and knock down an ancient cowshed on her ranch, they disturb a monstrous cowsprite that lives there. Rosie didn't know magic existed, but now all she wants is to regain control of her life.

"*Sparks* is a fresh and playful love story, told with wry, laugh out loud humor and populated with characters Anderson was a knack for making feel like your dearest friends. That would be enough reason to read this. But did I mention "amoral Barn-Sprites"? Because *Sparks* has those, too, and they are some *terrible fun*. Anderson uses a mischievous twist of magic to take her characters, and readers, on a cozy but exhilarating ride."

-Therese Oneill, NYT Bestselling author

WHEREVER FINE BOOKS ARE SOLD

ALSO AVAILABLE FROM NOT A PIPE PUBLISHING

Don't Read This Book

by

Benjamin Gorman

Magdalena Wallace is the greatest writer in the world. She just doesn't know it.

When she wakes up chained to a desk next to a stack of typed pages and the corpse of the person who read them, she learns just how dangerous her book can be. Rescued by a vampire, a werewolf, and a golem, she's on the run with the manuscript — and the fate of humanity — in her backpack, and a whole lot of monsters hot on her heels!

"…a whimsical, fast-paced, delight; snappily written, deliciously funny and smart, and full of affection for its characters."
- New York Times bestseller Chelsea Cain, author of *Heartsick*, *Mockingbird*, and *Gone*

"... smart, determined, and filled with really stunning prose ... maybe one of the best books I've read!"
-Sydney Culpepper
 author of *Pagetown*, editor of *Strongly Worded Women*

WHEREVER FINE BOOKS ARE SOLD

www.ingramcontent.com/pod-product-compliance
Lightning Source LLC
Chambersburg PA
CBHW072002190726
48293CB00001B/126

* 9 7 8 1 9 5 6 8 9 2 1 6 1 *